The Crimson Contract

The Volkov Illusion
Book 1

The Crimson Contract

The Volkov Illusion
Book 1

OPHELIA WREN

Trigger Warnings

- Characters being controlled, manipulated, or coerced into actions against their will
- Dark Power Dynamics
- Detailed depictions of panic attacks and emotional distress
- Detailed, graphic sexual scenes
- Drug and Alcohol Abuse
- Emotional and Physical Abuse
- Explicit power dynamics in sexual relationships
- Gun Violence
- Loss of Autonomy
- Murder, including detailed accounts of killings
- Non-consensual acts or implied coercion
- Non-consensual permanent marking of the body
- Parent-child abuse, including verbal and physical violence
- Physical altercations, including graphic descriptions of fights
- Sex Work
- Sexually Explicit Content
- Sexual Assault/Abuse
- Tattooing/Branding Without Consent
- Themes of human trafficking and exploitation
- Threats of Sexual Violence
- Torture

Content Warning

Sexual Assault

This book contains a scene depicting sexual assault. If you prefer to skip this content, please avoid pages 369—375 and continue reading after that point.

Torture

This book contains a scene depicting torture. If you prefer to skip this content, please avoid pages 380—389 and continue reading after that point.

Prologue

Damiano

One Year Earlier

I've always known I was different—not because people constantly told me so, but because I felt it, deep in my core. It wasn't just a suspicion; it was a certainty, something etched into my very being. Then again, anyone raised in *this family* would likely feel the same.

Deceive.

Lie.

Kill.

That's the foundation of this world, the unspoken creed we're all bound to follow.

Everyone has a role. A part to play in the dynamics of survival.

Mine? Kill.

And I'll do it by any means necessary.

When I torture, I don't see a person. I see a shell—a vessel holding the one thing I need: information.

They're already dead to me—no amount of pleading will change that. Given enough time, they all break, crumbling beneath the weight of their own desperation.

I grant mercy, but only once I have what I need.

Some endure longer than others, but in the end, they're no different. No one is unique. Every person has a weakness.

And I always find it.

Once you're in my *office*, it's over.

No one has ever left alive.

And no one ever will.

That's the reality of this life. Trust is a liability, and weakness gets you killed. I'd never put my family or myself at risk by letting someone walk away after I'm done with them—that's signing my personal death sentence.

Loose ends aren't an option. If something needs handling, I take care of it. Depending on someone else? That's a risk I won't take.

There's always an enemy. Always someone clawing their way to the top, forcing you to watch your back. Right now, that someone is Cristiano Fierro. He's the ghost I've been chasing, the loose end that refuses to be tied. Until his body is nothing but ash, I won't stop hunting him.

Word is, he's got a new girl—Contessa. I know the women he involves himself with, and because she's tied to Cristiano, she's as good as dead. Her worth is judged by the company she keeps, and she chose the worst. Intel places her with the cartel's leader tonight. If I can take them both alive and drag them back to my workshop, neither will leave breathing. But she alone would be enough. She's my key to Cristiano, and I won't stop until I get my hands on him.

Tonight's meeting is at an ordinary restaurant, nothing re-markable. That's probably why she picked it—to blend in without drawing attention. I've been watching for an hour, tracking who comes and goes.

My brother Andrei didn't give me much to go on: *"You'll know who she is the second you see her."* That's it. That and a grainy photo. From what I can tell, she's decent. However, I'd expect more from Cristiano, but then again, if you searched for trash on Google, his face would be the first result.

I lean back in my seat, letting my eyes roam over the street. Cars are parked neatly along the curb, their interiors dark and empty, reflections of the streetlights glinting off their windows. Foot traffic comes and goes—some lingering to chat, others rush-ing by. But none of them match the description.

She's supposed to be alone, standing out by trying not to. So far, nothing.

I check the time on my watch, exhaling slowly. It's been over an hour. If she doesn't show soon, I'll have to reassess the intel. Either she's running late, or she got word that something was off.

Boredom creeps in, but I remain focused. I drum my fingers against the steering wheel, scanning the entrance of the restaurant again. The bartender wipes down the counter inside. A couple waits near the host stand to be seated. A waiter steps outside for a smoke break, resting against the wall as he pulls out his lighter.

And then, *I see her*.

I sit up straighter, taking her in. There's no mistaking it—Cris-tiano's woman. The second my eyes land on her, I know. But I don't have the reaction I expected. I thought seeing her would make me sick, that I'd feel nothing but disgust. Instead, something shifts inside me, something I don't enjoy happening. Because this woman—the property of the man I hate more than anything—in-stantly makes me hard.

She moves toward the restaurant casually, her attempt at blending in almost laughable. Baggy pants that could fit three of her are held up by her hand awkwardly gripping the belt loop in a desperate attempt to keep them from falling off. A white tank top peeks out beneath a man's red plaid button-up, half-buttoned and rolled to her forearms. Long brown hair spills out from beneath a worn beanie, looking like it hasn't seen a brush in days.

Everything about her is a disguise. And yet, it makes her stand out more.

My gaze drops to her shoes—old and scuffed, as if they've endured countless miles, possibly more than I have in my hunt for Cristiano. I wonder where she even managed to snag a pair of dirty shoes like that. I'll give her kudos, though. Someone in her position would feel a sense of superiority—that even for an under-cover disguise, she's too good to wear dirty shoes like this. But here she is, as dirty as the street rats, just to blend in.

She steps into the restaurant, scanning the room before stopping a passing waitress. They exchange a few words, and the wait-ress gestures toward the bar.

She sits at the counter, pulls out her phone, and types quickly, but then pauses, looks around again, and tucks the phone back into her bag. I stay in my truck, watching patiently.

No man approaches her.

This could be a trap. Maybe they've caught on to me, and this is their setup—a plan to draw me out and eliminate me if I make a move. But there's no way. Nobody knows I'm here, much less that I'm going to take her out.

I fire off a quick text to Andrei, asking if we have a photo of the man she's meeting tonight. His response comes almost instant-ly, along with an image.

The man in the picture is older, his face weathered and lined. A thick mustache frames his upper lip, and a scar cuts through his cheek, adding to his hardened appearance. Dressed in a crisp button-up, he carries the unmistakable air of a man who's climbed to the top through blood and fear. He's the kind of man people don't cross and live to tell about it.

Andrei follows up with a message.

"I know intel says it's him, but there's no way he's showing up on this side of town. Someone else will take his place. No clue who. Keep your ears open."

He would definitely stand out like a sore thumb if he came here. Deciding I'm not going to keep waiting, I step out of my truck and head inside. When the same waitress makes her way toward me, I point toward the bar where my target is sitting, and the waitress offers a nod, gesturing for me to go ahead.

I take a seat near her, leaving one chair between us. She's eating quietly, her focus on her plate. When I glance at her, I'm momentarily struck by her beauty. If Cristiano ever did anything right in his miserable life, it was her. She's far more stunning than her picture. Even more stunning up close.

I order a drink, shrug off my coat, and drape it over the back of my chair.

I scan the room one last time, making sure I haven't missed the final piece to this meeting. But he's definitely not here. My gaze sweeps over the surroundings again before landing back on her. And just like before, my body reacts to her.

Not good.

This is not good.

I should pull back immediately—abort the mission and send one of my brothers in my place. But I don't. Instead, I stay seated, unwilling to walk away just yet.

The bartender sets a glass in front of me, and I nod. "Thanks." I slip a hand into my coat pocket, dropping my keys inside.

"Are you going to keep staring, or do you actually need something?" she asks, irritation lacing her voice as she takes another bite.

I settle back, turning my head forward, only to catch her watching me in the mirror behind the bar. Amused, I shift my attention back to her.

"Never been here before," I say smoothly. "Whatever you're having looks decent. Just trying to figure out how to order the same without having to pick up the menu."

She lets out a humorless laugh and takes a sip of her drink.

"So, do you come here often?" The moment the words leave my mouth, I know how pathetic they sound.

She rolls her eyes and looks back down at her plate, taking another bite.

I lean over slightly, trying to get a closer look at her food. "What is that, anyway?"

She doesn't look up. "It's a hamburger. What does it look like?"

"It looks like a hamburger with tentacles coming out of the sides."

Fries spill from every edge of her burger. I can't tell if she stacked them herself or if that's just how it was served, but either way, I'm willing to try it.

That earns the slightest twitch at the corner of her lips—barely there, but there, nonetheless.

"I'll have what she's having," I tell the bartender when he steps up to take my order. He nods and walks to the computer, tapping the screen, then moves to the far end of the bar to serve other customers.

"He didn't ask how I wanted it cooked. I'm assuming he's making it like yours. Please tell me that isn't well-done."

She takes a sip of her soda, turns her burger toward me to reveal the pink center, then takes another bite.

"Thank God," I mutter, loud enough for her to hear.

She's not one for small talk. She also hasn't touched her phone again, which means she either has a different way of knowing when the person she's waiting for arrives… or she thinks I'm him.

I hope she doesn't. I hope she doesn't look at me and see the kind of filth that runs with the cartel. I may not be a saint, but I'm not that.

And yet, as I study her, a different question pulls at me—how the hell did she get tangled up with Cristiano? And if she's here, does that mean Cristiano is close? Closer than I thought?

My eyes drop to the faint scars on her knuckles, then to the one along the side of her hand that extends to her forearm—a jagged line stretching nearly seven inches. A fight? An accident? Or did someone put it there?

A slow, unshakable possessiveness settles in. I will kill the person responsible for leaving such a mark on her skin.

I want to see if there are more—if scars mark other parts of her body. I want to trace them, commit them to memory, and make sure whoever has hurt her, pays for it.

And then there's the other part of me—the one that wants to press my lips to every single one.

Damn it.

And now I'm hard again.

The bartender returns, setting my plate in front of me before striding away. I glance down at it, then back at hers. She notices and just watches me.

"This looks completely different," I remark, comparing my neatly stacked burger to her chaotic mess.

She sets hers down and reaches over, pulling my plate toward her. She takes off the bun, stacks fries on top of the patty, drenches them in fry sauce, adds another handful for good measure, then smashes the bun back into place before shoving the plate along the counter back my way with indifference.

I catch it, staring down at the mess she just created. Shrugging, I pick it up and take a bite.

She stops chewing, waiting for my reaction.

It's good. Messy, but good. I nod as I wipe the corner of my mouth, and she seems satisfied, turning back to her own food.

I can feel her watching me in the mirror again. The urge to throw her own words back at her is tempting—to ask if she actually needs something or if she's just going to keep staring. But I have a nagging suspicion that my joke wouldn't land the same way. She's intense. Either she's having a bad day or she's in no mood to deal with me. Then again, maybe she doesn't even want to be here. Maybe she's just as disappointed as I am that he didn't show up. I think I would have enjoyed interrogating him.

She takes the last bite of her burger, wipes her hands, and motions to the bartender.

He approaches, and she tells him she's ready for the check. He pulls a leather bill book from his apron and sets it in front of her.

"Let me," I offer, already reaching for my wallet.

She quickly slides cash into the book and shoves it back toward the bartender before climbing off her chair, slipping her purse over her shoulder.

The words leave my mouth before I even think about them.

"Can I get your number?"

Just as quickly, she responds, "Fuck off."

As she strides toward the exit, the waiter calls after her, "Thanks, Rainey. Have a good night. Get home safe."

Rainey?

I stare after her, the name throwing me off completely.

I thought she was Contessa.

I sit in my brother Andrei's room as he pulls up the feed from the restaurant. Clear as day, I see that while I was so focused on the woman I thought was Contessa, I completely missed the real target walking in—right behind where I sat—to meet with the head of the drug cartel, a mere ten feet away. I missed the entire thing because I was so enamored by this other woman.

You can see it in the video footage, me sitting in my truck, eyes locked on *Rainey* as she walked away, completely oblivious to the meeting still taking place inside the restaurant. And then, I pull away, leaving behind my actual objectives.

I went there to bring Contessa back to my house, intending to get information from her before ending her life. But within minutes of spotting who I believed to be my target, my plans shifted. Instead of killing her, I began considering ways to take and keep her for myself.

Sitting next to her, I decided that's exactly what I was going to do, and I would kill anybody who tried to get in the way. Cristiano will be dead soon anyway; he won't mind if I take his girl.

Only to discover—*she isn't his girl at all.*

"I want everything on her." I point to the screen where the woman, Rainey, is frozen mid-motion.

Rainey.

Rainey Volkov.

Damiano and Rainey Volkov.

It has a nice ring to it.

Andrei pulls up the details, rattling them off like a list. "Rainey Lane, twenty-five. Dropped out of high school at sixteen to work. She's held a string of odd jobs ever since—waitressing, retail, janitorial, a brief time at a call center, and a few months cleaning motel rooms.

"Father's dead—killed in prison. Mother, Darla, is a drug addict and alcoholic with a gambling problem. Lives in Tin Can Trailer Park on the East Side, lot number thirty-seven. Darla's boyfriend, Ricardo, is another addict and gambler. Neither of them works. Ricardo has a record—petty theft, drug possession, domestic violence.

"The trailer is in Rainey's name, inherited from her grandmother after she passed. It was fully paid off, but Darla took out loans against it in Rainey's name, leaving her to shoulder the debt. She's been working to pay them off ever since. It looks like she covers all the bills—utilities, groceries, everything. No car. She either walks or relies on the bus to get around. No credit cards, strictly cash.

"Medical records show multiple ER visits over the years—mostly minor injuries: bruised ribs, a fractured wrist at nineteen, multiple concussions at twenty-two. But between the ages of eight and twelve, it was different—severe injuries. Deep lacerations, a broken nose, broken bones, multiple surgeries for wounds that were never investigated.

"No known boyfriends. No active social media, just an old Facebook account that hasn't been updated in years. No friends listed. Her phone number is linked to a burner she swaps out every few months. She keeps her head down, stays quiet. Doesn't cause trouble."

"Thanks." I pat my brother on the shoulder, then stride out of his room.

I just met the woman I'm going to marry.

Chapter

ONE

Rainey

The flip-flops aren't mine. They barely cling to my feet as I walk, the frayed strap on the right one threatening to snap with every step. I'd kiped them off someone's back patio this morning, slipping through the chain-link fence and grabbing them from the cement steps. They're old, worn thin, with someone else's footprints pressed deep into the soles, but they're better than walking barefoot.

Last night, Ricardo trashed the trailer again. I'd heard him screaming and breaking things as I curled up on Mrs. Mahoney's back porch, five trailers down. Her plastic chair was hard and cold, but it was better than staying within Ricardo's reach.

Mom had passed out with a needle in her arm hours before, and Ricardo… he was looking for someone to fight with. Someone to hit.

He attempted to take his anger out on Mom, but no matter how many times he hit her, she remained limp on the table, unresponsive to his attacks. Frustration twisted his features as he kicked at the chair she was slumped in, but his drunken stupor betrayed him. His foot tangled in the chair leg, sending him toppling sideways into the TV dinner tray stand. A pile of beer cans, empty takeout containers, and an overflowing ashtray came crashing down with him. By the time he scrambled back to his feet, his face was twisted with rage.

I watched as he scanned the room, searching for something—anything—to take his anger out on. He'd already tried Mom, but her lifeless form didn't give him the reaction an abuser craved. The chair had gotten the best of him, and somewhere in his fall, he must have cut himself; blood trickled down his forearm, though he didn't seem to notice. When he started knocking things over, I quietly closed my bedroom door and turned the lock. I held my breath, trying not to make a single sound, desperate not to draw his attention. But when I heard his heavy footsteps stomping down the hall, my stomach twisted with dread.

He'd remembered I was here. And now I was going to be his punching bag.

I barely had time to react before the door splintered open with a deafening crack. He stormed in like a raging bull, and before I could scramble away, his hand tangled in my hair, yanking me out of bed. Pain shot through my scalp as I cried out, my feet barely touching the floor as he dragged me forward. The fear was paralyzing, but the brutal sting of his first swing jolted me back to reality.

My cheek burned from the impact, the metallic taste of blood pooling in my mouth. I tried to shield myself, raising my arms to block his blows, but he was relentless. His shouts were a blur of fury and slurred curses, each one punctuated by another strike.

With every ounce of strength I had, I lashed out, my fist connecting with his face in a wild, desperate punch. The impact jarred my arm, pain shooting up to my elbow, but the sight of him stumbling back—even for a second—filled me with a fierce, fleeting satisfaction. My knuckles throbbed, but it didn't matter.

His anger only deepened, and I knew I couldn't win. Survival instincts kicked in, screaming at me to run. I wrenched free, the roots of my hair protesting with a sharp sting and bolted past him. My breath came in ragged gasps as I snatched my purse from the floor and darted through the broken doorway. Barefoot, dressed in pajama pants and a sweatshirt, I fled into the night.

I drifted into an uneasy sleep as the sounds of Ricardo's rampage echoed through the trailer park. The crashes and shouts somehow became a twisted lullaby, momentarily drowning out my own fear. I curled up tighter on Mrs. Mahoney's back porch, the hard plastic chair biting into my side, but at least it was safer than inside. When the first light of morning crept across the trailer park and I heard Mrs. Mahoney shuffling around her kitchen, I slipped away quietly, careful not to be seen.

I keep my head down, dodging glass shards and scattered trash on the sidewalks, my purse clutched tightly against my side. The dirt road beneath my feet shifts to cracked pavement, and the rows of rusted trailers give way to crumbling apartments and boarded-up storefronts. The cold air stings my face as I head deeper into the city, leaving behind the outskirts where the trailer park clings to the edge of town.

I don't have a plan. I'm running on fumes—lack of sleep, adrenaline, and a desperate need to get away. Where I'm going, I haven't figured out yet. Anywhere far from Ricardo is good enough for me. He'll sleep most of the day, and Mom will wake up clueless about what happened last night. But eventually, she'll see. She'll see my broken bedroom door when she goes to use the bathroom. She'll notice the drops of blood from Ricardo's cut arm. She'll take in the wreckage of the trashed trailer. But what she won't do—what she never does—is kick him out.

I round a corner, and it happens so fast I don't even see him coming.

A man crashes into me, his hand yanking the strap of my purse off my shoulder. The weight disappears before my brain can catch up. The force of his impact sends me sprawling onto the pavement, the rough scrape of concrete biting into my palms and knees. All I can do is stare at the ground, completely stunned, my heart racing as I try to piece together what just happened.

"Hey!" I shout, my voice cracking, but the man is already running away.

I try to scramble to my feet, but the flip-flops finally give up. The right strap snaps, the frayed threads giving way under the strain, and I stumble, frozen and helpless, watching the thief vanish down the street.

Rage burns through me as hopelessness settles in. My chest heaves as I stand there, unmoving, when suddenly, another figure emerges from the shadows.

This man moves with purpose. He closes the distance to the thief in seconds, his approach soundless as he lands a punch square against the thief's jaw. The crack of impact reaches me a second later, followed by the dull thud of his body collapsing to the ground, my purse tumbling from his hands.

The stranger bends down, picking it up without so much as a glance at the crumpled figure at his feet. Straightening, he turns toward me, his silhouette tall against the faint orange light creeping over the horizon. His face remains obscured beneath the hood of his sweatshirt and the brim of a baseball cap. But there's no mistaking the strength in the way he carries himself—controlled and intimidating.

He stops in front of me and holds out my purse. I reach for it cautiously, my fingers trembling as they wrap around the strap.

His knuckles are reddened, but his grip remains completely steady. I don't know why it surprises me. Maybe because every time I've been in a fight, adrenaline left my hands shaking and my pulse hammering too fast to keep still.

"Thanks," I manage as he releases it. The sight of it—the tattered thrift shop bag with its cheap faux leather peeling at the edges, the paint chipping off the clasp, and the tear I'd stapled shut on one side—makes my cheeks burn with embarrassment.

This? This is what he took down a thief for? The bag looks like it belongs in a dumpster, barely worth the effort of carrying, let alone fighting to get back. It wasn't worth his time—not the effort he spent catching that guy or the punch he threw to retrieve it.

"Thank you," I repeat. "For… getting this timeless artifact back."

He stares at me, his eyes tracing the damage on my face. Then, as if on instinct, he reaches out, his fingers barely skimming the skin beside my split lip. His touch is light as he pinches my chin, tilting my head to the side. He studies Ricardo's handiwork—the bruise spreading across my cheekbone—before guiding my face back toward him. His eyes flick between the swelling and the split in my lip, his jaw tensing slightly.

His hand stays for only a second before he pulls away. With a single nod, he turns and walks off.

It happened so fast, I'm not even sure it was real.

Did he actually touch me?

The phantom trace of his thumb still lingers on my skin. I can even recall how his sweatshirt sleeve inched up when he reached for me, revealing the tattoo wrapped around his wrist—a compass encircled by ropes, the black ink bold against his tan complexion.

His movements are as fluid as when he first appeared, his sweatshirt stretching snugly over his broad frame. I turn and head back the way I came, stealing a quick peek over my shoulder. For a moment, I think he's vanished, but then I catch sight of him walking with the thief, disappearing into an alley. Walking might not be the right word—he has the man by the back of his jacket, hoisting him like a cat carrying her kitten, steering him along as the thief squirms in a futile attempt to escape.

I half wonder where the man is taking him. Right now, I have nowhere to go and nothing to do. Maybe he's dragging the thief into the alley to beat the shit out of him. Honestly, I wouldn't mind watching. He knocked the guy out with barely any effort. I wonder where he got that kind of strength. Maybe he could teach me how to throw a punch like that. Hell, I'd like to get a few kicks in too. Little jackass tried to steal my stuff.

But even though the guy got my purse back, he reeks of danger. And I really don't need to keep throwing myself into shitty situations.

Buuuut… kicking the crap out of some scumbag in an alley still sounds better than going home. It might even help me burn off some of this anger.

Don't be stupid, Rainey.

I need to put some distance between myself and what just happened. The last thing I need is to be anywhere near it when the cops show up—and they will. Someone had to have seen what happened, and I don't need to get dragged into answering questions or explaining why I was even there. I have enough problems without adding this to the list.

I pick up my speed as I walk away even faster. I can't go back to the trailer. Ricardo will still be there, passed out for most of the day. And when he wakes up to a trashed trailer, nothing but empty beer cans and ashtrays full of cigarette butts surrounding him, he'll go off on another rampage. He always does.

My options are slim. The best one at the moment is going to Jules. She's been my only friend for the last year, and even though her moods have been unpredictable lately—thanks to her recent breakup with her on-again, off-again girlfriend—she's still my safest option.

I head toward her apartment, bracing myself for whatever version of her I'll encounter. Will she be the Jules who craves the world's attention, masking her pain with bright laughter and endless chatter? Or will she be the one who retreats inward, her heartbreak casting a shadow over everything, leaving me to tiptoe around the shards of her broken heart?

When I reach her building, I climb the narrow staircase to her floor, the cinder block walls streaked with peeling paint and faintly smelling of fried food from the neighboring units. I knock softly on her door—three quick taps.

A muffled voice comes from inside, followed by the shuffle of footsteps. The curtain beside the door shifts, and Jules' face appears, her phone still pressed to her ear. Her dark hair is pulled up in a messy bun, and her eyes widen slightly when she sees me.

I lift a hand in a small wave, managing a faint smile.

She holds up a finger and moves to unlock the door. The chain slides free with a metallic clink, and the door creaks open. She stands there, barefoot in sweatpants and an oversized hoodie.

"You look shittier than I feel." She leans against the doorframe, giving me a once-over. "What happened?"

I step inside, the door closing behind me, and shrug. "Long night."

She doesn't press for more details. Instead, she nods toward the couch. "You want coffee? Or… something stronger?"

Without waiting for an answer, she moves to the kitchen, grabs the coffee pot, and pours herself a cup.

I let out a long sigh, the events of the day sinking into my shoulders. "All I want is a shower, clean clothes, and a bed."

She waves her coffee spoon lazily over her shoulder in the direction of the bedroom. "Help yourself."

Her apartment is small. The living room holds a couch barely big enough for two, facing a TV mounted on the wall. The kitchen is compact, opening into a tiny dining area that could hardly seat three. A single bedroom sits just off the living room, with a queen-size bed shoved into the corner. A small closet overflows with clothes, more spilling onto the floor, leaving barely any room to walk. The bathroom is cramped, just large enough for a tub-shower, a toilet, and a tiny sink with almost no counter space—but Jules has managed to fill every inch of it with makeup and other essentials.

The hot water cascades over me, its warmth sinking deep into my skin, washing away the grime and sweat. It almost feels like I can breathe again. But the tightness in my chest remains. Even here, wrapped in steam and scalding heat, the suffocating feeling lingers, refusing to be rinsed away.

My scalp still burns from where Ricardo yanked me out of bed, and I probably should have checked to make sure I'm not missing a giant chunk of hair.

How is everything going so wrong? How did my life shrink down to this—trapped in a cycle I can't break? I should leave. I want to leave. But where would I go? No money, no plan, no one waiting for me on the other side of the door.

Every time I think about walking out, reality slams me back into place.

So I stay. I put up with mom and Ricardo's bullshit, swallowing the frustration, telling myself I can hold on a little longer. That something has to give.

But what if it never does?

My breath stutters, chest tightening as an invisible force clamps around my ribs. I suck in air, but it's not enough. The steam thickens, pressing in, swallowing me whole. My vision blurs at the edges, and suddenly, I'm on the floor, my back against the cool wall as my fingers claw at my throat. My head spins.

I can't breathe.

I. can't. breathe.

My arm knocks into the shelf, sending bottles clattering around me. The sound barely registers over the gasping, the rushing in my ears. My pulse hammers, my body locked in panic as if it's bracing for another blow that isn't coming.

Somewhere beyond the roar in my head, I hear my name. The voice is distant, warped, like it's echoing through a tunnel. The water shuts off, the sudden silence making the ringing in my ears worse.

"Hey. Look at me."

A firm grip tilts my face up, and through the haze, I see Jules crouched in front of me, her eyes wide with concern. She presses a towel against my shoulders, wrapping it around me, holding the two ends together.

"You're okay. You're safe."

I try to remain focused on her. My chest still aches, but the crushing weight starts to ease, the fog lifting just enough for me to move.

She helps me up, guiding me out of the bathroom, her arm secure around my waist. The next thing I know, I'm in her bed, wrapped in blankets, the faint scent of her citrus and Jasmine shampoo lingering on the fabric, comforting in a way I didn't know I needed. My body feels heavy, drained, and my breath finally evens out.

Jules doesn't say anything, just sits beside me until my eyelids grow too heavy to keep open. And then, mercifully, sleep takes me.

When I wake, the room is bathed in dim, golden light filtering through the blinds. The world outside murmurs softly—low voices, the occasional bark of a dog, and the rhythmic sound of a basketball being dribbled. A sharper scent pulls me from my haze—the acrid tang of cigarettes wafting in through the window.

I climb out of bed and rummage through Jules's closet, sifting through mismatched hangers and clothes shoved into every corner until I find a T-shirt and a pair of sweatpants. They're oversized, the waistband sagging around my hips, but they're clean and soft.

Rubbing my eyes, I step out of the bedroom and spot Jules standing at the front door, talking to someone outside. As I approach, she glances over her shoulder, noticing me. One of her downstairs neighbors leans casually against the railing, a cigarette dangling between her fingers.

"Hey, Rainey," the neighbor greets with a nod as I step into the doorway.

"Hey," I manage a small smile.

"I should get going," the neighbor mutters, dropping her cigarette to the ground and crushing it under her slipper before walking away.

Jules watches her retreat, taking a slow drag from her own cigarette. When the neighbor disappears down the stairs, she turns her attention back to me. "Feel better?"

"Yeah, thanks."

She flicks the ash off her cigarette. Her eyes narrow as she gestures with the hand holding it, pointing toward my split lip and bruised cheek. "Ricardo?"

"Yeah," I say again, my voice remaining flat.

"And Darla was passed out drunk or with a needle in her arm?" She takes another drag, this time exhaling slowly as she stares at me.

"Needle," I mutter, resting my shoulder against the doorframe.

She rolls her eyes, stubbing out her cigarette on the windowsill beside the overflowing ashtray before flicking the butt into the pile of crushed remnants. "Of course she was."

Footsteps sound on the stairwell, drawing both our attention. A delivery driver appears at the top, a plastic bag of food swinging from his hand. Jules barely acknowledges him, handing over some cash with a quick thanks as she takes the bag. The driver gives a wave and heads back down the way he came.

I follow her inside, shutting the door quietly behind us. She sets the bag on the coffee table, then pulls out containers of Chinese takeout, placing one in front of the open spot next to her before grabbing her own. She lifts the lid, picks up a pair of chopsticks, and settles onto the worn-out cushions.

She seems like the irritated version of Jules, so I stay quiet, trying to become one with the couch. She lazily flips through channels, her attention elsewhere, while I take in the bare walls. There isn't a single picture anywhere in her apartment. It almost looks like she just moved in, but she's been here for eight months.

In the year we've been friends, the only thing I really know about her is her history with her ex-girlfriend. Jules keeps things just as private as I do. Every time I ask her a question, she either dodges it or offers just enough to satisfy curiosity without actually giving anything away. But I don't press—because I do the same. She doesn't need to pry to know my life is awful, and she never tries. It's an unspoken understanding, like we exist side by side in quiet solidarity, each knowing the other is there without ever needing to say it.

"What's next?" she asks, breaking the silence.

I sigh, setting my half-eaten carton of food on the coffee table before settling back. My eyes stay fixed ahead for a long moment before I finally turn to look at her.

We hold each other's gaze, neither of us speaking. Then, I shrug. "I don't know."

"We could always hire a hitman to take out Ricardo."

I smile, liking the sound of that, but her face remains serious.

"As much as prison sounds more stable than going back home, I'd rather not spend the rest of my life in a cell."

"We wouldn't get caught."

I stare at her for a beat, then shake my head and steer the conversation elsewhere. Ricardo is the last thing I want to talk about. "How are *you* doing? Since the breakup."

She shrugs. "I have my moments."

I can tell she doesn't want to dive any deeper, so I let it go. "Well, I'm here if you ever want to talk."

"Likewise."

We watch a movie in silence, the weight of our unspoken thoughts filling the space between us. When it ends, Jules stands, stretching.

"If you want to crash on the couch, I'll grab you a blanket. Or I can save you a spot in the bed."

"I'll come to bed in a bit," I say, my voice quieter now.

I WAKE TO THE SOUND OF JULES MOVING WITH QUIET URGENCY AS SHE gathers her things. It's only four a.m., but she's in a hurry. I don't ask where she's going—it's not my business. Instead, I just watch as she moves around the room, slipping into her shoes, adjusting the beanie on her head, and pulling the hood of her sweatshirt over it, tucking her hair away.

Just as she reaches the doorway, she pauses and peers back. When she sees I'm awake, she offers a small smile.

"Sorry to wake you. I have to go. Please stay. You'll have the place to yourself. There's groceries in the kitchen. I'll be home late tomorrow night."

"Thanks," I mumble, still groggy.

She gives a quick nod before disappearing out the door.

I spend the entire day and the next stressing over the thought of going home and facing whatever waits for me.

Jules doesn't get back until around eleven p.m. She steps inside without a word, heads straight for the shower, and crawls into bed without a single explanation. And I don't ask.

After a full day of doing nothing but watching TV and lounging around her apartment, I finally work up the nerve to leave.

"Are you sure it's a good idea?" she asks, concern lacing her voice.

"Gotta face them sooner or later."

Chapter

TWO

Rainey

I drag my feet the whole way back, each step heavier than the last. I don't want to go, but I have no choice.

When I step through the door, the stench of stale beer and cigarette smoke hits me. The place is even more trashed than when I left—overturned chairs, new holes in the walls, and empty bottles littered across the floor. They didn't even try to clean up.

Dirty needles, crumpled foil, and burnt spoons cover the table, the aftermath of their latest binge. A large bag of meth sits beside the mess, untouched—for now—but it won't stay that way for long. Next to it, a flimsy credit card from a junk mail offer lies discarded, likely used to cut the lines of coke still waiting to be snorted. I wouldn't be surprised if they actually thought the "You're approved for $40,000!" was real and tried to spend it.

I just stand there, staring—not because of the horrific scene in front of me, but because of the laughter.

Mom and Ricardo sit together on the filthy couch, both of them looking like they got the shit beaten out of them. Ricardo took the worst of it—his face is swollen, every inch of him bruised and battered like he got jumped by a group of people who really wanted to hurt him. Mom, on the other hand, only has damage to her face, and I don't have to guess who did that. Whatever happened to Ricardo must have pissed him off enough that he turned around and took it out on her.

I should feel something about that. Maybe shock, maybe disgust. But all I feel is satisfaction.

Still, what throws me off isn't how they look—it's their voices. Light. Carefree. Like they don't look like hell. Like the destruction around them isn't real. As if everything is totally fine.

For them, it's just another drunken haze, another drug-fueled stupor.

For me, it's another night of walking on eggshells, waiting for the inevitable explosion.

Will they snap this time?

Will the cops show up?

"What the hell is going on?" I mutter under my breath as I walk past them, neither bothering to acknowledge me.

Then again, why would they? I'm twenty-six—I shouldn't be here. I should have my own life, my own place. And they should have theirs.

But this trailer—the one I grew up in—is mine. My Mimi left it to me in her will. And even though mom is a shitty excuse for a human being, every time I kick her out and the cops force her to leave, I feel sick when I find her living under the bridge with the rest of the homeless. So, I let her come back.

I should leave. It's the obvious choice. But I have nowhere else to go. If I walk away, I'll be the one under that bridge.

So instead, I stay.

I stay paying back the mortgage on a trailer that was already paid off—until Mom took out a loan against it in my name. I stay covering every bill just to keep the lights on, scraping together whatever I can from side jobs, so I don't lose the only home I've ever had.

And yet, Mom never fails to remind me that *I'd* be homeless *without her.*

The irony would almost be sad if it weren't so absurd. Because the truth is, they would be out on their asses if it weren't for me.

I make it to my room, but freeze when their voices carry through the thin walls.

"She just got home," Ricardo says loud enough for me to hear.

A beat of silence.

Then— "And just to be clear, it's just her?"

My entire body locks up.

Dread coils deep in my stomach, a sickening realization settling over me. He's talking about *me.* The unease turns to panic, and before I can stop myself, I storm out of my room, my footsteps hitting the floor so hard the pictures on the walls rattle.

"What the hell was that?" I snap, my voice trembling with a mix of rage and disbelief.

Mom's head jerks up, her glassy, unfocused eyes locking onto mine. She's high—her pupils are blown wide, her movements sluggish—but she still manages a crooked, unsettling smile as she steps toward me. Her hands are outstretched, a mockery of comfort.

"Rainey, baby, don't worry," she coos. "I know how much you want me to be happy. I've been in a little trouble, but thanks to you, my problems are about to disappear."

They've clearly been in trouble—again. Both of them look like they went a few rounds with MMA fighters and lost badly. I scoff, crossing my arms over my chest.

"What kind of scam are you part of now?"

The mask of sweetness falls away in an instant, her face contorting with fury. "You little skank," she sneers, venom dripping from every word. "You're no longer going to be my problem."

The words sting more than I ever thought they could. But I'm not going to let her know. "And how's that?"

Ricardo's low chuckle makes my skin crawl, and Mom rests against the counter, smirking like she's proud of herself.

"Pack your bags. Your ride will be here shortly."

"What the hell are you talking about?"

Mom's smirk deepens, her head tilting with a sick kind of enjoyment. "I made a deal with Lorenzo Volkov. *My debt, for you.*"

The words don't just hit—they shatter me. My chest tightens as I try to make sense of her meaning. Lorenzo Volkov is a sex trafficker. Everyone knows this.

"You traded me to a mobster?!" The disbelief rips from me.

"Lorenzo takes his deals seriously, so don't bother with any foolish ideas. This is already done."

I shake my head, backing up a step as my mind races. "I'm not going anywhere! It's your debt! Go spread your own legs to pay it off!"

Ricardo rises slowly, his arms crossing over his scrawny frame. "You don't have a choice. This is how the world works, princess. You'll learn that soon enough."

That's when my eyes land on the counter—a pile of cash sits there, thick stacks of bills thrown carelessly, as if they've already started celebrating their betrayal. The sight burns into my brain, the final confirmation that they're not bluffing.

They sold me to the mob.

The mob that deals in *sex work.*

Something in me snaps. Fury and despair crash together, a tidal wave of emotion that drowns out everything else. I shoulder past Ricardo, sending him stumbling into the couch.

"What the hell do you think you're doing?!" Mom screeches.

My fingers curl around a stack of bills, gripping them so tightly my knuckles whiten, and I bolt for the door.

Ricardo's roar echoes behind me, followed by the heavy thud of his footsteps.

"Rainey! Get back here!"

The screen door slams behind me as I burst into the night. I shove the money into my janky purse and high-tail it out of there.

They sold me to a mobster.

Ricardo is yelling somewhere behind me, growing fainter with every stride, but I don't dare look back. My heart pounds so hard it feels like it might burst, and tears blur my vision, but I keep running.

I don't know where I'm going. All I know is that I have to get as far away as possible—away from them, from this hell, and from the deal they made to trade my life for their freedom.

Chapter

THREE

Damiano

I wasn't expecting her to dart out of her house in the dead of night, nor was I expecting her to collapse onto a neighbor's porch and sleep like a stray dog. She's unpredictable, reckless, and entirely captivating. It's the kind of reckless abandon that makes people dangerous, but I know how to handle danger. And I'll take all the danger she offers just to have her.

When she took off into the city, I followed, keeping my distance. I parked a block ahead, waiting down an alley for the right moment to "bump into her." My plan was to slip a tracker into her purse and monitor her movements.

What I didn't anticipate was the scumbag who ripped her purse clean off her shoulder.

I watched him run straight toward me, his wiry frame barreling forward with her belongings clutched in his fist as she lay on the ground. I considered letting it play out—the meth head wasn't worth my time. But the thought of her stumbling further into chaos without that bag—without the tracker I planned to slip inside—forced me to act.

He never saw me coming.

The first punch shatters his nose, a wet crunch sounding as blood pours down his face. He lies sprawled on the ground, gasping for air, body twitching in pain. I peer down at him, unmoved by his whimpering as I step over his crumpled form and grab the purse from where it fell.

Up close, it's even more pitiful—the sides stapled shut in a last-ditch attempt to keep it from falling apart. She doesn't just need a new purse. She needs everything.

Soon, I'll make sure she has it.

I leave the junkie groaning on the trash-strewn pavement and stride back toward her. She's standing just up the way, her posture rigid, her eyes flicking nervously between me and the bleeding man on the ground.

I stop a few feet away, holding the purse out to her. She remains unmoving, so I hold it closer, making sure she knows this isn't a trick. She hesitates, her hand hovering midair, as if unsure I'll actually let it go.

Her fingers curl around the strap tentatively, her grip light at first. "Thank you," she murmurs. As I release my hold, she adds, "For… getting this timeless artifact back."

I meet her sapphire eyes, then drop to the split in her lip, to the bruising along her cheekbone, marks that weren't there a couple of days ago.

Every second I take in the damage fuels my anger and increases the amount of pain I will inflict on someone else.

Without thinking, I reach out, my fingertips brushing just beside the wound on her lip before tilting her chin to the side. My jaw clenches as I take in the full extent of the injuries.

She stiffens but doesn't pull away. Her breath hitches, and I feel the slightest tremor.

I force myself to let go, my hands dropping to my sides.

I give her a single nod, keeping my face neutral because if I let even a fraction of what's running through my head show, she might freak out.

I took my time after that. Meth heads don't learn unless you make an example out of them. When I was done, his face was un-recognizable—a grotesque mess of blood and swelling.

He'll be found slumped against a pile of garbage bags, with just enough drugs in his system to explain away his death. No one will ask questions. It'll look like a deal gone bad.

But the truth?

I wouldn't have beaten him so badly if Rainey's face wasn't already bruised. He messed with the wrong girl and the wrong guy on the wrong day.

The only thing that went right today was slipping the tracker into the torn lining of her purse before handing it back. She didn't notice the small, nearly imperceptible tear in the fabric—or the shadow I would now cast over every move she made.

I SHOVE THE HEAVY DOUBLE DOORS OPEN TO THE FAMILY MEETING room. The scent of polished oak and faint cigar smoke hangs in the air. Pa and my five brothers sit around the dark, sprawling table, their faces immediately lifting. There's a flicker of intrigue in their eyes, as they know I don't bother coming to the business side of the house unless it's absolutely necessary.

Unlike them, I don't waste my time sitting around discussing plans when there's work to be done. My focus is on results: extracting the truths people think they can hide, breaking them down piece by piece, and ensuring they'll never be a problem again. I prefer the physicality of it—the raw, unflinching reality of a job done with my own hands. Talking and making deals is for people that don't want to get their hands dirty. I'm not one of them.

Nobody looks away as I approach the head of the table. "Ricardo Benavidez and Darla Lane. Gambling and drug debts. Totaling one-point-nine million dollars. This is the contract I've drawn up for them to sign. We're paying off their debts."

Pa doesn't so much as glance at my brothers. He settles back in his chair, fingers clasped against his stomach as he studies me. He's waiting—calm and imposing.

I drop a thick stack of papers in front of him, the weight of it punctuated by a loud thud. His eyes flick briefly to the documents, then back to me, his expression as impenetrable as stone.

He's waiting for the catch.

"And what do we get in exchange?" he asks finally.

"Darla's daughter, Rainey Lane."

I flip to the page with her picture and point. Her image stares back at us—a snapshot of innocence amidst chaos. I've memorized every detail of that photo.

"And you have a personal interest in her?" His question isn't laced with judgment, just curiosity.

"She's going to be my wife," I state plainly.

"Why *this* girl?"

I don't need to explain that I'm obsessed with her, that I'll do *anything* to have her. So I settle with, "Because I want her."

"And you think her mother will… just agree and sign?"

I lean forward, my hands flat against the table. "They either sign, or I'll kill them."

The room falls into a heavy silence. I don't need to look to know my brothers are exchanging glances—some amused, others fully aware that I will absolutely kill those two low-life scumbags if they don't sign.

Pa flips through the contract. "She will be brought here under the guise of… working here?" His tone carries layers of meaning.

"Yes." My answer is curt and final.

"Son, if you want to marry her, I don't think this is the way to go about it. We can bring her here. But not as a worker."

"She won't willingly come. She's bullheaded."

"He tried to pay for her dinner, and she told him to fuck off." Andrei smirks.

I narrow my eyes at him, then straighten, turning my attention back.

"I'm going to break her down and build her back up."

Pa lets out a long sigh. "Do you plan on participating in the auction?"

"Yes."

Dante, my eldest brother, speaks. "No. You're not putting her in the auction."

I cross my arms and stare down at him across the table. "Do you plan on stopping me?"

"Son, you're going to marry this girl. You having intercourse with her should be a private matter, to make sure everything—"

I cut him off. "Do *you* have an actual objection?"

Pa doesn't concern himself with trivial things like the auction. He's never attended one and likely never will. His focus is always on the larger picture—the kind of business that keeps this family at the top of the food chain. Lately, he's been working abroad, handling affairs I haven't been briefed on. Not that I need to be. Those details fall under Dante's jurisdiction. As the eldest, he's the one groomed to take over the family empire when the time comes.

He holds his hands up in surrender. "Will we have a detox period?"

"She's clean," I state firmly.

He studies me, his dark eyes boring into mine. "I want her tested to be sure. Handle this properly, son."

"She's clean," Andrei chimes in.

Everyone turns to him. My father looks between Andrei and me, then lifts his brows.

"How long has he had you watching her?"

Andrei's attention shifts to me.

"A year," I answer for him.

I'm not ashamed to admit it.

Dad flicks his gaze to Dante, then shakes his head and hands the papers back to me with a nod. He tells my brother Giovanni, the second oldest, to make the wire transfers to pay off all the debts and get the documents to me as soon as possible.

Gio is already pulling up his computer, and Andrei is feeding him the information for the exact amounts.

I turn to Nikolai and Silvano before I leave. "I need backup to get the contracts signed. Let's go."

A FEW MILES DOWN THE ROAD, TUCKED AWAY IN THE SHADOWS OF THE city's outskirts, lies the crumbling trailer park where the local meth dealer prefers to operate. Nestled at the far end, surrounded by rusted-out cars and battered mobile homes, sits a lone trailer where he runs his operation. It's vacant, a skeletal husk of what it once was, with broken windows, warped wood, and gaping holes in the floor large enough to swallow someone whole.

It's the kind of place that should have been condemned, one that anyone in their right mind would avoid. But for the desperate and addicted, the risk doesn't matter.

I pay the dealer a visit, slipping him enough cash to make sure he'll play his part. His reputation precedes him—eager for easy money, willing to do just about anything for a payday, and slimy enough to keep his mouth shut. I instruct him to reach out to Ricardo and Darla with news of a fresh supply. It doesn't take much convincing. When he calls them, their excitement is heard through the phone.

"We don't have any money until Rainey gets home," Ricardo admits, his tone laced with irritation. "She's out being a tramp, should be back soon with some cash."

The dealer looks to me, and I give a curt nod. He offers them a solution, feigning understanding. "Don't worry about the money. I'll put it on your tab."

Their agreement comes quickly, their greed and addiction outweighing any logic or caution. They're already planning their trip to the park, oblivious to the trap they're walking into.

I watch from the shadows as they approach, their movements jittery. Ricardo's cigarette dangles from his lips, the ember glowing faintly as he mutters something to Darla, who clings to his side like a parasite. Her arm loops through his, but he shrugs her off roughly as they reach the steps. They don't knock. They just walk right in, driven by the need for their next fix.

I step forward from the shadows, placing my hand on the back of the door and slamming it shut behind them. The sound echoes like a gunshot in the cramped, filthy trailer.

Ricardo and Darla freeze, their wide eyes flickering between me and my brothers. Nikolai, standing to my left, casually rests a bat on his shoulder, with a faint, menacing grin. On my right, Silvano leans against the wall, arms crossed, his face a mask of cold indifference that's somehow even more intimidating.

"What's going on?" Ricardo's voice is high and strained. Darla attempts to hide behind him, and he shoves her aside. "Stop clinging like a damn leech."

I take a step forward, knowing my size from across the room is intimidating, but up close, it's frightening. "It's your lucky day," I tell them.

Pure fear is written all over their faces. "We... we have no debts with the Volkovs," Ricardo stammers, his hands lifting in a weak gesture of surrender.

Behind me, Nikolai lets out a low chuckle. He shifts the bat on his shoulder as if testing its weight. Silvano says nothing, his cold stare doing all the work.

"That's not entirely true," I reply, narrowing my eyes at them. "You have one-point-nine million dollars' worth of debts to the Volkovs."

Ricardo shakes his head, his face pale. "N-n-no, we never got in bad with you all."

I tilt my head, watching them squirm. "Not directly. But I took a personal interest in your debts. I paid them off this afternoon."

The realization hits them both. Darla gasps, her hands flying to her mouth, while Ricardo takes a shaky step back, nearly tripping over her. "Please," he sputters. "We aren't looking for trouble."

"Trouble found you." Nikolai taps the end of the bat against the floor.

I cross my arms, staring them down. "You owe me a lot of money now. I want to know how you plan on paying me back."

Ricardo swallows hard, then looks around the room searching for an escape route. Darla, however, lights up like a bulb, her desperation turning into something vile and opportunistic. "We can work out a deal," she says, her voice trembling with faux confidence.

I arch a brow. "I'm listening."

Darla steps forward, her hands clasped in front of her as if she's presenting a solution to all our problems. "My daughter—she could make back every penny."

Ricardo's head jerks toward her, his expression momentarily stunned. Then, as the implication sinks in, he nods eagerly, his self-preservation outweighing any shred of morality.

"She's young, pretty… she'd bring in more than enough money, doing… your kind of business," he says, his voice almost breathless.

I glance at my brothers. Nikolai looks stunned, while Silvano remains expressionless, fixed on the pathetic couple in front of us.

"You're offering me your daughter to pay off your gambling and drug debts?"

"She's not exactly obedient, but she can learn fast. You won't regret it. You can try her out if you want. I can get her home in an hour."

The sheer audacity of it, the absolute lack of humanity is disgusting. Trading her own flesh and blood just to save herself and her low-life boyfriend.

"If you don't bring her to me within the next week, I'll make sure neither of you ever sees the light of day again."

They nod frantically, their faces pale, their urgency eclipsing their fear. I pull a pen from my coat pocket and click it. Without taking my eyes off them, I reach behind me. Silvano hands me the contract.

"Read it. Understand it. Sign it if you're willing to accept and follow the terms." I extend the contract and pen toward them.

Ricardo snatches it first, flipping straight to the last page. He scrawls his name with a shaky hand and shoves the pen at Darla.

Before she can sign, I stop her. "You have sections to fill out. Sections that outline the work your daughter will be doing upon the boxes you check."

She signs the last page and works through the packet backward, checking every single box on all the pages, sealing her own daughter's fate. When she finishes, she places the contract and pen on the ground and takes a step back.

I pick it up, slide the pen back into my pocket, and hand the papers off to Silvano.

"Would you like to know what I plan on doing with her?" My voice is calm, but the anger inside me coils like a beast ready to strike. Because Rainey deserves so much better than this. Better than them.

Darla shrugs. "It's none of my concern."

"She's your daughter."

"She's your problem now," she counters without a trace of shame.

"Against the wall." I jerk my chin, motioning for her to move to the corner.

They just stare, blinking.

I take a step closer, my voice dropping, low and lethal. "Get against the wall. Now."

Darla scrambles, pressing herself flat against the stained wallpaper. Ricardo turns to follow, but I grab the fabric of his shirt and yank him back.

"I didn't say you."

His mouth opens, just as he tries to get a word out, my fist connects with his gut, knocking the air from his lungs. He folds, gasping for air, and I don't give him time to recover as I slam a right hook into his jaw.

"For every time you put your hands on Rainey." I drive my knee into his ribs.

He groans, doubling over. I grip his hair, forcing his head up.

"For the bruise on her face today."

The punch lands clean, his nose shattering under my knuckles. Blood spills instantly, streaming down his face, soaking his shirt, pooling on the floor. He stumbles back, hands raised, shaking, trying to stop the inevitable. A choked sound escapes him. But the pain barely has time to settle before his knees give out, and he crashes to the ground, hacking up blood.

I drive my boot into his ribs, sending him rolling onto his side with a strangled yell. He curls up, trembling, gasping for air, his body convulsing in pain.

I crouch beside him, gripping his chin, forcing him to look at me through swollen eyes.

"You ever put your hands on her again, and I won't stop at broken bones." My voice is quiet now. "I will bury you."

I release him with a shove, standing to my full height. He stays down, groaning, barely conscious.

I stare at Darla. She doesn't say a word. Doesn't move. Doesn't even breathe too hard. She just remains wide-eyed.

I flex my fingers, my knuckles bloodied and swollen. I adjust my coat, then turn to walk away.

"We're done here."

I pause at the door, tossing a roll of cash at her feet.

"Get off the drugs. Stay out of the casinos. You don't have another daughter to sell."

Darla flinches, then bobs her head in frantic agreement. I signal to Nikolai and Silvano and we step out, leaving Ricardo curled on the floor and Darla cowering in the corner.

As we walk away, his shouts echo through the broken windows. "Don't just fucking stand there, bitch. Help me up!"

"Well, that was fucking pathetic," Silvano says, getting in the driver's seat.

I knew I'd walk away with the signatures. I just didn't realize it would be her own mother who would willingly suggest her for the trade.

For three days, she keeps her distance, vanishing into the city like a ghost. I know where she's staying, and I know she's safe, so I wait patiently.

Thanks to the tracker I slipped into her purse, I know the second she heads home. My backpack is already packed, ready with everything I'll need. I've anticipated her next move. Now it's time to make mine.

Ricardo and Darla don't disappoint. I left them five thousand dollars in cash—more than enough to cover their bills for a couple of months since their little cash cow won't be around much longer. Predictably, they blew through half of it in hours—a quick stop at another dealer for drugs, then takeout, followed by a trip to the gas station where they stocked up on cartons of cigarettes, scratch-off tickets, and enough junk food to keep them rotting from the inside out.

My phone buzzes, an unfamiliar number lighting up the screen. I don't need to check to know it's Ricardo. Rainey's barely set foot inside the trailer, and he's already making his move. I answer, knowing exactly what he'll say. I'm parked across from their trailer, watching what's going down inside.

"She just got home," Ricardo bellows into the speaker.

"Great."

"And just to be clear, it's just her?" Ricardo asks, looking for confirmation.

For someone higher than a kite, I'll give him this. He's asking the right questions.

"What the hell was that?" Rainey shouts in the background, cutting through the exchange.

She enters the living room, looking furious, her purse still slung over her shoulder. Ricardo couldn't even wait for her to set her things down before making the call, and the idiot didn't bother keeping his voice down.

The commotion escalates. Muffled voices give way to a scuffle, followed by the line disconnecting, then Rainey bursting out the front door, her figure illuminated in the dim glow of the porch light as she sprints down the dirt road. My plan falls perfectly into place. Behind her, Ricardo stumbles after, his movements sluggish and erratic, the drugs in his system making him far too slow to catch her.

From our parked position, we wait. Rainey's figure grows smaller in the distance, her direction unmistakable. She's heading straight for the Greyhound bus stop.

Silvano maneuvers the SUV closer as we trail behind her. When we reach the curb, he slows to a stop, and I step out. Nikolai rolls down the passenger window, and I lean in.

"You're free to go once the bus leaves with us both on it."

They nod, and I straighten.

"See you in a couple of days," Nikolai calls after me as I turn toward the bus station, the plan unfolding exactly as I intended.

I hang back, my focus trained on her as she steps up to the counter and purchases her ticket. She clutches the small slip of paper tightly and heads toward the waiting bus.

I scan the station methodically for any sign of trouble. Anyone lingering too long. Anyone watching too closely. Satisfied that neither she nor we have been followed, I stride to the counter and buy a ticket for the same route.

It's late, the station is quiet, and the bus itself is sparsely populated. The lack of passengers is a relief, giving me the freedom to select a spot near her.

Boarding a minute behind her, I sit one row up and across the aisle. Close enough to keep her within sight but not so near as to raise suspicion. I sink into the worn fabric seat as the bus doors hiss shut and it rumbles forward.

Through the window, I spot Silvano and Nikolai. I offer a subtle thumbs-up before turning away, sliding in my earbuds. The music starts, drowning out the soft hum of the engine and the occasional shuffle of passengers settling in.

Leaning back, I allow myself a brief moment of calm. The bus is moving, the plan is in motion, and so far, everything is falling perfectly into place.

Chapter

FOUR

Rainey

I use the stolen cash to buy a bus ticket for wherever the next bus to leave is going. The destination doesn't matter as long as it's far enough to make me untraceable. The woman at the counter hands me the ticket with a disinterested look, her nails clicking against the counter as she taps impatiently, signaling for me to move along.

By the time the bus boards, I find a seat near the back, far from prying eyes. My heart pounds as I sit down, tucking my purse next to me in my chair. I keep checking my surroundings, scanning the few people boarding behind me.

Did Ricardo follow me?

Did Mom send someone else?

I crouch lower in my seat, trying to make myself as small and invisible as possible. The bus is fairly empty with plenty of open seats, and no one stands out immediately.

I can't relax. Even when the bus pulls out of the station and we're officially on the road, my nerves won't settle. I stare ahead, taking in details, focusing on the mundane to keep my mind occupied.

A few rows up, a woman with short, curly red hair sits silently, the frizzy ends catching what little light filters through the bus. Across the aisle, a gray-haired man rests his head against the window, clutching a balled-up gray hoodie in his arms. *Why not just use it as a pillow?* It's like those guys at ballgames who wear their caps backward only to shield their eyes with their hands.

Another passenger, a man with long, greasy blond hair, has limp strands sticking to the collar of his battered jacket, draping over his shoulders.

But one head of hair catches my attention—jet black and wavy. It belongs to a man sitting one row ahead on the opposite side, by the window. His hair is cropped shorter on the sides in a low fade, gradually blending into longer, loose waves on top, combed up and over. He's wearing a hoodie with the hood down, the dark fabric hugging his broad shoulders. From my angle, I can make out tattoos creeping up from the collar of his shirt. His ears have 10mm gauges in each lobe, adding to the striking impression he leaves.

I've always liked the look of earrings. There's something about them, simple yet expressive, that appeals to me. Mom, however, was adamantly against the idea of me getting my ears pierced. She called it frivolous, unnecessary, and something I'd regret later. When I was bitten by a wasp as a kid, she seized the opportunity to cement her point.

"That's exactly what getting your ears pierced feels like," she warned. "Now that you know, let's go get it done."

The thought of intentionally enduring that kind of pain terrified me. The idea of choosing to feel something similar? It's a fear I've never quite outgrown.

Still, I can't deny how much I like the look of them. His earrings, in particular, seem to fit him effortlessly. And yet, I can't quite explain why I care so much about the way they look on him—or why I keep noticing at all.

He's got earbuds in, staring out the window. I find myself watching him far longer than I should. I'm so lost in thought, so tuned into the steady rise and fall of his breathing, that I don't realize I've zoned out until he shifts slightly. My stomach flips, and I quickly look away, hoping he hasn't noticed.

The bus rumbles on, the vibrations humming through the floor beneath my feet, but I can't seem to fully relax. My mind flits from one distraction to another—the faint murmur of a phone call a few rows ahead, the distant rustle of a newspaper—anything to ignore the knot tightening in my stomach.

Then, unexpectedly, he moves. He turns his head, his eyes sweeping the aisle before landing directly on mine. The connection is fleeting, but it's enough to send a jolt of electricity through me, leaving me frozen as he rises from his seat and heads to the back of the bus to use the bathroom.

As he disappears down the aisle, my attention goes right back to his now-empty spot, where his backpack rests in the aisle seat and his wallet lies on the floor.

I hesitate, glancing around to see if anyone else has noticed, but the other passengers remain oblivious.

Slowly, I stand and cross the aisle, bending down to pick it up. My pulse quickens as I weigh my next move. I want to peek at his driver's license—I just want to know his name. To see if the name matches the gorgeous man.

Eww, Rainey, cut it out.

I consider slipping the wallet into his backpack, thinking it might be the safest place, but the thought feels like an even bigger invasion of his privacy. Maybe I should just leave it on his seat so he'll see it when he returns. But before I can make a decision, I feel it—the warmth of his presence.

He's already there, standing right behind me.

I turn, landing on his black sweatshirt before roaming up. My eyes widen so much I'm surprised they don't plop out of my head onto the floor.

"You dropped this." I hold the wallet out to him.

His dark eyes lock onto mine, and for a moment, he doesn't say anything. The silence stretches, and then he speaks—just one word. His voice is smooth, with an edge that makes my skin prickle.

"Intentionally."

I freeze, trying to process his response. *Intentionally?* Does he mean he purposely dropped it? Why?

"Do you want it back?"

I'm still holding it out, unsure if this is some kind of game.

"Sit down," the driver calls, his voice abrupt and annoyed.

We both glance toward the front of the bus before his hand moves, taking the wallet. His fingers graze mine briefly, and then he slips the wallet into his sweatshirt pocket.

He steps sideways past me, his broad frame brushing along mine. He's rock solid, and all I can think about is how I want to press myself against him, sliding up and down his body.

I sink back into my seat, glaring at myself in the window for even *thinking* like that. Whoever he is, trouble radiates off him. But for some reason, my body didn't get the memo.

No matter how hard I try to focus on the darkness outside, I find myself drifting right back to him. His profile is striking, with a razor-sharp jawline and high cheekbones—a face better suited for a movie poster than a beat-up bus in the middle of the night.

But he's here, which means he's running from something too. Nobody ends up on a bus like this for no reason. Whatever it is, I can't imagine it being worse than my life. Nobody is more screwed than me.

My stomach literally clenches at the thought. Because it is quite literal. I will be screwed in all the sinister ways that disgusting men can think of if I'm caught.

Still, he looks strong. Not just physically, but like someone who's been through hell and came out swinging. He looks like the kind of guy who could punch Ricardo's nose straight through his skull, and for some reason, the thought brings me immense joy.

I drift down to his hands resting on his lap. His knuckles are already scabbed over, the wounds still fresh. It's proof that he can throw a punch and come out on top, especially since his hands are the only part of him that looks even slightly damaged.

I trail back up his physique, my mouth actually salivating, until I'm staring at his face again. My heart skitters to a halt when I realize his head has turned toward me.

How did I not notice him looking back at me?

Our eyes lock, and I freeze, my breath catching in my throat. For a second, I can't look away. He doesn't seem surprised. If anything, he looks curious, like he's trying to figure me out.

Panic sets in, and I force myself to turn back toward the window, but I can still feel his gaze on me. I lace my fingers together in my lap, trying to act like I'm not completely mortified.

After a moment, I glance back, our eyes locking again. This time, he looks away, turning to the window like nothing happened.

He must think I'm such a weirdo.

The bus rolls on through the night. When it finally pulls into a rest stop, I scoot to the edge of my seat, my back and legs aching for a stretch.

"If you need to use the bathroom, this will be the only stop for the next several hours," the driver calls as he steps off to light a cigarette.

I consider holding it, but four more hours is too long. With a sigh, I stand and stretch, immediately drawn right back to the man one row up. His head rests against the window, eyes closed, breathing steady. I could spend the entire break watching him sleep, even taking a second to admire the softness of his lips.

Moving quietly, I steal one last look—he's effortlessly gorgeous—before heading down the narrow steps into the cool night air. I walk toward the women's restroom, scanning my surroundings. A few cars are scattered across the lot, a semi parked off to the far left. Probably people sleeping since it's so late.

Inside, the bathroom is eerily quiet. I push open the first stall. Then the second. Checking each one.

Empty.

Relieved, I lock myself in the last one, doing my best to finish quickly.

As I'm about to leave, footsteps echo against the tiled floor. At first, just one set. Then two.

The shadows beneath the door reveal them stopping, standing just one stall away from mine.

My pulse pounds as I steel myself, then push the door open.

Two men stand there.

They aren't from the bus.

They must have come from one of the vehicles in the parking lot. Almost everyone on the bus was asleep. Only two passengers got off before me, but they were outside with the driver, smoking.

"What are you doing out so late?" one of them asks with a grin, revealing a gap where his two front teeth should be.

"This is the women's bathroom." I try to keep my voice level as I walk past them to the sink. The faucet squeaks as I turn it on, and I focus on my hands, washing away the soap, pretending I'm not hyper-aware of their presence.

"You were on that bus, yeah?" the second man asks. His tone is casual, but there's a thinly veiled edge to it. "We have a car. Come with us. It'll be fun."

I ignore him, finishing up and reaching for the paper towels, but they block my way.

"Ready to get out of here, sexy?" Toothless Wonder smirks, taking a step closer.

"Get out of my way." I move to step around them, but they shift, cutting off my path.

"Move," I say firmly, but the calm veneer is slipping; panic is already clawing its way up my throat.

"We'll move," the second man says, grinning wide. "In and out of that tight—"

"Get out of my way, or I'll scream."

The knife is out before I can register the movement.

"Scream," he says coldly, "and I'll dump your intestines on the floor where you stand."

My hands shake as I press them behind me against the sink. "Please… just let me go."

As one of them moves closer, the bathroom door creaks open. A tall figure steps in, leaning casually against the wall.

"What's up?" His voice is deep, calm, and commanding.

The man holding the knife sneers. "This is the women's bathroom."

"Oh yeah? You got a pussy?" the newcomer asks.

When the guy holding the knife scoffs and turns to look at the man who entered, I flick my gaze to him too. Relief crashes into me the second I recognize the man from the bus. He still looks tired, a sleepy hint lingering in his features.

His eyes flick to me, then back to them. "Let's go," he says, his words directed at me. He raises two fingers, motioning me toward him.

"Get out of here, punk. Mind your own business," Toothless sneers.

I step forward, but the men grab my arms, pinning me in place.

"She's not going anywhere," Knife Man snaps, flashing the blade. "I suggest you leave now before you get hurt."

My bus hero tilts his head slightly. "Let her go," he repeats, his voice more dangerous.

The knife lunges toward him, but he moves faster. With a swift, controlled motion, he grabs the man's wrist, twisting it back until the knife clatters to the floor. A crack echoes in the room, followed by a scream as the man collapses, clutching his broken hand.

The second guy stumbles back, hands raised. "Whoa! We didn't know she was yours! We just—"

His words are cut off by a kick to the stomach, sending him sprawling. My rescuer steps onto the first man's neck, pressing down hard.

"Didn't you mention me getting hurt?" he asks darkly, his tone so cold it makes me nervous for the man on the ground.

The man gasps, his face red and panicked.

"Go back to the bus." His voice is softer now as he jerks his chin toward the door.

I don't second-guess leaving him alone in there with them. I rush out of the bathroom, my heart racing so fast I swear it's about to burst through my chest cavity.

Back on the bus, I slump into my seat near the back, trying to steady my breathing. Outside, the driver is still chatting with another man, his cigarette smoke curling into the air.

Minutes pass, stretching into what feels like an eternity, before the tattooed man steps back onto the bus, just behind the driver.

He sits catty-corner to me, in the same spot as before, pulling out his phone. His thumbs move quickly over the screen before he slips it into his bag, leans back, and puts his earbuds in, staring out the window.

It's only when my eyes trail down to his shoes, black running shoes with white soles, that I notice the faint red stains on the bottom.

Is that blood?

My gaze shifts to his hands. They're wrapped in bandages, the white cloth already soiled with crimson seeping through.

Before I can second-guess myself, I grab my purse and move seats, sliding into the spot next to him. He doesn't react until I reach over and tug one of his earbuds out, slipping it into my own ear.

He turns to me, one dark brow raised.

"Who is this?"

"Letdown," he says simply, his voice sending an unintentional shiver through me.

"I like it," I reply, letting the music wash over me.

His eyes linger on mine, searching, before he turns his attention back to the window. I take in his hands again, bloodied and bandaged. The sight pulls at me, a morbid curiosity gnawing at the edges of my thoughts.

What happened in that bathroom? Just how much damage did he leave behind?

The silence between us stretches impossibly long, and the occasional shuffle of passengers is the only sound filling the void. Neither of us speaks. Neither of us moves. Yet, at some point, without realizing it, we both lean slightly toward each other, as if drawn together by an unseen thread.

"Are you single?" The words spill out before I can stop them.

I instantly want to crawl into myself.

What the hell is wrong with me?

He looks at me, caught off guard.

"I'm alone," I add. "And I don't know why I'm telling you that. But… if you're single, and you're alone too… maybe we can stay together. I'm not good at much, but I can help us get by."

He stares at me for so long I start to feel self-conscious. Heat creeps into my cheeks, and I avert my eyes.

"You have a girlfriend," I state flatly, assuming his silence is confirmation.

"No," he says. "No girlfriend."

Relief washes over me, and I exhale softly. "Good. I'll go wherever you choose. I only have forty dollars left, but I can get more."

But I can't.

I'm nobody. I'm nothing.

I have no skills. My life is a mess. I've been sold into sex work. And I'm trying to drag an innocent man into my mess. If the Volkovs get their hands on him, he will be killed.

How selfish can I be?

An invisible grip tightens around my lungs, squeezing the air from them. *Not again. Don't do this now.* My vision tunnels. My pulse pounds against my skull, erratic and frantic.

Not here. Not now.

The walls of my mind cave in, drowning me in a surge of panic so sudden I can't fight it. I can't breathe. I can't—

His bandaged hand moves suddenly, resting lightly on my thigh. The unexpected touch sends a jolt through me.

"Breathe," he says softly, his dark eyes holding mine.

I'm on the edge of losing control.

"Breathe," he repeats gently, shifting slightly in his seat to face me. He demonstrates, inhaling deeply through his nose and exhaling slowly through his mouth.

I mimic his actions, focusing on his calm rhythm.

Inhale. Exhale.

Inhale. Exhale.

Each breath stretches the cage around my ribs. The tightness loosens, the panic ebbing away, leaving me drained.

I ease back in the seat, letting out a shaky sigh of relief. Exhaustion weighs heavily on me, and without thinking, I let my head rest on his shoulder.

His warmth and presence lull me into a fragile sense of security, and before I know it, sleep overtakes me.

"MISS, TIME TO GET OFF." THE DRIVER'S VOICE PULLS ME OUT OF MY dreamless sleep, accompanied by a gentle shake of my shoulder.

I blink groggily, disoriented as I look around. The bus is empty. The man who had been beside me is gone.

My stomach sinks, a hollow ache settling in.

He left me.

Grabbing my purse, I step off the bus. The near-empty parking lot stretches out before me. My eyes dart from one shadow to another, searching for any sign of him.

Nothing.

His earbud is still in my ear, playing music—the same song I had first heard when I took it from him.

He's close.

My heart leaps with hope, but then, just as quickly, the music cuts off. Silence fills the air, and with it, a cold realization.

He's gone.

Another person has left.

Another reminder that no one ever stays.

"Rainey. Get in the car."

The air catches in my lungs as I turn to face Ricardo. His disheveled appearance—the rumpled clothes, the dull glaze over his bloodshot eyes—nearly sends me crumbling to the ground. His presence feels like defeat incarnate, a nightmare come to life.

"Please." My voice trembles with desperation. "Just let me go."

My mind screams at the injustice. If the guy from the bus had stayed just five more minutes, he could have been here—a shield between me and Ricardo.

But he didn't stay.

It's just me.

Ricardo shakes his head slowly, his tone disturbingly flat. "You know I can't. They'll kill your mom and me if we don't hand you over."

He's high—higher than I've seen him before. But despite the haze in his expression, a flicker of guilt crosses his face, fleeting but there.

Even he knows how vile this is.

"You know what they'll do to me." Tears well up, blurring the glow of the parking lot lights.

"Sorry, Rainey." He shrugs with a casualness that makes bile rise in my throat. "My hands are tied."

I frantically scan the parking lot for any chance of escape. But then, Ricardo pulls a gun from his pocket. His grip is loose, but the threat is unmistakable.

"I got a new toy," he says. "Don't know how to use it yet, but after a couple of shots, I'm sure I'll get the hang of it. Let's go."

He motions toward the car he borrowed from the neighbor, the barrel of the gun leading the way.

And just like that, the final thread of hope snaps.

Chapter

FIVE

Damiano

Nikolai and Silvano are waiting at the bus stop when we arrive.

"Bathroom's handled," Nikolai says as I climb into the back seat.

That mess wasn't part of the plan. If I had time, I'd have made those bastards suffer for days before letting death finally take them. But time wasn't a luxury. I needed to be on that bus.

I didn't expect her to sit beside me.

Even less did I expect her to take one of my earbuds from my ear.

And when she asked if I had a girlfriend, I was momentarily confused, forgetting that she doesn't know she's mine yet.

I've spent the last year mentally creating a life with her, planning every detail, every step toward the inevitable. I wanted to tell her she'd be my wife soon.

She steps off the bus, turning in circles as she searches for me. A flicker of hope crosses her face as the music continues to play.

It almost makes me change plans entirely.

Almost.

But when I disconnect the signal, I see it—the hope drains from her eyes, replaced by cold, crushing reality. She's going back home.

"Think he's sober enough to get her back safely?" Silvano asks.

I watch the car we're following, and he'd definitely get pulled over if a cop were behind him. We'll just stay a barrier between them and anyone else.

Most of the drive, he stays under the speed limit. Other times, he goes so fast I can hardly believe the car can reach these speeds.

The bastard is so high, I'm surprised he can even find his way back.

Boris and a couple of our men are already in position, the van waiting for the signal.

Boris knows the rules. Everyone does.

Rainey is mine.

No one lays a hand on her.

When we near the trailer park, we cut ahead, parking far enough away to keep eyes on the place without being spotted.

The flickering porch light casts uneven shadows over the run-down trailer. Darla props herself against the warped railing, puffing on a cigarette.

Silvano types a quick message to Boris, letting him know it's time. The reply comes back instantly—a thumbs-up.

The neighbor's junk of a car rolls into view, and I straighten in my seat, watching it all unfold.

Rainey slams the car door as she gets out.

Darla grins. That smug, twisted expression makes me want to knock the last of her teeth down her throat. She looks past Rainey, right at Ricardo, and her lips curl into something darker.

That's when the black van pulls up.

Boris and Marko step out, clad in all black, and all three of their eyes widen.

Rainey spins to face her mother. "If you ever loved me, you wouldn't do this!"

Darla's response?

She locks her arms over her chest. "Have fun getting fucked, bitch." Her sinister laughter follows.

My jaw drops, and Nikolai turns to look at me, his expression mirroring my own.

"Did she actually just say that?"

Ricardo's hand lashes out, silencing Darla with a vicious backhand. The impact sends her stumbling, her hand flying to her cheek as she glares daggers at him.

"What if I refuse to go?" Rainey's voice cuts through the night.

But Boris and Marko don't give her the chance.

Rough hands seize her arms, dragging her toward the van as she twists, kicks, and screams. She fights like hell, but it won't change the outcome.

Nikolai glances back at me before handing over a tablet. The screen is already pulled up to a live feed from inside the van.

I watch as Rainey is shoved inside. She stumbles but recovers quickly, shooting a glare at Boris before dropping down next to one of the other girls. Even in this mess, she holds her chin high. Stubborn as hell, that one.

The van rocks slightly as it pulls away. Boris perches in the single bolted seat against the wall, his hulking frame taking up so much space that his size alone is enough to keep them in line. Up front, Marko lights a cigarette, exhaling a slow stream of smoke as he watches the road.

My eyes stay glued to the screen.

Rainey doesn't cry. Doesn't break down.

Instead, she sits rigid, her hands clenched into fists, staring straight ahead.

Chapter
SIX

Rainey

The van door slides open, and I'm shoved inside with enough force to make me fall. The air is suffocating, thick with fear and sweat.

Or maybe it's just my own fear and sweat I'm smelling.

Six other girls are crammed in the back, huddled together like fragile porcelain dolls, their faces streaked with tears that glisten in the dim light.

The van rocks slightly as one of the men climbs in, settling his massive body into a single seat against the wall. He's so big, he takes up more space than a normal person should. The other man moves to the passenger seat up front, but my attention stays fixed on the one in the back—his grin as twisted as his nature.

A dark part of me hopes the chair buckles beneath him. That it cracks, sends him crashing to the floor, and he hurts himself.

I let myself indulge in the thought, fixating on the chair, silently willing it to snap beneath him.

Just one thing.

If I get nothing else out of this, let the damn chair break.

But it holds firm.

I scan the girls' faces for signs of injury. To my relief, none of them appear visibly hurt. They seem well cared for—clean, their clothes unsoiled.

Meanwhile, I feel filthy. I haven't showered in days, which is a complete contrast to their almost pristine appearances.

"Where are you taking us?" I'm impressed that my voice comes out calm when internally, I'm shaking like a leaf.

The man's grin widens.

"Shut the fuck up, or I'll shut you up with my cock."

The vile threat makes me flinch.

He jerks his chin toward a girl curled in the far corner, her eyes still shut.

"Ask her."

My stomach churns violently as his words sink in.

What a fucking pig.

I shrink back, my gaze darting to the girl he's singled out. Even in the dim light, I can see the faint glisten of what might be blood on her lip, though it's hard to tell for certain.

The van lurches as it starts moving, and the harsh motion sends us all colliding into one another. The girl beside me reaches out, her fingers slipping into mine.

"I'm Tess," she says, her voice so soft it barely reaches me over the rattling of the van.

I turn to look at her.

"Rainey" is my only response.

As the van rolls forward, the passing streetlights cast fleeting slashes of light through the darkened windows. I glance back at the girl he pointed out.

Her lip *is* split, fresh blood staining the corner of her mouth. Her hair is a tangled mess, like someone had been yanking on it.

He wasn't bluffing.

Hours later, the van slows as we pull up to a sprawling estate— the kind of place that would be splashed across glossy magazine covers or used as the backdrop for a movie.

But instead of awe, a sickening dread tightens around my chest at the reality of why we're here.

Men in all black are stationed around the property, their postures stiff and professional. Bulletproof vests stretch across their chests, long guns slung securely over them. Their faces don't hold malice or curiosity—just focus. They're here for a job, to protect the people inside.

And to make sure no one leaves.

We're ushered out of the van near the side of the house, herded like cattle. Two guards stand stationed, their presence unmoving, their hands resting on their guns. At first, there's nothing but the smooth exterior of the estate, but as we're pushed forward, a hidden set of stairs is revealed beneath the cover of darkness.

As we walk, the massive man who had been in the back with us suddenly reaches out and smacks the girl with the bloody lip on the ass. The crack of his hand against her skin echoes in the night air, but she barely reacts—halting slightly before moving again.

I don't understand.

We're not handcuffed. We're not bound in any way. She could fight back. So why doesn't she?

My blood burns. I step out of line and barrel toward him. "Keep your fucking disgusting hands off her!" I yell.

Before I can fully reach him, a hand grabs my arm, jerking me back. I twist, wrenching against the hold, but the grip is firm.

It's the man from the passenger seat.

He doesn't say anything, just turns me back around, forcing me forward toward the stairs. My breath comes fast, my body trembling with rage, but I can't break free.

Then I realize—I may have just made it worse for her.

She's no longer walking with us.

He has her bent over the passenger seat.

Lifting her dress.

I try to look back, but the stairs are swallowing me whole, pulling me beneath the house.

By the time I reach the bottom, I can't see anything else. That's exactly what's going to happen to me. Men will take what they want from me whenever they want. I will now live with perpetual dread that any second of the day I could be assaulted.

The deeper we go, the colder the air becomes. It's damp and heavy, laced with the faint metallic tang of fear. At the bottom, two massive doors stand before us.

We're shoved into a room, lit by a single bulb, casting long, eerie shadows. The concrete floor is unwelcoming, and the walls are lined with metal handcuffs that glint ominously. My stomach drops further as I take it all in.

This isn't just a basement.

It's a cell.

A murmured warning beside me grabs my attention. "Don't involve yourself with other people's affairs."

I turn to Tess, startled by her words. "He spanked her."

Her eyes meet mine.

"And he can. *She's his.*"

I gape at her.

We don't belong to anybody.

The door creaks open, and a woman saunters in. She's both captivating and terrifying.

Sleek black hair, streaked with bold crimson, frames a flawless face. Her lips, painted blood-red, match the heels clicking against the cold concrete. Tight leather pants and a leopard-print top hug her curvy figure, every inch of her radiating danger and control.

It has to be around one in the morning, yet she's dressed to the nines.

She surveys us like a predator sizing up its prey.

"Come on, ladies," she purrs, her voice smooth as silk. "I don't know why those buffoons put you in here. This is where people get tortured."

She laughs lightly, as if she's made a joke. But there's no humor in her tone. And her words chill me to the core.

With a snap of her fingers, she beckons us to follow. We hesitate, but instinct pushes us forward.

She leads us up the stairs and into a sitting room that couldn't be more different from the basement. Lavish furniture, ornate rugs, and sparkling chandeliers fill the space. But the warmth it's meant to exude feels hollow, like a façade barely holding together.

She gestures for us to sit, and we comply, sinking cautiously into the plush cushions. The others ease back into the couch, their bodies folding into the softness.

I, however, perch on the edge, my back stiff, my fingers gripping my other hand in a desperate attempt to stay grounded.

Fear roots me there—too wary to let my guard down, too scared to even pretend I belong in a place like this.

The fabric is soft, but it feels foreign against my skin, as though it's rejecting me. I glance at the other women, each of them dressed in clean, well-fitted clothing that only highlights how out of place I am.

The pants I borrowed from Jules are covered in dirt, and the oversized sweatshirt hangs loose on me. They don't look like they came from the slums the way I do.

I half-expect her to sneer, maybe even throw down plastic wrap to protect her spotless floor from me. Or worse, make me undress and refuse to let my dirty clothes inside her home. But she says nothing as she scans each of us, and then realization hits.

"We're missing one," she notes, turning to the man who dragged me down the stairs.

"She's with Boris," he tells her.

She mouths a slow "Ahh" in understanding, like it all makes perfect sense.

But it doesn't make sense. A man gets angry at us, and that gives him the right to do whatever he wants? *I* made him mad, and somehow, she paid the price?

What if I'm next?

No—I can't think like that. If I do, I'll end up impressing this lady by puking all over her floor.

She takes her place across from us, lowering into an armchair with fluid grace, her legs crossing elegantly.

Everything about her radiates power. It's not just her beauty that intimidates. It's the aura of someone who knows she holds all the cards.

"I'm Valentina Volkov," she announces with a wide smile, and I realize this must be Lorenzo Volkov's wife.

"This isn't ideal, I'm sure," she begins. "But you'll grow to like being here. It's no surprise—you're all very pretty, and look much younger than your actual age, which will bode nicely in your favor."

She sweeps over us like we're objects on display.

"I have six boys—well, five who… let's just say they can't function without sex. They handle a lot of important business here, and you'll assist in keeping their stress levels low."

Her words hit like a slap, each one laced with implications so vile my brain refuses to accept it.

"I want to be transparent," she continues. "You'll be freshened up and pampered tomorrow afternoon to prepare for the auction."

Auction. Did she just fucking say auction?! As in, we are going to be auctioned?! They're going to auction human beings?!

"The first couple of weeks will be rocky, but you'll get into the swing of things. You'll be clothed, bathed, and fed. And all we expect in return is for you to keep the men coming in and out of this house happy."

Her tone is casual, as though what she's asking should be simple.

But she doesn't have to spell it out. I already know exactly what she expects from us.

"Each one of you sitting here has the same thing in common," she begins. "You're beautiful, and your innocence is still intact."

I feel violated just by her words.

That is something I never wanted anyone to know. Let alone the fact that they, too, are virgins.

"Don't get hung up on that, however," she continues smoothly. "You'll all be rid of that burden in a couple of days and ready to work. Some of my boys get a little rough, but don't worry—any injuries will be handled by our doctor." She smiles. "Your rooms are lovely. You ladies must be so tired. Let me show you to them."

She motions for us to follow, her heels already clicking against the polished floor.

Everyone rises and trails after her.

Except me.

I just gape.

The same hands grip my arm again, yanking me off the couch.

I stumble forward, hurrying to fall in step with the others. Tess glances over her shoulder, narrowing her eyes at the man behind me.

He chuckles—a quiet, amused sound—but I don't dare look back.

I don't have to. I can feel him right there.

As Valentina leads us down the long corridor, I catch snippets of her voice. "…your rooms are a place men like to go for their breaks."

At first, the words don't register. But then, realization crashes into me.

As in, anybody can come into our rooms at any time and…

Oh fuck.

We reach a massive spiral staircase, its golden railing gleaming under the soft glow of chandeliers.

At the base of the stairs stands the asshole from outside. The girl is nowhere to be seen.

He looks uninterested as we pass, his expression bored, until he spots me. Then, he smirks.

I narrow my eyes at him, and a strong hand seizes my arm, pushing me ahead. I yank free, proving I can walk just fine, and he doesn't argue.

The hallway stretches endlessly, lined with white doors, each adorned with intricate gold carvings. Every gleaming detail is a mockery of just how far I am from the life I once knew.

The others have already disappeared behind their doors. Only one remains open, with Valentina waiting beside it, her smile fixed on me.

"Come now, sweetheart," she coos, extending a hand in what's meant to be a comforting gesture.

It isn't.

I step forward, and her perfectly manicured, soft hands gently grasp each of my arms as she studies me from head to toe. Her gaze lingers on my face, and her features soften. She cups my cheeks, her thumb brushing over the bruise on my skin.

"You are extraordinarily beautiful."

One hand falls away while the other softly glides through my hair, from scalp to ends, her fingers trailing over every inch.

"Why don't you shower?" she gestures to my clothes with a faint wrinkle of her nose. "You can throw that away when you're done. There's an entirely new wardrobe in your closet. We'll get you polished up tomorrow."

She leans in and presses a kiss to my cheek.

My lips part in shock.

No one—not a single person in my life—has ever done that.

And yet, the woman preparing me for sex work just did.

For a fleeting moment, I almost relax.

Until I remember why I'm here.

Until I remember what I will be forced to do.

"If you need anything, just remember what it is and let someone know tomorrow."

With that, she motions for me to enter the room, then pulls the door shut behind me. The lock clicks from the outside, and her footsteps echo down the hall.

The room is breathtaking in a way that feels wrong. A massive king-sized bed dominates the space, its frame carved from dark wood and draped with silky, pale gold linens. Two matching nightstands sit on either side, each topped with a sleek lamp that casts a soft, warm glow. A cushioned chaise lounge sits elegantly in the corner, near a vanity stocked with expensive-looking makeup and perfume.

The attached bathroom is nothing short of incredible—marble floors, a soaking tub big enough for two, and a glass-enclosed shower with more settings than I can count. A massive closet stretches along one wall, and when I step inside, my breath catches.

It's full, overflowing with clothes. But not the kind I'd ever wear.

Racks of lingerie in every shade imaginable—delicate bras and panties crafted from lace and sheer fabrics that leave nothing to the imagination. Silk nightgowns so short they might as well be shirts. Shorts so tiny half my butt will hang out. Even the casual clothes—if they could be called that—are designed to cling and reveal. High heels in every style, color, and height line the shelves like trophies.

There's not a single modest outfit in here.

Not one.

I'm. A. Whore.

The words claw at my mind, branding themselves into me.

I step into the shower, the steaming water pouring down from a rainfall head as if it's trying to wash away the filth of the past twenty-six years. I let myself pretend this is normal—that this isn't a gilded cage designed to break me.

When I step into the closet, I sift through my options, each one more humiliating than the last.

Nothing in here was meant for comfort.

Eventually, I settle on a silk nightgown so short it barely qualifies as a shirt, so I pair it with cotton shorts that offer little more coverage. They don't match, but I don't care. It's the closest thing to full coverage I can find.

As much as I want to resist, the bed pulls me in.

The mattress cradles me, but sleep is reluctant, shallow, and restless. My thoughts keep circling back to the handcuffs bolted to the headboard.

And the skimpy little nightmares waiting in the closet.

I WAKE TO A SOFT KNOCK ON THE DOOR AND THE DISTANT HUM OF voices. My body feels heavy, my mind groggy. I barely slept, the tension in my chest never loosening.

The morning moves in a blur.

We're ushered downstairs, the scent of coffee and bacon filling the air as we enter the dining room. The table is set with an extravagant spread—fluffy pancakes, scrambled eggs, fresh fruit, and pastries. More food than I've seen in months.

"Eat," a woman instructs, her voice devoid of warmth. "You'll need your strength."

None of us speak.

The silence is thick, broken only by the clatter of utensils. My stomach churns, but the taste of the food almost distracts me.

Almost.

When breakfast ends, we're led down another corridor, this one longer and even more imposing than the last. We pass door after door, finally stopping at a set of double doors.

They swing open, and the sight stops me in my tracks.

It's a spa—an actual, fully equipped spa, right here on the property.

The faint strains of soft, calming music play in the background, mingling with the gentle scent of lavender and eucalyptus. Under different circumstances, it might have felt luxurious. But here, it feels wrong.

"You're being pampered today," Valentina announces, her voice sweet as she claps her hands together in excitement. "Massages, facials, manicures, pedicures, waxing—you'll look and feel perfect."

I glance at the other girls, and they all seem happy about this.

Happy.

Are they not grasping what's about to happen to us?

Who gives a shit that we're getting massages or our nails done?

We are going to be assaulted.

This isn't a gift.

It's preparation.

I'm led to a massage table, but as I lie down, my muscles tighten, refusing to relax under the stranger's hands. The woman kneads the knots that seem woven into my very being. The motions are meant to soothe, but they only make me more tense.

I want to ask her how she can stand to work here, but she probably doesn't have a choice either. Everyone working here is probably forced.

I hate every second of the facial. I find out immediately—I hate people touching my face.

The manicure and pedicure are unnervingly thorough, every detail of my hands and feet meticulously scrubbed, shaped, and polished. I didn't even get to choose the color. When Valentina handed the girl a bottle, she attempted to suggest a different shade, but Valentina shut her down with a firm, *No, this one is best.* Without further protest, the girl applied it.

As I finish, Valentina glides toward me, a satisfied smile on her lips.

"She needs her hair done," she says, tilting her head as she studies me. Then, with a flick of her wrist, she gestures toward a girl with blonde hair. "Add some depth to that color. Lighten it up, but make it look natural."

The girl's chin dips, and she immediately sets to work.

She sections my deep mahogany hair, applying the color with careful strokes. Time slips away, and when she finally rinses and dries it, I barely recognize myself.

My hair looks lighter, softer—but not unnatural. The brown base remains, but ribbons of warm caramel and golden honey weave through the strands. The added dimension makes it appear expensive, yet effortless.

I've never had my hair professionally done before. I've spent my whole life being a nobody, and right now, I'm struggling with imposter syndrome, feeling like I don't deserve this treatment.

But don't I?

I'm going to be fucked against my will.

I immediately want to mess up the beautiful style she created—the way she curled it, the new framing around my face.

This is hair that will draw attention.

And I don't want anybody's attention in this place.

When they bring out the wax, my body locks up.

"Everything," Valentina says. "Leave nothing behind."

My breath catches. I freeze, dread prickling over my skin.

The process is as painful as it is humiliating.

Each rip of the wax feels like a violation, every pull stripping away more than just hair.

It's invasive. Degrading. It leaves my face burning with shame and anger.

I want to lash out—partly because of the pain, but mostly because I wasn't given a choice. My hair is being removed when I don't want it to be.

By the time it's over, my skin feels raw.

Too smooth. Too exposed.

I glance at my reflection in a nearby mirror.

The person staring back looks polished and perfect.

But she's not me.

She's a stranger, molded to someone else's design.

I STARE OUT THE WINDOW OF MY NEW PRISON, A SECOND-FLOOR ROOM overlooking the sprawling estate.

The night sky stretches endlessly above, its beauty a cruel contrast to the suffocating reality I'm trapped in. The estate grounds are eerily still, bathed in pale moonlight that casts long, haunting shadows over the manicured lawns and perfectly trimmed hedges.

This will be my last night intact.

Okay, maybe I was never fully intact.

But my body was.

As my eyes sweep the expanse, a flicker of movement catches my attention. My stomach tightens painfully as I make out a group of men walking below, their low voices drifting faintly on the cool night air.

Then, I see him.

Him.

The man from the bus.

A spark ignites in my chest—relief, desperation, hope—burning so fiercely it almost hurts.

Without thinking, I pound on the window.

"Hey!" My voice is muffled by the thick glass, but the urgency is there. "Up here!"

The group stops.

Heads turn toward the sound.

My heart pounds as his gaze sweeps across the windows—until it locks onto mine.

For a breathless moment, I think he sees me.

I wave wildly, signaling him with every ounce of strength I have left.

Relief floods me, hot and overwhelming. I'm going to be saved. I can beg him to take me away, to bring me with him wherever he goes. Maybe he came for me. Or perhaps he had no idea I was here, but he'll be happy to see me.

Or maybe, with this new hairstyle, he won't even recognize me now that I no longer look like a bum.

The men exchange words, their voices lowering as they glance between each other, then back up toward the window. Their expressions are total confusion, as if they're trying to decide who I could possibly be calling for.

Then, they turn away.

"No, no, no!" I whisper fiercely, my voice cracking.

My fingers claw desperately at the window frame, searching for some way to pry it open. The glass is thick. The frame bolted tightly shut.

I push. I pull. I strain against it. But it doesn't budge.

Below, the men walk on. Their figures disappear around the corner of the house, swallowed by darkness until they're completely out of sight.

I slump against the window, my forehead pressing into the cool glass.

My last shred of hope is gone.

Slipping away with him into the night.

Chapter

SEVEN

Damiano

I walk the grounds with Dante, Nikolai, Silvano, and Giovanni.

It's late, but sleep doesn't come easy—not with her here.

She's in the house, close enough that I could reach out and touch her if I wanted. That thought alone is enough to set my nerves on edge.

"She's here now?" Dante asks.

"Yes."

He looks at me, waiting for me to give him something more. When I don't, he presses. "And how is she?"

I shrug. "Pissed she was brought here by force."

"Will you go through with the auction?" Silvano inquires.

"Yes."

"We can handle this another way, you know," Nikolai cuts in. "You could just tell her who you are and what your plans are."

I could do that.

I *should* do that.

All she's ever known is how cruel the world can be. That's one of the things her and I have in common.

She grew up poor, with a mother too strung out to protect her.

I grew up rich, raised in a family where power is absolute, and violence is just business.

Two sides of the same goddamn coin.

The only part of this life I've ever cared for is the killing.

The emptiness suits me—hollow, nothing, molded by blood and expectation.

But her?

She makes me want.

I want her to be mine.

I'll make her mine.

On the bus, she wanted to stay with me. I should've played it that way—taken her with me, let her think we'd run off together.

But I wasn't thinking straight.

A plan was already in motion, and there was no room for mistakes.

Not that this current plan will end well.

But I'll see it through.

"I'm doing the auction."

Nobody presses it further.

The sound of banging pulls all of our attention toward the house. I scan the upper windows—until my eyes land on her.

There she is.

Her frantic movements pull me in, her hands pounding against the glass, her silhouette bathed in moonlight.

She's so beautiful my chest clenches.

She lays her palms flat against the window like she's reaching for me.

"I'm assuming that's your girl trying to break the foolproof glass," Giovanni mutters, glancing at me over his shoulder.

"Good thing she won't be able to." My gaze never leaves her.

She keeps banging as we move on, the sound growing fainter with every step until silence swallows it completely.

"Tell us more about you trying to buy her dinner," Nikolai teases. "We never got the full story."

"Nothing to tell."

He grins. "Andrei showed me the video."

I lift a brow, wondering where he's going with this.

"Little fucker didn't show me the video," Gio quips. "What happened?"

"What happened was, he got fucked over since she made a disaster out of his burger and then refused him when he offered to pay for her dinner," Nikolai responds.

"Figures," Gio retorts.

"Dom asked for her number, and she told him to fuck off after they flirted for a solid hour."

Gio laughs. "You got rejected for the first time in your life and decided you were going to marry her? Hell yeah."

I let out a sigh, shaking my head, wanting this conversation to be over.

"We're just teasing, Dom. I'm happy for you," Gio says, clapping me on the shoulder. "Who would have thought you'd be the first one to get married? I think we all assumed you'd be the one who never settled down."

We round the corner, and the conversation shifts to business.

Giovanni updates me on Cristiano Fierro, who's been stirring up trouble again.

"I'm going to take his head."

"Pa wants peace," Silvano says with a shrug.

I let out a bitter laugh. "Peace? With Cristiano? He doesn't make peace. He waits for weakness, then buries a knife in your back."

They nod in agreement.

"I will kill him once I find out where he is," I tell Dante.

He lets out a sigh and nods.

I glance back at the house one last time, the image of her pressed against the window burned in my mind.

Hours pass before I finally make my way to her room.

The night has dragged on, each minute pulling at me, but now I have time.

Boris stands at the bottom of the stairs leading to the girls' rooms, leaning casually against the banister, a devilish grin plastered across his face.

"You want a condom, or you gonna raw dog it?" he snickers over his crude humor.

I don't even break stride—I just punch his arm as I pass, taking the stairs two at a time.

He laughs it off, trailing behind me as he pulls the key from his pocket and unlocks the door with a smirk. "She's feisty. Good luck."

When I step inside, she's still standing at the window, her face pressed to the glass.

Her body is tense, her shoulders stiff, as if she's been holding that position since she saw me.

I close the door softly behind me and walk down the short hall that leads into her room.

When the space opens up, I lean casually against the wall, hands shoved into my pockets, one foot crossed over the other.

I don't speak.

I just watch her.

She turns—and freezes when she sees me.

Her chest rises and falls with shallow breaths, but she doesn't look away.

We just stare at each other, the silence stretching between us.

Her lips part slightly—as if she wants to speak but can't.

My mind spirals, caught between restraint and desire.

I want to kiss her.

No—need to.

I want to shove my tongue so deep into her mouth that she forgets every ounce of fear she's feeling and drowns in me instead.

But I don't move.

"Are you here for me?"

I keep my gaze locked on her. "I am."

"Are we leaving?"

I shake my head. "No."

Her fingers tighten around the windowsill as she leans back against the glass, chewing on the inside of her cheek. "Then what are you doing here?"

"I live here."

She inhales deeply, then exhales slowly. "Were you following me?"

"Yes." There's no point in lying.

Her brows knit together, and I can almost see the questions racing through her mind—too many to sort through. Finally, she settles on one.

"The men in the bathroom… what did you do to them?"

"I killed them."

She gulps, loud enough I can hear it.

"Are you going to kill me?"

I shake my head. "No. But I've killed people for a lot less than stealing from me."

Her chin jerks back. "I never stole from you."

I smirk. "My earbud."

She pushes off the windowsill. "For starters, *you* left *me* on the bus, remember." Crossing the room, she stops at the foot of the bed, leaning against the post with her arms crossed tightly over her chest. "The polite thing to do would have been to wake me."

"Something urgent came up," I say smoothly.

"And you couldn't take me with you?"

"You're here now."

Her eyes narrow further. "And where is here?" She waves her hand around the room.

"Home," I reply with a casual shrug. "I guess."

"Okay, Mr. Mysterious." She tilts her head, sarcasm dripping from her tone. "What's your name?"

A slow smile curves my lips as I push off the wall.

I take a measured step forward, and she catches her lower lip between her teeth as I move in. It's all the confirmation I need that she wants me to close the distance between us.

Bracing my forearm against the bedpost above her, my gaze locks onto hers before drifting down to her mouth—watching the way she toys with that plump lip.

"Damiano."

Her eyes flicker, but she doesn't move.

"Do you want to know my name?" she asks, tilting her chin, positioning her face straight with mine.

"Rainey."

The single word makes her freeze.

She didn't think I knew who she was. She must be wondering how I knew that.

Her brow lifts, and she reaches out, hooking her pointer finger in my pocket and tugging me toward her.

"And what else do you know about me?"

"What do you want to know?" I counter easily as I let my body move to where she wants me.

Her lips tighten before she exhales. "Well, that's depressing," she mutters. "If you know about my past, it's not exactly a highlight reel."

"You think I'd judge your past?"

Her response is a shrug.

"Your father was a low-life snitch who got murdered in prison for his loose lips. Your mother is a drunk, a drug addict with a knack for bringing dirtbags home. But you?" I hold her gaze. "You're not any of those things. With everything stacked against you, you're still standing. I'd say you're doing just fine."

I watch her cheeks flush, a hint of pink rising as she realizes just how much I know about her.

She doesn't drop her gaze, though. There's fire in her eyes.

"Do you know why I'm here?"

She looked genuinely shocked to see me, which tells me she doesn't fully grasp what led to her being brought here. "In terms of the bargain your mother made?"

She shakes her head. "No. I was brought here to be turned into a whore." Anger burns in her eyes. "I'm a virgin, and I don't know how or when it will be taken, but if that's the last thing I can still control, I want to."

I watch her carefully, unsure where she's going with this. Then her hands slip into my pockets.

Her fingers curl around the fabric, tugging me even closer until there's no space left between us.

I don't resist.

Her hands trail up my chest, her touch tentative but electric.

"Are you seducing me?" I murmur.

"I'm trying. Is it working?"

I nod. "Very much."

"Good."

A slow smile tugs at my lips as I lean in. "And you want me to take that?"

She mirrors my smile. "Yes."

"Why?" My hand slides to her waist, slipping beneath the fabric of her nightgown, gliding over warm, bare skin.

"Aside from the fact that you're decent to look at?" Her tone is light, but there's no hesitation. "You saved me in the bathroom. This is the least I can do."

"Decent, huh?"

She smirks. "I'd say you're the most handsome man I've ever seen, but you already look like your ego doesn't need the boost."

I chuckle. "No one's ever called me handsome before."

"Then let's stick with decent." Her eyes gleam with amusement.

I nod slowly. "I should also mention, my favorite shoes got ruined." I brush my lips against hers.

She smiles against my mouth. "If you happen to find where they took my purse, you can have the forty dollars in it. I never got to spend it. Put it toward new shoes."

I can't take it anymore.

My lips crash into hers, hot and demanding, my restraint snapping like a thread pulled too tight. The kiss is raw, fueled by every ounce of hunger I've been holding back. I nearly lose control, my mouth devouring her.

I bend down, tighten my arms around her, and lift her off the ground. She responds instantly, wrapping her legs around my waist as I pin her firmly against the bedpost.

She pulls back just enough for her breath to brush against my lips. "The bed's pretty nice. We could get in."

Her fingers slide up the back of my hair, and she leans in, pulling my bottom lip between her teeth.

Part of me wants to. Needs to. But I can't. Not here. Not without her knowing the truth.

"Damiano Volkov."

Her mouth presses against mine, our tongues rubbing together in sync—until she suddenly stills.

I feel the shift before she even pulls away.

Her mind catches up to my words, and slowly, she leans back, blinking as realization takes hold.

Her body tenses in my arms, the fire in her eyes replaced with something colder.

"Say that again."

I don't look away. "My name is Damiano Volkov."

Her eyes flick between mine, her brows knitting together in confusion. "You're part of the family who made the deal for my life?"

I hold her stare, my jaw tightening. What can I even say? The truth is worse than she realizes.

It wasn't my family.

It was me.

I'm the reason she's here.

Her arms begin to tremble against my shoulders. "Who is Lorenzo Volkov?"

"My father."

Her mouth parts, her legs loosening from around my waist. I lower her to the ground, her feet silent as they touch the floor.

"And Valentina?" Her voice is lower now, laced with something bitter.

"My mother."

Her eyes widen, and before I can react, she shoves my chest.

"Your mother had my entire body waxed today!"

Her voice trembles with rage. Then, without warning, she rips off her nightgown top and hurls it at me before shoving down her bottoms.

She stands here, completely bare—furious, vulnerable, breathtaking.

And all I want to do is drop to my knees and worship every inch of her.

But this isn't for me. It's a statement.

She's angry.

"Do you even realize what this is for?" Her tone rises, teetering on the edge of hysteria as she motions up and down her body. "I'm going to have to fuck the freaks that come through this house!"

Her voice breaks.

"And this whole time… you knew. You were in on it! Why did you even bother protecting me from the douchebags in the bathroom?"

It was the honk of a passing trucker that woke me. When I looked around the lit bus, we were stopped, and she was gone. I was off the bus so fast.

I asked the driver if he'd seen her, and he motioned to the bathroom. As I got closer, I could hear men talking inside. I wasn't expecting them to have a knife to her. She wasn't physically hurt, just scared, and when I told her to get back on the bus, she left immediately.

Them threatening her felt like a personal attack. I stabbed them both multiple times in the neck with their own knife, left them to bleed out on the floor, and texted Nikolai and Silvano to let them know things went awry and they'd have to take care of the bathroom situation.

"I didn't want them touching you."

She blinks, her mouth opening slightly. Then it closes. "I didn't want them touching me either."

Her unfocused gaze lands on my ear, but I can tell she isn't really seeing it.

And then I notice her body locks up, each breath coming in sharp but not leaving. Panic flashes in her eyes. Her hands twitch, then claw at the air, as if searching for something solid to hold on to.

"Breathe," I say, stepping closer. "Breathe," I repeat, inhaling deeply so she can see.

She claws at her chest, then at her throat, gasping as her legs buckle. I reach out and catch her, lowering her gently to the floor. She drops to all fours, her body trembling, her breaths shallow and erratic.

I sit in front of her, splaying my legs wide as I bend forward—close enough to offer support without overwhelming her. "Breathe, Rainey. In and out. That's it."

Her gasps grow sharper, her chest rising and falling in jagged, frantic movements. But she's trying. I reach out, turning her gently until her back presses against my chest. My arms wrap around her, locking her in place, holding her tight.

"Breathe with me," I murmur against her ear. I inhale deep, exhaling slow, feeling her body start to sync with mine.

I begin to rock us, the motion grounding her as tremors rack her frame.

"Listen to my voice," I whisper. "In… and out. Don't think about anything else."

At first, she's gasping, pulling in air like she's drowning. But then she mirrors the rise and fall of my chest, her exhales no longer frantic.

"That's it," I murmur. "One breath at a time."

Sweat beads along her forehead, her skin cold and clammy. The door creaks open behind me, spilling a sliver of light across the room. I don't need to turn to know who's there—ma and Dante, their shadows stretching long across the floor as they watch.

But I don't acknowledge them.

I keep rocking her, my focus locked on her alone. "Good," I whisper as her breathing slows. "You're doing good."

I hold her until she settles, the tension draining from her body. Long enough for the door to close, leaving us alone in the dark once more. My cheek rests against her head, her soft hair carrying the faint scent of lavender—the same shampoo they give all the women here.

Gradually, she sinks into me, her muscles loosening as she relaxes against my chest. She's no longer resisting, and that's when I become acutely aware that she's completely naked.

My arms rest just below her breasts, their weight settling on top of them. The warmth of her bare skin against mine has my body reacting accordingly.

I don't know if it's my erection that has her gripping my hands and yanking them off her, but she angrily pushes to her feet, her shaky legs somehow holding steady as she swipes at her eyes, erasing the evidence of her tears. "Goodnight," she mutters, clipped and distant.

I rise as she moves to the bed and pulls back the covers. I wait, wondering if she'll extend another invitation, if she'll tell me to stay—or if she wants me gone.

She makes it clear.

She climbs into bed, yanking the blankets over herself with finality.

"I said goodnight," She snaps, rolling onto her side, her back to me. Her voice wavers, laced with bitterness. "My new career starts tomorrow. And as your mother said, my virginity will no longer be a burden after that."

I don't move. I stand there, watching the slight tremble of her shoulders as she sniffles into the pillow.

I could end this. Right here. Right now.

I could tell her the truth—give her a choice. I could take her to my house on the property, away from all of this. Tell her we will be married, that we will have a life together, the two of us, or that she could take her chances here, knowing what will be expected of her.

But I don't.

If she wants to spend another night crying, then so be it.

I've never been good at talking to women—hell, I hate it. I'm blunt, and most people don't want ripe honesty. I'm intentionally disrespectful when I don't need to be, but I hate small talk. I refuse to engage in conversations that serve no purpose, and the women who work in our house have nothing to offer me intellectually— nothing I need or could benefit from.

It was a woman who molded me this way.

I steal one last glance at her, her small frame curled into itself, and then the words fall from my mouth before I can stop them.

"Save your energy. You'll need it tomorrow."

I think she might not have heard me, but as I turn and walk away, the click of the door shutting behind me sets her off.

Something hard slams against the other side with a loud thud.

"Bastard!" she screams.

Boris smirks as he steps forward, re-locking the door.

Ma and Dante wait nearby, their conversation halting as their attention turns to me.

Dante lifts a brow. "That went well," he says dryly.

"I thought so too." I walk past them, not breaking my stride.

Chapter

EIGHT

Rainey

I couldn't sleep last night.

Damiano.

His name is Damiano.

The man from the bus—the one whose ID I was trying to nonchalantly peek at just to get his name. The man I practically begged to run away with me. *His name is Damiano.* And he's part of the reason I was brought here.

Maybe he has some weird fetish where he likes to watch men have sex with girls. Maybe that's what he's planning for me. Maybe he wants to watch while nasty men assault me.

Just the thought makes me furious. Furious because, even though I hate him right now, I still want him.

Yesterday, as we were escorted to the spa, we passed other girls lingering in the hallways. They were dressed provocatively—tight dresses clinging to curves, skirts so short they barely covered anything, and lingerie meant for the bedroom, not a public space.

Their eyes followed us, taking in the "new girls." Some smirked, while others looked bored, as if this was just another routine day.

Valentina's words still echo in my head: *Her boys like to have a lot of sex.* These girls are always ready, always available, waiting for their turn.

Those girls seemed happy—happy to be here, happy with their roles in this twisted place. How? How could anyone be *happy* in a situation like this?

Damiano.

He's probably been with all of them. That's what they're here for, isn't it? To cater to him and whoever else has the power to demand it. The idea slams into me, heavy and unexpected. Worse, it stings.

Why do I care?

I shouldn't. I don't want to. But the ache in my chest tells a different story, and it catches me off guard.

And now, I'm pissed.

Pissed at him. Pissed at myself. Pissed at the entire situation.

AFTER BREAKFAST, WE'RE ESCORTED INTO ANOTHER LARGE SITTING room. From one lavish space to the next, I can't tell if it's meant to disorient us, a subtle way to make us feel the sheer size of this house, or to remind us of all the places where horrors might unfold. Every corner of this mansion screams wealth and excess, the kind that doesn't just flaunt power—it chokes you with it.

I knew mafia men in movies were filthy rich, but this? This is something else. It's beautiful and monstrous in equal measure.

We sit in silence. My gaze shifts to the others. None of them look as terrified as I feel. Maybe it's resignation to the situation. I roam down to each of their hands. All of our nails are perfectly polished, painted in shades that feel chosen deliberately for some odd effect. Mine are crimson, glittering faintly under the room's bright light. They're all too perfect, unnervingly so.

The silence doesn't last long.

One by one, the seasoned girls start to saunter in, languid and confident, like predators entering a den.

They look like they belong here, their perfect skin untouched by any visible marks. My mind whirls with questions: Are we going to be beaten and assaulted? Are they all so flawless because they don't fight back? Or worse, because they don't see it as assault at all? How long have they been here? How long will it take for me to mentally check out the way they appear to have?

A girl with bleach-blonde hair and blood-red lips makes her way to us. She leans on the back of the couch, her manicured nails drumming lightly on the upholstery. Her eyes flick to one of the girls sitting at the far end, and she winks before letting her gaze rake over the rest of us.

"You all look so innocent," she mocks, her voice sweet but dripping with condescension. Her lips curl into a grin, baring her pearly white teeth. She lifts an imaginary camera, aiming it at us like she's snapping a picture.

"I love this night," she muses. "Girls come in looking innocent and are on the brink of death the day after."

Her words land with brutal precision, but I refuse to flinch. Instead of shrinking back, I meet her gaze head-on.

A bitter thought creeps in as I realize how heartless this girl is; she must have been shaped this way during her time here. I don't want that for myself—I shouldn't have kicked Damiano out last night. Maybe I should've begged him to stay, to protect me.

No.

Emotions can be a liability here, and I choose to master them. Survival demands strength, not surrender.

Noticing my unyielding demeanor, her grin falters. She thrives on fear, but I offer her none.

"Trixie, get out," another girl commands, firm and authoritative.

A tall brunette strides into the room, her striking green eyes locking onto Trixie. With a flick of her wrist, the brunette shoos the blonde away, as if dismissing an unruly pet.

Trixie doesn't argue. She saunters off, her entourage following.

The brunette advances into the room, her expression serene yet undeniably commanding. She appears to hold a position of leadership—or perhaps her extended tenure here has earned her the others' deference; the girls seem to heed her. She seats herself across from us, crossing her legs and reclining slightly, radiating dominance.

"I'm Em," she introduces herself, her tone gentler than Trixie's, yet still infused with control.

Her gaze sweeps over us, pausing momentarily on each individual, as though cataloging every flicker of emotion. Her look isn't cruel, but neither is it sympathetic.

"I remember my first day," she begins, her hands resting lightly on the chair's arms. "All the thoughts racing through my mind, all the questions I didn't even know I had yet."

She pauses, letting the silence stretch.

"So, let me tell you how this works."

Her words are measured, rehearsed, as if she's delivered this speech countless times.

"We are taken really good care of here," she continues. "The men who come in are clean and mostly respectful. If you're favored, you make Valentina really happy. And if you catch the attention of the Volkov men, you're practically Valentina's best friend. I think she's just hoping one of her sons will finally settle down and give her grandbabies." She winks.

"But if the men don't keep coming back for you, if you're not repeatedly utilized, you're either given another job in the house or…" She trails off. "Well, I don't know where the girls go when they're no longer needed. So make sure you are."

The silence is heavy.

Now that this conversation is happening, I wish I could rewind time, go back to last night, and tell Damiano I'll do whatever he wants—anything to stay in his good graces and secure better treatment. Especially if fucking him will keep Valentina happy.

"You need to adapt—quickly." Her tone is matter-of-fact. "Learn to read the men you're with. Figure out if they want a woman who wants them, or if they prefer someone scared and timid. Then become that. Whatever it takes."

Her words are clinical, detached, as if she's explaining a job description rather than laying out a roadmap for survival.

"If you're crying? You'll either get roughed up or ignored. Neither is good, unless you're into that sort of thing." She adds with a shrug. "Play your cards however you want. But remember—you're here to work. So do a damn good job."

I wonder if Em has done a "damn good job" satisfying Damiano. He 'utilizes' these girls too. How many times has she had sex with him? How many times has she felt his lips against hers, felt his smooth, bare skin against her own.

I marvel at her flawless dark skin, long legs, and thick, cascading curls. The thought of him inside her makes my stomach twist. It shouldn't matter—it has no right to matter—but the ache it leaves behind is undeniable.

"But," Em says, her tone sharpening, "everyone wants a Volkov. If you haven't seen them yet, you'll know why soon enough. They each have a type, and I can tell which ones of you will certainly catch their attention. But that's neither here nor there. Girls that are already in bed with them will slit your throat to keep their man. This is a dog-eat-dog world, so get their attention the right way. And don't upset the guests. You will be punished for it, and you won't like it.

"Tonight could be enjoyable for you if you allow it. However, it will most likely be the worst night of your time here."

She sweeps over us again. "My advice? Do what you're told. And if you're offered the chance to volunteer? Jump on it. Be first. You don't want to be last."

Her words are like a noose tightening around my neck. No one has explicitly said what tonight entails, but I know how auctions work. With us being the ones up for bidding and them talking about our virginities, I can piece it together.

From what I've gathered, we'll be living here. So with the auction, I don't know if the purchaser gets to take us home or if we'll have to go back to our rooms with them—which sounds even worse, considering we'll all hear what's happening in each other's rooms.

All I can hope for at this point is to get the guy with the smallest wiener and the two-pump chump.

Em offers to show us around, and though I have no real interest in seeing more of this place, I stay quiet. The thought of wandering through here makes me want to vomit, but as the others begin to move, Tess steps forward.

She holds out her hand to me, her expression softening. I hesitate, my pride warring with my exhaustion, but as her hand remains extended and waiting, I let out a slow exhale and take it. We fall in step together, following the rest of the group as Em leads us into the maze of hallways.

Everything stretches on endlessly, polished to perfection, every surface gleaming with a reminder of the power that looms over us.

Laughter floats toward us, light and careless. I wonder how the women in this house can find it in them to laugh. We pass a sitting room, and I'm immediately drawn to the sound.

Four men sit sprawled on a couch, deep in conversation, while Trixie and her girls hover nearby. Their giggles are sweet, their lashes batting as they hang on every word the men say.

And then I see him.

I lock onto Damiano, seated at the far end of the sectional. He leans back, his posture relaxed, one foot resting on the floor while the other leg stretches lazily across the couch. His arm is bent behind the cushion he rests against, exuding an effortless confidence.

He's devastatingly handsome, a portrait of control and power wrapped in disarming ease. But it's his eyes that hold me captive.

Those dark, burning eyes hold mine and everything else falls away—Em's voice, the soft murmurs of the other girls, the glimmer of laughter. It's just him and me.

The laughter dies instantly.

Trixie's grin drops, her features hardening into a glare. Her eyes narrow, and her jaw tightens as she takes me in, as if my existence alone is an offense.

I guess I know which brother she's possessive of.

The memory of last night crashes over me—his lips on mine, the heat of his body pressing against me, the way I felt both consumed and safe all at once. A mix of longing and resentment takes root, and I shove the thoughts aside.

"Dibs on that one," one of the girls ahead of us whispers.

Another girl responds, quieter, but no less awed. "I'd gladly let him tear the clothes right off of me."

Their words irritate me, and I force myself to look away. I'm sure their fantasies will be fulfilled soon enough. I want to march across the room and slap him—slap him for being so goddamn irresistible, for sitting there effortlessly flawless, and for making me feel things I have no right to feel.

I can feel his gaze on my back as the distance between us grows. I offered myself to him last night. No, I practically begged him to take me. If he'd just kept his stupid mouth shut, I wouldn't still be a virgin right now. And then I'd probably be exempt from the auction since I'd be *used*.

But he didn't.

Instead, he revealed who he is, shattered whatever illusion I had, and left me standing there completely exposed. Now, I walk away with the facade of my head held high, as if I'm unbothered, and I hope this bothers him.

THE WAITING GAME STRETCHES ON, EVERY SECOND DRAGGING LIKE entire hours until we're told to shower. How do I prepare myself for the unknown? How do I prepare myself for what's going to happen to me tonight?

Stepping out, I freeze at the sight of a dress lying at the foot of my bed. It's white and so short I wonder if it was even meant for me. Holding it up, I realize the fabric is so sheer that they might as well have had us arrive naked—both would reveal far more than I'm willing to give.

But I don't have a choice, so I put it on anyway. I don't really care to find out what would happen if I didn't.

The hem barely skims the tops of my thighs. I catch my reflection in the mirror, and a wave of humiliation washes over me. This isn't clothing—it's a message, an unspoken invitation for something I have no say in.

They didn't even provide us with underwear. I assume it's either an oversight or they figured we'd use what was already in the dresser, so I pull out a pair and quickly slip them on.

I sit on the edge of the bed, my hands trembling slightly as I wait. Time seems to slow, the air growing heavier with every passing second.

Then it happens.

Doors open down the hallway, the sound echoing like a signal it's time. My pulse quickens, the thud of my heartbeat loud in my ears.

Footsteps follow, growing louder as they approach. My body stiffens, and I force myself to sit up straight.

A shadow moves beneath the door, and then it pushes open.

The man who sat in the back of the van with us stands in the doorway, his expression blank as he motions for me to step out. My legs feel like lead, but I force myself to rise as I take the first step toward whatever comes next.

I glance at the other girls emerging from their rooms, their expressions mirroring my own—confusion and fear laced with resigned acceptance. Barefoot, I step into the hallway, the cold floor making my body react in ways I'd rather it didn't, especially when the guard next to me looks directly at my chest and grins.

We stand in a tense, unbroken line. No one dares to speak.

Valentina strides toward us, her heels clicking softly against the floor. She appears to be in an awfully chipper mood, which only amplifies the knot twisting in my stomach. She stops at each of us, placing a pair of white slippers on the ground.

"Put them on."

As she places mine next to me, her hands still. Then, without warning, she straightens and reaches under my dress, her fingers sliding to the sides of my underwear. Before I can react, she yanks them down my legs in one swift motion.

I freeze, humiliation surging through me. My face burns, and though my body moves on autopilot to step out of the offending fabric, shame knots tightly in my chest. Apparently, I'm the only one foolish enough to think wearing something extra would go unnoticed.

"Put them on." She gestures toward the slippers.

I nod quickly, sliding my feet into the absurdly soft footwear.

Once everyone is ready, Valentina cuts through the silence. "Follow me."

The line of girls moves, our steps muted by the slippers, each of us walking as if we are headed to the guillotine.

Outside, a black van waits for us. It's different from the one that brought us here; this one has proper seats—actual seats.

What a luxury.

"Inside," Valentina commands.

The girls at the front are already climbing in, seemingly unashamed that we can see under their dresses.

I keep my head down as I scoot in next to Tess in the first row. We sit shoulder to shoulder, packed tightly together.

I heard Valentina call the man with us Boris. He's the same man who guards the hall at night—and the same one from the first van. If he weren't so unsettling, he'd almost be ruggedly attractive. His sharp features and the way he carries himself resemble the Volkovs, making me wonder about his connection to them. He has to be related somehow. A cousin, maybe. He's around their same age.

I feel his gaze before I even glance up. When I meet his eyes in the rearview mirror, he winks at me, a smirk tugging at his lips. My stomach tightens, and I immediately turn to the window Tess is staring out of, desperate for a distraction.

The van lurches into motion, and I keep my attention outside, straining to make out the landscape. The scenery is somewhat connected—the trees and buildings of the estate passing by like fleeting shadows.

I don't really know what I was expecting, but being loaded into a van only to stay on the property wasn't it. As we drive down the paved road, the motion of the van and the silence around me leave too much room for my thoughts to spiral. Then the pavement gives way to dirt, the path narrowing as thick trees loom around us.

The drive isn't long, but it feels endless, each passing second dragging me deeper into dread. When the van finally eases to a stop, I stare out the front windshield, my pulse quickening.

We stop at the back of another massive house, but this one is different. Garage doors line the lower level along one side, as if the building is layered into the uneven ground, its design both imposing and strange. Boris drives into an open garage bay, the harsh fluorescent lights inside swallowing the van. As the garage door lowers behind us with a heavy, mechanical groan, my stomach drops.

Panic grips me like a vise. I'm trapped. Really, truly trapped. There's no escape—no way out of this.

I force myself to picture Damiano, his deep voice drifting in. *Breathe,* I imagine him saying. *In and out. One breath at a time.* I try to follow the imaginary command, fighting to regain control.

The van door slides open with a loud clatter, and the light floods in, momentarily blinding me. I squint, my heart racing as my body freezes, caught between fear and the suffocating inevitability of whatever is waiting on the other side.

We're pulled out one by one, directed where to stand in the sprawling garage. A door on the far side opens, and the guards lead us through, the one at the end locking it behind him.

We proceed down a long hallway, the walls seeming to close in, creating a sense of confinement. The corridor opens into what looks like a high-end man cave. Pool tables and casino-style games are scattered across the room, with a fully stocked bar gleaming in one corner. Couches and oversized TVs are arranged in a way that can host large gatherings. But nothing about this place is comforting.

Instead of entering, we veer right into another long, dark hallway. At the end of this passage stand two large black doors, flanked by guards whose stony expressions offer no solace. They sweep over us, assessing as if measuring us against some unspoken standard.

When we finally reach the doors, they swing open with a heavy groan, revealing a room that steals the breath from my lungs. My carefully guarded composure cracks; my wide eyes dart around the room, taking in every detail with a mix of horror and disbelief.

It's colder than it looks, the light casting a sickly yellow hue over the barren walls. My stomach churns as I take in the bed at the center of the room—a single mattress draped in a white fitted sheet. Handcuffs dangle from the corners, and ropes coiled neatly around its edges tell a much darker story. Chains hang from the ceiling like silent threats, swaying slightly.

To the side, a metal cart looms with objects I don't want to acknowledge but can't seem to tear my eyes from—ropes, chains, and an array of items that make my skin crawl: sex toys of every shape and size, clamps, collars, blindfolds, gags, and tools I can't even begin to name.

No one told us what to expect here, but the setup makes it painfully clear that whatever it is will take place right here—and it's nothing good. This is what Trixie meant when she said we come in innocent, and after tonight, we are on the brink of death.

What if they actually kill us?!

I might die tonight.

We're led to the far end of the room, where seven metal chairs sit in the shadows. The darkened section gives us a perfect view of the bed and everything surrounding it, like some grotesque stage.

Across the room, about twenty men sit in leather chairs, their suits crisp and expensive. Most of them are older, their graying hair and cold eyes gleaming with a warped pleasure. On the wall to the left, the girls who work here stand in a line, their faces blank—all except Trixie, whose devilish grin makes me want to slap it right off her face. It's clear she enjoys others being hurt.

She should be put in a lab and studied. There has to be some sort of medical term for that because she's not right in the head.

The door creaks open, and the sound of heels echoes against the cold walls. Valentina steps inside first, her crimson dress clinging to her figure like it's been painted on, the slit high enough to show off her incredible legs.

Behind her, five men follow, their resemblance to one another unmistakable. They're variations of Damiano—tall, broad-shouldered, and exuding raw power. They take seats in the front row, one of them speaking quietly to the others, who nod in agreement. Their presence is magnetic, but staring at them feels like watching a wildfire—dangerous, consuming, and impossible to ignore.

I recognize four of them. They were walking with Damiano when I was banging on the window like a psycho.

I notice the one in the middle flicks his gaze over to the wall where the other girls are standing. I follow his line of sight and see Em staring back at him. Then he looks away, and so does she.

Whatever brother that is—he's Em's.

Noted.

A single chair is positioned near the group of men—an outlier—and I wonder why it's set apart from the others.

Valentina has six sons. Five of them are right there. Where is Damiano? He's nowhere to be seen. He played a part in putting me in this shit, and the fucking coward doesn't even have the balls to watch what happens to me.

It makes me angry. So fucking angry. If I ever see him after tonight, I'll cut his dick and balls off and shove them down his throat.

Valentina begins to speak. At first, I hear her words—something about tradition, expectations, and opportunity—but the rest blurs when the phrase *bidding for virginity* leaves her lips.

My pulse pounds in my ears. The room feels smaller, the air heavier. It's actually happening. I guess my mind never let me believe that this was really going to take place. That perhaps they used those terms loosely, and the bidding portion was meant to scare us into submission.

"It begins now," she announces.

She strolls toward us, her gaze sweeping over the group. "Any volunteers to go first?"

Silence blankets the space. My body is so stiff with fear I don't think I could move even if I had to.

Her smile deepens, an unsettling edge curling her lips.

"Let me give you a piece of advice. You'll want to be the first. Trust me—you'll regret being the last."

My heart pounds so hard it feels like it might burst from my chest. The urge to run grips me, but my body refuses to obey. I don't even know if I'm still breathing. The tension in the room sharpens, pressing down with suffocating weight.

Then the door opens, and the atmosphere shifts again as Damiano steps in.

Chapter
NINE

Rainey

Every pair of eyes turns to him, the sheer power of his presence swallowing the room whole. His towering frame fills the doorway, the immaculate lines of his tailored suit only amplifying his intimidating aura.

Someone gasps softly from the line of staff at the far wall, and I don't blame them. He is utterly mesmerizing. And my god, in a suit, it should be illegal to look this good.

He strides forward with an ease that makes me feel smaller, as though he owns every bit of this space.

Valentina turns, her smile softening—a mother looking at her son.

"Ah, perfect timing," she purrs, stepping away from us and moving toward the center of the room.

Her voice takes on a sweet tone as she addresses him. "Are you here to play?" She reaches out and softly squeezes his arm.

Damiano says nothing, his silence speaking louder than words.

Valentina's grin widens as she turns back to the group of men seated across the room. "It's my baby boy's birthday, after all," she coos. "What better way to celebrate than to let him start the night off?"

I should be focused on what's waiting for each of us—the impending horror we're all about to endure. But all I can seem to think about is trying to figure out what day it is.

This is about to become the worst day of my life, yet somehow, I find myself noting that it's Damiano's birthday—and that seems worthy enough to remember the date.

Valentina turns, gesturing in a smooth motion toward where we all sit. "Would you like to take a closer look at the girls?"

But he's already locked on *me*.

The room feels impossibly still—the kind of silence that amplifies every heartbeat.

Damiano raises his hand, two fingers curling in a slow, deliberate motion—silent expectation woven into the gesture, leaving no room for misinterpretation.

All I can think about is how I wanted this last night—just him and me. But now, here we are, about to strip ourselves bare in front of an audience.

My eyes dart past him, scanning the onlookers, their leering faces turned toward us—an audience waiting for the show to begin. One man in the back row unzips his pants, his eyes locked on me. I don't want that creep—or anyone in this room—seeing me like this. And I sure as hell don't want Damiano exposed to them either.

When my gaze returns to him, his eyes narrow, and for the briefest second, something flickers across his face. It's subtle, almost imperceptible, but I catch it—a crack in the armor he wears so well. Then, with a jerk of his chin, he commands me forward.

Tess's hand clamps onto mine, as if she could hold me in place—as if her strength alone could keep us safe. I squeeze back before letting go.

With trembling legs, I push myself upright, hyperaware that the entire room is watching me. Every step feels unsteady, like the floor might give out beneath my feet. Honestly, I wouldn't mind if it did.

Our last interaction wasn't great—I kicked him out of my room, telling him to leave so I could prepare for my *new job*. And now, here he is, standing there. Not as an ally, but as my first... client?

I hate that my body is practically a neon sign broadcasting my fear. But I move forward anyway, stopping when we are a mere foot apart, tilting my chin to meet his gaze. He's just as devastating as I remember—every time I've been near him, he's undone me without trying. He's tall—so impossibly tall. His size and the way he looms over me make it feel as if the light in the room bends around him.

His stare burns straight through me.

"I'm scared," I whisper, the words barely escaping.

"Just breathe." His voice is smooth and controlled. He slips off his suit coat, then moves to loosen his tie.

I watch him unfasten each button of his shirt, revealing inch after inch of skin.

"Take off your dress."

He shrugs out of his shirt, letting it fall carelessly to the floor. Ink and scars mark his skin, the hard lines of muscle shifting beneath the dim light. My breath stutters, a reaction I loathe but can't control.

I roam over him—lingering on the sculpted planes of his chest, the chiseled contours of his abdomen, the strength in his arms. But then, something familiar stops me cold.

My eyes lock onto his wrist. A tattoo I've seen before. One I remember vividly—a compass encircled by ropes, the black ink stark against his skin.

No way.

It can't be.

How could he possibly be the one who got my purse back from the idiot who nearly tore my arm off to steal it? It doesn't make sense. It's not possible. Yet here he is, with the same tattoo, on the same beautiful skin.

He's standing right here.

"Take. Off. Your dress."

The belt slides free from his pants, the hiss of leather making me flinch.

Everything is happening at once—too fast, yet agonizingly slow.

He's the one who got my purse back. He was on the same bus as me. The one who saved me in the bathroom. How long was he following me?

And I might have led him straight to Jules.

My body refuses to move, every muscle locking into place. If anything happens to her, I'll never forgive myself.

With a single, predatory step, he closes the distance between us. His hands shoot out, gripping the front of my dress.

I don't even want to admit what he will soon find—the slickness between my thighs.

The sound of fabric tearing fills the air as he rips it straight down the middle, leaving me completely bare and exposed. The shredded material falls to the floor in tatters, and I raise my arms to cover myself—a futile attempt at preserving what little dignity I have left.

He seizes my wrists, twisting them behind my back. Pain shoots through my shoulders, and a small whimper escapes as he tangles his other hand into my hair, jerking my head back until his breath ghosts over my ear.

"You can make this easy on yourself if you do what I say." His tone is laced with a sharp edge.

The man I've encountered before today—the one who seemed almost human—is gone, every trace of him evaporated.

What's left is someone entirely different.

Someone dangerous.

"Is this how you like it? Rough?" I throw the words at him, masking the quiver in my voice with forced bravado.

"Is that how you want it?" he taunts.

"I want you to stop trying to rip my arms out of their sockets," I snap, glaring up at him.

A dark, low chuckle vibrates through the air, the sound echoing in my chest. His grip loosens just enough to offer a brief reprieve, but there's no retreat.

"Get on the bed," he demands coldly, punctuated by a shove that sends me stumbling toward the mattress, leaving one of my slippers behind.

Only my Prince Charming has turned into a beast tonight.

Anger flares, and I spin around, shoving him with both hands—the force of my rage driving me forward.

But he's faster.

He catches my wrists mid-push, spinning me around and forcing me down onto the mattress, the air rushing from my lungs as I hit the surface. Before I can gather myself, his hand clamps around my ankle, dragging me to the edge.

I yank off my remaining slipper and start smacking him on the head with it. His jaw tightens—until, unexpectedly, his head falls back, and he starts laughing.

If it weren't for the look of fury twisting his features, the sound might've been almost... sexy.

My legs are forced apart, solid weight wedging between them before he clamps around my wrists, glaring down at me.

"Drop it." The command is lethal.

I clutch the slipper tighter, even knowing my strength is no match. The hold around my wrists tightens, sending a sharp ache shooting through my arms.

Reluctantly, I let go, the slipper falling to the mattress beside me. He reaches out, takes it, and throws it over his shoulder—its location now somewhere over yonder.

He presses down further, leaning in closer. My wrists remain pinned against the bed, his control absolute.

"Try something like that again, and I'll chain your hands."

I'm just expected to accept this—to lay down and take it. His threat pisses me off, and I refuse to back down.

"You shove me down like that again, and I'll kick your teeth out."

Without breaking eye contact, he sits up on his knees, undoing the button of his pants.

Heat pools in my stomach, traitorous and unwelcome. I hate how turned on I am by him. I hate how badly I want to see him naked—to feel every part of him on me... in me.

I don't want to feel this way.

So I lash out, desperate to reclaim some semblance of control. My foot draws back, aiming for his stomach—but he's too quick, his hand snapping out to catch my ankle.

"You're fiery tonight," he remarks, shoving my leg back down with enough force to jostle the mattress. The amusement in his tone only makes my anger burn hotter.

He grabs the chains draped on the bed, snapping them around my wrists. Cold metal bites into my skin as I tug against them, testing their strength—but they hold firm.

He stands over me, his gaze sweeping over every inch—pausing on my breasts before drifting lower, stopping between my legs, then slowly dragging back up, settling on my chest once more before finally locking with mine.

I pull at the restraints again, regretting that I tried to kick him because I'm turned on in front of a room full of people—and embarrassed by it. His presence is both suffocating and addicting, and I can't decide whether I hate him for it—*or hate myself for the way my body reacts to the loss of his weight on top of me.*

I track his every move as he strips off his pants, letting them fall to the floor.

The air thickens between us as he steps closer.

Kneeling on the mattress beside me, he grips my leg and pulls it toward him, spreading me open. His other leg clamps over mine, keeping it immobile.

A shiver runs through me as warmth drifts across my skin, his face mere centimeters away.

Lips graze mine, teasing, before nipping at my bottom lip. The slow trail continues to the curve of my neck, where a deep kiss sinks into my skin.

Just as I'm caught in the softness of the moment, pain sears through me.

Teeth sink into my neck with brutal force, a scream ripping from my throat as the sting radiates outward. I thrash against the chains in a desperate attempt to get him off.

Muted whispers ripple through the room, swallowed by the relentless pounding in my ears.

His jaw is set, and I can't fathom why he's trying to bite a chunk out of my neck. My vision blurs—not from tears, but from seething rage.

If my hands weren't bound, I'd punch his nose right off his face. Hell, I'd bite him—harder.

When he pulls back, a bloody smirk curves his lips.

The bite was deep—so deep that my own blood paints his mouth.

"Perfect," he murmurs.

"Why did you do that?" I growl, yanking at the restraints again, hoping they'll give way so I can strangle him.

Only this time, as I jerk at them, a voice cuts through the room.

"Look at her perky tits bounce."

Okay, I'll strangle him too.

"I permanently claimed you," he says coolly, his tone almost smug. "Now everyone will know."

"Do I get to bite you back?" I snarl.

He pulls his bottom lip between his teeth, squeezing my thigh with barely contained restraint. "Do you want to claim me as yours?"

"I want to bite you back if that's what you're asking."

"Biting me means claiming me."

"Yes," I breathe. "I want to bite you back."

"Do your best, babydoll." He leans down, kissing me so softly that the tenderness of it momentarily disarms me.

He shifts, releasing my leg to lie on his side, only to hook his foot behind my knee, pulling it back between his legs at a new angle. His body presses close as he props himself up on his forearm, his hand gently resting on my hair. The other slides slowly up the inside of my thigh.

"You don't have to play around. Just do it. I wanted you last night, and my stupid body doesn't understand what's happening. She still wants you. So just... get this over with."

"Yeah? What's happening?" He rubs just beside my folds, teasing but not giving me what I need. All I want is for him to move just a little further—to where I'm desperately aching.

"Nothing if you don't scoot your hand over," I pant.

A predatory smile forms as his fingers part my lips, slipping between them, drawing a gasp from me.

I knew I was wet—I could feel it—but the full extent doesn't register until his touch finds me there.

His forehead rests against my temple as fingers circle the wetness then glide upward.

The instant contact finds my clit, a jolt of pleasure shoots through me.

My hips arch involuntarily toward his touch, and he slides back down, pressing one finger inside with an unhurried, torturous rhythm. My mouth falls open on a silent *O* as he rocks in and out, each stroke making my eyes roll. A brief withdrawal—then another joins, stretching me wider, pushing deeper.

"I want to taste you." His voice is thick with desire as his lips hover near my ear.

Yes. I want that—so badly. And I want him on my tongue.

Before I can think better of it, the words spill out. "You can... if I get to taste you too."

My eyes flutter open, locking onto his. He pauses, weighing my words as his fingers slow their pace.

"You bite me," he warns, "and I'll bite you back."

I nod, my heart pounding as he shifts. Rising, he hooks his fingers under the waistband of his boxers, dragging them down in an unhurried reveal. My eyes roam lower, drinking him in.

My god... he's glorious.

Strong arms slide beneath mine, lifting and repositioning me further up the mattress as though I weigh nothing. In one fluid motion, he straddles my chest—his broad frame caging me in, heat radiating from where he hovers just above my head.

His eyes darken, filled with the same raw hunger burning through me. Desire flickers across his face—he wants this just as much as I want him.

"Do I not need my hands?" I jerk against the restraints, testing their hold.

He reaches between us, pressing his thick shaft against me.

"Suck."

I obey, my head lifting off the mattress to take him in.

Wrapping my mouth around him, I begin to move. The angle feels unfamiliar, a little awkward, but the sharp inhale he takes tells me I'm doing something right. He tracks every slow, eager movement I make.

Then the first flick of his tongue unravels every ounce of control I have left. My hips jerk, and he doubles down, dragging me into the haze of pleasure.

His fingers slide inside, thrusting with a hunger that mirrors the relentless pace of his tongue. Pressure coils low in my stomach, spreading like a wildfire.

I move faster, suctioning tighter around him, taking him deeper. His cock flexes against my tongue, and then warmth spills down my throat.

I swallow instinctively, overwhelmed by the sensation, but there's no time to process it—euphoria crashes through me, dragging me under.

My thighs tremble, clamping around his head, but he doesn't let up. His fingers and mouth keep me teetering on the edge, wringing every last drop of ecstasy until I'm left shuddering beneath him.

Finally, he lifts away, his still-hard length slipping free as I collapse onto the mattress. I barely register the slow swipe of his thumb over the corner of my mouth. Then drags a hand casually down his thigh, wiping it clean, then swipes his forehead with his forearm, the faint sheen of sweat catching the light.

That smirk of his—the one that drives me crazy—returns as he stares down at me, confidence radiating from every part of him.

His grip tightens around my thigh, spreading my legs on either side of where he remains seated on his heels. I can only gape at his size, still reeling. I'm nervous to see how he plans on fitting that in my vagina. My jaw alone hurts just from having to hold it open so wide.

I tilt my head back, scanning the cart to see if there's any lube that we can use. There are different bottles, but he's not making any move to grab one. I guess we're just going for it.

Hovering over me, dark eyes capture mine, holding me there. I'm lost—drowning in everything unspoken between us.

"Did you not want to do this in private?" My voice comes out softer than I intended.

It's evident how much we both want this—how much the air between us crackles with it—but I don't understand why it has to happen here, with all these eyes on us.

"No." The simple, almost dismissive answer stuns me. I falter, searching his face for some kind of explanation.

"Why?"

"Because I want everyone to know you're mine."

The certainty in his words makes my pulse quicken, a tangled mix of emotions I can't even begin to unravel.

"And you have to take me in front of all these people?"

"No. I want to."

His mouth captures mine, silencing my protests with a kiss so consuming it erases all coherent thought.

His body shifts between my thighs, and my nerves take over— *it's time.*

"Are you going to keep me tied up?" I whisper.

"Are you going to behave?" he counters.

"Yes."

He leans in, his teeth grazing the edge of my jaw. His weight presses more firmly into me, and a hand slides between us, guiding himself to my center.

The moment his cock brushes against me, a quiet gasp escapes, anticipation pooling deep.

He lingers there, eyes flicking up to mine.

When he kisses the curve of my neck, trailing downward, my resolve crumbles.

I hook my leg around his thigh, pulling him in as he lowers himself, his mouth finding my nipple. His tongue teases, the warmth of his exhale and the gentle tug of his teeth have me on the verge of combustion.

He moves to the other side, the steady pull of his attention making me arch further into him, my body responding to every touch.

My hips tilt toward him, and the head of his cock presses against my center. My breath catches in my throat as the sensation overtakes me.

And then everything changes.

My eyes widen as he begins pushing inside me, the stretch sending a mix of heat and aching fullness radiating through my body.

"Maybe we need lube or something," I pant, pointing to the cart.

He rasps, "We're gonna be just fine. You're ready."

He moves slowly—pressing forward, pulling back, then pressing deeper.

My body coats a slick path for him to follow, the friction more intoxicating, every touch heightened.

Each new depth he uncovers is briefly painful before my body adjusts.

A soft moan fills the space, and for a fleeting second, I think it's someone else.

But then I hear it again, paired with a deep, guttural groan, and I realize—it's us.

Our sounds blend together, raw and unfiltered, filling the space with something so intimate it makes my heart ache.

This shouldn't feel this good, should it?

My mind blanks. His hips move in a way that's so hypnotic I can't even form a thought. He undulates against me, his body perfectly attuned to mine. Each thrust is slow, his body pushing into mine as if trying to fuse us together.

Then his pace quickens, his cock driving in and out with a relentless force that has my back arching off the mattress. He cradles my hips, holding me in place as he moves.

His lips find mine again, claiming them in a kiss so deep it steals every ounce of air from my lungs, replacing it with him.

His name escapes in a breathless plea, met by a low groan that rumbles between us. His tongue teases mine, and then my teeth graze his bottom lip. He moves with a need that borders on desperation.

Our bodies meld, slick with sweat, his whispers brushing my ear—words lost to the overwhelming rush taking hold. His voice alone is enough to get me off, rough and possessive.

A moan slips free as he leans down, his mouth finding my neck. Heat engulfs me, the ache inside tightening into an unbearable force—until it snaps.

Euphoria floods me, my body trembling as my release takes hold. My muscles spasm around him, pulling him deeper, and instinct takes over.

I bite his neck—hard—claiming him just as he claimed me.

He groans, his body stiffening as his release follows. A deep sound tearing from his throat.

Only when he stills do I let go, the tang of blood clinging to my tongue.

He stares at me. Then his mouth crashes onto mine—urgent and hungry.

When he sits up, I collapse onto the mattress, trembling with exhaustion.

He gestures over his shoulder, and someone steps forward to release the cuffs. The chains clatter to the floor, and I pull my arms to my sides, wincing as a dull ache radiates through them.

My head lifts as he pulls out, emptiness settling in. As soon as he's gone, my body clenches, trying to close off the loss—my vagina officially thoroughly used and abused.

Before I can process what's happening, his hands glide over my arms with unexpected softness. His thumbs circle gently, kneading away tension with a care that feels almost out of place.

I want to hate this—hate him—but I don't. I like him touching me. I like his attention.

He lazily trails down my stomach, his gaze following the path. Then, without warning, he wraps an arm around my waist, lifting me effortlessly and positioning me on all fours.

I gasp at the sudden shift. He grips my shoulder, guiding me onto my knees in his lap until my back is flush against his chest. His arm snakes around my throat, pulling my head back, and his mouth presses to my ear.

"Just relax."

It isn't a request—it's coaxing, almost soothing—but there's no mistaking the unyielding authority behind it.

My entire body tenses as his chest brushes my back. His lips graze the curve of my shoulder, leaving a trail of warmth.

The battle between my mind and body rages, but his touch— his voice—makes it impossible not to give in.

"It will hurt worse if you fight it."

His words make no sense. I'm more than ready for whatever position he puts me in.

And this one—on my hands and knees? I've seen this before. I've seen it a lot.

From what I've seen, it seems to be a favorite.

The thing about this position, though, is I always assumed there was only one hole used.

One hole for sex.

The other? *That's not for sex.*

At least, that's what my naïve thinking led me to believe.

But something in his tone sets off alarm bells in the back of my mind.

A tightness grips my throat as he tells me to lean forward and hold on.

I obey, gripping the sheets, my face sinking into the mattress.

My mind races with confusion and resistance as I feel him move lower, sliding his own semen back up—accidentally touching… that *other* spot. I flinch, and for a second, I think it was a mistake—a misstep.

I wonder if he's embarrassed that he touched me there, especially in front of all these people.

The mattress dips as he scoots in closer, one palm settling on my lower back, pulling me toward him.

I comply—until I feel the tip of him nudging into the wrong hole.

And then I understand.

It's intentional.

"Stop." Panic threads through my voice as I try to shift away.

He bears down on my back, holding me in place as he begins pushing into the same, wrong hole—just enough to breach me. I flatten onto my stomach, twisting to turn over.

"That's the wrong hole." I push against him as he leans over me.

He lowers himself, his face close to mine, his voice turning cold.

"Listen to me very carefully," he murmurs in my ear. "Any hole unclaimed when we're finished is fair game for anyone else in this room. So, you will let me put my dick in, or someone else will."

The words hit me like a punch. I struggle to process what he's saying—what he's threatening—but it doesn't make sense.

"I… I go to the bathroom out of there…"

"If you need to go now, try to hold it," he says flatly, his grip tightening as he pulls me back toward him.

Panic rises, suffocating, my body screaming to fight even as my mind falters. I really don't want this. I didn't want any of this in front of an audience.

But this.

I don't want him putting it in my ass.

When he inches closer, instinct takes over, and I crawl away, barely climbing to one foot before he has me pinned on my stomach, his arm wrapped around my neck, his body pressing into mine.

My face tingles as my circulation cuts off.

"If you think I'm going to let another man stick his dick inside you, you've lost your mind. I was going to be gentle, but now the image of someone else taking you has me pissed off."

His arm tightens, and he spits into his other hand—then that hand disappears, positioning himself against me.

Pressure builds, his cock pressing relentlessly against a space my body isn't prepared to accommodate.

I'm already as far into the mattress as I can sink, my body retreating instinctively, but there's nowhere left to go.

The only option is for his cock to push inside.

When he finally sinks in—inch by agonizing inch—a burning pain splinters through me. He pulls back slightly, only to go back in deeper, stretching me in ways that feel unbearable.

A whimper escapes, soft and involuntary.

I try to clench, to force him out, but it only spurs him on.

His determination grows as he shoves forward, forcing himself into a space that feels too small and completely wrong.

His movements turn rougher, each thrust sending sharp jolts through me. I squeeze my eyes shut, my fists clutching the sheets as I try to block it out.

I try to say "Stop," but the word catches in my throat, lost to the pressure.

Desperation takes over, and I pound my fists against his arm until he releases my neck, air rushing back into my lungs just as his hips slam into me.

The confusion is suffocating—a collision of pain and something else I'm not ready to admit. My body doesn't know how to react, torn between resisting and yielding.

"We can pretend, I won't tell anyone you're not in there," I whisper.

"I want it."

His hips press forward, forcing a gasp from me as I clutch the sheets tighter.

Then, he shifts.

Straightening, he pulls me upright with him, my knees digging into the mattress as he sits back on his heels. His arms wrap around my waist, holding me against him as he continues moving in and out of me.

I reach back blindly, needing something to hold onto, and my fingers tangle in his hair.

He groans—a low, guttural sound—and the rawness of it sends an unexpected shiver through me.

His panting fills the room, and against all logic, I feel my body responding. My hips begin to move on their own, pushing back against him, and I teeter on the edge of another orgasm.

"That's it," he breathes.

He positions me exactly how he wants me, lifting up and placing me on my stomach, his palms bracing against my lower back as he pumps into me so fast I scream out, clutching the sheets so tightly I might actually rip them.

He leans forward, burying his face into the curve of my neck, his groans muffled as he pushes deeper.

The intimacy catches me off guard. This should feel dirty, but instead, it feels deeply personal—something I never imagined myself doing. Yet, out of everyone in the world, he's the one I'm glad I experienced this with.

"Look at me," he murmurs, his voice hoarse.

I can't.

My eyes squeeze shut, and he takes my chin gently, forcing my eyes to meet his.

The intensity in his gaze nearly undoes me.

His movements turn frantic, and my body reacts, arching into him. Pleasure builds to an unbearable crescendo, every nerve in my body alight.

He stills suddenly, buried so deep I can feel every pulse of his release.

As he withdraws, an ache burns through me, and I wouldn't be surprised if the liquid I feel seeping out is blood.

I collapse onto the mattress, trembling and spent. Silence fills the room, save for our ragged breaths.

He presses a kiss to my shoulder, and for a moment, everything feels still—suspended in the aftermath.

He tells me to roll over, but I keep my face hidden.

I'm utterly humiliated. A room full of strangers just witnessed something I never intended to share with anyone but the person I chose to be intimate with.

When I don't respond, he repeats his request, his tone sharpening.

I still don't obey.

The sting of his palm against my ass jolts me.

I growl—more out of frustration than pain—as I roll over, glaring up at him.

His expression is intense, commanding.

"You bite me now, and I'll snap your neck."

His words confuse me—until their meaning sinks in.

"Open your mouth."

I take in the sight of him—hard, thick, and slick with blood.

Revulsion twists in my stomach, and my head shakes on instinct.

"No. Suck it yourself."

His fingers tangle in my hair, yanking my face toward him.

"No," I repeat, my voice steadier this time.

He leans in, his gaze pinning me in place. "You have five seconds."

"I already did that."

"And I want you to do it again."

The whiplash of emotions makes me want to scream.

He just had his cock in my ass, and now he expects me to lick the blood off of it.

He's sick.

And I fucking hate him.

He squeezes his fist, jerking my head forward.

I pinch my lips between my teeth, refusing as I push against his hips.

His fingers dig into my cheeks, prying my lips apart just enough for him to shove inside.

I gag, my body revolting against the intrusion.

His free hand brushes my jaw, and I glare up at his perfect face as he continues to fuck my mouth.

Time stretches endlessly.

Then his pace quickens, his breath turning ragged.

With one final thrust, he stills, his release hitting the back of my throat.

I gag again, but before I can spit it out, his hand clamps over my face.

"Swallow it."

I shake my head, but he straddles my legs, one hand over my mouth, the other against the back of my head.

"Swallow it and be done."

And so I do, even as my throat fights against it.

"Open your mouth."

I glare up at him but comply, letting him see I did as he asked.

"Good." He stands and grabs his pants from the floor.

He pulls them on, then extends his hands toward me.

I glare at him again before reluctantly letting him pull me to my feet.

"You destroyed my dress." I stare at the pieces of what remains, acutely aware that I have nothing to put on.

"You're not meant to have clothes on afterward," he says matter-of-factly.

With our fingers interlocked, he guides me toward the single chair along the wall, near where the men—I presume his brothers—sit.

As we walk, I take in the bed, and my steps falter.

My eyes fix on the sheets, now stained with a mix of blood and semen.

The stark contrast against the white fabric is jarring, a visceral reminder of what just transpired.

His hand tightens slightly, urging me forward. "Come on."

He sits down in the chair and pulls me onto his lap.

I settle there awkwardly, my body tense, while my mind reels.

My wide-eyed stare remains locked on the mattress, the image seared into my mind.

His arms wrap around my waist, pulling me closer.

"You're done. You did amazing, baby." His lips brush against my ear.

The intimate gesture sends a shiver through me, and I close my eyes, trying to ignore how his words make me relax—just slightly.

We barely have a chance to settle when someone approaches with a medical bag.

The girl looks nervous as her focus shifts between Damiano and the wound on his neck. She sets the bag down and begins pulling out supplies.

I forgot that we bit each other.

Funny how she doesn't even look at my injury—her focus is solely on his.

As she goes to reach toward him, he moves his head away.

"I'm fine."

She hesitates, uncertainty flickering across her face. "I really should—"

"Get away from me." His voice is abrupt enough that she flinches.

Her wide eyes shift toward who appears to be the eldest brother. He gives a curt nod, and she scurries off, clutching her medical bag.

I watch as Valentina reenters the room, an older gentleman in a tailored suit approaching her.

Her expression is poised and polished as she speaks. He nods along, his demeanor calm and collected.

I wonder if she left the room because she didn't care to see her son having sex—or if she never stays to watch, no matter which girl it is.

"Does it feel different... in the butt versus the vagina?"

The words spill out as I continue watching Valentina.

Damiano's head turns toward me.

When I finally meet his eyes, there's a flicker of surprise.

He shrugs, kissing my shoulder. "Both felt good."

"Just *good*? You ripped my butt open for *good*?"

A wicked grin spreads across his face as he shifts his hips so I feel the unmistakable flex of his still-hard cock against my back.

"Good is a good word," he murmurs.

I scoff, rolling my eyes as I playfully elbow him. "What's your favorite position, then? Or whatever."

His grin deepens, and he nips at my shoulder. "We still have a lot to try out."

Just as I open my mouth to respond, Valentina's voice rings out.

"We will begin the bidding," she announces, stepping forward.

Silence falls instantly, and her gaze settles on the six girls waiting. She strides forward, stopping just in front of them. Her eyes sweep over each girl, assessing. "Does anyone want to volunteer?"

Not a single girl moves. Their eyes remain fixed on the floor.

"Don't forget what I said earlier," Valentina warns.

Still, no one volunteers.

She surveys the row, her patience visibly wearing thin. "Fine," she snaps, stabbing a manicured finger through the air. "You. Come. Now."

The chosen girl stiffens, her body trembling as her wide eyes dart toward the others—silently pleading for help that won't come.

A murmur ripples through the back rows, low and eager. The men's eyes gleaming with dark anticipation as they drink in her terror. A few exchange glances, their breaths growing heavier, arousal feeding off her helplessness.

"I said go," Valentina bites out.

Tension coils through me, my toes pressing into the floor as I shrink back against Damiano. His arm tightens around my waist, one hand sliding down to my thigh, stroking it in slow passes.

When the girl doesn't move, two guards step forward, their hulking forms casting heavy shadows over her.

She barely has time to process that it's her turn as they seize her by the arms, yanking her upright.

Muffled pleas vanish into the void as they drag her forward, her slippers scraping uselessly against the floor.

A few of the men chuckle, their sickening pleasure heightening with every second she resists.

The guards deposit her in front of the mattress, unfazed by her frantic resistance. She stands there, shaking, as Valentina steps back.

My stomach twists as the reality of what's about to happen sinks in. I force myself to keep my focus steady, even as every instinct screams at me to look away. I flick my gaze to the other girls—some have their eyes in their lap, while a couple of them watch, expressionless. Their time is coming. It will happen to them too.

Only, unlike me, they won't have even the slightest, twisted consolation of being with a man they've shared any kind of history with.

I catch sight of a particularly sweaty man in the back row, his eager hands gripping the tablet he picked up the moment Valentina first asked for volunteers. The screen's glow casts an eerie light over his face, accentuating the sick grin. His attention flickers between the screen and the girls, as if already imagining what he'll do to one of them.

He wasn't given the chance with me, but the look on his face says he's already savoring his next opportunity.

"When do they change the sheet?" I whisper.

"After everyone leaves."

I stare at him, blinking slowly as his words sink in.

Is that why Valentina and Em said we'd wish we had gone first? Because every girl after will have to lie in the mess left behind by the previous one?

"Be glad you were first."

"Why?"

"We set the bar." He remains fixed on the bidding. "Every man after will try to raise it—to outdo the one before."

A lump forms in my throat. I already understand what he's saying.

"Whoever is last…" My words trail off, but I don't need him to finish.

The horrifying conclusion settles over me.

"She'll have it the worst," he confirms, his voice devoid of emotion.

"How often do I have to do this?"

"Never again." His answer is firm, and for a fleeting moment, relief washes over me.

But it's short-lived.

"They will, though." His gaze flicks toward the other girls, lined up like lambs to the slaughter. "They'll go through this many more times."

Chapter

TEN

Rainey

His words land heavier than I expect, and I struggle to swallow the lump rising in my throat. The thought of these girls being subjected to this again and again, their spirits chipped away piece by fragile piece, is too much to process.

"What do you mean?"

Before he can respond, his phone lights up on the table beside us. My gaze drops, catching the words on the screen.

> You have company. Three guests to be exact. Hopefully you're not tired out, birthday boy—you're gonna be going all night.

A muscle tics in his jaw as he types a brief reply—*Be there soon*. Then the phone is set down.

Adjusting to this place is going to take some time. I understand that we'll be forced to sleep with different men daily, but for some idiotic reason, I felt as though Damiano and I had a connection. I'm just now realizing how wrong I was. He's only using the flesh that's available for the taking. Probably getting some before I'm damaged goods.

Still, it's disgusting he hasn't even wiped me off him and is already setting up a foursome.

I zone out—this entire situation is really bizarre. Is the auction about making money? Or is it meant to break the girls in the most humiliating way possible—forcing us to understand what's expected? Maybe it's a twisted mind fuck, giving us a false sense of relief when everything that follows is just as inhumane, even if it feels less degrading in comparison.

I turn my head, looking at Damiano. He is literally the most gorgeous man I have ever seen. And I just lost my virginity to him. He looks at me, his eyes meeting mine, then shifts down to my lips. A soft smile forms, and he leans in, giving me a gentle kiss, then turns his attention back ahead. I stare a moment longer then shift to his brothers—*six gorgeous Volkov men*. Em was right; I did find out why everyone wants one of them. They are powerful and so goddamn sexy.

The one in the center is the most clean-cut of them all, his polished appearance setting him apart. There's something about him that makes him seem older, more refined, like he carries the most authority in the room. Even sitting, he radiates control.

To his right, a massive wall of muscle lounges back, his frame making the chair look almost small beneath him. He's clean-shaven like the one in the center, but where the other exudes precision, this one emanates sheer power.

Next to him, a man with glasses sits with an almost effortless poise. There's a certain intelligence in his expression, but he's still every bit as gorgeous as the rest of them. He also looks the youngest.

On the other side of the oldest-looking brother, another man leans forward, his perfectly trimmed beard only making him look more dangerous… second only to Damiano.

And then there's the last one, his long, wavy hair pulled into a bun on top of his head, giving him a rugged, almost effortless appeal. He looks like the most laid-back of them all. I don't even know him, but if I had to be left alone with any of them, aside from Damiano, I'd feel safest with him. Or the nerd at the other end. But definitely bun-head.

They're all devastatingly attractive, cut from the same impossible mold. But I'd still choose Damiano over any of them. He's the best-looking one—at least in my opinion. Then again, maybe I'm biased, considering I just had sex with him.

I scan back down the line, stopping on the oldest. My gaze drops to his hands—short, clean nails, trimmed cuticles—and I find the image of him getting a manicure funny. But also, those hands have probably felt every inch of Em's body. She probably sees them and melts.

He has a ring on his left pinky, but I can't make out what it is. I half wish my vision had zooming capabilities because I'd focus right in on it. Maybe a family crest or something.

I rake over his chest and the way his suit fits him so damn well, then trail up to his lips, his nose—until I reach his eyes. Eyes that are on me.

My heart screeches to a stop. His expression is unreadable, holding my stare for a beat before flicking to my boobs, taking in each one. Then, casually, he shifts his attention back to the mattress, looking completely unimpressed.

I shove down the painful hit to my self-esteem and shift my focus as a guard yanks the naked girl back toward her chair. The next one is dragged to the front of the room, and I tense when I see it's Tess. Her wide, terrified eyes dart around, pleading silently for help.

I can't sit still.

"Are you rich?" I blurt out. I meant for the words to just be for Damiano, but all his brothers turn in our direction.

He glances at me, caught off guard. "What?"

"Bid on her," I say urgently, as I nod toward Tess, who stands frozen at the front, her small frame trembling under the weight of every pair of eyes in the room.

His brows draw together, his confusion deepening. "I'd have to have sex with her."

"And?" I don't understand his point. He slept with me. He's about to sleep with three more after me. He can sleep with Tess. My voice edges into something frantic. "Just… bid on her."

"No."

"What do you mean, no? Bid on her." My panic floods every syllable. I clutch his arm tightly, desperation clawing at me as the first bid is called. "Please. Don't let them have her."

"No." His voice is colder now, his grip on me tightening, letting me know this conversation is over.

"I'll do anything you want," I plead. "Anything."

He hesitates for a fraction of a second, his jaw clenching as he looks down at me. His eyes search mine, but whatever battle he's fighting inside himself ends quickly.

"No." His tone is final.

A hollow feeling spreads through me as Tess is sold, the crushing weight of helplessness settling over me.

The winning bidder rises, shrugging off his coat and tossing it onto his chair. Tess stiffens, her eyes wide with horror as the man approaches—the one who is going to do unspeakable things.

My body sags in disappointment, and numbness weaves its way in.

My mind detaches, slipping into a hazy, weightless space where none of this feels real. It's the only way to survive it. The room blurs at the edges, the sounds dulling to a distant hum as I drift somewhere far beyond my own body. Even Damiano doesn't seem present, his attention fixed on my hand. It rests atop his, palm to palm, as his thumb idly traces over my skin, brushing against my ring finger absentmindedly.

By the time the fifth girl is dragged forward, I can't bring myself to look anymore. My stomach churns violently as three men step up, their cruel smirks searing into my mind even as I look away. The rustle of fabric, the unmistakable sound of them undressing, fills the air, and bile burns at the back of my throat.

"I need to go to the bathroom," I whisper, my voice shaky and barely audible over the muffled murmurs around us.

"You'll have to wait."

I swallow hard, the acidic burn climbing higher. "I'll pee on you." My desperation leaks through.

He exhales loudly, the sound almost resigned. "Fine." He gestures for me to stand. "Get up and lace your fingers behind your back."

I hesitate, but the nausea threatening to consume me leaves no choice. Slowly, I push myself to my feet, wincing at the ache radiating through my body. Stiff limbs protest as I interlock my fingers behind my back like he ordered.

His large hand engulfs mine, his grip firm and almost suffocating as he propels me forward. I keep my focus ahead, resisting the urge to acknowledge the way every man we pass scans me from head to toe. But once again, my gaze meets the brother in the center. This time, I look away first before he can give me any more of a complex.

Each step is fire, the raw ache between my legs and the sharp pain in my butt turning every movement into agony. I grit my teeth, willing myself to stay silent, refusing to let these sick losers hear me break.

The room feels impossibly large as he leads me across it, his hand an inescapable presence at my back. I want to tell every creepy guy staring at me to get a life because it's pretty pathetic that they have to resort to this in order to get laid. But I'd probably end up dead, or worse, have more of them violate me.

By the time we reach the single bathroom, my body is already giving up. His hand falls away, and I lurch forward, my legs barely holding me up. I don't make it far. My knees hit the cold tile in front of the toilet, and my stomach convulses. Bitter acid burns up my throat as I retch, the contents of my stomach splattering into the bowl. Each heave leaves my throat raw and burning.

Tears blur my vision, streaming down my face as my body shakes uncontrollably. I clutch the edge of the toilet for support as wave after wave of nausea grips me.

I can't do this. I can't be here. I don't belong here.

It's too much. Seeing what's happening out there, the awful things being done to the other girls. The items on the cart are actually being used on them. Their experience is far worse than mine, and the only reason mine wasn't completely incredible, aside from my butt being ripped open, was the men watching. Had it been just Damiano and me, I would have loved every second of the sex and foreplay.

But what they are enduring isn't fair. And I can't pretend it's not happening. Because it is. I can't ever go through something like this again, and none of them should have to either.

I remain on my knees, my palms flat on the floor as my head hangs in defeat. My body feels hollow, wrung out and broken, but I force myself to move.

Unsteadily, I rise to my feet, the room spinning slightly as I wipe my mouth with the back of my hand, avoiding my reflection in the mirror. I don't want to see the girl staring back at me. I don't want to see what I've become.

I turn to look at him. He's leaning casually against the counter, arms crossed over his chest, one ankle hooked over the other, exuding an infuriating calmness. It's as though none of this bothers him.

How many times has he done this? The thought sends a surge of nausea rolling through me.

Our eyes meet and nervousness grips me. Heat rises in my cheeks, and I quickly drop my gaze, unable to hold the weight of his stare.

I step toward the sink, desperate to rinse the sour taste from my mouth, to scrub the filth from my hands. But he stops me. "It's not allowed. You can shower back in your room."

I freeze mid-step, about to ask if he's fucking joking, but I catch my reflection in the mirror. My breath stutters as I take in the girl staring back at me—her tangled hair, her flushed cheeks, her hollow eyes that seem to belong to someone else entirely. A stranger.

"Can I get some water to rinse my mouth?"

He lets out a heavy sigh, uncrossing his legs as he turns to the sink. He cups his hand under the stream, letting water pool in his palm then shuts it off.

I blink at him, disbelief morphing into irritation. "Are you joking?"

He raises his brows, his hand still extended with the small puddle of water.

Rolling my eyes, I step closer. Reluctantly, I lean down, cupping his hand with mine as I take a mouthful. The metallic taste of his skin lingers on my tongue, but I rinse thoroughly, spitting the remnants of bile and water back into the sink.

When I glance up, he's annoyingly calm.

"Thanks," I mutter, wiping my mouth with the back of my hand.

His lips curve just slightly in a way that sends a fresh wave of irritation through me.

"Ready?" he asks.

The thought of stepping back into that nightmare makes me start trying to think of other ways to keep us in here longer. "If I say no… can we just stay in here?"

"Lace your fingers behind your back."

Noticing the door is unlocked, I latch onto a wild, desperate idea, and before I can think better of it, I lunge for the handle. I barely get it open when his hand tangles in my hair, pressing me roughly into the doorframe, the force knocking the air from my lungs.

Through the wide-open door, I catch glimpses of the girls waiting in the darkened area. They take in the commotion, and now they have two different shows to choose from. Maybe I can spice it up and punch the shit out of his face before he knocks my ass out.

"Try that again," he growls, his hand tightening painfully in my hair, "and I won't be so nice next time."

His other hand clamps down on my wrists as he pulls me from the wall.

"Walk," he orders, driving me forward.

Every step feels like a march toward my own demise, the room blurring around me as he steers me back to where we were sitting.

I can't stomach what's happening on the bed. The girl's screams cut through the room. The three men around her show no mercy, their movements ruthless and synchronized. I force my-self to look away, but the sounds still invade my mind.

As we get to the chair, he releases me, and I turn toward him, my chest bumping into his.

"Can we leave?" My voice is thick with desperation as I grip his pants pockets.

He bends down, smacking a kiss on my forehead. "No." Then grabs my hips to move me aside. "You'll be punished if you don't watch. Eyes are on you too."

I pull him closer to me, my bare chest pressed flush against his ribs.

"Please," I whisper. "I'd rather be punished than sit here and watch this."

He pinches my chin softly as he whispers against my lips. "I have two options for you."

I lift my brows, waiting to hear what they are so I can get on with one of them and tune out everything else.

"Get on your knees and suck my dick," he begins, "or you can ride me."

I try to process that. These are my options? Have sex with him again when my vagina feels swollen shut, or suck on his cock that was just in my ass? Neither of those sounds even remotely desirable.

"Can we just make out or something?"

He smirks. "My dick was in your booty, and you sucked it. You need to brush your teeth before we make out."

My jaw practically falls to the floor. He forced me to do that and is now making it seem like I'm gross for having my own ass in my mouth.

His face remains serious, and then he cracks a smile, leaning down and shoving his tongue in my mouth.

I'm not even sure what's happening. "Damiano," I scold, hitting his chest with the back of my hand, and he laughs as he steps around me, sitting back down.

I glance back toward the bed, and he taps my butt to get my attention.

What I see solidifies my decision.

"I'll go down on you."

He leans forward, grabs my hips, pulling me toward him.

"Get on your knees."

A sharp crack—a whip or something else—splits the air, followed by the girl's scream. I drop to the floor without thinking, my hands moving to his pants. My fingers fumble clumsily with the button, my heartbeat pounding so hard I'm sure he can hear it. I don't care how pathetic I must look. I'd do this all day, every day, if it meant blocking out the horrors happening behind me.

Finally, I manage to undo his pants, the fabric shifting as I open them just enough. My hand brushes against him, and the heat radiating from his body in the cold room is inviting. I'm not even sure how to do this. When we did it, we were moving together, and I didn't feel as self-conscious. But now, he just gets to sit here while I'm the one doing all the work.

I can feel the other girls along the wall staring, probably cringing with secondhand embarrassment at how awkward I look. But I'll learn to give the best damn head in this house if it keeps me from having to see any more.

"Look at me," he says, his voice quieter now but no less commanding.

I force my gaze upward, meeting his dark eyes. They hold me captive, pulling me into a connection I don't fully understand. Everything around us fades. The noise, the chaos—it all blurs into nothingness, leaving just the two of us staring at one another.

Another piercing scream rings out, and my hand tightens around him. I feel like I might break apart entirely.

His palm settles over mine, his thumb gliding across my skin.

Leaning forward, keeping my gaze locked on his, I take him into my mouth. His body relaxes beneath my touch, and he guides my hand, moving it slowly up and down. Once I find my pace, he leaves me to take over.

I feel the tension building in his body, the subtle shift in his breathing as he grips my shoulder. His release comes suddenly as his fingers thread through my hair, holding me in place. I swallow, my throat constricting with the act, and a low sound of approval escapes him.

He bends forward, his mouth near my ear. "Stand."

I do as instructed, rising to my feet with shaky legs. He takes me by the hand, pulling me with him. We sidestep the chair where we had been sitting, climbing the steps along the wall where the other men are seated. My stomach clenches, and my pulse quickens. I have no idea why he's bringing me up here, and the thought of having a better view of what's happening below makes getting right back on my knees and sucking him off for a fourth time sound really appealing.

Moving with purpose, he leads me to a leather chair positioned in the corner, lowering himself into it.

"Straddle me."

His hands slide up the backs of my thighs, guiding me closer.

I hesitate before finally climbing onto his lap, my body hovering uncertainly. His palm presses against my lower back, urging me down until I settle onto his thighs, flush against him.

The hardness of his erection nestles between us. He lifts me, adjusting my position, and then pulls me downward, his length parting my lips as it glides along my clit. A shudder runs through me, my breath hitching as our bodies align.

He takes his time, setting a rhythm, sliding me against him. The friction ignites sparks that undermine my attempts to stay composed.

I bite my lip hard, determined to suppress the sound trying to escape. I hate how my body responds, how it betrays me so easily, but I can't deny the way my skin prickles under his control.

Relief floods through me as I realize he's not trying to push inside me—at least, it doesn't feel like he is. But this, just like this, feels so incredibly good that I'm certain I could get off from it alone.

"The last girl is up," he murmurs.

I go to look, but he grabs my face, kissing me deeply.

"Just focus on me."

He keeps our hips moving against each other, my clit swelling with pleasure.

"I can't have anything in there right now," I whisper.

He smiles, a rare, genuine smile that throws me completely off balance. "I didn't plan on putting my dick back in you… right now."

His smile sends my thoughts spinning. It's beautiful—he's beautiful—and I'm a nutjob. He grips my hips tighter, holding me in place as his lips brush against my neck.

When he licks the sensitive skin, I tangle my fingers in his hair, pulling him closer. His tongue and teeth tease, and I find myself arching into him.

I suck softly on his in return, reveling in the quiet groan of approval he gives. The noise sends a thrill through me, and I hate how much I enjoy it, but I can't seem to stop myself. The intensity builds between us, every touch and sound drawing me further into his orbit.

Valentina's voice cuts through the air just as I reach that peak again—the edge where bliss waits on the other side. My hips roll faster along his shaft, and I pant as he grips my waist.

"Thank you all for coming," she announces.

A moan slips free, muffled against his ear as the wave crests. "Oh god," I gasp, my movements faltering as the orgasm crashes over me. My body seizes and I feel my walls spasming with another release. My forehead rests on his shoulder as I keep panting, really wanting water right now.

A slap on my butt makes me jolt, and I sit upright with a startled yelp. His chin jerks toward the center of the room, and I follow his gaze, dread sinking in.

The entire room's attention is on us. The six girls are lined up in front of the mattress, their faces pale and frozen. I want to throw myself down the stairs and hope that one of the steps manages to snap my neck.

"Whenever you're ready, darling," Valentina says, only her tone is so genuinely sweet that I know she's talking to Damiano.

I rise from his lap as he adjusts, tucking himself back into his pants, fastening them back up.

We've been down here for five hours.

A chill spreads through me as I take in the last two girls, their bodies quaking, covered in marks that will no doubt bruise. The very last girl's face is swollen, one eye barely open, blood trickling from random wounds, pooling beneath her. My gaze drags over her body—her nipples are bleeding.

The realization slams into me like a gut punch. They weren't lying. They warned us, and it was true.

I glance down at myself—my bare skin is marked, but nothing like theirs. Compared to them, I look almost untouched.

Damiano takes my hand as he leads me down the steps, depositing me in line with the others.

Valentina walks to him, kissing his cheek and rubbing her hand up and down his back. "Happy birthday, my boy." Then she turns to me and leans in, kissing my cheek, bringing her hand up to cup it as she smiles, almost in appreciation.

I'm so confused.

He grabs his discarded shirt from a nearby chair, slipping it on then retrieving his phone. The screen lights up, illuminating his face as he reads a message. His jaw tightens, as he types a reply before sliding it into his pocket.

My mind spirals. Will he shower first when he sleeps with them? Does it matter? Why am I even thinking about it? Who cares what he does? This is their world—this is what they do.

The final part of the night is just as gross. We're forced to stand here, filthy and exposed. Dirt, sweat, blood, and semen cling to our skin, some girls smeared with the remnants of those who came ahead of them on that vile mattress. And the men? They get to approach, inspecting us like animals.

Boris stands at the head of the line, his massive presence radiating authority. One man steps too close, his hand reaching toward a girl trembling at his proximity.

"Touch her, and I'll blow your fucking brains out," Boris growls, his voice a low, menacing rumble.

The man smirks. "I'll pay."

"Keep walking." Boris steps closer.

The man winks at the girl and strides off.

My eyes stay fixed on Damiano as he talks to his brothers, a couple of them grinning as they push his shoulder. He glances back at me as he continues talking, winks, then turns back to them, buttoning the last button of his shirt.

That subtle wink nearly sends me to my goddamn knees.

The men with virgin blood still on their cocks and the creepy onlookers all begin to filter out, their attention locked on us as they pass. Each one pauses, scanning the damage, their silent promises lingering in the air. Promises they'll be back.

Damiano and his brothers begin to head out, cutting a path through the crowd as he moves to the exit. My focus remains locked on him, and all I want is to be leaving with him. I don't see the man from the back row approaching until it's too late.

A sudden shove sends me sprawling onto the mattress, the impact making my head spin. Panic claws at me as his weight bears down, his rough hands already fumbling to position his readied penis at my entrance.

"No!" I thrash beneath him, but he's too heavy, his strength overwhelming. His hot breath fans across my face, and his grip tightens. My limbs flail, desperate to push him off, and then—wet. Warmth splashes across my face, startling me into stillness.

The room erupts into chaos. Girls scream, but all I can do is stare wide-eyed at the man on top of me. His expression frozen in shock, his mouth opening and closing soundlessly as blood pours from under his chin and mouth. A knife is lodged there, the hilt quivering as his body shudders.

The next moment, he's gone—shoved to the floor. My head jerks up to the man who lodged the knife there, and I see Damiano's gorgeous, fury-filled face, as he scoops me into his arms, cradling me against him.

I glance over his shoulder, my vision tunneling as I try to process what just happened. People are moving, some shouting, others rushing in with weapons drawn. All the Volkov men have each rounded up a group of girls and are ushering them out. But my focus lands on the man who had been on top of me, his lifeless body sprawled on the floor, blood pooling beneath him, the knife still lodged in his chin.

The world blurs, and I cling to Damiano, burying my face in his neck. The chaos fades as I focus on the rise and fall of his chest and the strength of his arms around me as he strides out of the room.

Chapter

ELEVEN

Damiano

Cristiano Fierro's men think they're clever. They managed to slip into one of our underground gambling rings, sniffing around where they had no business being. How they got in? I don't know yet. But I will. Soon.

They call me Mercy when I work. Not because I show it—God knows I don't—but because by the time I'm done, ending your life is the only mercy you'll ever get in the end.

Three of Fierro's men are tied up in the basement, waiting for me. Their fear is probably setting in now.

Good.

Fear makes people sloppy—it makes them talk.

Nikolai and Giovanni flank me, nudging my arm, grinning like idiots.

"Can't believe you went through with it," Nikolai says, his tone half-teasing, half-impressed.

"Best birthday ever, huh?" The smirk on Giovanni's face widens as he claps me on the back.

In truth? It is.

I *claimed* Rainey on my birthday.

Their voices fade as the conversation shifts to Cristiano. Just hearing his name makes my anger flare. He's the root of every problem in my life.

"Make sure Rainey gets back to her room." My gaze shifts to her, the crowd around us blurring as our eyes lock. I wink, and her cheeks flush as she looks almost nervous. I turn back to my brothers, locking eyes with Nikolai to ensure he understands that he is personally responsible for getting her back to her room safely and untouched.

"Go handle it," Dante says.

Silvano claps my shoulder. "Then crawl back to your girl's bed."

I nod and push my way toward the exit. The noise of the room melts away with each step, but something nags at me, pulling me back. I want to feel her lips on mine one more time before I leave.

I pivot, threading back through the crowd, but my steps falter as the bodies part.

Rainey's being shoved onto the mattress by a man who already has his pants down, his intent written all over his face. Her scream pierces the air, and my vision narrows to red.

I storm toward Boris, ripping the blade from its sheath on his thigh. The crowd barely registers my presence as I close the distance, grabbing the man by his hair and jerking his head back. His eyes widen in shock, but I don't give him the chance to speak.

The knife drives upward into his chin, the steel meeting resistance before tearing through flesh. My chest heaves with fury as I press the blade deeper, his gurgled breaths echoing in my ears.

I wrench him backward, tossing his lifeless body to the floor like garbage. My gaze snaps to Rainey. She's frozen, wide-eyed, blood splattered across her face, her trembling form radiating shock.

The crowd is scattering in chaos as I bend down to scoop her up. She doesn't resist, her body limp against mine as I cradle her to my chest and carry her away.

I WAS ALWAYS DIFFERENT. EVERYONE WHISPERED IT WAS BECAUSE MY mother was pregnant with me when she was held hostage for three months and tortured. She was weeks away from giving birth when my father rescued her.

That might be why most people think I'm different. It's an easy assumption to make. But the truth is, what she went through likely wouldn't have affected me in the womb.

No one talks about the car accident that nearly killed me when I was three. The impact left me with severe brain trauma, and I had to undergo brain surgery. The damage was concentrated in the prefrontal cortex—the part of the brain responsible for processing emotion, empathy, and impulse control.

I didn't speak a single word until I was seven. The years between were filled with treatments, speech therapy, and endless attempts to retrain a brain that refused to function the way it was supposed to.

But silence had its advantages.

I became an observer. While others spoke, I listened. While they revealed themselves, I studied every detail—the way people tic, the subtle shifts when they lie, the small tells that betray their thoughts.

I learned quickly it wasn't just actions that got people killed. More often than not, it was their inability to keep their mouths shut.

I was five when I saw my first kill. My father pulled the trigger, the sound loud and final. It didn't bother me, not even a little.

It was a lesson. Life had rules, and in our world, breaking them meant dying. Simple as that.

I stared at the dead body for a long time, watching the blood seep from his head, his lifeless eyes fixed on nothing. I felt nothing.

The house staff whispered that it was then I changed, but they were wrong. It wasn't change. It was fascination.

By the time I turned fourteen, I felt my first true emotion—rage—the kind that scorches your soul and leaves nothing but ash behind.

That was the year my mother's friend decided I was her target.

During one of the endless parties my parents hosted, I accidentally walked in on her with four men. She didn't even seem bothered, and neither did they. They carried on as if I weren't there.

I didn't care—what people did behind closed doors wasn't my business. I turned and left, with no intention of saying a word. Who someone else's wife screws means nothing to me. By the time the door clicked shut behind me, I had already forgotten what I'd seen. That's how insignificant she and her activities were.

But she didn't see it that way.

I became her sole target. At first, it was subtle—brushing up against me, sitting too close, letting her hand linger in what appeared to be innocent gestures. I ignored her. I'd intentionally go anywhere she wasn't.

I was fourteen, and she was a grown woman. I looked older. I know I looked older. But it didn't matter. I was fourteen. I didn't want it. I didn't want her. But she didn't care.

One night, she cornered me in a hallway, backed me up against the wall, and whispered things in my ear that she wanted to do to me while she rubbed at my pants, only to find I was completely limp.

She kissed me, and when I pushed her away, she fell to the floor, looking at me like *I* was a monster. She called me a pussy and said I'd regret it if I ever pushed her again. She said I will make it up to her.

She was drunk. She wouldn't remember. That's the story I told myself.

But she *did* remember.

It got worse.

One weekend, I was sent to stay at her house to help watch the younger kids. I told ma I couldn't. She said I was the only one available and that I could help for just one night. It was either that or go to an opera. Watching kids seemed like the lesser evil.

There were always enough teenagers around that I could slip out back and wait for the night to end. That was my plan.

When we arrived, Ma and she talked in the kitchen while I stood nearby. I was handed a drink and told it was juice. I shook my head, but my refusal instantly embarrassed ma, and she shot me a look, the kind that didn't need words. The look that said if I disrespected her friend, I wouldn't hear the end of it.

So I drank it.

She kissed me goodnight, saying she'd see me in the morning.

I was the first to show up.

No one else came.

That was the plan all along.

She drugged me.

I woke up tied to a chair, my head spinning, my body heavy and unresponsive. She was on her knees, sucking me off, trying to get a reaction out of me. I remained completely limp.

When she tried rubbing herself on me and attempting to make it go in, she still couldn't manage, so she did the next best thing. She forced my fingers inside her, riding them like they were her own personal dildo.

My fingers, my fourteen-year-old fingers, bent and broken under her relentless grinding and screaming on them.

The pain was blinding, but the humiliation was worse.

She didn't stop. She untied me, laid me on the couch, and climbed on top of me, grinding against my face, smothering me with her pussy.

I couldn't move, couldn't fight back. She shoved her tongue in my mouth, whispering how much she loved the taste of herself on me.

My fractured fingers throbbed, my chest heaving with rage.

I stayed silent because she threatened to tell her husband I raped her if I ever said a word. That was the world I grew up in—lies and leverage, power used to destroy.

After that, I told my father I wanted to learn to kill. Not because I enjoyed the thought of death, but because I needed a way to channel the fire inside me. He didn't hesitate. He put me through training, taught me how to turn rage into precision, into control.

I've carried that rage ever since. It's shaped me, hardened me. Now, when I take a life, I think about her—about how she fractured more than just my fingers. And every time, I make sure the people I deal with feel a fraction of what I felt.

It's not justice. It's not even revenge. It's survival.

And survival is the only thing I've ever been good at.

I was seventeen when Dante walked into our father's office and found me tied up, tears streaking my face as she rode my fingers—just like she had for years. The room was dim, the air thick with her sick, twisted control.

For years, nobody understood why my hands kept breaking the same way. Fracture after fracture. But Dante saw everything that night. He didn't just see it—he became a part of it.

He told her to get out.

For a moment, I thought it was over, that this nightmare might finally end. But she didn't leave. Instead, she turned, her smile as cold as ice, and pulled a gun, leveling it at him.

"You think you're going to play hero here, Dante? You want to save him? Go ahead, tell someone. I'll just tell everyone it was him forcing himself on me. What do you think your family will do to a boy like that, huh? What will they do to him? He's sick, Dante. Everyone knows there's something wrong with him."

He froze. I could see the gears turning in his head, calculating the fallout, the danger. He was smart enough to know she wasn't bluffing. She was too cruel, too crazy to lie about something like that.

I silently pleaded for him to tell. To get out of there. I thought he could read that in my eyes, that he knew it was what I needed from him.

I knew I would be killed. I wished for death every time she was done with me. I just never imagined I could want it more than I did after this night.

"Why?" He didn't want to know the answer, but he asked anyway.

"Because I love him," she spat. She turned back to me, her gaze hungry and manic. "I've loved him for years. But he's broken. Completely useless. You know how many times I've tried? How long I've worked to fix him? He's still broken."

I wanted to vomit. My body felt like a cage, my skin too tight, my shame suffocating me.

She tied Dante up. He begged her not to, but she didn't care. She made him sit in that chair, helpless, as she unfastened his pants to find that he *wasn't* broken like me. His body reacted as a man's should when someone offered sex.

She took it as an invitation and straddled him. She moaned my name with every move, staring straight at me like I was the one inside her, like I was the one responsible for all her sick desires.

When she was done, she climbed off him, her face flushed, her breath coming in shallow gasps, while his head hung in shame. He couldn't even look at me.

She turned, her eyes angry as she started hitting me, one slap after another. Then she untied me, letting me crumple to the floor before climbing on top of me again. Her wetness smeared across my face as she pressed her thighs to my cheeks and my mouth.

She put my own brother's semen on my face.

She kissed me afterward, her tongue forcing its way into my mouth as she whispered how much she loved me.

Months later, we found out she was pregnant. Only he and I knew it was Dante's child. We stayed quiet. What could we say?

But silence wasn't enough for me.

The night I slit her throat. She bled out on the floor, her eyes wide with shock, and for the first time in years, I could breathe.

Her husband found her diaries later—pages and pages of delusional ramblings about me, about a love affair that was entirely one-sided. That was all it took. The war began.

Dante told my family. He thought it would help, that exposing the truth would ease the weight crushing down on me. But all it did was ignite my father's rage. Not at me—never at me—but at the world, at the circumstances that allowed it to happen under his roof.

Since then, his fury has kept him distant, his anger barely contained every time he looks at me. My father—the most feared man in the city—unable to protect his own son. His guilt manifests in other ways.

I get everything I want—money, power, respect. Nobody questions me because they pity me. And they fear me.

I kill with no remorse.

The worst part of the entire incident? It's all etched into film.

It was recorded, captured in footage from one of the hidden cameras in our house. A house meant to be a fortress, a symbol of our strength. Instead, it became the stage for my humiliation.

Everyone saw it. The worst moment of my life, laid bare for my family to witness. My mother watched it over and over, her sobs echoing through the halls until my father couldn't take it any-more. He destroyed it, smashed the tape into a thousand pieces.

But the damage was already done.

That tape was like a ghost in our home, haunting us even after it was gone.

Dante and I both had to have extensive therapy afterward. We were told we developed a trauma bond over what we went through together.

I know anger.

I know rage.

I know fury.

But nothing prepared me for the anger I feel now—seeing Rainey like this. Broken. Hurt.

The warm water cascades over both of us as I wrap my arms around her in the shower. Blood swirls around the drain, disap-pearing into the void, but she doesn't move. Her eyes stay fixed on the floor, glazed over with a hollowness.

She sits on the shower bench as I grab the soap, lathering her hair, my fingers gently massaging her scalp. The scent of blood clings to her skin, mixing with the water as it flows down her body. I rinse her hair, then move to her arms, her shoulders, her back—washing away the evidence of what she's endured... be-cause of me.

But she doesn't react. Not a word. Not a flinch. Her body is here, but her mind is somewhere far away, trapped in the horrors of tonight.

After she's out of the shower and dressed, ma and my brothers step into the bedroom.

"She's in shock," Dante says, stepping closer to the end of the bed.

"No shit," Nikolai retorts. "She just watched a man get killed in front of her after Damiano's big cock fucked her."

Right now, I need to kill. I need to destroy.

"I have to go." I walk past them out of the room.

"I'll stay with her," Nikolai calls after me.

I HEAD TOWARD THE BASEMENT, MY SHOES HEAVY AGAINST THE POL-ished floors. As I push open the heavy steel door, the stench of sweat and blood hits me immediately. The three men are seated in metal chairs, their wrists bound tightly behind them. One of them looks up, his face already battered, his left eye swollen shut. The others keep their heads down, but I can see the tension in their shoulders. They know what's coming.

"Evening, gentlemen." My voice is calm and measured.

No one responds. The one with the swollen eye shifts uncom-fortably, his chair scraping against the concrete floor. I take my time, rolling up the sleeves of my shirt as I pace in front of them.

"Let's keep this simple." I stop in front of the first man. His head stays down, so I grab a fistful of his hair and yank it back, forcing him to look at me. His face is pale, beads of sweat trickling down his temple. "Who sent you?"

He doesn't answer, just stares at me with wide, fearful eyes. I sigh, letting go of his hair and delivering a punch to his stomach. He doubles over, gasping for air, the chair wobbling beneath him.

"I'll ask again. Who sent you?"

"I… I don't know," he stammers, his voice shaky. "I don't know anything, I swear!"

I shake my head. "Wrong answer."

I move to the second man, who's trying—and failing—to keep his composure. His hands tremble against the ropes binding his wrists, and I can see his pulse hammering in his neck.

"You," I say, crouching in front of him. "Do better than your friend here." I stab a knife right above the other man's knee.

He swallows hard, his Adam's apple bobbing.

"We didn't know it was yours," he blurts out. "We were just told to scope it out, that's it! I swear. We didn't mean—"

"Who sent you?" I cut him off.

"Fierro!" he yells, panic overtaking him. "It was Cristiano Fierro!"

I stand, crossing my arms as I look down at him. "And how exactly did he find out about my operation?"

"I don't know. We're just the runners. Please, we were just following orders."

I glance at the third man, who's been silent this whole time. He's younger than the others, his jaw clenched tightly.

"You," I say, stepping toward him. "You're awfully quiet. Got something to add?"

He doesn't answer, just glares at me. I chuckle, grabbing the knife from the nearby table and twirling it between my fingers.

"Here's how this is going to work. One of you is going to tell me how Fierro found out about my ring. If none of you talk, I'll start cutting pieces off until someone does. Understood?"

I let the threat hang in the air for a moment, watching their reactions.

The young one finally breaks, blurting out, "There's a girl. She's been passing information. I don't know her name, but she works for him. She's the one who told us where to go."

I narrow my eyes, stepping closer. "Where is she now?"

"I don't know," he says quickly. "That's all I know."

I nod slowly, tucking the knife into my back pocket.

"Good. That wasn't so hard, was it?"

I grab a pair of pliers from the table and turn back to them, my lips curling into a cold smile.

Tonight, they'll learn why they call me *Mercy*.

Chapter

TWELVE

Rainey

I was never cared for—not even as a child. Cops were a regular presence at our house, their flashing lights and authoritative voices becoming part of my normal. When CPS came knocking, I'd climb out of my bedroom window and hide in the woods behind the trailer park, holding my breath until the social workers left. Stealing became a necessity for things like shampoo or food.

Mom's boyfriends were always cruel. Most nights, they would use her as their punching bag, but when she was too strung out on drugs to fight back, their fists would find me instead.

I never thought my life could end up worse than it already was. I thought I had hit rock bottom, just trudging along until I could finally begin to climb my way up. Apparently, life had a really big shovel and decided to dig me even deeper.

The image of the knife lodged in that man's throat refuses to go away. It replays in vivid, gruesome detail—the shock in his eyes as he stared at me in horror, the way his body jerked before collapsing, the sound of his last breath as the life left him.

For the first time in my life, I had watched someone die—and it wasn't just a faceless tragedy on the news. It was real. It happened right in front of me. On top of me.

The guilt gnaws at me. The man's death, his blood spilling out, his body being shoved to the floor. I had been the reason for it. Or was I?

What was his reason for dying? Was it because he hadn't paid to have sex with me? Is that how it works?

I don't understand these twisted rules, and I'm not sure I even want to. But why, if he wanted me so badly, wouldn't they have just let him pay afterward?

Damiano's words come back to me when I asked how often I will have to do that: *Never again.*

I don't know the rules here. I only know that man had bad intentions, and now he's dead.

But even knowing that doesn't erase what happened. I still feel the weight of him pressing me into that filthy mattress. I remember every desperate scream, every frantic flail of my arms as I fought him. And I remember the end—when the blade sliced through flesh, silencing him forever.

His blood is on me, mixed with my own from the horrors of the night.

Now, as Damiano steps into the shower with me, still fully clothed, it feels like stepping into another life entirely. He sets me gently on the bench as though he does this on a nightly basis.

The steam rises around us, curling like a ghost, as warm water cascades over his suit and down my bare skin. Blood-tinged water pools momentarily, swirling down the drain, reminding me that no amount of scrubbing can make me clean again.

The stain isn't just physical—it's etched into my soul.

I can't forget why I'm here. I won't let myself forget.

My mother gambled with my life to erase her debt, trading my freedom for her failure. The Volkov family accepted the terms, reducing me to nothing more than a commodity, a body meant to be used and discarded. It's vile and dehumanizing.

And Damiano… he's complicit. The man standing in front of me, soaked to the bone as he scrubs the blood from my scalp, is part of this. No matter how gentle his touch, or how safe he makes me feel right now, he's still part of the reason I'm here.

He's a bastard.

Warm water continues to pour over us, turning pink as the blood washes from my skin. I can't stop staring at the swirling streaks, hypnotized by the way they vanish, as if it never happened.

I sit there, numb, as he picks up a washcloth and begins to clean my body with a care I don't know how to process. His touch is so soft and unhurried, and I can't comprehend why someone is tending to me—not as an obligation, not out of anger, but with something almost resembling tenderness.

And yet, it's him. The same man whose blade spilled blood onto me, who's saved me three times but only because he's the one who placed me in danger to begin with. My body is caught between repulsion and reluctant trust, and I hate that I can't tell which is winning.

I don't even know where I am anymore. Everything feels like a blur. I remember the van ride around the property, being carried through what looked like a hidden entrance in the forest, then another house. It all blends together now, a haze of confusion and exhaustion.

When he finishes, he crouches in front of me, his eyes searching mine. I can feel his gaze trying to pull something from me, but I can't meet it. I look away, focusing instead on the water rushing over his shoulders.

"You're shaking." His voice is softer than I've ever heard it.

"Breathe," he murmurs, his hands lifting to cup my face. His thumbs brush over my cheeks, wiping away tears. His touch is infuriatingly gentle, a contradiction to everything I know about him.

And yet, for a moment, it feels good. Too good.

I force myself to snap out of it, anger flickering through the fear and grief. I glare at him. "Don't tell me what to do."

His thumbs pause their soft strokes. "I'm telling you because I've seen this. I've felt it. You're in shock."

"Of course I'm in shock!" I snap. "I just watched a man die! And his blood splattered on my face!" I lean forward, shoving at his chest.

But he doesn't even budge.

"He was going to hurt you." His tone is so infuriatingly calm.

"*He* was?! I was brought here to be hurt daily!" My voice cracks, and I shake my head, my words spilling out in a rush. "He was going to do what all of you are going to do to me. Why did he die? Because he didn't pay? Did *you* have to pay? Or do you get freebies because it's your birthday?"

I bury my face in my hands, my shoulders shaking as the tears come.

He doesn't say anything, but I feel him shift closer, his hands settling on my knees.

"Nobody else is going to touch you."

What does that mean? Valentina said we are here to sexually satisfy the men that come into this house. Men will have to touch me for me to do—that. Men like the creep that was forcing himself on me.

"I hate you." The words tumble out, and in this moment, I've never meant anything more.

His face hardens, his jaw tightening as he processes my outburst. He straightens, pulling himself up to his full height as he begins peeling off his clothes.

"There's a towel right outside the shower for you," he says, his tone almost detached. "I don't have women's clothes here, but there's a shirt and sweatpants on the bed. A guard is outside the front door. If you don't feel safe with me, he can escort you back to your room."

His words confuse me. Why bring me here just to send me back to my room? And what the fuck does he mean if I don't feel safe with him? That is almost laughable. He might be a dick, but he's saved me more times than anyone else ever has. Like it or not, he's the only person in this world who makes me feel safe. And after what he did—killing a man for trying to touch me—I doubt anyone else will dare to try.

So right here is exactly where I'm staying.

He begins scrubbing his hair, then washes his face and body while I watch in silence.

At least he will be clean for the three girls waiting for him.

He shuts the water off, swiping his hands down his face, then reaches for a towel, wrapping it around his waist. He picks up a second towel and holds it open toward me.

I glance at him, then down at my hands. They're clean, but they don't feel that way. Standing, I step forward, letting him wrap it around me. Once it's secure, he turns and walks to the bedroom, and I follow, torn between not wanting to lose sight of him and wanting to be as far from him as possible.

The muscles in his back ripple as he grabs a pair of boxers from the bed, sliding them on. When he turns, he's holding the sweatpants he mentioned, the waistband stretched open in his hands. "Unless you'd prefer to do it yourself," he offers.

I hesitate before stepping closer. He bends down, holding the pants for me to step into. The fabric pools around my hips as he slides them up, the waistband far too loose to stay in place. He rolls them down a few times, trying to make them fit better, but they still threaten to fall.

As he glances over his shoulder, my gaze follows his, landing on the four figures now standing in the doorway—Valentina and three of the brothers, all of whom had been in that room. There's no point in being bashful now. They've already seen everything. And I can't shake the sinking certainty that it's only a matter of time before each of them has me.

Damiano grabs the T-shirt and slides it over my head. His fingers graze my arms as the fabric falls into place, sending an unwanted tingle across my skin. I hate that I feel anything at all when he touches me.

"That wasn't supposed to happen," Valentina says from the doorway.

I snap my head up, meeting her gaze with disbelief. She has to be joking, right? How was that *not* supposed to happen? I'm literally here for men to use and abuse me. Isn't that the deal?

The room tilts, and I'm not even sure if I'm breathing. Everything—the voices, the movement, the sound of footsteps—blurs into a muted haze. My focus stays on the doorway, unblinking, as though staring hard enough might force some logic into this mess. It doesn't.

She steps closer, sitting gracefully on the edge of the mattress. Damiano pulls back the bedding on the massive bed and guides me to climb in.

"Rainey, honey," Valentina says softly, "we have a doctor coming to check you for injuries. Dinner's being brought over too."

Her words float around me, muffled and distant, like they're coming from underwater. I don't respond. I can't. My throat feels tight, my body alien, as if I'm watching myself from outside.

"She's in shock," one of the men says, stepping closer to the foot of the bed.

"No shit," another retorts. "She just watched a man get killed in front of her face after Damiano's big cock fucked her."

The crude comment barely registers. It skims the surface of my awareness, fleeting and meaningless.

Damiano's voice slices through the room, cold and detached. "I have to go."

That's it. No reassurance. No pause. Just a statement—an excuse to leave. As if I wasn't even here.

"I'll stay with her," one of the men says, and all the others nod in acknowledgment.

He strides out without a backward glance, muttering something to the oldest brother as he leaves.

Valentina places a hand on my arm, her touch unexpectedly light. She murmurs something, her tone soothing, but her words don't reach me. They're swallowed by the thick fog clouding my thoughts. I stare at the doorway, trying to convince myself it's all a dream. A nightmare. Anything but real.

The door opens again, and the doctor steps inside, carrying a bag of supplies. Someone tells me to lie back, and I do, my body responding without thought. It's as though I'm disconnected from the world around me. I lock onto the ceiling, my breath shallow as her hands begin their work.

The doctor speaks softly in another language. The murmurs of the others in the room blend together in the same unfamiliar tongue—Russian, maybe. Though I can't understand them, the meaning becomes clear when the doctor's hands pause, her tone carrying a note of certainty. One of the men responds firmly, and the low conversation continues, passing between them like a decision is being made without my input.

"Stitches won't be necessary with *this one*," the oldest interjects.

Stitches.

The word should spark panic, should send adrenaline coursing through me. Instead, it drifts over me like a whisper in the wind, distant and meaningless.

Won't be necessary with this one.

I'm not a person here—just *this one*. A thing to be patched up, then put back on the shelf. My chest tightens, but no tears come. I'm too drained, too hollow for that.

The doctor nods and sets a small tray of supplies on the nightstand. "I'll come back in the morning to check on you," she says, taking a step back, her role in this surreal tableau complete. She's gone as quickly as she arrived, leaving the room heavy with silence.

Valentina rises from the bed, her heels not making a single noise on the carpet. She leans over me, brushing a kiss against my hair like a maternal figure. "Thank you."

Thank you?

The words make no sense. I've done nothing but sit here, frozen and useless. If anything, I've doomed them all. By morning, there will be police, handcuffs, questions I can't answer. Their entire operation—whatever it is—will crumble, and I'll be right there in the rubble. But the thought doesn't bother me.

Not anymore.

She straightens, smoothing the front of her dress, and walks out. Her footsteps echo down the hall, fading into the distance.

A while later, a tray of food is brought in—plates arranged neatly. But I don't even try to eat. Then again, I shouldn't be that hungry, considering my stomach is full of Damiano's sperm.

Eventually, the oldest brother and the one with a beard exit, leaving only the brother with a bun—the one I told myself I'd feel safest with. Apparently, I practically willed this scenario into fruition.

He sits in a chair in the corner, pulling out a tablet and scrolling through it idly. The soft clicks and swipes of his fingers fill the silence.

I stay where I am, still staring at nothing, letting the events of the night settle over me.

My gaze shifts to the man. His posture is relaxed, and the faint glow of his tablet lights up his face. He looks exactly like Damiano—the sharp jawline, the intense eyes, even the way he carries himself, though there's something calmer about him. Less storm, more steady tide. These men are so good-looking it irritates me.

I stare at him for a long moment, then finally speak. "What's your name?"

His eyes flick up to me, assessing, before he sits up straighter in his chair. "Nikolai."

"Are you Damiano's brother?"

"Yes. Older. By one year."

"And the others?"

"Our oldest brother, Dante. Then Silvano."

So I was right about the one being the oldest. I glance at the tray of food on the nightstand, the soup's aroma rising faintly.

"Is this poisoned?"

His lips twitch, not quite a smile but close. "Damiano would skin us alive if it were."

The brutality of his words should alarm me, but I don't doubt them for a second. There's something raw and undeniably dangerous about Damiano, a constant undercurrent of control and power that seems to radiate from him. You can see it just by looking at him.

I pull the tray closer, testing the soup with a small sip. The warmth spreads through me, and before I realize it, I've finished every bite.

"What is your family's organization? Are you guys like pimps or something?"

Nikolai looks up at me again, then offers a simple, "No."

"Drugs?"

"No."

"Then what?" I ask, confused.

"We run gambling operations," he says casually. "Underground poker games, casinos, betting rings."

"Illegal gambling?" I ask, arching a brow.

He shrugs. "Depends on who's asking. The wealthy and pow-erful don't care if it's legal as long as they get what they want."

"Is that it, or is there other random stuff? Like loan sharking?" I press, already knowing they must be, since I am now here.

"Sometimes people need help. We give it to them. They don't pay us back? We remind them of their obligations."

"And they're allowed to negotiate their debts with their daugh-ter's body?"

That seems to take him by surprise. His eyebrows knit together.

"I think this is a conversation for you and Damiano."

"No thanks." I lean back, pulling the covers higher.

He goes back to looking at his tablet, and I continue staring at him. I don't understand how such gorgeous men have to rely on sex workers to get laid. It's insane.

"Does everyone here have STDs?"

His eyes flick up to me, and once again, he seems genuinely confused.

"Nobody has any sexually transmitted diseases. Are you think-ing you got one tonight?" He lets out a laugh, and now I'm the one confused about why he would find that funny.

"You all sleep with all the women here. Men come and sleep with the women here. Men leave and sleep with women elsewhere, then return and sleep with the women here. It's unsafe."

"Everyone is tested regularly."

"And are *you* currently clean?"

"I am," he responds confidently.

I chew on the inside of my mouth, then push the covers back. "Do you want me to take these back off? They aren't mine, and I don't think your brother would like them getting ruined."

This man's expressions are a roller coaster—confusion, reali-zation, then back to confusion with every question I ask.

"I'm not going to have sex with you," he says, as if my impli-cation is ridiculous.

"Because I'm not your type, or…?"

"Because the bite mark on your neck was a warning to any man wanting to have sex with you that if they go near you, they will end up dead."

"And once it's healed? Then you'll have sex with me?"

"He will make sure that never heals," he says casually, looking down at his tablet.

"And the rules don't go both ways?"

This time, he looks up, his brows furrowing slightly like he's trying to decipher a foreign language. The way he doesn't immediately answer only makes my blood boil.

I let out a condescending laugh. "You all are disgusting."

I wait for him to say something—to get mad, or yell. But he doesn't, and that pisses me off.

"Okay… then what? He just didn't get his fill tonight? He had to go sleep with three more girls?" I glare at him.

When he looks at me with confusion, it fuels my anger.

"I know how to read. He got a text when we were in your guys' creepy dungeon cave, and it said he had company… three guests, to be exact."

He stares a moment longer, the realization of my words sinking in. His eyebrows raise in understanding, but then he masks it, looking back down at his tablet.

"Whatever," I mumble. "I'm sure you are stationed here on guard duty. When you see your brother, tell him to keep his disgusting penis away from me. Actually, better yet, tell him he can go sleep in one of those girls' beds because if he brings his slimy dick anywhere near me, I'll cut it off."

And then I roll over, flicking off the lamp and pulling the covers up.

Chapter

THIRTEEN

Rainey

Sleep came in fitful bursts throughout the night, fragmented and restless. Each time I managed to drift off, vivid dreams or lingering pain jolted me awake.

When morning finally comes, sunlight spills through the curtains, painting the room in muted warmth.

I sit up, my body heavy with exhaustion. My mind is groggy, and a dull ache pulses between my legs.

In the bathroom, the ache intensifies, turning sharp as I lower myself onto the toilet. My vagina feels swollen, tender beyond anything I've ever experienced, and even the stretch of my other hole burns, raw and unbearable.

The pain brings tears to my eyes, and I bite my lip, trying to keep quiet as I finish. When I stand, I see a small jar sitting on the back of the toilet. It's the same ointment the doctor applied last night.

Grateful for the small mercy, I grab the jar, unscrewing the lid. I hurry to apply it, the cool ointment easing some of the searing discomfort as I gently rub it over both areas.

I exhale shakily, closing the jar and setting it back down, making my way back to the bedroom. Every step is cautious, my body still protesting.

When I enter the room, I stop short. Damiano is there, leaning casually against the doorway, his arms crossed and his gaze locked on me.

We stare at each other for a long, tense moment.

"Did you talk to Nikolai?" I mirror his stance as I cross my arms and glare at him.

"I did."

"Then why are you here?"

His lips curve into a smirk as he pushes off the wall, approaching with an unhurried ease. He walks toward me, his presence suffocating in the large room.

"Well," he begins, closing the distance. I press my back against the wall, trying to keep space between us, but he doesn't stop. He raises one arm, bracing his forearm against the wall above my head, his body so close I can feel the heat radiating from him.

"If I had listened to Nikolai," he murmurs, his voice dripping with mockery, "my disgusting, slimy dick wouldn't get to be near you."

Hearing him use the exact words I told Nikolai to say almost draws a laugh from me, but everything about him makes it hard to focus. He inches closer, and I turn my head, hoping it's clear I don't want him to kiss me.

But it doesn't stop him. His face moves closer, his teeth grazing my earlobe in a soft, teasing bite. A shiver runs through me despite my anger. My eyes flutter shut, betraying how my body responds even as my mind protests.

"Don't," I whisper, though my voice lacks conviction.

He doesn't answer, but I can feel the smirk on his lips as his teeth graze my skin again, leaving me torn between shoving him away and pulling him closer.

"You know," I begin softly as I swallow hard, "I owe you a thank you."

"Oh?"

"For getting my purse back…"

Pulling back slightly, he tilts his face to meet mine and places a gentle kiss on the tip of my nose. "You already thanked me for that."

"So it *was* you!"

A slow, knowing smile spreads across his face, one that only fuels the heat rising in my chest. I swat at his stomach, my palm connecting with his solid frame. He barely reacts, chuckling as his arm snakes around my back, pulling me firmly against him.

"All I remembered was the tattoo on your wrist."

"Yeah?" He closes the remaining space, pressing his lips to mine.

They're soft. I melt into him, parting my mouth. My arms loop around his neck, pulling him closer. He lifts me, and my legs curl around him as my back meets the wall.

"What happened to the man?"

"He OD'd," he says, resuming our kiss.

A pattern is forming—any time someone tries to hurt me and Damiano is around, they wind up dead.

"With a little help from you?"

"Maybe." He smirks, his tongue brushing mine.

The sound of someone clearing their throat snaps us out of the charged moment. I shove his chest, and he sets me back down before stepping back, smirking.

I turn to see Valentina standing in the doorway, her ever-elegant posture impeccable. Beside her is a man who looks like an older version of Damiano. His hair is slicked back, a salt-and-pepper blend that only makes him look more distinguished. His tailored suit clings to a broad, solid frame, and there's something in his eyes—a cold calculation—that tells me this is the man in charge.

Lorenzo Volkov.

He steps into the room, his presence alone enough to make my knees feel like they might give out. His gaze drifts over me before settling on his son.

"Was the problem handled?" His voice is smooth.

"Of course," Damiano replies with a casual confidence.

Lorenzo nods once. "Good. I want a full debriefing over lunch."

Damiano doesn't respond, but the silence must suffice because Lorenzo's attention turns to me.

I'm not sure what to expect as he approaches, but the closer he gets, the more nervous I become. When he stops in front of me, he extends a hand.

"Lorenzo Volkov," he says, his voice surprisingly… polite.

I just stare at his outstretched hand, unsure of what to do. Then, I reach out and take it. The softness of his grip catches me off guard. I half-expected him to crush my fingers, to squeeze until my knuckles turned purple and I whimpered in pain. But his hold is gentle.

As I pull my hand back, an automatic reflex kicks in, and I wipe it on my shirt without thinking. The moment I do, my stomach tightens in realization. I just disrespected the mob boss.

Lorenzo either doesn't notice or doesn't care to react. "Get dressed." His tone is curt but not unkind. "You'll join us for lunch."

He turns without waiting for a response, his hand resting on Valentina's lower back as he holds his other hand out for her to go first. Even that catches me by surprise.

I step away from the wall, intending to follow.

"What are you doing?" Damiano's hand clamps around my arm.

Just like that, whatever spell he had me under breaks. The thought of where he's been, who he's been with, sours the mood completely. My jaw tightens as I rip my arm free. "Getting ready for lunch."

He doesn't argue. Instead, he turns and leads me through his absurdly massive house—far too big for just one person to live in alone.

At the end of a long hall, he opens a door and steps into a garage so enormous it could swallow the entire trailer park I grew up in.

The overhead lights flicker on, revealing a space that is immaculate. The walls are stark white, creating a sharp contrast against the black toolboxes, safes, and workbenches that are seamlessly built into them. Everything is meticulously organized, each item in its designated place, like a showroom rather than a working garage.

I take in the three blacked-out vehicles, lined up with almost military precision. The first is a luxury sedan, its glossy finish reflecting the overhead lights like liquid ink. Beside it sits an all-black truck. But it's the third vehicle he heads toward that has me lifting my brows in confusion.

An all-black ATV, rugged and monstrous, looking like it belongs in some dystopian wasteland.

I stare at it, unimpressed. "That's fucking ugly."

Damiano doesn't even blink. "Doesn't matter if it's ugly. It'll get us back to the house without you destroying your feet and whining about blisters."

He stares for a beat longer, arching a brow. "Would Her Highness prefer a car instead?" He gestures lazily toward it.

I roll my eyes but climb in anyway.

He leans down, reaching over me to buckle me in like I'm a damn toddler before shutting the door and walking around to his side.

The moment he starts the engine and revs it, I know I need to brace myself. His hand grips the stick shift, shifting gears, and I barely have time to process what's happening, he turns and winks at me—a silent warning.

Then we're off.

He drives like he's trying to set a record, the ATV jerking forward with raw power as he tears across the property. Every sharp turn makes my stomach lurch, and I'm convinced we're about to flip at any second. But somehow, he maneuvers it with expert ease, handling the clutch and gears like it's second nature.

By the time we skid to a stop behind the main house, my death grip on the seat loosens. I turn to glare at him, my pulse still racing.

He bursts out laughing, completely unbothered, then leans over and unbuckles me.

I climb out on shaky legs, slamming the door way harder than I need to and stalk off down the path toward the back. He strides quickly to catch up to me and lazily drapes his arm over my shoulder, pulling me in to kiss the top of my head. I hit his chest and knock his arm off me as I try to walk faster, but he easily stays next to me.

Movement in one of the upstairs windows catches my eye, and I look up to see Trixie scowling down at me.

Perfect.

I meet her glare, narrowing my eyes before flipping her off. Her exaggerated eye roll only fuels my smirk, but when Damiano looks up, his reaction is instant. His glare locks on her, and the confidence in her posture crumbles.

She quickly lowers her gaze and steps away from the window, retreating like a scolded child.

I glance at Damiano, and he meets my gaze with a playful smile. The fact that he did that to Trixie brings me so much satisfaction that I might just forget about him leaving last night.

Back in my room, I head straight for the shower, letting the hot water soothe my nerves. Once finished, I towel off and head to the closet, hoping to find something simple and modest.

Instead, I'm met with the same rows of tight, revealing dresses and barely-there lingerie. My heart sinks as I sift through the hangers, realizing I have no real choice. Every outfit is designed for one purpose, and none of it is meant to make me feel comfortable.

I pull out a black dress that's slightly less offensive than the others, but it still clings to my body in all the wrong ways. Is this really what I'm expected to wear to have lunch with the mob boss?

Then, a darker thought settles in my mind. What if this isn't just about a meal? *What if I'm expected to… sleep with him?*

Valentina doesn't look like she'd be okay with that. She'd likely kill me herself. Not that it matters—I feel like I'm already living on borrowed time.

I shake the thought away and move to the mirror, styling my hair and applying makeup. If I have to endure this, I might as well make a good impression. As the curls fall perfectly into place and my makeup enhances every feature, I steel myself with new resolve.

I pull on the black dress and find that it's practically transparent, plunging low across my chest. This is what I have to work with, and damn, my boobs look good.

I grab a red thong, slip it on, and then step into a pair of red high heels, intentionally leaving off a bra.

Walking downstairs, I keep my shoulders rolled back and my head held high, ignoring the stares from the other girls. Their eyes follow me, but I don't give them the satisfaction of acknowledging their whispers, or the fact I know they witnessed what happened to me last night.

When I enter the kitchen, I hear voices down the hall and follow the sound until I step into a large dining room. The moment I enter, the room falls completely silent.

The Volkov men sit around a massive table, Valentina among them, perched beside Lorenzo. Their conversation halts, and all eyes turn to me.

Damiano's gaze rakes over me until his eyes land on my boobs. He doesn't bother hiding the way he stares. Finally, he stands, his expression unreadable.

"Baby, do you want to wear something over that?"

I glance down at the dress, then back up at him.

"I'm a whore." My tone remains flat. "This is what was provided."

The tension in the room deepens, but I refuse to back down, meeting his gaze head-on. Whatever this lunch is about, I won't let anyone think I'm ashamed of who *they* are making me.

The men on the opposite side—Nikolai, Dante, Silvano, and another man they called Giovanni—don't even bother hiding the hunger in their eyes. It's the kind of look that tells me they'll devour me whole when they are given the chance.

Damiano pulls out a chair for me, gestures to it, then takes the seat beside me. On his other side sits a brother I haven't met, his face only familiar from the auction, the nerdy-looking one with glasses. Valentina sits further down, poised and elegant as always, while Lorenzo presides at the head of the table, radiating an authority that keeps everyone in check.

"Problem?" Damiano asks.

The men across the table snap out of their trance, shifting uncomfortably under his gaze. Their eyes flick to him, then toward Lorenzo.

"Not at all," Dante says smoothly, turning toward their father. He picks up the thread of an earlier conversation, his voice dropping into something more serious.

"There's a concern with the profits from the Emerald casino," Dante begins, tapping his fingers lightly against the table. "The high-stakes tables are drawing too much attention. Last week, someone started asking questions we didn't like. We'll need to move the bigger games to the warehouse and tighten security on the floor."

Lorenzo nods thoughtfully, his fingers steepled under his chin. "Good. And the laundering? Is it still flowing smoothly through the clubs?"

"It is," Giovanni interjects. "The nightclub fronts are solid. We've got three more investors lined up, and all of them are eager to clean their cash. We're considering opening another spot uptown. It'll be exclusive—invitation only. High rollers, no amateurs."

"Make sure the invites are discreet," Lorenzo says firmly. "The last thing we need is another leak. And keep an eye on the dealer rotations at all locations. We can't afford any slip-ups."

The conversation shifts to a party being hosted tonight, something about welcoming a new business partner. It sounds like a high-profile event, with guests who are likely just as dangerous as the Volkov family themselves.

"All invitations have been sent out for the auction in four days," Valentina says, smiling at her husband.

My heart sinks at the mention of the auction. The blood drains from my face, my stomach twisting into tight knots. I feel like I might be sick right here at the table.

I try to keep my breathing steady, but the words echo in my head, each syllable hammering at me.

Another auction.

Four days.

Damiano squeezes my thigh, and I blink, realizing my entire body must have stiffened. I look down at his hand—the same hands that touched me in front of all those perverted men. With my thumb and pointer finger, I flick it as if it were a bug on my leg, letting him know I don't want him to touch me. His jaw flexes, but he removes it.

The conversation around the table drones on, each word about business or logistics bouncing off me like distant echoes. My plate sits untouched, and all I can think about is the auction in four days.

I force myself to keep still, to look like I belong here, but inside, I'm unraveling. How am I supposed to endure it again?

When lunch finally finishes, Lorenzo turns to Damiano. "I'd like a word with you. In private."

Damiano nods, rising from his seat as the others begin to disperse. I slip out behind Dante, keeping a careful distance as I follow him down the hall. He walks with purpose, eventually stepping into a room and closing the door behind him.

I wait, glancing around to ensure no one is watching, then slip inside.

The room exudes power—like something pulled straight from a mafia movie. A dark wood desk dominates the space, and a sleek leather chair sits behind it. Dante is seated, head bent as he rifles through papers.

When the door clicks shut behind me, his eyes lift, irritation flickering across his face. But the moment he registers that it's me, arousal overtakes his features.

I take my time crossing the room, sauntering toward him. His gaze tracks my every movement, never wavering as I close the distance between us.

Leaning against the edge, I position myself close to him, my hip brushing the corner as I look down at him. "Buy me at the next auction," I say softly, my voice carrying an edge of desperation.

His brows knit tighter, confusion deepening. "What?"

"Damiano doesn't go to those things," I continue, my words rushing out. "But you do. I'll behave. I won't fight you. Just… please."

His jaw tightens, and I think he might be considering it. But then he shakes his head. "As much as I'd love to fuck you," he says bluntly, his voice low, "Damiano claimed you first."

"Fuck Damiano," I snap, stepping closer.

His focus drops to my chest, mouth parting slightly before he turns away, locking onto the chairs across from his desk as if forcing himself to look anywhere but at me.

"Look at me," I whisper, letting seduction creep into my tone.

A pause. Then, dark eyes flick back up, dragging over my body in slow assessment. His breathing deepens, lingering on my breasts before finally meeting my gaze.

"Take me how you want me."

His chest heaves, and I see the strain against his pants, the bulge pressing against the fabric. His hand moves to my hip, sliding down my leg and back up beneath my dress.

The door suddenly opens, and I freeze, my heart leaping into my throat. For a moment, I'm convinced it's Damiano, ready to end us both.

But it's not.

It's Em. She stands in the doorway, eyes wide with surprise before narrowing at me. "What are you doing here?" she hisses, stepping inside and quickly shutting the door behind her. "Are you trying to get us all killed? Get out before Damiano sees you!"

She said it's about surviving. That's what I'm trying to do. Survive. I've seen the way he stares at me. He's my best shot of having someone familiar take me at the next auction.

Dante stands abruptly, his hand grabbing my arm and squeezing.

"Don't ever come back in my office again. Get out," he snarls.

I stare at him, startled by the sudden shift in his tone, then yank my arm free. Em glares at me, holding the door open, her impatience palpable.

Without another word, I hurry out, the door slamming behind me.

I stand in the hallway, my thoughts spinning. The abruptness of Dante's mood change, Em's words, the way he pushed me out so quickly.

And then I hear it.

Something crashes inside the office. I flinch, but it's followed by another sound, one unmistakable—skin slapping against skin, the breathy moans cutting through the heavy silence.

My stomach twists, and realization hits me. That's why they wanted me out. She was there for him.

She can thank me later for being the one who had him hard and ready.

Chapter

FOURTEEN

Damiano

I'm being pulled in a million directions at once. Ma had to make a big deal about me working so much away from the house, especially with Cristiano and his men still out there. Now, I'm stuck with orders to stay on the property, and the work is being brought to me.

Normally, I wouldn't take the order seriously. But Rainey is here now, and that changes everything. If staying on the property means I can spend more time with her, then I'll play along.

My youngest brother, Andrei, is a tech genius. His setup in the main house is incredible. He has the biggest suite, with a massive space that almost feels excessive. The walls are lined with book-shelves crammed full of everything from tech manuals to novels, and there's a sleek glass desk tucked into one corner with a single monitor for his more casual work.

The connected living room has been completely transformed into Andrei's personal tech command center. The space feels more like a high-level operations hub than a part of the house. Monitors of every size cover the walls, displaying live feeds, code, and maps. The hum of servers and the soft click of cooling fans fill the air, a constant reminder of the power flowing through this room.

Cables run along the edges of the room in neat, intentional patterns. Andrei's no slob, and every wire, every device has a purpose. A black sectional sits in one corner, untouched except for the occasional nap he takes when he's been working for days straight. The coffee table is littered with notebooks, highlighters, and empty energy drink cans.

His main workstation is a custom-built desk that looks like it was designed for a sci-fi movie. It's loaded with multiple keyboards, touchpads, and a dizzying array of monitors that wrap around his chair like a cocoon. A massive, curved screen displays live maps of the city with areas of interest highlighted in bright red.

Everything Andrei does is methodical. He doesn't just monitor the property; he monitors everything—our team, the network, hell, probably the weather if it helped him catch a lead. Nothing gets past him, and if it does, he finds a way to correct the error so it never happens again.

I sit back in one of the leather chairs in his room, my hands resting on the smooth surface while I tap lightly against it. His eyes dart across the screens, his fingers flying over the keyboard with an intensity that makes you wonder if he's even aware of anything else around him.

"Show me what you've got."

"We've got abandoned warehouses here, here, and here." He gestures to one of the maps displayed on the largest monitor. "Surveillance is already in place on the first two, but the third just went live."

"And Cristiano?"

Andrei glances at me with the faintest flicker of frustration. "If I had him, you'd know."

I shift forward, elbows on my knees, staring at the screen. "He's hiding somewhere close. He has to be."

"He's smart," Andrei mutters, almost to himself.

"And the tech team?"

"Monitored," he replies. "If they slip up, I'll know before they do."

I lean back, watching him work as we go over possible hideouts for Cristiano and his men.

"That's odd…" His voice pulls me from my thoughts, his focus narrowing on a single monitor. He enlarges a satellite image of an abandoned industrial building, zooming in on details I would have overlooked.

"What?" I scoot in, following the cursor as it highlights something near the building's perimeter.

"This one's got fresh power usage," he says, tapping a few keys. "Looks like it's drawing electricity from a nearby substation. It's subtle, though—could be intentional, or just a front."

"Subtle doesn't feel like an accident. Could be them."

Andrei types furiously, his screen shifting to display an overlay of heat signatures. "There's movement inside. Small, but consistent. Could be equipment or people. I'll tap into the nearby traffic cams and see if anyone's been coming or going."

"Set up surveillance."

He nods, already way ahead of me. Another screen lights up, showing a grid of live traffic footage. He toggles between cameras, rewinding feeds and speeding through hours of data in seconds. "There," he mutters, freezing a frame. A black SUV pulls up to the building, the driver staying inside for several minutes before leaving. "Same car's been spotted twice in the past three days."

"Can you track it?"

"Already on it." He pulls up a license plate database, cross-referencing the SUV's details with local traffic records. "It's stolen. Swapped plates."

"Of course it is," I mutter, pinching the bridge of my nose. "Anything else?"

"Give me a second." He switches to another monitor, accessing thermal satellite imagery. "There's a heat signature near the north side. A van parked for hours with no one moving in or out. Could be a surveillance vehicle or part of their operation."

"Isolate it. I want to know what's inside that building and who's running it."

"I'll patch into nearby business security cams and see if they caught anything."

My leg starts to bounce impatiently, the energy building in me with nowhere to go.

"You're going to wear out my floor."

I don't respond, but my leg doesn't stop. He glances at me, sighs, then pulls up a new window. Suddenly, one of the monitors displays a live feed of Rainey sitting in one of the living rooms. One of the other girls is beside her, animatedly talking, while Rainey sits with a pillow over her lap, her fingers threaded through her hair.

My leg stills immediately.

"Better?" Andrei asks, smirking as he goes back to working on his other monitors.

I scoot right in, my eyes locked on the screen. "Zoom in."

He complies, the image sharpening to show her face in clear detail.

I stare at her, completely captivated. The way her lips part as she responds, the subtle nod of her head as she listens—it's mesmerizing. There's a calmness to her that I can't look away from, a strength beneath the surface that's impossible to miss.

The only thing about this picture I don't like is that she doesn't have a ring on her finger yet. I wonder what kind of diamond she'd want. Something simple? Flashy? She deserves the best. Something unique, like her.

The feed catches movement as Trixie walks into the room from the side, Cherry trailing behind her. Rainey doesn't seem to notice. Trixie leans over, whispering something to Cherry, and they both start walking toward the girls.

"What are they doing?"

Andrei pauses, his eyes darting to the monitor before going back to work. "You're about to find out."

Trixie nudges Cherry playfully, the act exaggerated. Then Cherry bumps back into Trixie, and the cup of liquid in her hand tips, splashing over Rainey. The reaction is immediate—Rainey gasps, her hands shooting up as the cold liquid soaks through her already tight dress. The expression on her face says it all: she's furious.

She stands, shaking her arms as if trying to fling off the droplets. A heated exchange takes place between the four girls, but I can't make out any of the words.

Rainey's expression hardens, and she storms out of the room, her body tense with anger. Behind her, Trixie and Cherry dissolve into laughter.

"Switch the feed."

Andrei switches the view to another camera that follows Rainey as she stalks down the hall. I watch her shoulders rise and fall with every breath.

"Switch it to a front view," I say, my eyes still glued to the monitor.

Andrei raises a brow, his fingers pausing for a moment over the keyboard. "Really?" he asks, a hint of amusement in his tone.

"Just do it."

With a shrug, he taps a few keys, and the feed shifts. My smile widens instantly as the camera captures her from the front, her wet dress clinging to every curve. The thin fabric has turned almost transparent, giving me a clear view of her perfect tits as they bounce with each frustrated step she takes.

"Perv," Andrei laughs, shaking his head as he turns back to his other screens.

"She's sexy." I grin, unable to peel my eyes away from the monitor.

As she disappears from the cameras into her room, I start to think about how I should get one installed in there so I can watch her while she's alone. She's undressing right now, and I'm dying to see her naked again.

Andrei leans back in his chair, stretching his arms over his head, locking his fingers behind his neck. His eyes flicker from one monitor to the next, then finally land on me. "What ever happened with that car? The one with the four girls?"

I glance at him, the memory flashing back from just three weeks ago. "No complications. All four healing."

We got word of the vehicle—a beat-up van carrying four women and one man. A tip came through from one of Cristiano's enemies who decided it was worth more to cross him than stay loyal. Said the van was headed out of the city loaded with drug mules. I didn't wait for the details. I gathered only Nikolai, Boris, and Marko, and we hit the road.

Tracking them wasn't the hard part. They thought they were subtle and careful. But they were in a caravan of death and drugs on four bald tires.

When we finally cornered them, it wasn't elegant. It never is. We boxed them in on an empty stretch of road, our SUVs creating a wall they couldn't get through. Guns were drawn as the first shot rang out. A firefight erupted—short and loud. None of ours were hit, and by some miracle, none of them were either.

I remember the driver's face as we pulled him from the van. Fear and anger—it was all there. But it was the women I didn't want any part to do with. My job would begin when I brought the driver back to interrogate. Nikolai is the ladies' man. He's a smooth talker and people immediately trust him. The women sat huddled in the back, their eyes wide and blank like they'd already accepted their fate.

Four women, each one carrying a piece of Cristiano's empire inside their bodies. They didn't move, didn't scream, didn't even flinch as Nikolai walked up and crouched in the door and began talking to them. As I loaded the man into the SUV, I turned back and saw the women nodding and climbing out of the vehicle, grabbing Nikolai's arms.

He took them to Sterling Point—one of our compounds. A safehouse with doctors, housing, kids, and women who have been through hell and survived—now under Volkov protection. It's a place Cristiano's reach doesn't touch. Though it's not for lack of trying on his part.

The doctors worked through the night. The girls had implants, drug bundles in their stomachs, even stuffed up inside them. It wasn't the first time we'd seen it or heard of it.

The driver spilled everything after a few hours with me. Said there'd be four more cars, coming every other week for three weeks. And if those shipments didn't make it to their destinations, the girls' family members would be killed.

I reached out to Nikolai, who stayed at Sterling Point with them before, during, and after their surgeries, and he asked each of them what family members were being held hostage to keep them complicit. They all said the same thing: they were homeless. No one to look for them. No one to miss them. That's how Cristiano found them. Vulnerable and disposable.

I've dealt with a lot of scum in my life, but Cristiano? He's in a class of his own. A man who builds his empire on the backs of the broken.

Andrei's voice cuts through my thoughts, bringing me back to the present. "What's the next move?" he asks, not even looking away from his monitors.

"We let them think the next shipment's going as planned, and we follow them to their drop off point."

Chapter

FIFTEEN

Damiano

I don't realize how late it's gotten until Andrei speaks up. "Party's wrapping up."

I glance at the clock—one a.m. Rainey's probably asleep by now. I should head back to my house, but the idea of not seeing her while I'm here doesn't sit right. I'll stop by her room, just to kiss her cheek.

I haven't seen her since lunch with my family five days ago. Dad had pulled me aside after to talk.

"How are things going?" he'd asked, keeping it casual. "Now that she's here, do you still want to marry her?"

"Of course I do." If anything, I want to marry her even more.

"Her family? Will they be any trouble?"

"No. I've got eyes on them."

He studied me for a moment. "And you? How are you hold-ing up?"

"I'm good," I replied. And that was the truth.

When I'd gone to leave, he pulled me into one of his rare hugs, his hand firm on my back. "I love you, my boy. You always make me proud."

When I returned, Rainey was storming off toward her room. I didn't know what had set her off, and I wasn't about to get my head bitten off finding out. I left her to cool off, figuring time would sort it out.

But now, five days later, I'm done waiting.

I slip into her room silently, closing the door behind me. She's standing by the window, just like she had the first night I came in here. The moonlight silhouettes her figure, highlighting her body in that damn tank top and those tiny booty shorts that ride high. Goddamn. My body reacts instantly, and I'm left standing here with an erection. She's the sexiest woman I've ever seen.

I lean against the wall in the same spot as the first night, mim-icking the same casual stance—hands in my pockets, foot crossed over the other ankle. I watch her, memorizing the way her fingers comb absently through the ends of her hair.

She turns and halts when her eyes lock on mine. For a heart-beat, I think she's happy to see me. Her face softens, but then it's gone, replaced by fury.

"Get out," she snaps, striding to the bed.

"No."

Her dramatic eye roll makes me smile.

I walk toward her as she yanks at the bedding, seizing her arm to turn her toward me. I just want to look at her, take her in, only for a moment. Then I'll leave.

"Fuck you!" she shouts, shoving my chest with surprising force.

I don't know what's pissed her off, but my grip tightens as I pull her closer and press my mouth to hers. She melts into it, her body yielding to mine. But then she jerks back, her hand swinging up.

The slap lands hard, snapping my head to the side. The sting ignites darkness inside me—a flash of rage, sharp and blinding. *Carmella.* Her face, her voice, her touch floods my mind. The violation, the humiliation. The broken fingers. The way she forced herself on me. I want to strangle her, to make her pay a thousand times over.

This isn't Carmella.

This is Rainey.

My Rainey.

My nostrils flare, and my chest heaves as I force myself to step back, dragging air into my lungs. I turn, heading for the door. I need to walk it off before I say or do something I'll regret. No woman has ever put her hands on me like that since Carmella, and I'm using every bit of strength I have to keep my legs moving. But just as I reach the door, I turn back. I can't leave like this.

"Fucking dick!" she screams.

The vase of flowers I'd left on her nightstand is hoisted high above her head then sails through the air, colliding with my head, the crash reverberating through the room like a thunderclap. Glass and water explode outward, raining down in glittering shards. Everything seems to pause, suspended in the aftermath.

Slowly, I turn toward the mirror to my right. The reflection staring back at me shows a large shard of glass embedded in my hairline, blood streaking down my face like war paint. That's definitely going to need stitches.

Reaching up, I grasp the shard firmly as I slowly pull it free. The faint sound of it sliding out of my skin is drowned out by the steady thrum of my pulse. The pain is nothing. I've felt worse. I've survived worse. I hold the shard up, blood dripping from the thick tip, and stare at it before letting it fall. It lands on the broken pieces littered across the floor with a soft clink.

My boots crunch over the broken glass as I take a step toward her.

She backs away, until the bed presses against the backs of her legs. Her gaze locks onto mine, wide and frantic.

Her hands come up, palms out like she's trying to calm me. "Damiano," she starts, her voice trembling, a thin thread of fear laced with regret.

My clothes cling to me, soaked with water and blood. I know I must look unhinged—face cut, chest heaving as I prowl toward her.

"Damiano, I—"

"Don't," I snap. My fury is barely contained, teetering on the edge of eruption. "You—" I start, then pause. "—just had to push me, didn't you?"

I reach for her, too fast for her to react. My hands close around her waist, and I lift her, tossing her onto the bed. She lands with a soft thud, her body bouncing slightly on the mattress.

She scrambles to sit up, her eyes still fixed on mine.

"I was going to leave you alone tonight!" I roar, my voice echoing in the room.

She doesn't flinch. Doesn't cower. Her gaze meets mine with the same fire that's burning me alive.

I reach for the collar of my shirt, yanking it over my head. Her eyes drop, flicking over my chest, and her throat bobs as she swallows.

"Dom…" she says, her voice softer now. "I'm sorry—I didn't mean to—I was—."

I glare at her, and whatever courage she had vanishes. Without breaking eye contact, I grab the waistband of her shorts and slide them down her legs. She doesn't resist, lifting her hips and feet to let me remove them.

I undo my pants, and she watches, tracking every motion.

"Take off your shirt," I command.

She obeys without hesitation, pulling the tank top off and tossing it aside.

My eyes roam over her. Her skin is smooth, glowing in the dim light. Her full breasts rise and fall with each breath. The curve of her waist, the dip of her hips—she's perfection.

When I kneel on the bed, she lies back, parting her legs in invitation. The sight of her like this—open, vulnerable, waiting—sends a rush of heat through my veins. I position myself between her thighs, pressing my knees under hers so her legs rest on mine.

My heart pounds, an unrelenting rhythm that drowns out all other sounds of the women arriving home.

My hands slide up her thighs, one remaining on her hip, the other brushing against her heat. I feel the undeniable proof of her arousal—she's soaking wet. I let out a slow exhale as I position myself at her entrance.

I pause there, allowing the anticipation to build. The way her body trembles beneath me. The way her thighs tighten against my hips, as if her body can't wait any longer. My gaze flicks back to hers, and I see it: her trust, her surrender, her need, all laid bare.

I push forward enough to feel her warmth envelop me. I'm met with resistance, and the snugness is incredible. A low groan rumbles in my chest as my head tilts back, eyes shutting briefly. Her hands grip my waist as she pulls me in, allowing me to sink deeper. The slow stretch of her body tries to keep me out, but she doesn't seem to care. She wraps her legs around me, tightening them to draw me in deeper.

She clenches around me, her walls pulling me in, holding me there. My heart pounds harder, and my head feels light—whether it's from blood loss or the sheer, unrelenting pleasure of being inside her, I can't tell.

"Fuck," she pants, her body arching beneath me.

I press in fully, my hips meeting hers, and for a moment, I'm still. Just feeling her. Just letting myself savor the way her body grips me so perfectly. Her lips part and another moan tumbles out.

Her head tilts back, exposing the smooth line of her throat, and I lean down, brushing my lips against her neck, her shoulder, her collarbone. My free hand trails up her side, curving around her waist, holding her steady against me as I begin to move.

Each thrust is slow, my body basking in every inch of her. Her gasps grow louder, our moans blending, the rhythm between us building. Her body yields to mine, stretching to accommodate me, making my head spin.

She's heaven. Pure, unfiltered heaven. As I bury myself inside her, my chest tightens—if I die here, like this, with her wrapped around me, it would be the perfect way to go.

I flip her over, relinquishing control to her, placing her body on top of me. She looks stunned as her hands press flat against my chest and she stares down. She's tense as her knees press into the mattress on either side of my hips. I don't know how someone can look so fierce and so timid at the same time, but she does.

"Move," I growl.

Her gaze locks with mine as she tentatively moves, testing the motion. Uncertainty fades, replaced by the spark of friction. She finds her rhythm, rolling her hips, grinding on me.

I grip her waist, guiding her. My hands roam higher, cupping her breasts and squeezing. She gasps, head tilting back as her confidence grows.

"Just like that," I murmur, my words blending with her soft moans.

One of my hands slides to her neck, wrapping firmly around her throat. Her breath catches, her eyes snapping open, wide and full of desire. I pull her down to me, capturing her mouth with mine in a kiss that's wild and consuming. I drink in the soft whimpers that escape her as our tongues tangle.

Her hips roll faster as the pleasure intensifies between us. The friction increases, and my grip on her neck tightens enough to make her face redden.

"Damiano," she whispers as her rhythm falters, her body caught on the edge of release.

I thrust upward so deep she cries out, her nails digging into my chest. Her body tenses as she shatters, a moan ringing out. My release rips through me, raw and unrestrained, leaving me breathless beneath her.

She stills on top of me, her body trembling, her hair a wild mess around her face. I stare up at her, my chest heaving, completely lost in the sight of her. She's a masterpiece, a vision of chaos and beauty, and I'm hers. Completely and utterly hers.

Then, she pulls away, her expression shifting. She slides off me, and I reach for her, but she's too quick, scooting to the end of the bed and remaining on her knees.

"Get out," she snaps as she points to the door.

Her words don't make sense. One minute she's riding my cock, and the next, she's kicking me out. I let out a sigh, my head falling back onto the mattress, my arms splaying wide.

She slides off the bed, disappearing into the bathroom.

I stand, grabbing my pants and pulling them up with more force than necessary, then stomp my shoes back on.

My shirt is soaked, so there's no point in trying to put that back on. When I hear the toilet flush and she comes out of the bathroom, I stride over, grabbing her by the waist and flipping her over my shoulder.

"What the hell are you doing?" she snarls, her fists pounding against my back.

I don't answer. I don't owe her an explanation. I stride forward, crunching through the broken glass on the floor, and jerk open the door.

"Oh my God, Damiano, you're injured!" Trixie's screech cuts through the hallway as I step out.

Of course, she's here. Of course, she couldn't help but linger outside Rainey's room. She was probably hoping it was another man with his dick inside her.

"Put me down, Damiano!" Rainey's voice rises.

I deliver a firm slap to her bare ass. The sound echoes in the hallway, and she goes silent. Good. I need her quiet long enough to get us out of here without the whole house coming to see what's going on.

At the bottom of the stairs, Boris turns, his expression blank until he catches sight of us. His brows shoot up as he takes in the scene.

"Her room needs to be cleaned," I tell him flatly, not slowing down.

I hear the patter of feet down the stairs, then Trixie's obnoxious voice. "Damiano needs medical attention! His head is bleeding!"

That woman can't seem to stay out of my business.

Rainey's useless struggling continues all the way to my ATV, where I set her in the seat and fasten the strap across her. "Calm down, or I'll handcuff you."

She glares at me and immediately reaches for the buckle. With a sigh, I open the front compartment, pull out a pair of handcuffs, and snap one around her wrist, securing the other to the bar above her.

Ignoring her curses, I walk around and climb in. She stays quiet for most of the ride back, but as we approach the house, the swearing starts up again.

I pull into the garage, park, and go around to unbuckle her seatbelt then undo the cuff. She flings the seatbelt off, which only makes it easier for me to scoop her up and carry her inside. As soon as we step through the door, I set her down.

"What is your problem?" she snaps, crossing her arms as she glares up at me, her eyes full of fury.

"Go shower," I order, slipping off my shoes and setting them neatly outside the door in the garage.

She opens her mouth to argue and then it snaps shut again.

"Your room is covered in glass, in case you forgot."

Her eyes flick up to the cut on my forehead, and I see her protests die in her throat. With an exhale, she turns and walks away, back through the house toward the master suite.

I asked Monique, our stylist, to get Rainey a proper wardrobe and she delivered. Quite literally to my house. I pull out a simple pair of cotton panties, sleep shorts, and a loose top from her closet. None of the lingerie that fills her drawers back in her room—just comfortable clothes. I set them neatly on the edge of the bed so she'll see them when she comes out of the bathroom.

Grabbing the first aid kit from the hall closet, I make my way to the second suite. I want to give her space. She's mad, and I don't need more wounds tonight. I need to cool off too before I go back to her.

In the bathroom, I flip on the light and catch sight of myself in the mirror. Blood streaks my face, the gash on my forehead still sluggishly oozing. It's worse than I thought. I pull out the butterfly bandages and carefully clean the injury, the antiseptic stinging as I press it into the cut. My hands are steady, though the sight of the deep gash would make most people queasy. I, however, have patched up plenty of damage.

Once the wound is closed and secured, I strip off my bloodied clothes and step into the shower. The hot water beats against my shoulders, washing away the blood, flower water and sweat. I scrub my hair, feeling the tension start to ease as the steam rises around me. The water turns pink as it swirls down the drain, and I watch until it remains clear.

When I step out, I grab a towel, wrapping it around my waist as I head to the mirror again. The bandage on my forehead holds firm, but I'll definitely need it stitched up.

Stepping into my room, the light from the bedside lamp casts a warm glow over her. She's curled up under the covers, her head resting on the pillow, but her eyes meet mine as I walk in.

Her gaze follows me as I cross the room. There's no anger there now, just exhaustion. The fire from earlier has dimmed, leaving only the bare embers of her emotions visible.

Reaching my side of the bed, I pull the covers back and climb in. The mattress dips slightly under my weight, and I feel her shift, rolling to her side to face away from me. She pulls the blanket up higher, cocooning herself in its warmth, her breathing already beginning to even out.

I lay there propped up on one elbow, watching her silhouette in the darkness. Her hair spills across the pillow, and there's a stiffness in her shoulders that hasn't fully left.

Reaching out, I let my hand hover over her for a second, then pull it back. She needs space. I need patience. But damn, it's hard not to touch her.

I settle back into my pillow, my eyes fixed on the ceiling as her soft breaths fill the silence. Each inhale and exhale is a reminder that she's here, with me. I want to pull her close, to feel her body against mine, but tonight isn't the night.

Instead, I turn onto my side, facing away and mirroring her position. The distance between us feels like miles, but I'll take this over us being under different roofs.

Chapter

SIXTEEN

Sunlight filters through the curtains, brushing against my face, waking me slowly. The other side of the bed is empty, the sheets cool to the touch. I'm not surprised he's gone, and honestly, I'm relieved. I don't think I could stomach looking at what I did to his face.

What was I thinking? I threw a vase at him, for God's sake. A vase. And not just any vase—one that shattered like something out of a movie. I didn't even know they could do that outside of staged stunts. The worst part is, I wasn't even aiming for him. I thought he'd left. I was aiming for the wall, trying to let my frustration out. But he stormed back in at just the wrong second, and by the time I saw him, it was too late. The crash, the glass, the blood—it all happened so fast.

A part of me wants to make excuses, to tell myself that I made it right by letting him have sex with me. Maybe the pleasure would dull the pain I caused, smooth over the rage I saw brewing. Maybe it would stop him from snapping and retaliating in ways I don't even want to imagine. I mean, it has to be some unwritten rule of the mob—don't injure the mob men. And I didn't just injure him. I *big time* injured him.

But that's not why I slept with him. Not entirely. The truth is, I crave him in ways I don't understand, ways that make me feel wild and eager. Even after swearing I'd never willingly let another man inside me—not after the only other time left me sore and humiliated—none of that matters when I'm around Damiano. My body forgets everything else. All I want is him. To feel him. To make him mine in a way that no one else can. And last night... he was better than I remembered. Perfect. Incredible. Completely, irrevocably mine.

I tried to kick him out afterward. Not because I didn't want him there, but because I couldn't stand the sight of what I'd done. The gash on his forehead made me queasy. I thought I might throw up right then and there, adding to the mess of shattered glass on the floor.

I got half of what I demanded. He left, alright… taking me with him back to his house. And then there were the clothes. Clothes that fit me perfectly, like they were there specifically for me. The thought stirs a pang of jealousy. Who else has worn these? Whose were they previously? Did she stand here the way I am now?

Screw these pajamas. As soon as I get back to my room, I'm throwing them in the trash. But for now, I can still smell him faintly on the fabric, and that thought alone keeps me from tearing them off right this second. I hate how much I want him, even now, even after everything. But more than that, I hate how he makes me feel like I'm his.

I make the long trek back to the main house, trying to get back quickly despite how sore my legs are.

I slip in through the back door, careful to close it quietly behind me. My feet ache, a dull throb settling into the soles with every step I take. They're filthy—caked with dirt from the gravel, grass clinging to the damp spots, and the grit from the paved sidewalks.

The kitchen is empty, so I cross the room, ignoring the sting in my heels as I make my way to the counter. With a sigh, I hoist myself up onto the smooth surface, swinging my legs up and placing my feet in the sink. The cold water rushes over them as I twist the faucet on, sending dirt swirling down the drain. I flex my toes, wincing slightly as I rub soap between them, working out the grime. The soreness is worse than I expected, but that's what I get for walking half an hour barefoot.

The quiet sound of a drawer closing makes my head snap up. Dante walks toward me casually, a folded towel in his grasp. I freeze, half expecting him to scold me for treating the sink like a foot bath, but he doesn't. Just steps up and extends the towel.

I reach for it cautiously, waiting for the reprimand, but it never comes. "Thanks," I murmur.

I dry my feet quickly and twist to hop down—only Dante's hands settle on my waist, and he lifts me off the counter. His grip lingers a second longer than necessary before he steps back.

"Thanks," I repeat, quieter this time, then turn and walk away.

He must not have seen Damiano yet. That, or he's putting on a front. Maybe he knows I'm about to get my ass handed to me and wanted to throw me off, lull me into a false sense of ease so I'm blindsided when it happens.

To my surprise, my room is immaculate. Spotless. As though last night's chaos never happened. The shards of glass, the water, the blood—all of it is gone. Even the bed linens have been replaced, and the bed is neatly made. It's eerie, like a reset button has been hit on a nightmare that's still haunting me. Relief washes over me briefly. The mess is gone, scrubbed away as if erasing it could also erase my guilt. I cling to that feeling, pretending that maybe I won't have to face the consequences of what I've done.

I dress quickly, slipping into a skin-tight black dress. The neckline plunges low, teasing more than revealing, while the hemline is modest enough to cover my butt completely. Beneath it, I opt for black lace panties that feel like a tiny shield against the vulnerability I always carry here. Once dressed, I head downstairs, my bare feet padding softly against the polished floors. The house is unusually active, alive with murmurs and shifting bodies as all the girls gather in the large seating room. When I spot Tess, I weave through the crowd to stand beside her.

For the first time since the auction, the girls who arrived with me are all in one room. Their faces bring back the surreal weight of that night. Yet, they seem… oddly fine. Even the girl whose face had been swollen beyond recognition is smiling and chatting with the girl next to her. The bruises have faded into light shadows, and her demeanor is casual. It's odd, like they've all collectively decided to pretend none of it happened. Or maybe they've been conditioned to cope in ways I can't understand.

Valentina enters, commanding attention without having to speak. She radiates confidence, her good mood written in every calculated movement. I take her in, noting the flawless makeup, the expensive tailoring of her dress, the way her hair shines like it was styled by angels. If I looked like her, I think, maybe I'd be in a good mood all the time too.

She glides to the front of the room and clasps her hands together, her bright white smile just as stunning as the rest of her with her painted on red lips. The soft hum of murmurs dies instantly, replaced by total silence.

"Very important people are coming today," she announces. "Make sure the men are satisfied."

Her words are a dagger to my stomach. I glance around, trying to gauge the reactions of the other girls, but their faces remain neutral. How do they not understand what she means? Or worse—maybe they do, and they've just accepted it. My ribs feel like they're caving in, but I keep my reaction carefully masked.

Valentina's gaze sweeps the room, her attention settling on those of us who were auctioned. Her tone shifts, taking on a warmth that feels almost maternal.

"I'll have you ladies serve drinks tonight. You all worked very hard this week." Her smile widens with what looks like genuine pride as she combs over each of us until she settles on me. Her expression shifts. She takes a step forward and tilts her head. "How are you, sweetheart?"

The softness in her voice is almost disarming. Her question feels rhetorical, a prelude to whatever punishment she's about to deliver. Unease coils through me as she sweeps over me. She studies the hickies scattered across my skin, her lips curving into a smile, then takes another step closer.

"Would you like to guess how many stitches my son received last night because of your little stunt?" Her voice is calm... *really* calm.

I press my lips together, refusing to respond. My heart pounds as I feel the entire room shift to me. I should have known better than to think she wouldn't find out. Trixie's big mouth aside, how could Valentina not notice her son's head ripped open?

"Since he has a concussion and has been ordered to do absolutely nothing today, you will care for him."

The room seems to close in around me. I want to protest, to tell her that seeing his stitched-up face will only make me feel worse, but maybe that's the point. Maybe I deserve to feel this guilt. Maybe being confronted with the consequences of my actions is exactly what I need.

My lips stay clamped shut as I nod. Valentina's smile widens, satisfaction radiating from her. "Despite his injury, he was… happy. And for that, my dear… thank you."

She turns and strides away, leaving a heavy silence in her wake. Did she just announce to the entire room that Damiano and I were having sex? No, worse—she implied we had wild, reckless sex that led to his injury. My heart pounds as I peer around the room taking in all the curious stares bearing down on me. Everyone knows what happened last night—or at least they think they do.

They were all there at the auction. They know Damiano and I aren't strangers to each other's bodies, but this is different. This was consensual. This was… something I still can't fully comprehend myself. And now, every single person here knows about it.

I don't even know why I concern myself with what they think. We are all here to have sex. That is literally our job. I need to stop letting sex embarrass me so badly, because until I can find a way to escape this place, it will likely become a daily occurrence. And while I find it incredible with Damiano, it won't always just be him.

Trixie's glare burns into me, jealousy and contempt emanating from her. I don't even get the chance to return the look. Tess steps up beside me, a sly grin curling her lips as she nudges my arm.

"Tell me it was during sex that you injured him," she teases.

I try to think of a way to deny it, to brush it off, but words fail me. My cheeks burn as I realize I'm too flustered to come up with a convincing lie. Tess' smile stretches, and she shakes her head knowingly.

"Oh, don't even try," she says with a laugh. "I could hear you both. Moans loud enough to wake the dead and screaming each other's names. We share a wall, remember?"

We do share a wall, but I assumed she'd be asleep—or at least pretend not to hear anything. Whenever I hear men going to their rooms, that's exactly what I do. I bury my head under my pillow, drowning out every bit of noise. Right now, all I want is to escape this conversation.

"If it makes you feel any better," she says with a shrug, "stitches don't hurt because they numb you first. And mine are already almost healed—and trust me, they're in a much more sensitive spot than a forehead. He'll survive."

She walks away, leaving me frozen in place. Her words replay in my mind, dragging a memory to the surface—the doctor examining me, someone saying, *"Stitches won't be necessary on this one."*

The words had struck me as strange at the time, but I hadn't had the capacity to question them. Now, the puzzle pieces start to shift, and Tess's offhand comment only deepens my confusion.

Where had she needed stitches? She said a far more sensitive region. My stomach turns as the realization creeps in. Was she talking about… her vagina?

I shove the questions aside, unwilling to dwell on something I might not be ready to understand.

As I step into the kitchen, the scent of fresh bread and deli meat fills the air. Damiano stands at the counter, casually assembling a sandwich, completely unfazed by the gash across his head, now held together by pristine stitches. The sight is both gruesome and oddly fitting—like a battle scar that suits him. And the thought that any woman who looks at him will know I'm the one who left a permanent mark brings a strange sense of gratification.

On the other side of the counter, Trixie leans against it nonchalantly, her body angled in a way that screams for his attention. Her dress is pulled dangerously low, just enough for the tops of her nipples to peek out, and the way she shifts makes it clear she wants him to notice.

I move to the opposite side, deliberately placing the cold, sturdy granite as a barrier between us. Crossing my arms over my chest, I lean against it, my gaze fixed on him. "I get to be your babysitter today." My tone light enough to feign indifference.

He glances up, a slow grin spreading across his face. "Oh yeah?"

"Yeah," I reply, arching a brow. "Because you decided to barge into my room last night and assault me."

The knife stills, and he looks at me through his lashes. "I think this classifies as *you* assaulting me." He casually points the knife at his forehead.

"*You* assaulted *me* when you crawled into my bed like a savage beast."

A glint of amusement sparks in his dark eyes. "Are we calling it assault when you were on top of me, riding my dick?"

I bristle at his audacity and want to yell at my nipples for hardening at his words. "Call it whatever you want."

Trixie seizes the opportunity to insert her desperation into the conversation, laying her hand flat on the counter toward him with a sultry smile. "If she doesn't want to take care of you, I'd be glad to," she purrs.

Damiano doesn't even spare her a glance. Instead, he finishes making a second sandwich and slides it across the counter toward me. I catch the plate, my fingers curling tightly around its edges as I glare at him, trying not to feel anything by this small act of kindness.

He steps around the island and rests one forearm and one elbow on the surface as he casually takes a bite. With a playful smirk, he bumps his shoulder into mine—an almost insignificant gesture, but it sends butterflies racing through my stomach.

Out of the corner of my eye, I catch Trixie's reaction. Her fists clench, her jaw tightening as she fights to maintain her composure.

In the adjacent living room, Nikolai, Boris, and two other men sit comfortably, girls draped over the arms of the chairs and couches like accessories. One of the men tells an animated story, his words punctuated by bursts of laughter and commentary from the others. Even Damiano is drawn into the conversation occasionally, chiming in without breaking his relaxed demeanor.

"Come on, baby." He smiles as he walks past me, delivering a firm slap to my butt.

I freeze, stunned by the brazenness of it, before tossing my trash into the bin and following him out of the kitchen. As I pass Trixie, I don't miss the venom in her glare. Her jealousy is practically radiating out of her.

A condescending smile curves my lips as I lock eyes with her. It's petty, but I can't help myself.

When we reach the couch, Damiano turns to me. "Take off your dress."

I gape at him, heat rushing to my face. I scan the room, catching the amused stares of those nearby. The air feels like it's been sucked out of the space. "No," I whisper.

He raises a brow. "I can help you out of it if you prefer."

Panic flares through me. "I'll just lift my dress," I offer quickly, hoping to find some middle ground that won't leave me completely exposed.

He lets out a deep, throaty laugh that unsettles me. Grabbing the collar of his tank top, he pulls it over his head, revealing the sharp lines of his chest and the muscle beneath. "I'm not trying to have sex with you. I want to take a nap."

I blink at him, dumbfounded, unsure how my dress will interfere with his ability to take a nap. But relief washes over me regardless because I won't have to have sex with him in front of more people. I lower my dress as he requested, feeling the heat of every gaze on me, but he steps forward and slips his shirt over my head. The familiar scent of him surrounds me, a mix of cedarwood, citrus, and jasmine. It's strangely comforting.

"Move," he says to the two seasoned girls sitting on the couch, and they immediately scoot over, giving him space.

He turns back to me, his expression softening. "Lay down." He points to the newly cleared spot.

"Why?"

"Why do you question everything? Just lay down."

Swallowing my nerves, I do as he says, stretching out on the couch. I barely have time to process what he's doing when he climbs on, positioning himself between my legs. He lays on his stomach, his head resting directly on my chest. The weight of him presses into me, solid and so, so good. He exhales deeply, letting out a sigh that sounds like pure contentment.

His fingers begin tracing the bruises on my leg, the lightest touch skimming the edges of the discolored skin. He doesn't press down, doesn't aggravate the tender areas, just moves around them as though he's mapping every mark he's left on me.

"Admiring your handiwork?"

He lifts his head slightly, his eyes locking onto mine. "Do you admire yours?" he shoots back.

My face falls as guilt floods through me. The memory of what I did punching deep.

"I'm teasing," he whispers, his voice gentler now. He presses a kiss to my chest, then rests back down as his touch glides over my skin in slow, delicate patterns.

I wrap my arms around his shoulders, tracing gently along his bare skin, mirroring the way he's skimming over mine. His body feels solid and warm, and I feel the tension melt away from his muscles. The sounds of conversation around us fade into the background, blending into a distant hum as his breathing slows.

His hand stills against my leg, and I realize he's fallen asleep. The gentle rise and fall of his body against mine is calming. I relax deeper into the couch, continuing to brush his back lightly.

This. This is happiness. I don't think I've ever felt it before— not like this. Not something so genuine and consuming.

When I wake, the room is still. The chatter has faded, and the girls are gone. Nikolai is sprawled on the long part of the sectional, his head tilted back, sound asleep. From this angle, he looks just like Damiano—only smoother around the edges, a calm shadow of the man lying on top of me.

I glance down and see he's awake, watching the TV. His body hasn't moved, still pressed against mine, but there's a subtle shift in his breathing that tells me he's fully aware.

"How long were we asleep?" I ask, my voice raspy as I stifle a yawn.

"Couple hours," he murmurs.

"You didn't want to get up? I'm all sweaty," I tease, running my fingers absently over his hair.

He shifts slightly, lifting his head to rest his chin on my chest. A mischievous grin tugs at his lips. "I'm definitely up."

My brows furrow in confusion until he reaches down between us, adjusting himself. When he settles back against me, the undeniable press of his arousal sends a jolt through me. His thick cock is resting perfectly against my center, and my body arches into him.

"I see," I whisper, my voice coming out breathy and uneven. "Did you plan on doing something with it?"

"Did you?"

I smirk, half-laughing. "I can't move."

He shifts, pulling the waistband of his joggers down just enough to free himself. His cock grazes me as he moves my panties to the side, sliding between my folds. He leaves it just like that, then relaxes back down, his weight pinning me, the delicious friction making my breath hitch.

"You're a tease," I murmur as I tilt my hips toward him. A soft whimper escapes me as the sensation of him sliding against me sets every nerve on fire.

His groan rumbles low in his throat as he presses back, meeting each subtle roll of my hips with his own. The slow grind builds between us, our bodies moving together in a rhythm that's so incredibly perfect.

"That feels good," I whisper, my voice breaking as a shiver courses through me.

He hooks his fingers under the neckline of his shirt, tugging it down. One of my breasts spills free, and his lips close around my nipple, his tongue flicking over the sensitive peak as his slow thrusts continue.

My head falls back, a quiet moan slipping free. My hands slide around his shoulders, gripping him tightly as I feel the heat coil deep in my core.

"Are you going to put it in?" I pant, my voice shaking as I fight to keep my breathing steady.

Time feels suspended, every inch of me focused on the sensation of him against me. I thread my fingers through his hair, squeezing as another whimper escapes.

The spell shatters as I gape up at Giovanni, who's smirking from right above us.

"What the fuck are you doing?" I gasp.

Damiano releases my breast, his head snapping up. His expression shifts instantly, irritation transforming into amusement.

"Ma has summoned us." His grin widens before he casually turns and walks away.

I rush to pull his shirt back over my boob, my face burning with embarrassment. I'm clearly settling into this new role nicely, considering I was just encouraging intercourse right here in the living room.

"How long was he standing there?" I groan, watching as Damiano adjusts himself with zero concern.

He shrugs as he climbs to his feet. "He probably just got here," like any amount of time he spent watching us wasn't a big deal.

I glance over at Nikolai, who's stretching and yawning. He doesn't comment or acknowledge whether he heard or saw anything, and I mentally thank him.

Damiano holds his hand out to me, and I take it, confused when he starts leading me toward the back doors.

"I need to check on some stuff," he explains, "and we can change really quick." I barely get a chance to ask what he means when he scoops me up.

"Damiano," I protest, but he just smirks, cradling me against his chest as he carries me to my chariot.

This time, as he drives us back to his house, he doesn't speed like a maniac, giving me time to take in the beautiful scenery.

When we step inside, he sets me down gently, lacing his fingers with mine.

He leads me through his home to his closet. But calling it a closet feels like an understatement—it's a whole other room.

I pause, taking it all in. To the left and right are separate areas, and directly in front of us stands a black velvet bench and a full-length mirror that reflects the space back at me. He gestures to the right, and I follow his gaze.

The room is massive, with white shelving units lining the walls and a large island dresser at the center. Though most of the closet is empty, sections around the room have things in them. Dresses, shirts, pants, and coats hang neatly in designated areas. Shoes are arranged perfectly—from sneakers to heels, sandals to boots. Even lingerie has its own spot, all with tags still attached.

I turn back to him and raise a brow.

He grins, leaning casually against the dresser. "They're all yours. Wear whatever you want."

When I don't move, he steps past me, rifling through the clothes.

He selects a floral dress, holding it up to inspect it and drapes it over the island. He grabs a loose-fitting cardigan to match, followed by a pair of white panties, placing them neatly on the counter. He heads to the shoe wall, picking out white sandals and white heels, setting them beside the clothes. Then turns back to the shoe wall, grabs a pair of black sneakers, and playfully adds them along with everything else.

"If I were to choose," he says with a smile, gesturing to his picks. Then leans in, pressing a kiss to my cheek before disappearing to the left side of the closet.

I stand there staring at the outfit he chose. The dress is beautiful—white with large floral patterns, soft and flowy yet fitted in all the right places. As I slip it on, the fabric hugs my chest and waist before flaring out loosely around my hips, ending mid-thigh. It's soft, luxurious, and unlike anything I've worn since arriving here. The cardigan adds an extra layer of comfort, wrapping me in a sense of protection.

The panties are simple and so much more. They fully cover both my butt and vagina, and that feels refreshing. Even the sandals are cushioned and comfortable, their soft soles cradling my feet as I step into them.

I walk to the mirror in the center of the hallway, taking in my reflection. I look... pretty. Not provocative, not like I'm a whore, but genuinely beautiful. I turn slightly, checking the back. The dress isn't revealing at all, and for the first time since I got here, I don't feel like I'm being reduced to an object.

Damiano steps up beside me, pulling my attention away from the mirror. He's dressed casually in dark jeans that fit him perfectly and a black V-neck that hints at his tattooed chest. His full sleeves of ink stand out, each piece of art bold and striking. The man exudes confidence, and it takes everything in me not to start drooling.

He's sexy.

"I'm hungry," he says, leaning down to kiss the top of my head before slapping my ass playfully.

"Me too," I mutter, watching his delicious ass as he walks.

He chuckles and turns back, reaching an arm out and wrapping it around my neck as he pulls me into his side.

Chapter

SEVENTEEN

Damiano

Tonight, the estate is alive with preparations for a large-scale event. Men from across the city—filthy rich bastards who spend millions in our underground gambling rings—will gather here for a night of indulgence. It's more than a meet-and-greet; it's a showcase of the Volkov family's empire, a glimpse into the world of power and vice we've perfected.

Tables are already being set up for the gambling portion of the evening. Giovanni will take his place there, as he always does, wiping the floor with these fools and stacking their money into neat piles of humiliation. The man's a genius with cards, and his calculated charm seems to make their loss more bearable.

But gambling is just the bait. The real allure is the girls. These men will drink our top-shelf booze, ogle the women, and for those who are curious enough, there will be… options. Sampling, choosing, observing—it's all laid out for them, a buffet of temptation. The ones who show the right amount of interest, the ones who loosen their wallets with the right level of enthusiasm, will receive exclusive invitations to the next event in the *Round Room*. That's where the real money is made, during one of our elite gambling nights. Free booze and pussy mean drunk men with lowered inhibitions—and bottomless pockets.

Ma, of course, is in full hostess mode, orchestrating every detail. She thrives in this environment, knowing exactly how to charm these men while keeping them in their place. I usually remain in the background of these things, only mingling when necessary. My concussion, however, is getting me out of having to attend altogether, and I'm happy to oblige by 'staying out of the way.'

I told her Rainey would be taking care of me. She smiled, saying she would make sure it was handled. Rainey isn't thrilled about having to 'babysit me,' as she called it, but when she was told she had the night off, she seemed more than relieved.

The shuffling around the house makes my head throb more than it has been. My elbows rest on the kitchen island as I sit, my palms propping up my face. Rainey is behind me, her arms wrapped around my waist as her chin rests on my shoulder. A couple of guards are in here talking with Dante and Andrei while Cleo, our chef, places a plate of food in front of me.

"Eat it all," she tells me in Russian, pointing to the food, then to me.

I know she slipped something into my dinner—some pain med disguised in the sauce or the seasoning. It's only confirmed when I look at the food on Rainey's plate and Cleo hits me with a towel, telling me to eat my own food.

Discussion over tonight's plans continues as Dante gives Marko orders to make sure all his men are stationed in their guard areas on high alert. We have extra staff tonight and plainclothes security blending in as guests, roaming the house. This is to protect the women as well as the family.

At first, I follow along, tracking the conversation as it moves between them. But then the words begin to stretch and distort, muffled like they're coming from the other end of a tunnel. The haze from whatever Cleo dosed me with settles in, wrapping around my senses like a heavy blanket.

Dante claps me on the shoulder. "Head on upstairs and lie down. We've got this."

I glance at my watch, the numbers swimming slightly. The guests will be arriving soon. The house will fill with exaggerated laughter, overly loud conversations, and the kind of tension that comes with obscene wealth and fragile egos. Gio can handle the high rollers at the tables. Andrei will monitor the tech. Dante and Silvano will talk business while Nikolai takes my place, observing everyone. Me? I'll be upstairs in the living room with Rainey, just above the party.

When we reach the oversized sectional, I settle in, lying on my side with the throw blanket bunched at my waist. I lift the edge and glance at her. "Come here."

She climbs in with a soft smile, settling on her back beside me as I tug her closer. My leg slips between hers while the blanket is adjusted over both of us. The TV flickers on, subtitles flashing across the screen while the sounds from downstairs drift up—the familiar mix of music, laughter, and overlapping conversations.

The ottoman is tucked against the corner of the couch where we're lying, my laptop resting on top, its screen glowing with live camera feeds covering every angle of the house. I know I should unplug, but old habits die hard. Ignoring what's happening below isn't an option. A message pops up in the corner of the screen, Andrei's name flashing beside it.

You have a concussion. Shut your laptop and relax with your girl. I've got the cameras covered.

Rainey notices the message but doesn't react, simply returning her focus to the TV. Her dress has ridden up slightly, exposing the soft plane of her bare stomach. My fingers trace lazy patterns across her skin. She doesn't pull away, doesn't say a word. Instead, she shifts, pressing closer, molding herself against me.

The drug Cleo gave me has fully taken effect, dragging me into a sluggish, numbing fog. My hand continues its movements, but the rest of me feels weighted, almost disconnected. I'm unsure if I'm even still blinking at this point.

Guests pass by with girls as they're led to private rooms in the house. It's typical for people to enter cautiously or avoid the room altogether when they see me inside.

Trixie never cared. She's made her intentions clear since the day she arrived, and I've made mine even clearer—she will never, in a million years, end up in my bed.

She saunters into the room, leading two men behind her. If I had the energy or control over my body right now, I'd tell her to turn right back around and take these men anywhere but here. Instead, my gaze remains fixed on the TV, though I catch glimpses from the corner of my eye as she drops to her knees in front of them—facing me.

Rainey notices too. Her head turns, visceral disgust taking over. She doesn't avert her gaze, though. She keeps watching, lips parting slightly as if on the verge of speaking, yet no words come.

Trixie either doesn't see her or simply doesn't care. She's too caught up in the spectacle, her exaggerated movements designed for attention. Rising to her feet, she strips completely, letting the men have her right there by the railing. Her moans pierce the room, loud and theatrical, the kind you'd expect from a low-budget porno. Below, the party carries on, and I'd bet more than a few guests are watching her get hammered.

"Fucking freak," Rainey mutters under her breath, her eyes still locked on Trixie.

She shifts onto her side, draping a leg over my hip before gripping my face and turning it toward her. Her lips press into mine, pulling me into a deep kiss. I hope my mouth is responding properly—it feels like it is—but my reaction time is delayed. Even though this might be the best kiss of my life, there's a chance she might be making out with me in a comatose state.

Trixie's moans escalate, turning more desperate, as if she's fighting for attention. Rainey doesn't waver. She rolls me onto my back, straddling me, the blanket settling over her hips in a way that keeps us just barely covered. She shifts between us, adjusting until my length is pressed against my stomach, still trapped in my pants. Then she lowers herself slowly, rolling her hips over me.

I need more friction. I need our clothes gone. But she isn't actually trying to take this further. She's putting on a show, making it look real without any intention of following through.

Apparently, it's enough to set Trixie off. Two new guys enter the mix, settling on the far end of the couch as she wastes no time climbing onto his lap. Another man steps in behind her, and together, they take her right there. I have no idea where the other two disappeared to, but they're gone, and still, Trixie refuses to look away.

Rainey doesn't let up. Her hips continue their slow grind, pressing into me with a steady rhythm. I can't tell if the moans I want to let out ever make it to the surface as I try to keep my eyes on her. I can feel how ready she is, but we both know I'm in no condition to perform. Not that it matters. What does matter is the possessiveness in her touch.

Trixie learns that Rainey isn't messing around and will only continue to do this until she rubs my entire dick off. As soon as Trixie saunters away, Rainey rolls off me, groaning at how sore she is.

She keeps shifting, searching for a comfortable position, until she finally settles on her side, throwing her legs over me. We stay like that, her gaze fixed on me before she suddenly covers my eyes with her hands, forcing them closed. "Shut your damn eyes and stop fighting sleep."

SHE'S STILL FAST ASLEEP BESIDE ME WHEN I WAKE. I WATCH HER FOR A while, then press a kiss to her cheek. No reaction. I move to her jaw—still nothing. I trail down to her neck, sucking lightly until I feel her stir.

When I pull back, she shakes her head and taps the same spot, silently telling me to keep going.

"You like that?" I murmur, my mouth finding her skin again.

A soft moan is my only answer.

I take my time, kissing, licking, and savoring every inch of her until she's completely satisfied.

She shifts onto her side, resting her head on her palm. "Do parties like that happen often?"

"Yeah. It's about business and making connections."

She nods, seeming to understand. "You fell asleep, and I overheard something about a casino night in three days. What's that about?"

I shake my head. "Nothing you need to worry about."

"So, just because I don't need to worry about it, I don't get to know what it means?"

I don't want to tell her because I don't want to scare her. We deal with corrupt, wealthy people, and she already thinks the worst about us. Knowing what happens on casino night would only reinforce her preconception of my family.

"There are certain aspects of this life you won't be privy to—and that's for the best."

"K."

The way she says it tells me she's not thrilled with the answer, but it's the truth. She won't be there, so there's no reason for her to be concerned with any of the details.

"I'm gonna go shower," she says, sitting up and sliding off the couch.

Muffled voices from downstairs drift up. My mind is still sluggish, but I catch enough to recognize Silvano's voice and the urgency in his tone.

"Another van is going out tonight," he says. "Same route."

That's all I need to hear. I push up from the couch too fast, my vision tilting before leveling out. I ignore it, rushing down the stairs after him. "I'm coming with you."

Silvano barely glances at me as he heads toward the door. "Not happening."

I follow, keeping pace. "I didn't ask."

That makes him pause. He turns, arms crossed, looking me over like I'm some reckless idiot. "You've got stitches in your face and a concussion. You're staying put."

Nikolai exhales sharply. "Just let him come. His eyes aren't stitched. He can still shoot. He's moving slow, but guessing from the bedhead, that's because he just woke up." He grins.

Silvano exhales through his nose, his patience running thin. He glances at Nikolai, then back at me. A silent debate passes between them, one I don't give them time to finish.

"You either take me with you, or I follow on my own. Your choice."

Silvano curses under his breath. "Then get dressed. Fast."

I don't waste time. My suite in the main house is dark when I step inside. The outfit I left ready on the bed is still there. I yank on black tactical gear, then grab a holster and strap it on.

Returning, I find Silvano, Nikolai, and Marko are already loading up. Nikolai hands me a Glock, and I check the magazine before sliding it into my holster. A blade follows, sheathed at my thigh.

Silvano eyes me as I move, but he doesn't argue again. Instead, he hands me an extra clip.

"Try not to pass out on us," he mutters.

"I'll do my best."

With that, we head out.

DANTE'S GOING TO LOSE IT WHEN WE GET BACK. WE WERE SUPPOSED to be gone for a short trip, not several days. Ma's already furious that I left the property, saying I pull this every time she leaves the country. It took Nikolai stepping in to calm her down while Marko and Silvano sat back, laughing at the whole thing.

By the time we return, the casino and *Round Room* event will already be in full swing. We'll have a quick meeting with Dante—he refused to talk to us over the phone. He's trying to remain calm. When he gets heated, he has sex and then feels better. So, hopefully, by the time we get back, he will have gotten laid and be level-headed. After that, I'll have to go to Rainey's room and grovel for being gone for days.

Chapter

EIGHTEEN

Rainey

We were warned that tonight's outfits would be left hanging on the doors of the girls who were working. The thought alone twists my stomach into knots. I stay frozen just inside my room, watching the faint sliver of light under the door. My pulse quickens as muffled footsteps draw near. A shadow moves past, and I exhale slowly, relief settling over me. It looks like I won't be needed in what they so ominously call the *Round Room.*

I assumed I wouldn't be working since Damiano said I didn't need to be concerned with whatever tonight is. But he's been MIA for days now, and nobody is saying a word about his whereabouts.

He confuses me more with every passing second. He acts like I belong to him, though what that means in his mind, I couldn't say. There is a closet full of clothes he stocked specifically for me, yet he never explained what we are to each other or why he intervenes when others try to have sex with me. I know my role here—or at least what it should have been—but he makes sure I never have to do the disgusting parts of that role. And while I'm grateful for his interference, I can't live like this, perpetually bracing myself for someone to assault me, hoping he'll appear at the last second to stop it.

Tonight's rules were made painfully clear: we aren't allowed to refuse anyone. The only acceptable response is *yes, sir.* They even gave us an example. If we're asked whether we want them to cut off a nipple, the only suitable response is *yes, sir.*

One of the girls whispered to another that disobedience means losing your tongue, and I'm quite fond of mine, so I'll do whatever it takes to keep it as a functioning part of my body.

I sit on the bench at the end of my bed, trying to decide how to pass the time. I have a TV—I guess I could binge something. At the very least, I'll put it on for background noise. Not that it matters. I already know I'll spend the next few hours the same way I always do—staring out the window for Damiano, periodically glancing at the doorway, hoping to find him standing there. But he never is.

A sudden shuffle of feet yanks me from my thoughts. My head snaps toward the door, and I freeze as a shadow passes beneath it. The soft clink of metal follows, the unmistakable sound of a hanger being placed. A few seconds later, a door further down the hall clicks shut. My stomach twists painfully keeping me rooted in place.

I don't want to verify what I already suspect—that *I am* in fact working. That I'll be in the *Round Room,* the one where refusal isn't an option unless I want my tongue cut out.

But ignoring it won't change the reality. Slowly, I crack the door open and peer out. The outfit sways from the hanger, its crude design a cruel reminder of what awaits.

It's a twisted blend of seduction and humiliation. Thin leather straps form tonight's attire, the bare minimum to conceal my nipples from view. The narrow band wrapped around my breasts is just thick enough for my nipples to be covered but the rest is bare, leaving most of the skin exposed, the straps stretched taut as if designed to highlight rather than hide.

A single strap runs down the center of my torso, connecting the top to the bottom, dividing my bare stomach with a harsh line of black leather. The bottom is no less revealing—a low-cut design with straps forming a minimal shape over my hips, leaving my waist and most of my backside on full display.

I don't recognize the person staring back at me in the mirror. The collar sits heavy in my hand as I stare at it, unwilling to put it on.

But the knock at the door and the barked orders leave me no choice. I slip it around my neck like the noose that it is. It covers the only remaining hickey Damiano left on my skin, aside from the scarred bite he put there—but the collar hides that too. The cool metal snaps into place with a soft click, a trap closing around me.

Trixie's smirk is waiting for me the second I step into the hallway, and it instantly pisses me off. But I swallow down the words threatening to escape. Telling her to suck a dick feels pointless—chances are, both of us will be doing just that before the night is over.

She falls in step behind me, and I can feel her scheming already, probably planning to trip me or pull some other petty move to get a rise out of me.

"Nice ass, fresh meat," she whispers. "Let's see how you're walking when we come back."

I turn to glare at her, but her grin has the words spilling from my mouth before I can reel them back. "My ass handles Damiano's big cock every night."

Her nostrils flare with anger as she attempts to keep her composure. "I hope you get to meet Mr. Jack tonight. The things he does—I'd pay to see him do to you."

I don't know who Mr. Jack is, but I pray I, in fact, don't meet him tonight.

"Were you always this nasty? Or did the endless line of cock rot your brain and turn you into this heartless little snake?"

"Oh, sweetie," she purrs, "it's going to be my life's mission to make sure you never know a second of peace in this house. Every time you close your eyes, every time you turn your back, someone will be there, ready to fill that disgusting cunt. Count on it, bitch."

She shoves past me, her shoulder knocking into mine hard enough to make me stumble a step. Her laughter echoes in the hallway as she strides toward the front.

A man I've never seen before stands at the open van door, his expression blank as he methodically cuffs each of us. When it's my turn, the cold steel closes around my wrists behind my back, pinching my skin. The combination of our current attire and the fact that we are being handcuffed tells me nothing good will come from this.

Alarm bells ring out in my mind.

I am actually in danger this time.

The drive feels endless, the van rocking slightly with every bump in the road. I know where we're going—the same place as the auction. My breath is shallow and my heart pounds, but I don't dare speak.

When we arrive, the door slides open, and I squint against the sudden flood of light. Guards with guns are everywhere, their cold eyes scanning us as we're hurried inside.

The hallway they force us into is unfamiliar, separate from the auction room. The walls are jet black, swallowing the light overhead. To my right, doors stretch down the corridor, green lights glowing above each one. To the left, a set of double doors swings open, and the deep pulse of music spills into the air.

We're led into a large, circular room, the polished black floor so reflective I can see my own distorted image staring back at me. The walls are black and bare, except for a single strip of red light winding along the ceiling, casting the room in an ominous glow.

The line shuffles forward, and I watch, horrified, as the first girl is grabbed, her collar clipped to a chain leash that hangs from the wall. She faces the cold surface, barely able to move, like some grotesque display. Bile rises in my throat as the men work methodically down the line, grabbing girls and securing them in place.

Three women stand in the center of the room in tiny dresses, holding tablets while they talk. I don't even understand what we're doing here—why these girls get to hold tablets while we're being chained up.

When it's my turn, two men step forward, their grasp rough as they spin me around and shove me forward, clipping the leash to my collar. My knees threaten to buckle, leaving me completely helpless and trapped. I have maybe six inches of slack, just enough to adjust slightly and attempt to look around.

Positioned next to the others, spaced about ten feet apart, my heart pounds so loudly I can't tell if it's my nerves making my legs shake or the vibration from the bassline.

The chain rattles as I shift slightly. The position is impossible, humiliating even. My wrists ache where the handcuffs bite into them, and the wall is close enough that my breath bounces back toward me, hot and uneven. I try to focus, but the pressure on my neck keeps me trapped.

I truly thought the auction would be the worst thing we would endure, but I was wrong. Nothing has happened yet, but I already know this will be worse. Especially since we are all handcuffed with no way to fight back against what's coming.

I attempt to turn my head as much as I can to see what's happening. From my limited angle, the women with tablets are approaching three men. One by one, the men walk with them, inspecting the girls like they're browsing merchandise. My knees weaken when one of them reaches my side of the room, scanning each girl he passes, then stopping at the one right before me.

My head can't turn enough to see what's happening, but I catch a glimpse from my periphery of the tablet's glow illuminating the woman holding it and the tall figure beside her. They exchange a few words until the device dings softly, its green light glowing. "Enjoy," she says.

A guard steps forward, ensuring only what was paid for is taken.

I catch sight of another girl being led out, her collar tugged as she walks behind the man holding the leash. I force myself to look back at the wall, only to hear the man beside me bark an order.

"Wider."

I try to stay focused ahead, desperate for the scene to fade away, but curiosity—or morbid self-preservation—wins out. Peeking through my lashes, I catch when he shoves his hand between the girl's legs. She remains still, her face a mask of apathy, her eyes squeezed shut as if she's not even in her body. A wave of nausea rolls through me so violently that I think I might collapse. Hanging actually sounds more appealing than what she's experiencing.

The roar in my ears drowns out everything else. My breath comes in shallow bursts, my heart racing so hard it feels like it might just stop.

Then, I feel a presence behind me. My chest tightens as his body brushes against mine, just barely. I didn't hear footsteps, didn't hear the usual chatter of the women with the tablets. Just someone, all of a sudden, there.

"Rainey."

The voice is low, right by my ear. It's familiar—too familiar. I shut my eyes, willing the sound to belong to anyone else. Swallowing hard, I finally speak.

"Dante."

Chapter

NINETEEN

Rainey

His exhale skims the curve of my ear, a sensation that leaves my nerves on edge. I want to confirm that it's really him, but the chain keeps me pinned and helpless. His hand braces against the wall beside my head, and when I finally open my eyes, there it is—the ring I had wanted to see up close, right in front of me on his unmistakable hand.

It is him.

"You're becoming a problem for me." The words are quiet but heavy, his tone strained.

I blink, trying to piece together what he means, but my mind draws a blank. A problem? For him? Did Em give him a hard time for me cornering him in his office?

I stayed away after that. I immediately realized I fucked up as soon as I got back to my room and wanted to die of embarrassment. I hoped I'd never see him again. And the times I have seen him, I don't even think he noticed me. He never acknowledges my presence. In fact, he seems to purposely avoid or ignore me.

I just assumed it was because I'm a nobody whore that works in the house.

My mouth feels dry as I swallow back the urge to protest. To tell him I'm sorry for going into his office. To tell him it won't happen again. Or maybe he means I'm a problem because I injured his brother. That's more likely. But no matter the reasoning, I can't defend myself, so I stay quiet.

"I'm having a bad day. And to make it worse… you somehow ended up here… I can't stop thinking about you," he murmurs. "It's pissing me off."

I'm unsure how to respond. *Yes, sir* doesn't seem fitting for the context of this conversation.

We both remain quiet, and I take that as him expecting a response. I muster up a simple, "I'm sorry." The words are placating—anything to keep him calm.

His fist clenches against the wall near my face, the tension in him palpable. I don't dare move. The music pounds on, oblivious to how much it's adding to my stress. I want to tell him if he unhooks me, we can go somewhere quiet and try to talk this out, but I already know what his response will be.

"How can I rectify the situation?" I ask cautiously, knowing we aren't allowed to refuse anyone. That was the *one* rule. And I quite like my tongue. So if he tells me to get on the floor and lick his boots, I'll have them shining.

He doesn't answer, just stays there, close enough that I can feel the heat of him radiating against my back. The silence stretches on as I wait for him to speak, but I'm met with nothing. His hand slides to the chain, gripping it. I stare at it, then gently rest my chin on it.

His cheek presses against mine as he lets out a slow exhale.

"Do you need something from me?"

He subtly nods.

"Do you want to touch me?"

His other hand wraps around my waist. The chain rattles softly as I tense under his touch.

"Do you want me to touch you?" His voice is quieter now, switching from anger to arousal.

"If that's what you want." My response is mechanical, measured—an effort to stay neutral. But the truth is, I *do* want him to touch me. He's the one I sought out after the auction because he's the one I would want taking me the same ways Damiano did.

His lips softly brush my ear. "It's what I want."

"Okay." I nod, my movements constrained by the collar and the cuffs.

The chain rattles softly as Dante's fist falls away. One hand slides upward, tracing the curve of my torso, pausing between my breasts before settling on one and squeezing. The other ventures downward, grazing the thin barrier of fabric between my thighs. My breath catches, and I shift slightly, widening my stance.

His exhale is warm against my neck as his palm fully cups my pussy. I rest my forehead against the wall, my body reacting to the proximity and control he exudes. With an almost casual ease, the strap of leather is pulled aside, baring me to his touch. When his fingers pinch the sensitive peak of my nipple, I moan, unable to keep my composure.

Time feels warped, the pounding bass of the music muffling everything else as his fingers explore further. A soft, restrained sound escapes me when he finds the most sensitive part of me, circling in a rhythm that makes my knees weak. My head spins as he drifts lower, his fingers sinking in deep. A shiver courses through me when he curls them just right, and I lift onto my toes, rocking my ass back against him. My hands align perfectly with his erection, and I attempt to grab it through his pants.

He breathes heavily in my ear. "You want it?"

Yes keeps my tongue. *No* means I lose my tongue.

"Yes," I manage, the word tumbling out before I can second-guess myself.

Everything comes to a halt. He withdraws his hands, leaving a cold ache where his warmth had been. "Give me a minute," he says softly, stepping back.

"Where are you going?" My voice wavers with confusion.

The metallic click of the cuffs releasing echoes through the room, and I let out a soft sigh as one wrist is freed. I brace against the wall, but before I can process the relief, the solid warmth of his bare chest presses against my back. The heat of his skin is a stark contrast to the cool air, and I arch toward him, silently inviting him closer.

He turns my head gently, as much as the chain allows, and I see him clearly. He's utterly breathtaking. The intensity in his gaze holds me captive, and when our lips meet, the kiss is urgent, consuming. His tongue brushes mine, pulling me further under his control as he positions himself at my entrance.

I gasp as he pushes forward, the sensation shocking in its depth. I shift higher onto my toes, the instinctive motion an attempt to slow him down, to adjust to the unfamiliar pressure. His hands are steady on me, one sliding to my hip to guide me, the other trailing upward to my chest again.

"You're tight," he mutters, his voice strained.

"Is it okay?"

"No," he groans.

My voice stutters. "Sorry," I huff at the same time he thrusts into me. It's not my fault I'm chained and can barely move.

"You're as good as I feared you'd be. I should never have given you up."

He thrusts in so deep my eyes cross, and I try gripping the wall as a moan slips past my lips. Each stroke sinks deeper, more purposeful, drawing a sound from me that I can't suppress. My body locks up, the sensation overwhelming as he doesn't let up, driving into me while exploring every inch of my skin. My fingers curl behind me in his hair as wave after wave of pleasure builds until it crashes over me, leaving me lightheaded and weak.

Even as I cry out, he doesn't stop, his pace quickening. His body tenses behind me, stilling as a low groan escapes him, and I feel the change in him as he finds his release.

The silence that follows is heavy, save for the faint bass of the music that has become background noise. I can feel him moving, but I'm too dazed to process it fully.

"Douche," he says, and for a minute, I think he's calling me one—until he says he's going to pull out. When he does, a towel is pressed between my legs.

I catch sight of him standing beside me, adjusting his pants before buttoning up his shirt. It's over. At least, I assume it is.

I'm startled as something thin pushes inside me. My body stiffens at the unexpected sensation, and before I can fully process it, liquid cascades out of me—cold and foreign.

It happens again—twice—each time leaving me even more disoriented. The towel returns, pressed firmly against me as if to clean away the remnants of what just transpired. My mind races, trying to make sense of the routine precision of it all. I feel exposed, vulnerable, and utterly thrown by his actions, unsure whether to speak or remain silent.

He gapes absently, then drags his hands down his face, visibly stressed. Without warning, he starts pummeling the wall—over and over and over. Instinct drives me to retreat, but the chain holds me in place.

I stare, wide-eyed, as the commotion erupts around us. Men rush in to stop him, shouting for him to calm down. Another guard steps in, snapping the handcuff back around my other wrist.

Dante throws his arms up. "Don't fucking touch me."

I don't even know what's happening or why he's losing it, but blood smears the wall, and when his fingers push into his hair, I see the damage—his knuckles are torn and raw.

"Dante," I call, trying to break through the rage he's experiencing.

He doesn't stop. He doesn't look at me. He just shoulders past the guards and disappears.

The weight of the chain pulls at the collar, yanking me back into the reality of my confinement.

I remain still, my forehead pressed against the wall as my mind reels. Whatever just happened—whatever this is—I can't begin to comprehend it. The calculated intimacy, the abrupt detachment, the violent outburst, and then storming out of here.

Hands adjust the straps back in place over my boobs and vagina, and then the woman steps away.

I wish he had taken longer so I could avoid any other interactions tonight. My nerves are so fried right now, and I'm trying my best just to hold it together.

Chapter

TWENTY

Rainey

Voices.

A man speaks behind me, his timbre deep and distinct. The vibration of his words hums in the air, though I can't make out the exact ones. I blink, the wall in front of me reflecting the faint glow of the tablet behind me. His cologne lingers—heavy, cloying, suffocating.

Then, her voice cuts through, dripping with unsettling sweetness. And all I want is for Dante to come back.

"Just touching, or are you looking for the full experience?"

His response is little more than a low murmur, detached and indifferent. My chest constricts when I hear her say my name. I wanted to believe they weren't talking about me, but now there's no denying it.

"It's her first time," she says lightly, as if it's some enticing feature. "So she's more."

The man grunts in acknowledgment. "It's no issue," he replies.

"One hour. Private room. No restrictions," the woman states, and her words hit me like a hammer.

The dreaded ding follows—loud and final—as her tablet lights up green. Just as quickly, my chain is unhooked and passed off. The man takes hold, and my entire body locks up. My legs refuse to move. My mind screams at me to fight, to run, but my muscles betray me, keeping me frozen in place.

The first tug on the leash drags me forward, the force of it making me stumble. The cuffs around my wrists dig into my skin as I struggle to steady myself. He doesn't look back, doesn't care if I fall, doesn't see me as anything more than a body he's just purchased for the next hour. He gets to do whatever unspeakable things he wants to me.

And this is just the beginning. After this, I'll be dragged back in, chained to the wall, and left for another man. And then another. For six more hours.

Rage rises inside me, and I want to wrap the chains around his neck until I choke the life out of him. But the cuffs render me powerless as I'm yanked forward like a dog on a leash.

We exit the room, and the hallway stretches endlessly ahead, the only interruptions being the red bulbs glowing ominously above each door. My heart pounds harder with every step, the muffled sounds leaking through the walls—moans, laughter, whimpers. Each door we pass feels like another nail in my coffin, and all I can do is walk, dragged forward into the unknown.

We stop at a door with a green bulb glowing above it. The guard unlocks it with a swipe of his card, the light switching to red as he pushes it open. My stomach plummets as the man holding my leash starts to lead me inside. Every muscle in my body tightens in resistance, but his pull is unrelenting.

"Not going to happen," a voice growls.

My head snaps up, and my heart stutters. Damiano. He strides down the hallway, flanked by Nikolai and the other man who helped kidnap me. His approach is a storm waiting to break. His eyes burn with fury, his jaw clenched so tightly the muscle twitches with each step.

The guard holding the door stiffens, his posture rigid as he begins to stammer an explanation.

"The gentleman already signed and paid," he says quickly, his voice uneasy.

Damiano doesn't slow, his approach brisk as he closes the space between us. In one seamless motion, his rough grip locks around the collar at my neck. The leather bites into my skin as he tears it free, the buckle snapping open with a vicious tug.

"What the hell is that?" He points to the mark on my neck.

I freeze as his glare snaps to the guard, whose face drains of color. The man stumbles over his words, his fear palpable.

"A… a claim, sir," he manages to choke out, his throat bobbing as he swallows.

"Did you put it there?" Damiano barks, his voice echoing through the narrow hallway.

He blinks in confusion. "No, sir. Of course not—"

"Did you put it there?" Damiano cuts him off, rounding on the man who paid for me.

"…No?"

Damiano's attention zeroes in on me. "Who left that mark?"

I straighten my spine before answering. "You did."

His slow nod feels dangerous. "I did." Then his voice erupts, roaring through the hallway like thunder. "Why is someone with a claim down here?"

The guard flinches as though struck, his head bowing slightly. "I… I don't know, sir. I just escort the girls from the *Round Room* to the private rooms. That's all."

I see irritation flash across the face of the man who paid. "She's mine for the next hour," he bites out. "You'll get your chance when I've had my fill."

The air grows colder. In a single, fluid motion, Damiano pulls a gun from his waistband. The metallic click of the slide echoes through the hall as he chambers a round and presses the barrel against the man's temple.

The hallway seems to hold its breath. Another man with a chained girl is led past, none of them sparing a glance.

"Go back and pick someone else," Damiano snarls, his voice lethal. "This one is mine."

The man's sneer doesn't fade. "If she's yours, why was she on the menu?"

"I plan on finding that out. Now get your erection away from my woman before I blow it off."

His jaw flexes as he considers another way to protest.

"Damiano," one of his men says, clapping him on the shoulder—maybe to calm him down, though I have no idea what they were thinking. What if that startled him and he pulled the trigger?

The man's eyes widen with realization. Finally, he steps back, holding his hands up in surrender. "Sorry, Mr. Volkov, I didn't recognize you. My apologies to you and your Mrs. Accept my purchase as a token of goodwill." Then, he backs away down the hall.

Damiano turns to the two men flanking him. "I want every girl checked for a claim," he commands.

They nod, then disappear down the hallway. The sound of their retreating footsteps is the only noise in the suffocating silence that follows.

Damiano turns back to the guard, his glare cold. He reaches for my arm, pulling me forward. His touch feels possessive, a silent declaration of authority as he leads me into the room I was just about to be dragged into.

He pauses just inside the doorway, his eyes flicking to the guard who lingers awkwardly in the hall. "I'll be out when I'm done." His tone is flat and dismissive.

The small room is clearly not meant for comfort. It's oppressive, with dim lighting casting shadows that seem to shrink the already confined space. The walls are a cold, dark gray, their surface unadorned except for the metal cuffs bolted in various positions—high, low, even horizontal—designed to accommodate whatever twisted scenario might unfold. The air is thick with the faint scent of leather and cleaning chemicals, sterile yet suffocating.

In the center of the room sits a large, plush chair upholstered in a deep, luxurious purple. The fabric is immaculate, its velvety texture catching the light in subtle ways that make it seem almost inviting—if not for the grim context. The chair's design is elegant, with a wide seat and a high, slightly reclined back, but the lack of armrests makes its purpose obvious. Nothing blocks the way of the woman straddling whoever is beneath her.

Flush with the wall on one side is a cupboard with a seamless glass front. Inside, neatly folded white towels are arranged with precision, their crisp, clean appearance adding an unsettling touch.

Once the door clicks shut, I turn to him. He looks pissed. He moves across the room to the chair in the corner, sinking into it as he lets out a long, controlled sigh.

"I—" I begin, but the words don't seem to form. I don't even know what I'm trying to say, and he doesn't give me the chance to figure it out.

"Come sit," he orders, flicking his eyes to his lap.

I pause, feeling like I'm dealing with Jules again. Right now, I'm not sure which version of Damiano I'm approaching. He just had a gun to a man's head, and I was almost positive he was going to pull the trigger.

"Which way?"

"Face the door." He jerks his chin in the direction.

I pivot, hoping that maybe a subtle tease of my ass might lessen his bad mood before lowering myself onto his lap.

His fingers brush against my wrists, then comes the click of the handcuffs releasing. My arms drop forward, sagging with relief, but the ache remains. I rub at the raw marks the cuffs left behind—evidence of how tight they were. My skin is red, tender, and stings under my touch.

When I peer over my shoulder, his furrowed brows are illuminated by the glow of his phone, his fingers moving quickly as he texts. I don't need to ask to know the message is about me.

If I wasn't supposed to be down here, it explains why there wasn't an outfit on my door in the first place. When they were being put out, mine was skipped. Then later, something was left for me. Someone had taken an outfit from another room and placed it there. Intentionally.

Realization sets in. It had to have been Trixie. She was the only one with that smug, satisfied smirk when she saw me wearing an outfit that wasn't even mine—like she already knew I wasn't supposed to be going.

He tucks his phone into his pocket and looks up as his hands settle on my hips. He draws me backward, aligning my body against his. One arm wraps around me, the other presses flat against my chest as he buries his face in the curve of my neck, inhaling deeply.

I ease back slightly, feeling his erection pressing into my back. "Rough day?"

"Something like that."

I nod slowly in agreement. "Since we have a room that's paid for, can I take care of this for you?"

I shift, my almost completely bare ass moving up his length.

His hold secures around me. "What are you doing?"

"Attempting to make you feel better," I whisper. "I'm not very good at this when I've spent the last hour trying not to hurl my brains out from being so petrified."

"You weren't supposed to be here."

His admission pisses me off. I wasn't supposed to be here? I'm here because I was forced into this life. I'm here because Mom made a deal with them. Yet I'm not supposed to be here—in this underground, sick, fucking freak show?

"How so? We were told the girls working tonight would have an outfit hung on their door."

"And you weren't supposed to have one."

I sit up abruptly, turning to face him. "I was brought here to be a fucking whore."

He scoffs.

I stand, gaping at him. "This is funny to you?"

His expression darkens instantly, and he closes the distance between us in two strides. He grips my jaw, pressing me against the wall as his nose brushes my cheek.

"The man you'll be a whore for is me. You got that?"

It's my turn to scoff. His hold on my jaw tightens—not enough to hurt, but enough to remind me of his dominance. His free hand slips between my legs, and a thrill runs through me.

He drags the thin leather to the side, his pointer and middle fingers pressing my lips together, holding them firmly. He glides up and down in opposite directions, trapping the swollen bundle of nerves between them. I arch into him, seeking more, needing more.

His middle finger dips between my folds, gliding effortlessly along my slickness. The motion sends my hips jutting toward him, every nerve alive and thrumming. When he presses against the spot I ache for, a shudder runs through my entire body. His touch is slow, torturously slow, as his face stays pressed close to mine.

Two fingers slide back down, circling my entrance before curling inside me, filling me completely. My legs part wider, giving him everything he needs to work me over. He moves in a steady rhythm that has me clinging to him, barely able to stand.

Instinct takes over, and I begin to rub my clit, chasing the pleasure that's building too quickly to control. I'm teetering on the edge, my breath coming in shallow gasps, and though I bite my lip to hold them back, soft, needy whimpers escape.

I'm so close, so close I can almost taste it. The world narrows to this moment—his fingers, my touch, the unbearable need consuming me. Just as the ache deep inside me is about to shatter, everything stops. He withdraws, and his hand covers mine, pulling it away.

"What are you doing?" I manage, my voice shaky with a mix of frustration and confusion.

He steps back slightly, his demeanor calm, his tone dismissive. "We're leaving."

"No." The word bursts out of me, edged with disbelief. My chest heaves as I glare at him. "You're going to finish."

I reach out, desperation guiding me as I try to shove his fingers back inside me.

Anger unlike anything I've seen twists his face, making my blood run cold.

In an instant, I'm pinned against the wall again. He squeezes my throat so hard that my vision darkens at the edges. Air locks in my lungs, panic rising as he leans in, his voice a low, dangerous growl.

"You ever try to shove my fingers in your pussy again, I'll rip your intestines out while I'm in there."

The threat isn't so much a threat as it is a promise. I can't think, can't move. My chest burns as he releases me, and I gasp for air, my lungs heaving as I try to comprehend the abrupt change in his mood. He was just fingering me, practically panting against my face. Now, he nearly snapped my neck for trying to put his fingers back where they were not even five seconds ago.

He steps back, his hands flexing open and closed like he's struggling to rein in his temper. Without another word, he stalks to the door and yanks it open, the force rattling the frame.

"Walk," he orders.

I roll my eyes, masking my fear with defiance, and storm past him. "Dick," I mutter.

His long strides overtake me easily as he reaches out, clamping around my wrist. He pulls me toward Nikolai and the other man waiting in the middle of the hallway.

Damiano jerks his head toward the man, a silent command for him to speak.

"Yours was the only woman claimed," the guard reports.

Damiano's brow furrows. "How?"

Nikolai responds, "Andrei's checking the cameras. My guess is someone swapped the uniform."

Damiano nods. "And Dante?"

My stomach plummets. What does he mean, and Dante? Is he asking if they killed Dante? I feel like I'm going to puke at even the mention of him. *We messed up.* Damiano just pulled a gun on a man for attempting to have sex with me after he paid for me. Dante literally just fucked me senseless against the wall. Even the thought has me squeezing my thighs together to stop the tingling from trying to create moisture.

"Broken hand. They want him in surgery in the next couple of hours. He's wrapping up some stuff in the casino," Nikolai says.

Damiano lets out a long sigh at the same time I do. I thought they killed him for what we did.

"I knew he'd be pissed. I didn't know he'd be this pissed we left. I'll let him cool off and come to me when he's ready to ream me."

Wait. Does Damiano not know that Dante and I just had sex?

I send up a silent prayer, hoping he doesn't. I may not like the situation I was put in, but I do enjoy breathing. I don't want it to end because I did my whore duties. I could use the *yes sir* rule to defend myself. We weren't allowed to say no. But I'm not going to throw Dante to the wolves like that.

Though I'm not sure how I could even turn the tables to make it seem like maybe I initiated it.

The faint sound of a door opening pulls my attention, and the light above it flickers from red to green. I look down the hall just as a man steps out, his shirt clinging to sweat-soaked skin. His face is flushed, and his hair is tousled like he just rolled out of bed. He doesn't spare anyone a glance as he strides away.

Then Trixie emerges. Her hair is a tangled mess, though she's clearly tried to smooth it down, and her eyeliner is smeared into dark streaks that only highlight the redness in her flushed face. A single handcuff dangles from her wrist, the faint clinking sound echoing as she walks.

The guard closest to Trixie barely looks up. "Fix your makeup before we head back," he orders gruffly, nodding toward a room at the end of the hall. Turning slightly, I catch the open door, revealing a vanity and mirror inside.

She starts walking in our direction, her attention locking onto Damiano. As she approaches, she flashes him a flirtatious smile, her voice dripping with seduction. "Hey, handsome."

But then her focus shifts to me, half-hidden behind him, and her entire demeanor changes. Her smile vanishes, her expression falling flat. Her fists curl at her sides, and for a second, I think she might lash out. Instead, she just continues past us.

A short time later, two women appear. They're in sleek black dresses that seem more appropriate for a cocktail party than janitorial work. One pushes a mop bucket while the other carries a tote of cleaning supplies. Their faces remain expressionless as they make their way straight into the room Trixie just exited.

The faint sounds of bottles clinking and a mop swishing echo down the hall as they begin their work. It's clinical, cold, and unsettling, like they're erasing whatever happened in there, sanitizing the space as if nothing ever occurred.

As Trixie moves away, I catch sight of her butt and freeze. Her cheeks are exposed in the same leather we're all wearing, and the evidence of what just happened is painfully obvious. Deep red handprints welted across her entire ass. The sight churns my stomach, and I have to look away.

I search for any sign of a reaction from Damiano—anger, pity, anything—but his expression remains unreadable, still fixed on the current conversation.

I look back one more time, and that's all I need to see. I try to pull away from Damiano, but he keeps talking, only pausing when he notices my attempt. I go still under his stare, but all I want to do is punch him in the face. He didn't even acknowledge Trixie. She just went through… whatever happened to her in that room, and he couldn't care less.

But it's too much. The rawness of what I just saw, his complete lack of reaction—it ignites something inside me that I can't control. Before I can stop myself, I rip my wrist free from his grasp and pull the gun from his waistband, my fingers curling around the cold metal as I take a step back.

My chest heaves as I level the weapon, my hands trembling slightly. The gun feels heavier than I expected, but the anger coursing through me far outweighs it.

"You're all pigs!" I spit, my voice shaking with fury. "Let me go, or I swear to God, I'll shoot every one of you."

The hallway is silent. All eyes are on me, their expressions uneasy, as if the girl who's never held a gun before might accidentally take out everyone in one wild shot. Damiano remains still, standing there, perfectly composed.

"Baby." His voice is infuriatingly calm, with a hint of mockery. "If you're going to shoot us, you might want to take the safety off first."

His bored delivery pisses me off. My grip tightens around the gun as I glance down, trying to figure out how to disengage the safety. I've never done this before.

With exaggerated ease, he reaches out and flicks it off with a single, lazy movement before stepping back to where he was.

I lift the gun again—this time steadier, this time with purpose. I want to pull the trigger. I want to wipe that smug, detached expression off his face.

The door farther down the hall creaks open, and I look toward it. Another sweaty man steps out, followed by a girl with flushed, red-marked skin. Only, she's smiling and holding his arm. My stomach twists violently as I take in the welts on her.

The sight burns itself into my mind, the final push that breaks whatever fragile restraint I had left. I clutch the gun tighter, my vision blurring with unfiltered rage.

"Fuck all of you," I spit, my voice cracking from my anger.

Damiano's expression is impassive. The absence of emotion feels like a deliberate insult.

And then… a sharp, brutal impact lands at the base of my skull, and everything spins. The gun slips from my grasp as my knees buckle. The last thing I hear is Damiano's voice, though I can't make out the words. My vision darkens, the world tipping sideways, and I hit the floor.

Chapter

TWENTY-ONE

Damiano

The loud crack of something colliding with Rainey's skull reverberates down the hall as she collapses to the floor. Annoyance prickles at the edge of my thoughts, but I keep my expression neutral. Nikolai lets out an exaggerated sigh, dragging his palms down his face like he's trying to pull himself together.

"Well," I say evenly, "at least we didn't have to find out how bad her aim was."

"What the hell is going on?" Dante's voice cuts through the air as he approaches, his steps purposeful.

A thick white bandage and brace wrap around his hand as he strides toward us, and it looks like I'll be facing his wrath a lot sooner than I expected.

He's never had this sort of outburst from us disobeying an order. I think this might even be his first broken bone. I can't think of a single time he's ever been injured.

His gaze lands on Rainey's unconscious body, and his expression hardens, irritation flashing across his face. "What the fuck happened here?"

"She just tried to shoot us," Nikolai blurts, gripping the back of his neck.

"Relax. The gun was pointed at me," I say, glancing down at her.

"She doesn't even know how to use a gun," Nikolai counters. "She would've peppered us all with bullets."

Dante exhales heavily, frustration etched across his face as he crouches, slipping his arms under Rainey's limp body and lifting her. "What a goddamn mess," he mutters.

"I don't need you playing the hero. Go to surgery. Your hand is shattered." I step forward, arms outstretched to take her from him.

"She pointed a gun at us," Nikolai reiterates, his voice rising.

"She doesn't even know how to fucking use it!" Dante fires back.

He sidesteps me as he strides purposefully toward the door.

"Where the hell are you going? Give me my girlfriend," I bellow, my voice echoing through the hallway as I follow him, my irritation building with each step.

"She needs a doctor," Dante growls, not bothering to glance back at me.

"She does?!" I demand, incredulous. He needs surgery, and he's worried about a bump on her head. "She's my problem. I brought her here. I'll deal with this."

He stops, his head whipping around as his nostrils flare. "Yes, *you* did… didn't you?" Then turns and keeps walking.

I follow him through the house, guards stepping aside and opening doors for him as he approaches. He walks straight out back, where my truck is parked, making a beeline for the passenger door.

"If I want to put a bullet in her head, I will. If I decide to let her bleed out on the floor, that's my call—not yours."

He stops abruptly again, turning to face me, his eyes blazing as he holds her securely. "If you want to act like a fucking asshole, go ahead. But right now, she needs help. And if you won't get her medical attention, I will."

His words register, but I don't give a damn what he's saying. He's holding what's mine. I shove past Nikolai, my strides quick, but even then, it's a struggle to keep up with how fast he's moving.

He walks straight to my truck and gets into the passenger seat, Rainey cradled in his lap. "Get the fuck in and drive," he commands as he slams the truck door shut.

Marko and Nikolai climb into the back, and I grip the steering wheel tightly as I pull out, the truck growling down the road through the thick trees as I wind back through the property to my house. From my periphery, I see Dante staring down at her.

"What's the plan now?" Nikolai finally asks.

"You're gonna get on your fucking phone and call for medical," Dante snaps. "Have them meet us at Damiano's."

Then he shifts to me, his voice dropping but still carrying that edge of authority. "And you'd better not punish her for me stepping in."

"I can do whatever I want to her. She's mine."

"Yes," he agrees. "You brought her here to be your wife, not treat her like this."

He has a point. But she threatened me with my own damn weapon. She will be punished for it. And since she's *mine*, I will punish her how I see fit. I keep my focus on the road, saying nothing, my jaw clenched so tight it aches.

By the time we pull into the driveway, the medical team is already waiting. They waste no time, rushing to the truck and attempting to take Rainey from Dante's arms.

"Just get the fucking door," he bellows as he climbs out, still carrying her.

They hurry ahead, and he turns to me. "Get your shit together."

Then, he follows the medical team inside, leaving me standing there, seething.

Rainey lies motionless on the bed. The medics move quickly, their faces blank as they get to work. One kneels on the mattress, gloved and already inspecting the back of her head.

"She's got a decent-sized contusion back here," the medic murmurs, tilting her head slightly to expose the swelling at the base of her skull. "No open wound, but we'll need to monitor for a concussion or worse. Possible skull fracture."

The other medic pulls out a penlight, prying one of her eyelids open to test her pupil response. "Reactive," he says after a beat. "No signs of brain swelling so far, but we need to keep her still and sedated."

A portable IV kit is retrieved, and I watch as they set up the line, threading the needle into the vein on the inside of her arm. They hook her up to a saline drip, the fluid running through the tube in steady drops.

"She'll need fluids to stay hydrated, and this will keep her stable for now," one of them explains to Dante.

I step forward, arms still crossed tightly over my chest. "You can explain it to me." My gaze locks onto his, and when he flicks his attention between me and Dante, I take another step forward, knowing this immediately makes him nervous.

His eyes widen slightly, and he nods, bringing his focus back to Rainey. He turns her carefully onto her side, propping a pillow against her back to keep her supported as his fingers trail lightly down her spine, checking for any other signs of injury.

"She's breathing evenly," the second medic adds, her tone calm but focused. "Vitals are stable. She'll need to be monitored closely for the next twenty-four hours."

The medic near her head glances up at me. "She'll be out for a while. We gave her a sedative to keep her calm and still, just in case she wakes up disoriented."

"Good," I reply curtly.

One of them steps back, motioning to his partner. "We'll leave instructions for monitoring her. Call immediately if anything changes."

I give a nod, dismissing them. They pack up their equipment quickly then hurry out of the room.

Dante and Nikolai stand near the door, their gazes bouncing between me and Rainey.

Dante finally speaks. "If you're not feeling up to watching her, I'll stay."

"I've got it," I bite out.

He studies me, his jaw flexing before he exhales a long, resigned sigh. "Fine," he says, turning toward the door. "But if you need—"

"I won't." My tone cuts him off, and he nods once before glancing at Nikolai. Without a word, they both step out.

The silence that follows is absolute. I look back at Rainey, still unconscious, her face pale. My gaze hardens as I turn and walk to the closet, pulling out a single long-chained handcuff.

I grab a drill from the toolbox tucked in the corner of the garage, then head back to the bedroom and kneel at the side of the bed. I secure the chain to the bedpost at the foot on her side.

I clamp the cuff around her ankle, making sure it's tight enough that she won't be able to get it off.

Straightening, I take a step back, watching her. Finally, I turn and leave the room.

Chapter
TWENTY-TWO

Rainey

The pounding in my head drags me awake, each throb like a hammer striking the inside of my skull. I groan, disoriented, my eyes squinting against the light streaming in from somewhere. It feels like knives slicing through my brain, making the ache worse. Slowly, I sit up, my hand flying to the back of my head where a painful goose egg has formed. The tender spot makes me wince as I rub it, and I try to push past the fog clouding my thoughts.

The room tilts and spins as I try to make sense of my surroundings. It's unfamiliar at first, but then recognition hits. The rich, dark wood furnishings, the sleek black bedding, and the faint scent of leather and cologne—I'm in Damiano's room. The realization floods my mind with vivid memories.

The collars.

The room with the chains.

The private rooms with their dark intentions.

The swollen handprints on Trixie's body.

My stomach churns, and a new wave of anger surges through me. I push the blankets back, ready to swing my legs out of bed and confront him—or anyone else who dares to cross my path. But as I move, I feel the tug.

I glance down and freeze. My ankle is chained to the bed. A sturdy cuff circles my skin, the metal links extending to a bolt securely fastened to the bed frame. I stare at it in shock, convinced my eyes are playing tricks on me. I reach for the restraint, gripping it and tugging, but it's not coming off anytime soon.

Looking out the wall of windows, I see the courtyard. Damiano is there, walking with Trixie and another man. She looks perfectly fine—laughing, smiling, like the events of last night never happened. My teeth grind together as I watch her, the image of her body flashing through my mind. How can she act so normal after everything? She's even walking like her ass hadn't been abused.

The three of them head toward the main house, their voices too far away to hear, and fury rips through me. "You son of a bitch!" I yell, my voice echoing through the room.

My anger has me thinking I might be able to hulk-smash this entire bed into pieces—maybe rip out a post and beat the shit out of him and Trixie. I must look deranged, yanking at the restraint and screaming like a lunatic. My head throbs from the effort, and my hands ache. But it doesn't budge. I'm trapped… again. Chain after chain, I'm locked up.

I'm a prisoner.

"Fuck!" I scream, punching the mattress over and over.

Defeated, I flop onto my side, staring out the window at the bright sky.

I watch for hours as birds fly by, careless and free. Not chained to the horrors of mankind. If I had wings, I'd soar high above it all, weightless, untouchable. No pain, no restraints, no monsters lurking in the shadows. Just the wind against my skin and the sky stretching endlessly ahead, an escape no one could steal from me.

I hear the front door close, but I don't move. My gaze stays fixed on the window, pretending—if only for a moment—that I'm a bird. Heavy footsteps approach, and I know it's him. I can feel his presence.

He leans on the same bedpost my foot is chained to, hands stuffed in his pockets. "You're awake."

I don't respond, I keep my focus on the sky, my jaw clenched tightly. Obviously I'm awake. He can see that my fucking eyes are open. His silence stretches, his patience clearly waiting for me to acknowledge him.

Finally, I glance over. "Get this off me," I say through gritted teeth.

He flicks to my foot and back to me. "You pulled a gun on me. Actions have consequences."

"Fuck off," I retort, staring back out at the window.

"That sounds like an attitude begging to remain as you are."

Fury surges through me, and I glare at him. "Then get the fuck out."

He raises an eyebrow, amusement written on his face. "I live here. Why would I leave?"

"Then get me out of your house."

"This is both our house."

"This is *your* house," I correct.

"You live here now, too."

I turn back to him, studying his face, trying to figure out what his angle is. But for once, it seems like he might not have one.

"Then why am I in your room? Can't I be locked up in my own?"

"You *are* in your room," he replies evenly, the faintest trace of amusement tugging at his lips.

I narrow my eyes. "And your room is where?"

His smile widens as he saunters over to the chair in the corner—the same one Nikolai had occupied before. He sits down, lounging comfortably, his eyes never leaving mine.

"We share this one."

"Why?" I ask, my tone laced with sarcasm, hoping it conveys just how ridiculous I find this entire conversation.

"Because you are mine, and I am yours. It ensures things like last night won't happen again."

"So, what, you're like my boyfriend now?" I laugh mockingly.

"Something like that."

I arch a brow, the laughter fading from my voice. "So, you're my boyfriend, and yet you tried to choke me to death when I wanted you to continue fingering me?"

"You tried to force my hand inside of you," he corrects, his smile vanishing.

"If you don't enjoy doing that, then why start in the first place?"

"I do enjoy touching you."

The sincerity of his tone throws me off, leaving me confused. I blink at him, waiting for more of an explanation. When one doesn't come, I settle on rolling my eyes and letting my gaze shift back to the window. I'd rather stare blankly outside than try to untangle anything he's saying.

"Since we're both here," he drawls after a beat, his voice taking on a teasing edge, "wanna have sex?"

My head snaps toward him, my eyes blazing with fury. "You're a grotesque piece of trash," I spit. "The only way I'd ever sleep with you is the same way you've ever been able to get in my pussy—by forcing me."

He chuckles. "Alright. Take your clothes off."

I can't tell if he's being serious, but if he is, he has got to be one of the stupidest people I've ever met. "Pretty sure I have a concussion from whoever hit me."

"Shouldn't have pointed a gun at me."

The anger in me bubbles over, and it surprises even me when it comes out in a slow, dangerous smile. "You should come closer." Then, I let the smile drop. "Because I'm going to kick your dick so far into your chest cavity you'll have a vagina."

His lips curl into a grin, and he stands, unhurried, walking to the bed. His hands grip my legs, yanking them apart as he climbs between them. My brain takes a second too long to catch up, and when it does, I lash out, swinging for his face. But he's faster—much faster. He pins my arms above my head effortlessly, his weight pressing down, making any attempt to escape impossible.

He laughs—his infuriatingly beautiful laugh—then leans in, sinking his teeth into my skin. Not hard enough to hurt, but enough to send a jolt through me. A soft, wicked chuckle escapes his lips as he starts to suck, the sensation equal parts infuriating and intoxicating.

And just as abruptly as he pinned me, he lets go, standing over me with a grin that feels like a challenge. He steps back, straightening his shirt like nothing happened.

"Thanks for kicking my dick into my chest cavity." He smirks, already heading for the door. "I've got an urgent situation to handle, but we'll blow off some real steam when I get back."

THE SUNLIGHT SHIFTS ACROSS THE ROOM, MARKING THE SLOW PASsage of time—the light disappearing, then rising again, only to begin fading once more. The chain around my ankle clinks softly as I adjust my position, a constant reminder that I'm stuck. The silence stretches thin, amplifying every creak and groan of the house.

But tonight, he doesn't return.

Hours stretch into a bleak, agonizing eternity. Hunger gnaws at my stomach, and the only water I've had is from the single bottle on my nightstand.

I've gone twenty-nine hours without food. My body is weak and trembling.

When the need to pee becomes unbearable and still he doesn't return, I give up. I crawl off the bed, crouch on the floor, and relieve myself there. I grab his pillow, using it to wipe myself before tossing it onto the mess of urine.

The smell fills the room, matching my disgust for him.

I crawl back onto the bed, curling into the same spot as before, my gaze fixed on the window. The outside world feels like a distant dream—unattainable and indifferent.

When the door finally opens, my heart skips, expecting Damiano's return. But the sharp clack of heels on the floor sends a chill through me. This isn't Valentina; her steps are softer, and she rarely comes out here.

Blonde hair gleams in the soft light as Trixie steps into the room, her expression smug and her posture oozing superiority. She's wearing a sheer red mini dress, and she knows exactly how sexy she looks in it.

Her arms cross over her chest as she leans against the doorframe. "Hope your head still hurts. I hit you as hard as I could."

My mouth falls open in shock. "Why would you do that?"

Her welted ass cheeks were the entire reason I pulled a gun on Damiano. What was happening to all of us was fucked up. But once again, I had been saved from the harsh reality of what we are. Not Trixie, though. She wasn't saved from it. She was one of the first to be led out of the room. The welts on her bare butt were so prominent, he had to have been spanking her really hard. So why she would hit me when I was trying to protect us is lost on me.

A cruel smile curves her lips. "Of course I did. Someone had to stop you. You were pointing a gun at the only man I've ever wanted."

A bitter scoff escapes me, the absurdity of her logic pushing past my anger. "Damiano will never want you."

Her grin doesn't falter; it only grows wider, her eyes gleaming with malice. "I'm here because he told me to meet him. Something about thanking me for saving his life."

Doubt begins to creep in.

No. There's no way. She's lying.

As if on cue, the front door opens, the sound of heavy footsteps echoing through the house. Trixie's face lights up with triumph. "His favorite color is red… just like this dress. He asked me to wear it. Don't worry. I'll close the door so we don't disturb you with how loud it gets."

My heart hammers, each beat echoing in my ears as I strain to hear what's happening beyond the door. Muffled voices—a man's deep timbre and a woman's softer tones—reach me, and my mind races. It has to be Damiano and her. But he wouldn't sleep with her.

It doesn't take long for me to be proven wrong. The laughter hits me first—light, playful giggles echoing faintly through the walls—followed by her unmistakable, over-the-top moans. The pornstar kind. The kind designed to be heard, to be a performance.

Then come the deep, guttural grunts of a man, low and rough, mixed with the unmistakable sound of skin slapping against skin—rhythmic and unrelenting.

My chest tightens as the sound reverberates through the space. Blood roars in my ears, louder than the obscene symphony coming from beyond the door, but not loud enough to drown it out. The world tilts, and I lean over the side of the bed, barely making it before my body rebels.

I retch violently onto the pristine carpet, the force wracking my body as everything I had inside comes up. Acid burns my throat, my stomach clenching again and again until there's nothing left but dry, hollow heaving. My ribs ache, and my head pounds as I slump back onto the bed, feeling utterly drained.

I sit there, staring out at the darkened sky through the floor-to-ceiling windows. My body feels heavy, my mind numb, but the knot of frustration and pain twists tighter with every passing second.

He's cruel. This is the cruelest thing he could have ever done. He might be even more evil than Trixie. They deserve each other.

The door opens, the sound pulling me from my daze. I don't turn, but in the reflection of the glass, I see Trixie. She walks to the bathroom, her movements casual, her posture smug. When she returns minutes later, she doesn't head straight for the door. Instead, she pauses at my side of the bed, her figure outlined in the faint light.

"You're pathetic, and it stinks in here." Her nose wrinkles in exaggerated disgust as she eyes the mess on the floor.

She lingers, as if savoring the moment. "If you think I'd let him go after he just fucked me like that, you've lost your mind. I'll feel his big cock for days to come."

And she will. I know because I've felt it.

"Oh, and if he fucks you tonight, just know—his cock was in my ass, and his mouth was on my pussy." She grins wickedly, then strides out, leaving the door wide open.

Her words hit their mark, gutting me. I stare blankly at the open door, unable to process anything except the pain settling in the deepest depths of my heart. As much as I want to block it out, as much as I want to pretend I don't care, I do.

Tears sting my eyes, and before I can stop myself, they spill over. I cry, the crushing reality of everything pressing down on me, suffocating and inescapable.

Through the window, I see their silhouettes—hers, walking confidently back toward the main house, and his, tall and unmistakable, trailing beside her. A fresh wave of sobs wracks through me, and I curl into myself, trying to make it stop, trying to will the pain away.

Chapter

TWENTY-THREE

Damiano

The interaction with Rainey went decently, given the circumstances. I should unchain her, but I'm hoping that by the time I return in a couple of hours, she'll be mad enough that we can get rough. I told her we'd blow off steam when I got back—a long, hard night in bed will make us both feel better while reminding her who she belongs to.

I would have ignored Andrei's text and had sex with her now, but he said urgent, and when Andrei says urgent, it's never something to brush off.

The hallway feels heavier as I make my way to his suite. When I push the door open, tension hangs thick in the air. Silvano sits with his elbows braced on his knees, a deep scowl etched into his face. Nikolai paces near the window, restless energy radiating off him. Giovanni leans against the desk, flicking the safety on and off his pistol.

Andrei is at his station, his fingers flying across the keyboard, the glow of his monitors casting shadows across his face. The screens flash with maps, live feeds, and lines of data that I don't need to decipher to know we're dealing with something serious.

"You're late," Silvano mutters without looking up, his voice low and accusing. He rubs his hands together, frustration rolling off him in waves.

Nikolai doesn't miss a beat. "Leave him alone. He's got a feisty woman to wrangle." His smirk is fleeting, more reflex than genuine humor.

I ignore the jab and pull the Glock from the back of my waistband, checking the clip. Seeing Gio idly messing with his pistol puts me on edge. "So, what's up?" I ask, snapping the clip back in place.

Andrei doesn't look away from the monitors. "Warehouse activity spiked about an hour ago. Vehicles have been coming and going. I ran the plates on one of them, and it's registered to a guy who works for Cristiano."

My jaw tightens at the mention of his name. Just the thought of him sends a surge of rage through me, my fingers itching to blow the entire warehouse sky-high.

Andrei glances over his shoulder, his expression grim. "That's not all. Nikita's location puts her at the warehouse."

Gio straightens abruptly, his pistol swinging in his hand as his voice sharpens. "What the fuck? She's not actually there though, right?"

"She's not answering her phone," Andrei replies as he pulls up a new screen. "I've been tracking her phone, and it hasn't left the warehouse in over an hour."

Nikolai freezes mid-stride, his pacing halted by Andrei's words. "That's a problem. If Cristiano's men figure out who she is…"

No one finishes the sentence, but the implication hangs heavy in the air. It doesn't need to be said, if Cristiano figures out her true identity, she's as good as dead.

The urgency in the room propels us forward as we file into the armory, lined with racks of weapons, shelves of ammo, and gear meticulously organized for situations like this.

Silvano yanks open a heavy cabinet, revealing rows of firearms, blades, and tactical equipment. Nikolai is the first to grab a rifle, checking the chamber before slinging it over his shoulder. Gio straps a knife to his calf, his expression set like stone. Ammo clips clatter onto the central table as I toss them from a nearby drawer.

I step toward the wall, selecting a blade and strap it securely to my thigh. "We need to move faster."

The armory fills with the mechanical clicks of guns being loaded and the muted snap of Velcro as holsters are secured.

The speaker in the room suddenly crackles to life. The opening notes of *I'll Make a Man Out of You* from *Mulan* fill the space, and the moment *"Let's get down to business"* plays, we all freeze, glancing around at each other.

Andrei.

Nikolai huffs out a laugh, shaking his head as he adjusts the straps on his vest. "Fucking Christ."

I glance up at the camera in the corner of the room, the red light on, indicating he's watching. I lift my brows, then turn back to them, making sure my voice carries while we gear up. "Nikolai and Silvano will enter through the south side. Gio, you'll take the east side. Stay outside, scope it out through the window. Andrei's heat map shows about twenty people inside. If Niki's there, you extract her—whatever it takes. If she's not, get intel and get out. No unnecessary risks. We move fast, we move quiet."

Silvano gives a single nod.

"Earpieces," I remind them, grabbing a small device from the table and slipping it into my ear. The others follow suit, each inserting the nearly invisible earbuds that link us to Andrei's comms.

I tap the mic near my collar to test it. "Sound check."

"Good, boss," Andrei says.

Silvano adjusts his earpiece and speaks. "Silvano."

Nikolai taps his mic. "Nikolai, good to go."

"Gio, ready."

Andrei comes through our earpieces. "All channels are open. I have eyes on your positions. Stay connected, and I'll guide you as needed."

"Copy that," I respond.

I grab a Glock from the wall, securing it in the holster at my side. "I'll stay in the car," I add. My gaze sweeps across the room, landing on each of them. Silvano raises a brow, knowing I'm usually the first to insert myself into the action.

"Ma will have my nuts if she finds out I left the property. And if she finds out Rainey's chained to my bed, I'm as good as dead."

Silvano smirks. "Real noble, playing the getaway driver."

"Stick to the plan," I growl, grabbing the keys. "Find her. Get her out."

Silvano gives me a nod. "Understood."

With the plan set, we move out.

THE VEHICLE HUMS QUIETLY AS I PARK NEAR THE WAREHOUSE, KEEPing it hidden in the shadows. The surrounding darkness stretches like a barrier, isolating us from the world outside. Andrei filters through the earpiece as he tracks Nikita's movements. "Her phone hasn't moved. She's still inside. No sign of activity."

In the backseat, Silvano and Gio speak in low, measured tones, hashing out the final pieces of their approach.

"This is as close as I'll get without drawing attention," I say, cutting the engine.

Silvano adjusts the blade strapped to his thigh one final time before opening the door. "Alright. Let's move."

Gio smirks, flipping his knife in a quick, practiced motion before sheathing it. "Want me to bring you a present to play with tonight?"

"If they might have info on Cristiano's whereabouts, yes. But I'll have enough work when I get home. I don't need extra from here."

He claps me on the shoulder. "Don't say I didn't offer."

"Just get her and get out."

Silvano meets my gaze, then nods. "We've got this."

They pile out, their shadows disappearing into the night as they approach the warehouse. I watch them go, my grip tightening on the wheel. I hate being the one waiting in the car. I don't do well sitting still when they're walking into possible danger. I need to be in charge of the situation.

I keep my eyes on the darkened building, waiting for them to return.

My earpiece crackles, Andrei chiming in. "Still no movement. Everything's quiet."

Too quiet. Minutes tick by, stretching into an unbearable eternity. Each second feels heavier than the last. I scan my surroundings, making sure nobody has spotted me. No vehicles come or go. No noise anywhere. Utter silence.

Forty minutes pass, and unease churns in my gut like acid. My pulse pounds in my ears, each beat amplifying the wrongness of the situation.

The silence is suffocating. My fingers drum against the steering wheel in rapid succession. The SUV's interior suddenly feels too small, almost forcing me out.

I give it five more excruciating minutes, then my patience shatters. "Check-in." My voice is tight. "Silvano, Gio, Nikolai—status?"

Nothing.

"Andrei, what's the heat map showing?"

A brief pause. Then, the earpiece hisses with static.

No. Our communication didn't just go out.

"Silvano. Gio. Nikolai. Check-in."

More crackling.

I press the comms harder against my ear. "Check-in."

Dead air.

Forgive me, Rainey.

I'm out of the vehicle before I can second-guess myself. I stride to the trunk, yanking it open, grabbing a rifle with a scope, securing it against my back, then turn toward the building.

A guard leans against the wall, lazily puffing on a cigarette, his eyes half-lidded. He doesn't even notice me until it's too late. My arm slips around his neck, and with one quick motion, the sickening crunch seals his fate. His body collapses, lifeless and silent, crumpling to the ground.

I peer through the small window and catch movement. I crack the door open and slip inside, staying in the shadows, my ears tuning to the low hum of voices. The scene unfolds before me as I crouch behind a stack of crates.

Gio kneels on the concrete floor, a gun pressed to the back of his head. Silvano and Nikolai stand nearby, their hands raised in surrender, their weapons strewn across the floor. A dozen men surround them, postures tense, fingers twitching near their triggers.

Twelve men.

I move quickly, keeping low as I reposition behind a higher stack of crates with a clearer line of sight. I unshoulder the weapon, position it on top of the crate, and press my eye to the scope. The crosshairs hover over the man holding the gun to Gio's head.

He doesn't even get the chance to blink.

The shot is clean. He drops like a marionette whose strings have been cut, the gun clattering to the floor.

Gio wastes no time, diving for a weapon, snatching it up just as chaos erupts.

A barrage of gunfire shatters the silence, the echoes ricocheting off the warehouse walls. Smoke, shouts, and the scent of gunpowder choke the air.

My breathing remains slow and controlled. I shift my aim and squeeze the trigger. Another body drops. Then another.

Silvano and Nikolai explode into action, elbows slamming into ribs, fists cracking against jaws. Silvano knocks one man back, sending him crashing into another before pivoting to take on the next.

Nikolai intercepts an attacker raising a gun, grabbing his wrist and twisting hard enough to force the weapon upward. A shot fires, striking another enemy rushing in. Nikolai yanks the gun free, turns it on its owner, and pulls the trigger. The man drops instantly.

Silvano ducks under a wild swing, driving his knee into his opponent's gut before shoving him aside. Nikolai seizes the opening, diving for his weapon and rolling to his feet. Gun in hand, he fires at another enemy closing in too fast. They move in sync—calculated, efficient, unstoppable.

The remaining men spin around, their guns snapping up—but I'm quicker.

My focus narrows as I line up my next target. One by one, I take them down, my bullets finding their marks with brutal efficiency. Six drop in rapid succession.

Seven men vanish into cover, their shots coming from unseen angles. They're smarter, more calculated. I press against the crate—my location is known by now—and each second stretches, every corner I peek around a gamble with my life.

Silvano and Nikolai move like wraiths, their shots ruthless and precise.

But before I can fire again, a flash of motion draws my attention.

A gunshot.

Giovanni staggers.

Blood.

And then he drops.

Chapter

TWENTY-FOUR

Damiano

I shove the rifle onto my back, draw my Glock, and push forward—dead or alive, I'm getting him out of here. If he's left behind, the vile things they'll do to his corpse… It would kill Ma.

Blood spills from his leg and chest. His hands are pressed to the wound, his face pale, contorted with pain. He's not getting up—just lying there, vulnerable.

Bullets slice through the air, some so close I can feel the heat of their passage. My Glock empties with a click, the slide locking back. No time to reload. I toss it aside, grab Gio under his arms, and haul him up. "Hold on."

"Fuck!" he yells as I jostle his leg. His blood is everywhere—on me, on the floor, soaking through my clothes. I grit my teeth and keep moving, his weight dragging me down but not enough to stop me.

"Stay with me!" I bark, more to keep myself focused than anything else. "The only one getting killed today is me when Rainey gets her hands on me."

I hear Silvano shout something, but the blood roaring in my ears drowns it out. The exit looms ahead, the cold night air spilling through like salvation.

Gunfire erupts behind me, and I stagger, my grip on Gio slipping for a moment. A searing pain tears through my side as a bullet finds its mark. The burn is unmistakable—familiar, even. I've been shot before.

I grit my teeth, barely flinching, and keep moving. No time to stop. No time to even acknowledge it. Every muscle in my body screams with effort, my legs growing heavier with each step, but I push forward—driven by sheer will, the need to get him out alive, and the promise to myself that I will get home to Rainey.

The SUV screeches to a halt just as I burst out. Silvano is out in an instant, his face a mask of urgency as he swings the back door open.

"Get him in!" he shouts.

I all but throw Gio into the backseat, climbing in after him. The door slams shut behind me.

"Go!" I bark, and the tires squeal as Silvano tears down the road.

Gio groans beside me. Blood pools beneath him, staining the seat. His breathing is ragged and uneven. Too much blood.

I yank my belt free with one hand, looping it around his leg just above the wound. "This is going to hurt," I warn.

I tighten the belt, twisting it until the bleeding slows. He lets out a strangled noise, his body jerking against the seat.

"Stay with me." My voice is low. "You're not dying today."

As soon as the tourniquet is cinched, I shove his hands out of the way and apply pressure to the chest wound.

"You'll be fine." I press down harder, trying to stop the flow.

Silvano glances back for a split second. "You okay?"

I nod, though every inch of me burns, adrenaline and fear warring in my veins.

Blood soaks through Gio's jeans, crimson spreading across my hands as I press down hard on the wound. His face twists in pain, his breaths coming in shallow, uneven gasps. His eyes flicker open for a second before fluttering shut again.

"Stay with me, Gio," I urge, pressing down harder, his blood seeping through my fingers.

Nikolai groans, slumping against the passenger seat, clutching his arm, blood oozing from between his fingers.

The SUV screeches as Silvano swerves onto the highway, the tires howling in protest against the asphalt. The engine roars as he pushes it to its limits. His voice cuts through the speakers as he barks into the phone. "We need medical ready, now. Gio's leg is torn apart, chest wound is bad. Nikolai, Dom, and I are hit too. Surgery center better be ready when we get there."

The vehicle lurches as Silvano threads through traffic, a horn blaring in our wake. Gio's eyes crack open for a fleeting moment, his lips moving soundlessly.

Neon streaks pass in a distorted haze, the city slipping by in fractured glimpses. The muffled drone of traffic fades beneath the thunder of my pulse.

Silvano doesn't let up, the vehicle screaming down the final stretch toward the family's private surgery center. The tires screech as he pulls into the lot, and the world narrows to the immediate need to get Gio inside.

The medics don't waste time. Giovanni is wheeled straight into surgery, the gurney disappearing behind swinging double doors. The urgency in their voices is a low hum, fading as they disappear.

The rest of us are ushered into an adjacent room, the air heavy with the metallic tang of blood and antiseptic. My shoulders sag as the adrenaline begins to ebb, replaced by the dull throb of exhaustion and pain.

Nurses and doctors come in, teams splitting up to join each of us as we remove our gear, waiting to assess our injuries.

One by one, I unstrap the weapons clinging to my body. The knife holstered at my thigh is the first to go, the blade glinting faintly as I toss it onto the nearby table. Next, I remove my empty gun holster.

I unfasten the last set of straps, stripping off the gear and tossing it onto the chair with a dull thud, still loaded with spare ammo.

Finally, I grip the hem of my blood-soaked shirt. The fabric clings to my skin, sticky and stubborn, and I wince as I peel it free. Fresh air hits the exposed flesh, intensifying the sting, but I grit my teeth and shove the pain aside. Blood trickles sluggishly down, pooling at my waistband.

I toss the shirt aside, the bloodied fabric landing in a heap on the floor. The nurse steps forward, her gloved hands moving with steady precision as she surveys the damage. I brace myself, muscles tensing instinctively.

Silvano's eyes widen as he catches sight of the wound. "How the fuck did you carry Gio out after getting hit?"

I glance down, shrugging as if the burning sensation isn't making every nerve in my side scream. "It's nothing."

"Sure doesn't look like nothing," Nikolai grumbles from the chair next to me. His shirt is gone, revealing a bullet wound clean through his bicep. Blood trails down his arm as a nurse works quickly to sterilize and stitch the area, and he hisses when the needle pierces his skin.

The room buzzes with gloves snapping, instruments clinking, and low murmurs of reassurance from the nurses. Silvano leans against the wall, one hand bracing himself as a medic patches up a shallow graze on his shoulder. His face is grim, his eyes tracking everything like he's still on high alert.

The first wave of drugs kicks in—a numbing fog that starts at the edges and works its way inward, and exhaustion takes over. One by one, we begin to drift off, the adrenaline finally giving way to the pull of drug-induced sleep.

I WAKE UP GROGGILY IN A HOSPITAL BED INSIDE THE SURGERY CENTER. My body feels heavy, the lingering effects of painkillers dulling everything.

Dante's voice booms through the room. "Pa is going to fucking kill us all!"

I blink, my brain still fogged from the drugs. Em stands beside him, fists planted on her hips, her expression a mix of fury and concern.

"And how dare you!" she snaps, pointing at me. "Where is Rainey? Does she even know you got shot and had to have surgery?"

Her words jolt me fully awake. I sit up too fast, my head spinning.

"Uh-uh, mister," she scolds, jabbing a finger at me. "Lay back down before you fall over."

"I have to go," I argue, swinging my legs over the side of the mattress. "Rainey is chained to my bed."

The room falls silent. Em's face twists in pure disbelief. "She's what?" she snarls.

Dante steps in. "You chained her to your fucking bed like a goddamn animal?!" he bellows.

"Yes." It's my only response.

"Unbelievable," Em mutters.

"I need to get home," I insist, ignoring the stabbing pain in my side. Gritting my teeth, I reach up and yank the IV from my arm, ignoring the sharp sting as blood beads at the insertion point.

My legs protest as I push myself to stand, but I force them to hold steady.

"You're staying here. You got shot. I'm going to check on her," Dante says, looking furious.

"I said I am!"

"You think she wants to see you? When this is how you treat her?" Dante retorts.

"You think you can treat her better?!" I glare at him. It's a pissing match right here in the surgery center.

Em steps in. "Excuse you. Don't make Dante out to be the bad guy when you treat your girlfriend this way. You're probably the last person she wants to see, and could you blame her?"

"Nobody asked for your opinion. I suggest you get back in your place before I put you in it." I sit in the chair next to my bed and begin lacing up my boots.

I hear a doctor come in and begin talking to Dante about Gio, and they both walk away briskly.

Em narrows her eyes, visibly wrestling with whatever lecture she's holding back. After a long, exasperated sigh, she steps forward. "Fine. Let's go. But don't think for a second this conversation is over. And don't you dare act like I have no credibility here."

She strides to the bed, dropping a duffel bag onto the mattress with a thud. Unzipping it, she rummages through the contents and pulls out a clean shirt. "Put this on." She tosses it toward me, and I catch it with one hand, shaking out the fabric before pulling it over my head.

Nikolai approaches, running a hand through his disheveled hair as Em pulls out a pair of pants and another shirt. She hands them over, and he takes them, slipping the shirt on then stepping into the pants.

On the drive back, Em apparently tries her best to contain her anger and disappointment, but it finally boils over. "You can't chain your girlfriend to your bed, Damiano! One day, Rainey is going to be the mother of your children, and how the hell do you think they'll feel knowing you treated their mother like this?"

I grip the armrest, my glare fixed on the window. Slowly I turn my head toward her. "Let me make something very clear to you. Rainey is mine. I'll do whatever I want with her. Either learn to mind your own business, or I'll make sure you never have to worry about anyone else's again."

"You're threatening to kill me when I'm the only reason you're even going home right now?" Em's laugh cuts through the air. "Enjoy your tears alone when she never falls in love with you. You don't give her a reason to."

"I'd ask the same thing about your kids, but everyone knows nothing will ever come from you and Dante."

Her hands tighten on the wheel, knuckles whitening. "You're a prick. At least Dante would never tie me to a bed and leave me there."

"No, he wouldn't, would he?" I fire back. "He just ties you to the bed, takes what he wants, then unties you and sends you on your way until he has another need."

Her mouth opens in shock, but no words come. Then it snaps shut, her jaw tightening as she struggles to hold back her response. She finally opens it again, but Nikolai cuts in before she can erupt.

"We had a shitty night. Can we save this for later?"

I don't answer, and neither does she. The silence that follows is deafening.

She's right. I can't expect Rainey to love me if I keep treating her this way.

When we pull up to the estate, Nikolai doesn't wait. He climbs out and heads straight inside, muttering about checking in with Andrei. Em follows, hurrying up the front steps—probably to go cry.

I head toward my truck, parked near the side of the house. My thoughts are a tangled mess, but one thing is certain—Rainey is going to flip when I walk through that door.

As I pull up to my house, Trixie stands near the porch, arms wrapped tightly around herself. Her face is blotchy and streaked with tears. She looks like a mess.

"Jesus Christ," I grumble under my breath, cutting the engine and stepping out of the truck. The last thing I need right now is another problem.

The moment she sees me, her tears flow harder, and she stumbles toward me, sobbing uncontrollably. "Damiano," she chokes out, grabbing onto my arm as if it's the only thing keeping her upright. "I came out here to talk to you, and… someone attacked me. I'm so scared. Please, can you walk me back to the house?"

I let out a long, frustrated sigh. The idea of walking her back is the last thing I want to entertain, but I should touch base with Andrei too.

"Fine. Let's go."

Trixie lowers her gaze with a small smile as we start walking.

Chapter

TWENTY-FIVE

Rainey

"**G**ood God," Damiano's voice cuts through the silence. I hear his footsteps approach, and when he lifts the pillow on the floor, he groans with disgust.

He drops the pillow back down with a thud, his expression twisting. "Get up," he says, moving to unhook the chain from the bed. "Shower. Now."

I don't move, my body leaden with exhaustion and anger.

He steps out and returns moments later with a tray in hand, setting it gently on the bed. On it rests a white food container, a bottle of water, and a can of Coke. "You can eat first if you want. Though I don't know how you'd manage to keep anything down with that smell."

I still don't respond, my gaze fixed out the window, refusing to acknowledge him. The battle between my pride and my hunger nags at me, but I stay silent, my body unmoving.

He walks around to my side of the bed and slaps my butt, the gesture casual, almost teasing. If I weren't so furious, I might have thought it was meant to be playful.

"Don't fucking touch me, you piece of shit!"

I kick out with my leg, my foot barely grazing his hip before he grabs my ankle. He stares down at me, his expression confused, like he can't fathom why I'm this pissed. As if chaining me up wasn't degrading enough. He left me here—no food, no way to get to the bathroom—and I can't even think about what happened with Trixie.

I know this is the kind of world he comes from, but he plays with emotions, dangling hope in front of my face just to rip it away. He pretends he cares about me, and all that talk about me being his girlfriend? Just more bullshit, because he turned around and slept with another woman under "our" roof.

"Something urgent came up. I got back as soon as I could." He holds onto my ankle like he has every right to touch me, his gaze fixed on mine, still wearing that look of confusion.

"Something urgent came up," I mock.

His brows draw together as he stares at me, like he's genuinely perplexed by my reaction. The sheer audacity makes me want to scream. Maybe I should invite someone into this room, let them fuck me on this bed, and see how he likes it.

He finally releases my foot, turning on his heel and striding out of the room. The faint murmur of his voice drifts back to me as he makes a phone call, but I don't bother trying to make out the words. Moments later, he reappears, grabs the tray off the bed, and vanishes into the bathroom.

When he comes back, he picks up the chain from the bed and, without warning, gives it a yank, pulling my foot off the mattress.

I sit up in a flash, swinging my fist at him, but he catches it mid-air.

"Do you want an apology? Is that it?" he asks, his tone exasperated. "Fine. I'm sorry I didn't get back last night. I should've called and had someone bring you food. There. Happy now? Will you stop trying to hit me?"

I wrench my hand free from his grasp and immediately swing at him again, unable to hold back my frustration.

He lets out a low, irritated groan, sidestepping my swing. His hands are on me, hoisting me up, flipping me over his shoulder like I weigh nothing. I thrash against him, but he ignores my protests as he carries me into the bathroom and sets me down on the edge of the large soaker tub. Then, he strides across the room, sits on the counter, and rests his hands in his lap.

I glare at him, but the smell of the food he carried in lingers, teasing me. My stomach growls, and I decide I don't care if he watches me. I grab the hamburger and take a bite, then wash it down with a drink of Coke. I hate that I feel so vulnerable eating. I would have felt better if he was eating too.

The silence is broken by the shrill ring of his phone. He leans to the side, pulls it from his pocket, glances at the screen, and sighs heavily before answering.

"Ma," he says flatly.

Her voice explodes through the phone, loud enough for me to hear every word. "You were given orders to stay on the property, and then you and your brothers leave and all get shot?" she bellows.

He pinches the bridge of his nose, his expression shifting to one of annoyance mixed with resignation. At the word "shot," I freeze, the bite of hamburger in my mouth suddenly feeling like lead. I sit quietly, watching him, caught between anger and curiosity as the conversation unfolds. I can pick up on half of it, but the rest is in Russian.

"Papa and I are flying home now. Are you okay?" Her voice softens, the concern palpable.

"All good."

"And your brothers?" she presses.

"Ask them," he says dismissively.

Shot? When was he shot? He doesn't look injured—not even a limp or a scratch. Maybe I really don't know what's going on. The realization makes me feel like an intruder, eavesdropping on something I have no right to hear. The feeling settles heavily in my chest, and suddenly, I can't stomach another bite of food.

I set the half-eaten hamburger back on the tray and stand, heading straight for the shower. His eyes follow me as I walk across the room, but I ignore him, focusing instead on turning the water on. The sound of the spray fills the silence, and I begin peeling off my clothes, letting them fall to the floor in a heap before stepping into the warm stream.

When I finish, the room is quiet.

He's gone.

Good.

The faint murmur of voices drifts from the other room, so I follow the sound. The stupid chain trails behind me, clinking against the floor with each step as I head toward the bedroom.

Still damp, water dripping from my hair and skin, I step into the bedroom—completely naked.

The sight that greets me stops me in my tracks. Two men are there, armed with cleaning products and a carpet shampooer, clearly tasked with addressing the mess I made. All three men freeze when they see me, their eyes widening in surprise.

I stand there, unfazed. "I assume I'm getting chained back to the bed?" I point.

Damiano's jaw tightens, and for a moment, I think he might explode. "Bathroom. Now," he snarls, pointing toward the open doorway.

This time, I don't bother with attitude. His anger is evident, and even I know when to back off. I turn on my heel and walk away, the sound of his footsteps following close behind.

He gestures to a shelf by the sink. "The towels were right here if you had bothered to look!"

"Meh." I shrug, my nonchalant response only fueling his anger.

He storms out, then returns, throwing a set of clothes onto the counter before leaving again.

I take my time getting dressed, not out of defiance but because I feel drained. When I finally exit the bathroom, Damiano points, making it clear he wants me gone from the space where these men are working—and where I just exposed myself to them. I stride past, heading straight for the living room.

A knock at the front door draws my attention, and I glance toward it, my heart sinking as I see Trixie's familiar silhouette through the glass. Rolling my eyes, I turn over on the couch, facing the backrest. I want no part of this interaction.

"Hey," Damiano greets her, his tone casual as he steps outside.

Peeking over my shoulder, I see them walking away from the house. They stop just at the bottom of the stairs, their conversation muted, but the sight alone twists my stomach. I will myself not to care, but the knot in my chest only tightens.

The door opens and closes, but I don't bother turning to look. I try to block everything out. Even as the cushions shift beside me, I ignore it.

"Puked on the floor, huh?"

I turn to find Nikolai sitting there, a playful smile plastered on his face.

"Your brother has me chained to his bed like a dog," I snap. "And he didn't feed me for over a day."

Nikolai raises an eyebrow, then reaches out and grabs my ankle, jerking it onto his lap.

I try to yank my foot free, but his hold tightens. He bends to the side, reaching into his pocket and pulling out a ring of keys, then starts flipping through them. He pauses on a small, slim object tucked amongst them—a lock-picking tool disguised as part of the set.

He separates the tool from the ring, clutching the keys in his hand while he inserts the pick into the lock, his other hand gripping my ankle firmly to keep it steady. His fingers twist and adjust the tool inside the mechanism. I watch, transfixed, hoping it actually works.

Then, with a satisfying click, the lock pops open. The cuff falls loose around my ankle, and he swipes it to the floor.

I stare at my now-free ankle, blinking in disbelief, then hurl myself across the couch into his arms, squeezing him tightly.

He groans, and I lean back, startled, trying to figure out how I hurt him. I doubt my hug was that strong. My eyes catch on the edge of a bandage peeking out from under his shirt. Sitting back, I grab his sleeve and pull it up.

My mouth falls open. *They really did get shot.*

"What happened?"

He peers down at the bandage as if it's nothing, then shrugs, a grin spreading across his face. "Got shot."

I blink at him, my mouth still hanging open. "I can see that. How?"

"With a gun," he says with a wink.

"Wow," I mutter, crossing my arms. "You're just as annoying as your brother."

The sound of footsteps echoes from the hallway, and the two men step inside, their cleaning equipment in tow. "All done."

"Sorry. And… thanks," I say awkwardly, shifting back to my original spot.

The door opens again, and my stomach tightens as Damiano walks in. His eyes immediately lock onto the chain lying on the floor and my now-free ankle. His expression is unreadable at first, but then a small smirk curls at the corner of his mouth.

"Pops says we're having dinner tonight," Nikolai says casually, his tone almost bored. "And before you think of an excuse to get out of it, he specifically said the five of us better be there."

Damiano raises a brow, a smile spreading across his face. "Rainey and I can't wait."

Nikolai stands, shoving his hands in his pockets. "Don't leave us alone with him. He's pissed."

Damiano's smile doesn't falter. "We'll be there."

I straighten in my seat, curiosity tugging at me as I look at Nikolai. "Can I be your date?"

Nikolai opens his mouth to respond, but Damiano cuts him off before a single word can escape. "No, you'll be mine."

"Trixie can be yours," I snap, glaring up at him.

Damiano strides over and sinks onto the couch beside me. His arm snakes around my shoulders, pulling me against his side. His warmth seeps into me as he tilts his head down.

"You will be mine."

Chapter

TWENTY-SIX

Rainey

The dining room feels more like a battleground than a place to eat. I'm seated next to Damiano, who sits calmly. On his other side, Andrei leans back in his chair, while Valentina sits beside him, composed but watching everything intently. Across the table, Giovanni, Dante, Silvano, and Nikolai occupy one side, their expressions ranging from irritation to barely concealed anger. Well, everyone except for Giovanni, who looks half dead. Lorenzo commands the head of the table, his presence impossible to ignore as his eyes sweep over his sons.

Plates of food sit untouched, though the aroma of roasted meat and garlic fills the room. I want to eat, but nobody else is, so I don't know if we're allowed to.

"I should go," I whisper to Damiano.

"Say it to the table, dear?" Lorenzo calls out, making my private conversation public.

I glance up at him, aware of everyone's eyes fixed on me. Clearing my throat, I try to keep my voice steady. "I was just saying that this feels like a family matter, and I don't want to intrude. I was going to excuse myself."

Valentina cuts in. "You'll stay right where you are. You're part of this family now, and your boyfriend made a reckless call. Perhaps if he weren't such a hothead and hadn't chained you to your bed, you might have talked some sense into him." She stares pointedly at Damiano.

Part of this family.

I shouldn't care, but the words settle over me, leaving behind something unexpectedly comforting. Even the way she called Damiano my boyfriend sends a flicker of happiness through me, despite the anger I'm still wrestling with.

"You're reckless. All of you," Lorenzo says finally, his voice cutting through the silence. "I told you to hold back, and yet you still went ahead."

Silvano straightens in his seat. "What were we supposed to do? Let a threat on Nikita slide? Pretend it wasn't real?"

Lorenzo fixes his gaze on him. "Nikita can take care of herself."

"And we're just supposed to hope she can?" Damiano interjects. "We're her brothers. We don't sit back and do nothing when someone threatens her."

I blink, trying to process his words. A sister? My gaze darts around the table, wondering if I misheard, but the conversation continues without pause.

"And I already told you," Lorenzo says, his tone hard, "I had everything set into motion to pull her out. But you didn't wait. You didn't listen."

"You didn't move fast enough," Damiano retorts.

Lorenzo leans forward, his voice rising. "Fast enough? You think getting yourselves shot is the solution? You think nearly dying is what protects this family? Don't forget who got Niki into this mess in the first place. You don't just get to make calls only when it's convenient for you."

"Convenient for me?" Damiano's body radiates anger.

"Yes, son, convenient. Convenient for you to overlook your brothers' safety while rushing to get your sister out of a hairy situation—one she ended up in because she was doing *your* bidding."

Valentina, coming to the same conclusion as everyone else—that Damiano looks like he's about to lose his temper—chimes in, her voice calm but carrying an edge. "You boys are lucky to be alive. Do you understand how dangerous this was? Damiano, did you even think about Rainey when you ran into gunfire?"

"I was thinking about Rainey when I stayed in the car to play getaway driver. I was thinking about my brothers coming out of the warehouse alive when they failed to check in."

"You had no business being there!" she snaps. "You were told to stay on the property until Cristiano is dealt with! You just don't listen!"

Damiano's jaw tightens, but he doesn't respond. Silvano is the one to finally speak.

"Do we want to talk about what really happened?" He looks pointedly at Valentina, then Lorenzo. "We were surrounded. Gio had a gun to his head. If Damiano had stayed in the car like you wanted, we'd all be dead."

Valentina's eyebrows knit together. "I didn't want him sitting in any car. I wanted him staying on the property!"

"It was his kill shot that got the gun off Gio's head. And his next twelve shots that took out the men who had guns on all of us."

A heavy silence falls over the table as the weight of Silvano's words sinks in. Lorenzo's face hardens, but he doesn't interrupt.

"And when Gio got shot in the chest and leg, going down hard," Silvano continues, his voice softening, "it was Damiano who ran straight into the gunfire. He got shot himself but still managed to carry Gio's big ass to safety. While the rest of us were just trying to survive, he was the one who made sure Gio didn't bleed out on the ground."

"He shouldn't have had to," Valentina fires back. "You're brothers. You should be looking out for each other, not putting yourselves in situations where one of you has to play hero."

"We *do* look out for each other," Silvano says firmly. "That's exactly what we were doing there. Looking out for our sister."

Nikolai, who has been silent, finally sets his fork down. "The threat on Nikita was real, and we handled it. What else were we supposed to do? Sit back and hope for the best?"

Lorenzo's palm slams onto the table, the sound loud enough to make me flinch. "You wait because I told you to. You wait because I'm in charge. Everyone knows how far you'll go for her. You've just painted a bigger target on her back."

Damiano leans forward, his elbow brushing mine. "And if we had waited and something had happened to her, would you have been able to live with that?"

Lorenzo glares at him, the room falling silent under the weight of the unspoken challenge.

Dante shifts in his seat, speaking for the first time. "Letting them think they could threaten Nikita and walk away unscathed makes us look weak. Last night sent a message."

"A message," Lorenzo spits. "A message that makes this family look vulnerable. Do you think showing how much she means to us makes them back off? No. It makes them come after her harder. Now they know exactly how to hurt us."

"She's your daughter, for god's sake," Nikolai spits.

I glance at Damiano, then at Andrei and Valentina. Everyone seems to know exactly what's going on, but I'm lost. My mind spins. Who the hell is Nikita? Why hasn't Damiano ever mentioned her?

"This conversation is over," Lorenzo declares, his tone final. "Nikita will be home soon, and I'm sure she'll love hearing how you all got shot. Especially you." He points his fork at Nikolai.

The room falls silent as Lorenzo begins to eat. I follow his lead, picking up my fork and taking a cautious bite. I can feel his gaze sweep across the table, but I keep my eyes down, focusing on chewing.

"Everyone but Rainey is dismissed," Lorenzo says as he continues eating.

A ripple of confusion spreads as everyone shifts their attention to one another. Lorenzo lifts his head. "She's the only one eating. Get out." He flicks his fork in a dismissive motion, signaling them to go.

The room is quiet as everyone picks up their utensils and begins stabbing into their meat.

One of the girls walks past, and Valentina calls her over, rising from her seat to speak discreetly. The girl nods, then quickly leaves.

The silence stretches on, and I pray Damiano finishes soon so we can get out of here.

The click of heels echoes down the hall, and I glance up to see Em and five other girls entering the room, positioning themselves along the wall. My gaze lingers for a moment before I turn back to the table, trying to ignore the unease settling in my chest.

Dante is the first to rise. He strides over to the group, holding out a hand to Em. She takes it, and the two disappear together. Next, two of the girls walk over to Giovanni, hooking their arms under his as they help him stand.

It doesn't take long to realize they've been brought here for each of the men. I have to count multiple times how many girls are standing there, trying not to puke at the number. Anyone who tries to leave with Damiano will leave with my knife stabbed through her eye.

A wave of relief washes over me when Damiano stands and says, "We're going home."

Silvano meets us at the end of the table. "I'll be ready in an hour."

Damiano nods, and we head out through the back door. As we step outside, I glance over my shoulder through the glass and catch a glimpse of the others leaving with their chosen girl.

I drift upward to the right side of the house. Trixie stands at her window, arms crossed, her expression thunderous. Even from here, I can see the fury in her posture, the way her fingers dig into her arms.

I quickly look away, refocusing on the path ahead, and keep walking.

Chapter
TWENTY-SEVEN

Rainey

When we get home, Damiano heads straight for his closet. I watch him disappear inside, but I don't care what he's doing. My thoughts drift, wondering if I'll be chained to the bed again once he leaves. Silvano had said he'd be ready in an hour, but no one bothered to mention where they're going— or why.

I walk to my side of the closet, tugging at the edge of my shirt as I search for something to sleep in. As I begin undressing, he steps out. Moving toward the door, he pauses in the small hallway that connects our closets.

"Stay dressed. We're going out," he says, his voice even but carrying finality.

I turn to face him, my brows knitting together in question. My gaze drops to the compact duffle bag he's holding. He's dressed in dark jeans, a fitted T-shirt, and a thin jacket. Effortless, simple—yet annoyingly sexy. I hate how my stomach knots at the sight of him.

As he strides out of the room, I hesitate before deciding to change. I slip on a black dress that skims mid-thigh and throw a gray cardigan over it. Black boots complete the outfit. I leave my hair loose, its soft waves cascading down my back. I don't know what he has planned or if my choice is appropriate, but something about the uncertainty feels charged, like the calm before a storm.

I glance toward the door he disappeared through, debating whether I should ask all the questions I have, but I can't bring myself to. Instead, I follow, unsure what we're even doing.

We step outside, and I watch as he tosses his duffle bag into the trunk of the SUV. He opens the back door, pausing to look back at me. Without a word, I stride past him, sliding into the center of the seat. He follows, settling in beside me.

Noticing Silvano behind the wheel and Nikolai in the passenger seat, I shift toward the opposite side, creating some space.

The drive stretches on, the silence thick enough to choke on. I scan each of the brothers, wondering what they were doing to get injured. Surely whatever it was, they aren't going back… with me here.

I'm surprised they're not in the hospital or on strict rest. I guess I just always assumed that after surgery, you had to stay off your feet for like six weeks.

My gaze shifts between them once more, and the question spills out before I can stop myself. "Weren't you all shot? Aren't you supposed to be in bed or something?"

Nikolai's lips twitch into a faint smile as he meets my eyes, the expression laced with amusement and a hint of *I told you so* as he flicks to Damiano. He shakes his head in a subtle, almost imperceptible motion before turning his attention straight ahead.

"Were you not shot?" I direct the question at Damiano.

He lets out a sigh and turns his head to me.

"Why don't you slide over here and check my body for injuries?"

I roll my eyes and look back out the window.

Nobody else speaks for the rest of the drive. We seem to be heading to the middle of nowhere, and when the vehicle finally begins to slow, I sit up straighter, peering out the window. The outline of a massive industrial structure looms ahead. The headlights sweep over a chain-link fence topped with barbed wire, and my stomach tightens.

We pull up to a warehouse, which looks more abandoned than it should. The lights meant to illuminate the property are dim, some flickering, others completely burnt out.

Out of nowhere, a man steps in front of the chained-up gate, unlocking it before pulling the heavy metal open. Silvano flashes him a peace sign as he drives through. The man nods in acknowledgment, then disappears back inside a small structure near the entrance—probably where he had been waiting.

Rounding the back of the massive building, I take in the unexpected sight—cars. A lot of them. Silvano pulls right up to the heavy metal doors at the rear and rolls to a stop. For a moment, nothing happens. Then, with a groan, the doors creak open.

The vehicle glides into the cavernous space, the tires crunching over gritty concrete, amplifying the uneasy feeling clawing at my gut. This is every scene from an action-packed drama, and I'm pretty sure I won't make it out alive. Part of me wants to start begging Damiano to let me live, to promise him I'll do whatever he wants. If he demands I get on my knees right here, I will. Or maybe I should just shut up because, deep down, I know he didn't bring me here to murder my ass.

The moment the engine cuts, muffled noise seeps in—shouting, cheering maybe.

I survey the area, taking in the scattered pallets and rusting equipment that dot the floor.

Damiano opens his door, and the sound swells, no longer muffled. Definitely cheering. He steps out of the SUV with unhurried confidence, strides to the trunk to retrieve the duffle bag, then circles around to my side. He swings the door open and extends his hand toward me.

I flick my eyes to his outstretched hand briefly, my face twisting in disgust, before stepping out on my own. I make sure to side-step him, avoiding even the briefest touch as I pass, then fall in step with Nikolai.

He smirks over his shoulder at Damiano, who's been pissed off all night anyway, so I don't think much of it when he strides right past us, leading the way.

We move through what looks like a run-down kitchen, its faded tiles and rusted appliances giving off an abandoned feel. Damiano strides up to a large industrial freezer door, grabs the handle, and pulls it open. Then, he steps inside.

I stop dead in my tracks. Absolutely not.

Nikolai's hand presses gently against my back, urging me forward. I glance up at him, searching his face, and he nods once. Swallowing hard, I reach around, gripping his wrist as I take a step. I want to climb him like a spider monkey and hold on for dear life, but even his body remains completely at ease.

Inside, it's bigger than I expected. No hanging slabs of meat. No icy air biting at my skin. It doesn't even feel like a freezer.

At the far end, two men pull open another set of doors, the sound ricocheting off the walls. It's not cold—it's loud.

Cheers erupt from beyond the doors. Damiano disappears through them, taking the stairs down. I follow, still gripping Nikolai's arm.

The air shifts the farther we descend. It's thick, stifling, laced with sweat, and blood.

The room pulses with energy, packed to the brim with bodies. Bleachers line the perimeter, all facing a massive cage at the center. The crowd is electric, their faces alive with wild, almost feral excitement as they roar—the noise nearly deafening.

Inside the cage, two fighters collide, their bodies slick with sweat and smeared with blood. Every move is calculated, every strike punishing. A heavy punch lands with a bone-jarring crack. One man staggers, his face swollen and battered, but he doesn't back down. He charges again, animalistic in his determination.

The scene is overwhelming, my senses struggling to keep up.

We descend the concrete stairs toward the cage, and with each step, the heat and noise press in tighter. My palms grow clammy, my heartbeat quickening as my eyes dart around.

What are we even doing here?

"Stay with Nikolai and Silvano," he says, his voice cutting through the noise.

I don't know where he thinks I'd even run in a place like this, but I have no intention of leaving their side. I flick a glance at him, but his expression is unreadable, his gaze already scanning the crowd. Before I can say a word, he turns and strides away, vanishing into the throng of people.

Nikolai and Silvano shift closer, a silent wall of protection.

I force my eyes away from the cage, away from the sheer brutality playing out inside.

"Why are we here?"

Neither of them answers. Their focus stays locked ahead.

The clamor and jeering around us only amplify the tension, the occasional brush of curious gazes making my skin crawl. I don't like the attention. I keep my head down, trying to fade into the background, but even my heartbeat hammers with a frantic rhythm,

The match ends abruptly with one fighter crumpling to the ground, blood pooling beneath him. The crowd roars in approval, the noise so loud the ground vibrates.

The body is dragged out, leaving a smear of red in its wake. Someone rushes in with a mop, wiping away the evidence.

Before I can process it, another fighter steps into the cage.

This one is massive—easily twice the size of the last two. Every step he takes under the harsh fluorescent lights sends his muscles rippling, his presence alone a challenge.

The spectators explode, their excitement palpable—a static charge electrifying the air.

Then I see him.

My entire body goes rigid as Damiano steps into the cage. His coat and T-shirt are gone, leaving him in just a black wifebeater, jeans, and sneakers. My breath catches. Before I even realize it, I take a step forward.

Nikolai's hand clamps down on my shoulder, stopping me cold.

"No." I shrug off his grip. "Why is he in there?"

"He's releasing anger," Nikolai replies over the raucous crowd.

I shoot him a glare before snapping my head back toward the cage. "And he has to do it *this way*?" Disbelief seeps into my voice as I turn back to him.

He shrugs, unfazed. "I didn't see you eager to help him release any."

My jaw clenches, and my retort comes just as quickly. "He didn't give me a chance. He was too eager to fuck Trixie. It's not my fault she couldn't satisfy him enough to keep him from having to come do this bullshit."

Nikolai and Silvano both look at me, their brows knitting together, then Nikolai smirks like I'm joking.

I roll my eyes then fix my attention back onto the cage.

Damiano circles his opponent, his movements controlled.

Then, without warning, the fight begins in a sudden blur of motion.

The other man swings, a punch so forceful it looks like it could shatter bone, but the hit is avoided with a grace that feels almost surreal—especially for someone who was recently shot.

They collide, fists flying in a ruthless display of power and precision. Damiano lands a clean, devastating uppercut, his knuckles driving into the man's jaw with an impact that would drop most men. But not this one. The brute barely stumbles, shaking it off before retaliating with a vicious hook to the ribs.

The impact reverberates through Damiano's body, sending him back a step. Pain flashes across his face—but only for a second. He absorbs the hit, adjusts his footing, and lunges forward, unshaken. Blood drips from a cut above his brow, a single crimson trail slipping down his cheek, blending with the sweat that clings to his skin.

The crowd roars, feeding off the violence, but I barely hear them. My focus is locked on him.

His opponent is pure force—reckless, wild, throwing heavy-handed swings. Damiano, on the other hand, is controlled and methodical. He reads the man's attacks, anticipating the next strike before it comes.

A wild haymaker comes flying toward his head. He ducks at the last second, the air splitting where his face should have been. In one seamless motion, he pivots and slams his elbow into the man's ribs.

The man stumbles, but Damiano doesn't wait. He drives a knee into his gut, then follows with a right hook to the temple.

The brute grunts in pain, blinking rapidly as if his brain is struggling to keep up. Damiano's breathing is heavy now, his chest rising and falling in quick, measured bursts. Blood trickles from his split lip, yet his expression remains impassive.

The man shakes off the hit and charges, barreling forward like a wrecking ball of muscle and fury. Damiano stands his ground until the last possible second—then sidesteps, hooking his arm under the brute's and using his own momentum against him. The man stumbles, momentarily off-balance, and Damiano capitalizes.

His fist collides with the man's jaw, then another—each hit landing with punishing accuracy. The sound of knuckles meeting flesh echoes through the space, raw and unforgiving. His head snaps back, sweat flying from his skin, but Damiano doesn't stop.

A left jab. A right cross. A knee to the ribs.

Blow after calculated blow, until the man's legs buckle beneath him. His massive frame crumples, hitting the ground in an unconscious heap.

The crowd erupts.

My pulse pounds—not from fear, but from something darker, something I can't deny. Watching him fight like this—unforgiving, relentless—I realize I've never truly seen this side of him. I knew he was dangerous, but this is something else entirely. The sheer intensity of him is intoxicating.

He stands back from his opponent, his chest heaving, his face smeared with blood—some of it his, most of it not. He doesn't gloat. Doesn't revel in the victory. He simply wipes the back of his hand across his mouth, flicking the blood away.

The defeated man is dragged out, leaving a trail of blood that's quickly wiped away.

But I don't care about him. My eyes are locked on Damiano.

He stands in the center of the cage, shoulders squared, chest rising and falling. Not winded. Not shaken. Just standing there exuding an untouchable, lethal energy.

Then his gaze lifts, sweeping over the crowd, searching—until it finds me.

The moment our eyes meet, something inside me snaps tight, the air around us charged, crackling like a live wire.

Heat pools deep in my core. It's not just the way he looks, standing there bloodstained and victorious. It's the way he owns the moment, as if he was built for it. Built to destroy.

And God help me—it does something to me.

Another opponent steps in, and I find myself leaning forward, drawn in, unable to look away. It should disturb me—how badly I want to see him fight again. But I don't care. He's a force, lethal and incredible, and I want to witness every second of it.

The bell rings.

This time, he doesn't wait.

He strikes first, a vicious right hook that sends the man staggering before he can even react. His opponent barely has time to blink before another hit lands, a relentless storm of fists and elbows.

The man swings wildly. The attack is sloppy, easy to dodge. A quick weave past it, a low duck, then a fist drives straight into the guy's ribs. He gasps, clutching his side—but there's no mercy given.

He pivots, slamming a knee into the man's gut over and over, followed by an elbow to the jaw. The fighter stumbles—a perfect opening.

He's seized by the back of the neck and pulled straight into a knee to the face. Blood sprays from the man's nose as he crashes to the mat, motionless.

The fight is over.

Relief flickers, a fleeting sense of ease slipping out before I even realize I'm holding it. But it vanishes just as quickly.

Because Damiano doesn't leave.

He rolls his shoulders, his blood-smeared hands flexing in measured control.

And that's when I realize—he's not finished.

He lifts his shirt to wipe his face, and my eyes catch on the bandage beneath—soaked through with fresh blood, dark against his skin.

The sight jolts me from the horny induced trance he had me under.

A third man steps into the ring, his smug grin radiating confidence.

"Enough, Dom!" I scream, my voice cutting through the uproar as I shove my way toward the cage. Gripping the cold steel, I press myself against it, locking onto him. "You're done!" I snarl.

The new opponent flicks his gaze to me, his smirk widening. "This your bitch?" he taunts, barely getting the words out before—

Crack.

Damiano's fist collides with his jaw, snapping his head to the side. The grin vanishes, replaced by wide-eyed shock.

Then, all hell breaks loose.

He unleashes, fists flying so fast, each hit lands harder than the last, fueled by anger. There's no calculated control this time—just rage.

The other man gets in a couple of swings, solid ones, but Damiano barely reacts. Doesn't even slow down. His movements are like a force of nature—merciless and unstoppable.

He lands an uppercut that sends the fighter crashing to the ground.

But he doesn't stop.

Not this time.

He follows him down, driving his fist into his face, again and again, until there's nothing left of that arrogant smirk—just blood and brokenness.

The ref rushes in, dragging Damiano off his opponent, and only then does he finally stop.

Chapter
TWENTY-EIGHT

Rainey

Damiano steps out of the cage and moves through the throng of people. Before I know it, I'm following.

There's an entire locker room down the tunnel the crowd surrounds. Fighters who had been knocked out are stirring, medics tending to them—checking pupils, wrapping gauze, stitching wounds. Some are even laughing with their former opponents, as if the violence inside the cage meant nothing once the fight was over.

He lowers himself onto a bench, straddling it, his knuckles raw and smeared with red. Even bloodied and battered, there's an undeniable pull to him.

Two medics move in—one tending to the cut above his brow, the other carefully cleaning his knuckles. When the first finishes, he kneels at Damiano's side and begins peeling away the bandages on his abdomen.

The bruise surrounding the stitches on his back is dark and ugly. I hadn't realized the gunshot wound was this bad.

Why the hell is he fighting when he's this injured? Surely Nikolai was lying when he said he needed to release anger in one way or another. It sounded like he was aggressively pounding Trixie. Guess she's not all that great. I could have told him that.

My gaze traces the ridges of his back, the ink stretched across muscle, the way sweat glistens along every carved line. Every part of him looks lethal, sculpted for dominance.

I shouldn't want him. But resisting is a battle I've already lost.

All I can think about his how badly I want to run my tongue over every inch of him—taste the heat radiating from his body. He's devastatingly sexy.

I take a slow step forward, weaving around the medics tending to him, and lean casually against the lockers next to the bench. His focus stays on his knuckles as they finish wrapping them.

"So," I say, crossing my arms. "You brought me here to watch you get beat up?"

Finally, his eyes lift to mine. That infuriatingly smug expression spreads across his face, his lips curling into a smirk.

"Did it look like I got beat up?" His tone is edged with challenge.

"You're an asshole," I mutter, unable to suppress the mix of irritation and desire mixing together inside me.

The medics finish bandaging his wounds, then step away, leaving us alone.

I move closer, straddling the bench in front of him, mirroring his posture. The closeness only amplifies the crackling energy between us.

"What were you thinking? You were shot."

Without waiting for an answer, I reach out, cupping his face in my hands. His skin is sweaty under my palms, and it only turns me on more.

I lean in, pressing my lips to his. It's not gentle. Not tentative. It's urgent—a hunger I can't contain. The taste of sweat only drives me further. His mouth claims mine just as desperate, matching my intensity with his own.

My hands move between us, fumbling with the button of his pants, my fingers working fast. Without breaking the kiss, I shift onto his lap, straddling him. I don't care that we're not alone, that the room isn't private.

"I'm still mad at you," I pant against his lips, lowering myself onto him.

The stretch is immediate, and I gasp at the sensation, but I don't stop. I begin to move, my body taking what it needs.

His head tilts back slightly, a groan rumbling deep in his chest. "I'm sorry for leaving you chained to the bed," he murmurs, his voice rough, thick with need.

His grip tightens on my hips, guiding me into a rhythm that's both primal and consuming. The sounds of the locker room fade away—nothing else exists but this. The friction, the unrelenting push and pull between us. Neither of us cares who's watching or what they think.

It's filthy—fucking in this rundown locker room while fighters come and go, while injured men groan in pain a few feet away. But I don't care.

And clearly, neither does he since he has a full erection.

My lips crash against his—hard. "That's not what I'm maddest about," I gasp, leaning into him, my nails digging into his shoulders. "I'm mad at you most for fucking Trixie."

A guttural growl rumbles from his chest as I roll my hips against him, pulling a broken moan from both of us. His fingers dig into my waist, gripping me like he needs to keep himself tethered to me.

"I never touched her," he pants, voice rough, thick with frustration and urgency.

"Bullshit. I heard you," I bite out, my pace quickening, each motion fueled by anger and need. Every thrust sends another wave of heat crashing over me, the tension between us reaching its breaking point.

He shakes his head. "That's a lie."

His hips surge upward, meeting mine, demanding my full attention. The heat between us is unbearable.

The world blurs around us, everything narrowing to the feeling of his body pressing into mine.

"I'm still mad," I gasp, my voice breaking as pleasure coils tight.

"Fine," he rasps, his lips grazing my neck, teeth dragging over my skin, making my body arch into him.

I cry out, my body convulsing as I shatter. My forehead presses against his, nails raking up his skin as my orgasm rips through me. His release follows, unrestrained, his moans vibrating through me.

Even after, my hips keep moving, desperate to prolong the sensation, to chase every last ounce of pleasure. My fingers weave into the damp strands of his hair, pulling him closer until our foreheads press together.

The high fades slowly, leaving me breathless, trembling, utterly wrecked in his arms. His hands loosen their grip, gliding up my back, his touch lingering as if steadying me.

Beyond the walls, the muffled roar of the crowd drifts in— voices rising, still drunk on the mayhem. I can understand the appeal—there's an energy in it, something primal in watching two people battle with everything they have. But what I can't wrap my head around is how anyone who cares about the fighters—their friends, their family—could stand to watch them lose. To see them beaten, broken, brought low—it must be unbearable.

But then my thoughts shift to Damiano.

He wasn't beaten. He was unbelievable. The way he moved—fast and lethal, always a step ahead. No matter how massive his opponents were, he never went down. He never lost.

I stare at him, my pulse still racing—not just from the fight, but from the anger that refuses to leave me.

I want to hate him—especially now, with his blatant lie about Trixie. Why deny it? He's never struck me as the type to lie. And the fact that he is?

Really, really ticks me off.

Him lying makes me want to fuck him all over again. Only this time, aggressively. I want to hit him, choke him. And I want him to do the same to me.

Finally, I pull myself off him, adjusting my panties and smoothing down my dress. My legs feel unsteady, a mix of lingering adrenaline from the bloodlust and the aftermath of having sex in a public setting.

Straightening, I glance at him, frustration still coiled in my chest. I can't shake it.

"Can we leave now?"

"Yeah." His voice is rough but even.

He grabs a new shirt from the duffel bag and pulls it on, the fabric clinging to his sweat-dampened skin. Reaching for the bag, he slings it over his shoulder before extending his hand to me. I step forward, letting his fingers lace with mine as he leads me toward the door.

The surge of bodies slams into me the instant we step out of the locker room. The fights are still going, the atmosphere electric, and the brutal sounds of bodies hitting the cage echo through the space. The energy has only intensified, and it seems like the number of spectators has doubled since we first arrived.

People press in from all sides, their movements restless and eager as he steers me through the packed space toward Nikolai and Silvano.

Nikolai's grin stretches wide as he takes us in. "Better?"

"Much," Damiano says as he guides us back upstairs.

The crowd thickens near the main doors. Damiano easily clears a path for us, his large size making people move aside as we walk. Behind us, Nikolai and Silvano both scan the sea of people.

When we finally step out into the warehouse, the fresh air is incredible after the hot and stifling room we had been in.

Chapter

TWENTY-NINE

Damiano

Once we get back to my house, we head inside. I tell Rainey I'll be back after a while and jerk my chin to Nikolai. "Stay with her until I return."

She doesn't respond, just turns and walks to the bathroom. A second later, the shower kicks on.

Silvano, Nikolai, and I remain in the living room, the silence stretching until Nikolai jerks his chin at me. "What's up?"

"I split a couple stitches. Gonna get them checked, then talk to Andrei." I exhale, running a hand over my jaw. "She was madder than I expected about the whole chaining-her-to-the-bed thing. I shrugged it off, but then she said she's mad at me for sleeping with Trixie."

"Yeah, she mentioned that back at the fights. Why the fuck does she think that?" Nikolai asks. "When would you have even had time? Before, during, or after we got riddled with bullets."

I shake my head. "No clue. But somewhere in the last forty-eight hours, she got that impression."

Nikolai lifts a brow, then exhales heavily. "Hurry back. I don't want to deal with her wrath if you're gone too long. And I sure as hell don't want her grilling me about something like that."

I nod, grab my keys, and head out with Silvano. We take my truck, leaving the SUV for Nikolai to use later when he heads back to the main house to pick up his own. He lives just half a mile from me, but most nights, he stays in his suite at the main house instead of going home.

Some nights, he crashes in my guest suite—actually, more often than not, he does. But ever since Rainey arrived, he hasn't. He's never mentioned it, so I haven't either, but I wouldn't mind if he kept staying. It's not like he's in the way, and I can't imagine Rainey would care. She seems comfortable around him. More so than any of my other brothers.

I send a quick message to our doctor, asking her to meet me in Andrei's room. As soon as we get back to the house, Silvano follows me upstairs. I stride in, finding Andrei at his desk, working away with music playing in the background.

He pauses the track and swivels his chair to face us. "Feel better?"

"Yeah," I say, but my focus shifts as the doctor walks in, a medical bag slung over her shoulder.

She motions for me to sit, already prepping supplies as she assesses my injuries. I barely acknowledge the sting of antiseptic as I turn my attention back to Andrei.

"Rainey thinks I slept with Trixie, and I want to know why."

His eyebrows lift in surprise, then he turns back to his computer, pulling up different camera feeds.

"Did you tell her you would never?" he asks, eyes still on the screen.

"Yeah. She's still mad."

He huffs out a breath, clicking through more footage. "Then let's figure out what the hell put that idea in her head."

The three of us watch the footage on fast-forward as Andrei scrubs through the timeline. Then, there she is—Trixie, slipping into my house. Andrei pulls up additional feeds, tracking her movements.

And just like that, I see the exact reason Rainey was pissed. My jaw tightens as the scene plays out. What the hell was Trixie thinking? And more importantly, why did she involve one of my guards? A guard who will now pay for the mess she dragged him into.

Andrei transfers the footage to a tablet, setting it up for playback. Rainey deserves the truth. And I deserve to not get my face kicked in because she thinks I was unfaithful.

They follow me through the house to Dante's office. When I step inside, he's stretched out on the couch with Em straddling him.

"Fucking Jesus," he bites out. "Ever heard of knocking?"

"Get out," I say, jerking my chin toward Em.

"No. You can wait until we're finished," he snaps, his hands tightening on her thighs to keep her from moving.

He's been in pain since his hand surgery. This is probably the only natural painkiller he's utilizing, but Em can come back later.

"It's about Rainey."

His grip loosens instantly. Without another word, he nods for her to get off him.

Em looks furious—if looks could kill, I'd be deader than dead. She yanks on her clothes and moves to storm past us, making sure we all know exactly how pissed she is.

"Fucking asshole," she mutters.

I react on instinct, reaching out and seizing her by the neck, slamming her into the wall. Her breath catches as my grip tightens. "Try that again," I warn, my voice low as I press in closer.

Her eyes flick to Dante, who's calmly tucking his shirt back in, not the least bit concerned.

"Don't forget your place here." I press harder, just enough to make her gasp for air. Then, just as quickly, I let go. She stumbles, coughing, a hand flying to her throat.

"Sorry," she murmurs before rushing out, not daring to look back.

Dante sighs as he settles into his desk chair, lifting his gaze in silent expectation.

Andrei steps forward, handing over the tablet while I explain.

"She was pissed I cuffed her to the bed but seemed fine when I left. We were obviously gone longer than I intended with the shootout, and when I got back, she had puked all over the floor and was even more upset than I expected. Beyond mad about being chained up." I drag a hand down my face, still trying to make sense of it. "After the fights, we had sex in the locker room— only for her to turn around and say she's mad I slept with Trixie."

He lays the tablet on the desk and leans forward, forearms resting on the surface as his good hand traces the palm of his bandaged hand—a typical Dante gesture when he's calming a storm. When his eyes flick up to mine, I know he's mad.

"I'm not even touching the topic of you leaving the property again because it's starting to feel like you're begging to be killed. As for Rainey, I'm going to make myself perfectly clear. She is not to leave this property under any circumstances until Cristiano is dealt with. Is there any part of what I just said that you didn't understand?"

My nostrils flare as I stare down at him.

"We all have your back, Dom. We'll help you through these new changes. But I'm drawing the line with Rainey. You're not endangering her."

He's absolutely right. I brought her with me to the fights because I thought she could use time away from here, and I wanted to make up for pissing her off. It was reckless and dangerous, and I don't think straight around her.

"Understood." I nod.

Dante exhales, leaning back, his hands resting over his abdomen.

"As for Trixie—" he trails off waiting for me to fill him in.

"I'm going to handle Matthews," I tell him.

He shakes his head. "He's a good worker. We don't know the reason he was there. To me, it looked like he just wanted some pussy."

"He knew it was my house. He knows Trixie doesn't belong there. He knows he shouldn't be inside, especially if I didn't invite him. I'm not asking for permission—I'm telling you what I'm going to do."

"Let me get this straight. You're pissed that he broke the rules at the same time you were also breaking the rules?" Dante lifts a brow. "But he deserves to be punished?"

"I'm a Volkov."

Dante nods. "You are. And I'm proud of it. But you're not punishing someone for chasing tail when you only know about Trixie because Rainey wasn't putting out, and it set off alarm bells. I'll talk to him."

"I'm going home to show Rainey the footage. I'll be back tomorrow to take him downstairs."

I turn and stride out, my brothers exchanging glances before Silvano and Andrei fall in step behind me.

Dante knows he has until I return to find out what role Matthews played. I can't think of a single scenario that will change his fate. If anything, Dante should tell him to enjoy his last night alive.

Chapter

THIRTY

Rainey

When we get home, Damiano informs me he'll be back in a little while and that Nikolai will stay with me until he returns. I don't bother asking where he's going—it's none of my business.

When I step back into the bedroom, wrapped in my robe, I lower myself onto the edge of the bed and grab the lotion from my nightstand. The familiar scent of lavender drifts through the air as I work it into my skin, the repetitive motion meant to soothe me. But as my fingers glide over my legs, my mind wanders back to Trixie.

She had sex with Damiano—just a room away. Only a thin wall had separated us while I was forced to listen to the sounds of their pleasure. My stomach twists at the memory, a brutal reminder of the reality I've been trying to ignore.

I know what this place is, what it demands. The men take what they want, and sex is just another part of the equation. I told myself I understood that. I told myself I was fine with it because I didn't care about him. But deep down, I *do* care about him. I care about him more than I've ever cared about another person. I'd started to believe that he truly was mine.

But now, that illusion lies shattered at my feet. He's not just mine, and I'm not just his. Bitterness rises in my chest, and I scoff.

"Here," Nikolai says. He steps forward, holding out a steaming cup of tea. "It's hot."

"Thanks." I force a smile as I take it from him. I lift it to my lips, blowing gently before taking a cautious sip. The warmth spreads through me, though it does little to ease the ache in my chest.

I finish the tea and place the mug on my nightstand before returning my focus to smoothing lotion over my leg.

"So, your brother—what? Had to run off to tend to Trixie?"

Nikolai's features shift, caught somewhere between surprise and discomfort at my question. Leaning to the side in his usual spot in the corner chair, he props his face against his fist, studying me. "Dom doesn't tend to women. Not ever." His tone is calm but pointed. "He tends to *you*—his woman. Singular. But not women."

A hollow laugh escapes me, devoid of humor, lingering awkwardly in the quiet room.

"And you're with him all day to know when he's having sex?"

"I don't need to be with him to know you're the only person he's sleeping with," he says confidently.

"Do you have sex with your brothers?"

I want to burst out laughing at the look on his face. He looks so confused, then repulsed. But he never answers. I think my question shocked the words right out of him.

"I mean, you all sleep with the same girls. Every girl in the house has probably slept with all six of you. And when you put your dick inside one of them, it's like you're touching the same spots your brothers did. Is that not gross?"

"It's pretty fucking gross when you word it like that."

I smile at his reaction. "Next time you have sex, just remember—your brothers' skin cells sloughed off inside her, and their penis skin is now on you."

"I have never in my life wanted a conversation to end so badly. Where the fuck is Dom?"

I start laughing as I lean back against my pillows.

"Why the long hair?" I ask, still watching him.

"I hate getting my hair cut. And women love a good man bun." He winks.

"Can I see it down?"

"Sure." He sits up, removes the tie, and shakes it out. His curls are beautiful—thick, shiny, and healthy.

I stare, just taking him in like this. With his hair down, he looks… almost innocent. Like a nice guy who would feed birds for fun and volunteer at a soup kitchen on the weekend.

He waits for me to say something, and I smile. "You're really handsome."

"I know," he sighs playfully.

"Can I braid it?"

"Sure. I've never had it braided before."

I smile, climb out of bed, and point to the floor below where he's sitting. He scoots to where I indicated, and I settle into the chair behind him. He leans back between my legs as I comb my fingers through his hair, his head tilting into my touch.

"When I was in second grade, my teacher used to have me come into class before school started so she could brush my hair and braid it. I was probably the most disgusting kid, but she didn't care. She made sure my hair was always fixed. Toward the end of the year, she bought me a doll that stayed in class, and she taught me how to braid using it. We called her Sunshine."

I work through his soft curls, braiding them as best as I can. He'd actually look sexy with some Viking braids, but I doubt he'd let me do that.

"What happened to Sunshine?"

"At the end of the year, Mrs. Jensen let me take her home. My mom's boyfriend at the time got drunk or high—who really knows, maybe both—ripped her head off, and peed inside her body."

Thankfully, I'm holding the braid tight because he whips his head around, staring at me with his mouth hanging open. I laugh, slide a finger under his chin to push his mouth closed, then tug the braid until his head is straight again.

"Did you ever have toys?" he asks as I guide his head down.

"Only Sunshine."

I think about my brown-haired, blue-eyed doll and how upset I was when she was ruined. I cried for days over her. Mom's boyfriend teased me relentlessly, calling me a baby for crying over a doll. I was even relieved when third grade started and Mrs. Jensen wasn't at the school anymore. I had been so scared she would ask how I was enjoying Sunshine, and I'd either have to lie and say I still loved her, or I'd break down, cry, and get in trouble.

Nikolai seems so bothered by this that he absentmindedly lifts my foot onto his lap and rubs my toes.

We sit in silence, and I can feel how much this unsettles him. I don't have words that can make him feel better when I couldn't even make myself feel better at the time. I guess the only good thing that came out of it was that I never wanted toys again—I knew they would just be used to snuff out any happiness I might have felt. I even stopped reminding mom of my birthday. It didn't matter. The only time I ever remembered myself was when the school would tell me happy birthday in elementary school and give me a pencil and a piece of candy.

The sound of the front door opening cuts through the air, followed by heavy footsteps in the hallway. They grow louder as

Damiano strolls in, Andrei and Silvano right behind him. They all halt, turning to look in our direction, appearing unsure of what they're even looking at.

"It's called a braid." I lift a brow at Damiano as I lean forward, pull the hair tie off Nikolai's wrist, and secure the end. Then smooth my hands over the sides and lean around to check my work.

I smile at how good he looks.

Andrei taps Damiano's shoulder with a tablet, and he turns to take it, messing with the screen before stepping toward me and holding it out. His face is calm, but there's something behind his eyes that makes my stomach tighten.

"What?" I ask, my brows knitting as I glance between him and the device.

He doesn't answer, simply holds it closer.

Nikolai reaches out, takes it, and presses play on the video. We both lower our gaze, and the queasy feeling I had that day instantly resurfaces.

It's camera footage.

The first image shows Trixie entering the room with her confident strut. I remember every detail of this.

I jerk the tablet from Nikolai's hand and hold it out. "Cool. I already know."

"No, you don't," he says, pushing it back toward me.

I let out a sigh and hold it out in front of me and Nikolai. He's still playing with my toes, and I want to tell him to massage my feet harder because I'm overly stressed right now.

The footage shifts. The camera follows her as she leaves the room, and my hands start shaking. Nikolai takes the tablet, and we watch as the door shuts behind her.

I literally think I hate him. I hate him for forcing me to watch his betrayal. And when I'm done, he can deal with me destroying his house. If, by some miracle I get my hands on a weapon, I'm going to kill him.

My hands tremble slightly, and I rest my elbow on Nikolai's shoulder, my chin propped against my fist while my other arm crosses over my stomach. I'm going to puke all over again.

I glance up at him, searching his face for some kind of reaction, but he gives nothing away. Does he enjoy causing pain? What kind of monster does this?

The footage shifts again, and I know this is where I'll see my gorgeous man come inside and fuck Trixie. Except… instead, a guard enters the house. Trixie reappears, her attitude completely different.

Did they have someone watching them?

She moves toward him, and within seconds, it turns explicit.

My mind can't comprehend what's happening. Trixie fucked Damiano. I heard them. But it's not right. Damiano isn't here. It's the guard. She said it was Damiano…

I clap Nikolai on the shoulder in shock as I sit up straighter, my mouth hanging open as I watch.

It shows a side-by-side image of Trixie being plowed and me on the bed, my hands over my nose and mouth as I listen, then start crying.

My gut tightens for the me on that bed.

The guard grabs her hips, pulling her closer. The two of them have sex right there, shamelessly, in Damiano's and my home. Disgust churns in my gut, and I look away, but Damiano nudges the back of the tablet, silently urging me to keep watching.

The scene shifts again, showing Trixie and the guard leaving through the front door. He walks around the patio and disappears around the side of the house while she lingers on the steps. The camera cuts to a new angle, showing Damiano pulling up moments later. He steps out of the truck, his stride steady as she approaches him.

Trixie bursts into tears when she sees him, her hands gesturing dramatically as she speaks. I can't hear her words, but I don't need to. The exaggerated display is enough to make my teeth clench.

Then comes the part that makes my blood boil. She points back toward the main house, clearly asking him to walk her there, and he agrees. The guard she had just been with is nowhere to be seen, off doing who-knows-what.

She played me.

That manipulative bitch played me.

I stare at Damiano, my mouth slightly open, words caught in my throat. My mind races as the pieces fall into place. Without breaking eye contact, he reaches out, takes the tablet from Nikolai, and calmly passes it back to Andrei, who nods silently.

Nikolai's eyes widen, and he lets out a breath that sounds like he was holding it before standing. "That was fucking brutal. Sorry you thought he would ever do that to you. I'd go rounds on him for you if he had." He winks, then they all stride out, leaving us in silence until the front door shuts.

Damiano walks to the bed and leans against the bedpost, his expression frustratingly self-assured, the hint of a smirk tugging at his lips. "Wanna take that robe off and blow off some steam?"

"She's fucking crazy!" I stand and throw my hands in the air.

Trixie had me on the side of the bed, puking, convinced she was screwing Damiano—and for what?

He chuckles softly, reaching his hand out to me, and I walk to him. He snakes his arms around my waist and pulls me in, pressing his lips to mine.

"You almost killed my erection back at the fights when you accused me of sleeping with her," he says, grinning. "Figured, with you trying to punch me the second I walked in the door, something must have set you off." His voice is teasing, but there's an edge of sincerity in his tone. "I'm sorry you had to hear that and think it was me," he adds softly.

"How would you have felt?" I ask, my gaze locking with his.

"I'd have murdered the guy first and asked questions later."

"Well, now that I know you're not a heaping pile of shit…" I trail off with a playful smile, untying my robe and letting it fall to the floor. "Why don't you lose this?" I tug at his shirt, my fingers brushing the hem. "Because those fights have me all hot and bothered."

His grin widens. "Yeah?"

"Yeah," I murmur, leaning up to kiss him, my hands moving to the button on his pants.

He grabs the back of his collar and pulls the shirt off, discarding it on the floor, then scoops me up and carries me to the bed as I squeal with excitement.

Chapter
THIRTY-ONE

Rainey

I wake to a searing, burning pain on my neck, the intensity of it pulling a groan from my throat. I reach for the spot, brushing against something taped over the area. A sting shoots through my body, making me wince as I sit up, my mind foggy and disoriented.

Sliding out of bed, I shuffle to the bathroom. My reflection in the mirror stops me cold. Confusion flickers across my face as I tilt my head, catching sight of the taped bandage covering my skin.

Who the hell put this on me?

I carefully pick at the edges, peeling it back. The sting worsens as the adhesive tugs, and when the bandage finally comes free, I stiffen.

My eyes widen as I stare at the fresh tattoo inked onto my neck. Crawling up onto the bathroom counter for a closer look,

I lean toward the mirror, my fingers trembling as they graze the swollen, reddened area.

The design isn't just any tattoo—it's a *bite mark*. Damiano's bite mark. The one where he tried to bite my skin off during the auction. It had already scarred. And now, it's permanently inked.

Right in the center of it, his name is scrawled in bold handwriting that could only belong to him.

I gape at it, torn between disbelief and anger. The audacity of it leaves me speechless.

"This… this isn't real," I whisper. But the pain tells me otherwise. This isn't a joke, and it's definitely not a press-on tattoo.

I jump off the counter, adrenaline surging through me. Leaving the bandage half-peeled, I storm out of the house, my tank top and shorts barely covering me.

Was this punishment for falling asleep last night in the middle of us having sex? Exhaustion hit out of nowhere. I think it was from the overwhelming emotions of believing he was showing me a video of him having sex with Trixie. I don't think permanently marking me is the punishment I deserve for that.

I'm practically sweating by the time I near the back of the main house. Girls in skimpy bikinis lounge by the pool, their laughter pissing me off even more. My eyes scan the area, locking onto a group of men near the edge of the patio.

There he is.

He stands with his brothers and a few other men I don't recognize. Valentina is nearby, chatting with two other women, her appearance as poised as always.

"What the hell did you do?!" I shout, storming toward him.

The girls fall silent. The men turn to look. Valentina pauses mid-sentence. The group steps aside, giving me a clear path to Damiano, who watches me with calm amusement.

"You branded me!" I yell, shoving him hard in the chest. He doesn't budge. "You tattooed your name—and your stupid teeth—on me! Forever!"

"That was the intention." He smirks like this is all some joke.

"Because I fell asleep while we fucked?" I ask in disbelief.

"I'd have been impressed if you managed to stay awake with the sleep aid in your system."

My brows knit together in confusion before my gaze snaps to Nikolai. "You drugged my tea!"

He doesn't confirm or deny it, offering no reaction at all. But he doesn't need to—I already know the truth.

Turning back to Damiano, I catch sight of the bandage on his neck. Without a second thought, I grab the edge of the tape, yanking it off with enough force to hurt, but he doesn't stop me.

And there it is.

My bite mark, tattooed onto his skin, with my signature inked right in the center. Memories from last night resurface in fragments—his voice urging me to bite his neck when the room began to blur, his request for me to write my first name on a piece of paper. I had been too out of it to question him.

"Wow." My fingers hover over the ink.

"Do you like it?" he asks, and I can't tell if he's genuinely curious or just trying to get a reaction.

Shaking my head, I turn abruptly and stomp toward the main house.

"Baby," he calls out, laughing like he has no idea why I'm upset.

"What did you do, son?" Valentina's voice rings out as I storm past her.

Reaching the kitchen, I yank open the freezer and grab an ice pack, pressing it firmly against my burning neck. The cold offers a small reprieve from the sting, but it does nothing to soothe the rage.

Tess approaches, her eyes widening as she notices the fresh tattoo. "Does it hurt?"

"Obviously," I snap.

"It looks really good, though," she says admiringly, her gaze lingering on the ink every time I pull the ice pack away.

I glare at her. "It's permanent. It will never go away," I remind her, my voice edged with bitterness.

"I think that's the point. Damiano's making it clear—he's never letting you go."

Trixie saunters into the kitchen, popping a grape into her mouth as she rests casually against the counter. Her glare is unmistakable, and the way she carries herself radiates smugness. She opens her mouth, ready to deliver one of her trademark snide comments—when Damiano enters.

The shift in her demeanor is instant. Her confidence drains, and she takes a step back as he walks toward me.

Strong arms encircle my waist from behind, pulling me in as he kisses my unmarked shoulder.

"I thought a permanent claim would be better than leaving hickies all over your beautiful body," he says smoothly, as if branding me with his name was the most logical solution.

"Maybe I like the hickies," I retort, tilting my head slightly to meet his gaze.

His lips curve into a slow grin. "Then I'll give you as many as you want," he murmurs, his teeth grazing the side of my neck.

"No." My voice is firm as I shrug my shoulders, trying to dislodge him. He doesn't budge. "You don't get to make me feel good when I'm mad."

His grin widens against my neck as he presses another kiss there, completely unbothered by my protest.

The atmosphere shifts as men file into the house—some dressed in plain clothes, others unmistakably guards. Two of them look worse for wear—sweat glistens on their foreheads, their clothes are rumpled, blood staining their knuckles.

One of the guards steps forward, holding up three fingers to Damiano.

His expression hardens, a flicker of something cold crossing his face. He presses another kiss to my shoulder before speaking. "Punish me when I get back." His words are punctuated with a firm slap to my ass as he releases me and strides out of the kitchen, his presence lingering even after he's gone.

As he disappears, Valentina walks in with Nikolai, Dante, Giovanni, Andrei, and Silvano following close behind.

"Get lost," Nikolai says to Trixie, jerking his chin toward the door.

She hesitates, her posture stiff, refusing to move. All eyes fall on her, and her discomfort grows.

"Are you deaf? Get the fuck out," Dante snaps.

The defiance drains from her in an instant, and she quickly turns on her heel.

"We got word of a mole," the man who signaled Damiano says, scanning their faces. "Turned out to be more than one."

Dante takes a step forward. "Where are they now?"

The man's mouth twitches into a hint of a grin, not quite a smile, but something darker. "About to meet Mercy."

I don't know who—or what—Mercy is, but the way he says it makes me really uncomfortable. The word suggests something kind, something forgiving, but his tone and the charged tension in the room leave no doubt that there's nothing merciful about it.

I stay quiet, my eyes darting between the brothers as Nikolai walks into the kitchen. He stops beside me, resting his forearms on the surface, his gaze fixed on his brothers for a moment before turning to me.

He reaches up, pinching the edge of the bandage still clinging to my neck between his pointer and middle finger. "You gonna take this off, or is this a fashion statement?"

"It's an '*I'm going to kill your brother*' reminder," I say flatly.

His grin widens. "You're the only one he'd let that close to his throat."

"Well, then he should watch his back." I adjust the ice pack against my neck, wincing as the cold numbs the throbbing pain.

Reaching over, I grab his phone off the counter and open the camera app, flipping it to the front-facing view. The bandage hanging crookedly on my neck and the fresh tattoo underneath stare back at me, a forever reminder of Damiano's claim.

Rolling my eyes, I sigh and set the phone back down.

"Chicken wraps sound good?" Nikolai asks the chef before glancing at me. "How do you like yours?"

"Surprise me," I say, setting the ice pack down. "I need to change. I'll be back."

I head toward the back door, but Tess calls out, "You still have clothes in your room upstairs if you don't feel like walking all the way back to Damiano's."

I pause, considering, then nod. She walks with me upstairs, and I step into the familiar closet. Rows of tight, revealing dresses greet me, their bold designs daring me to choose one. After sifting through a few options, I finally settle on a sleek black dress. The plunging neckline and high slit running up the side are so revealing I might as well not wear anything.

I pair it with strappy heels that elongate my legs, giving the outfit the finishing touch. Standing in front of the mirror, I adjust the fabric slightly, then roll my shoulders back and straighten my posture.

When I return to the kitchen, Nikolai is waiting by the counter, eating. When he looks up, he stops chewing, his eyes roving down my body in slow motion. Then he swallows, unable to look away.

"Is that mine?" I point at the extra plate as I walk toward him.

He blinks, then looks down and pushes it toward me.

"Thanks." I accept it and stand next to him.

I take a bite of the wrap, my attention drifting to the living room. The men have shifted from their earlier conversation and are now lounging on the couches. Trixie sits perched on one guy's lap, whispering in his ear, while another girl giggles as her partner trails kisses down her neck.

The man Trixie is sitting on nods in my direction. He says something I can't hear, but Dante and Silvano follow his line of sight, their attention landing squarely on me.

"Damiano's," Dante responds quietly.

Both men's reactions are immediate. The one already halfway through foreplay with the girl on his lap whips his head toward me, his expression shifting to pure surprise.

"Damiano?" he repeats.

"Yeah," Dante confirms.

The man eye-fucks me a little too long. "That's too bad. She looks tight."

"You'll never find out," Dante snaps, cutting him off with an edge to his voice.

Whatever claim Damiano has on me, making me off-limits to others, is painted across this entire room. And not everyone seems happy about it—the men because they can't fuck me, and Trixie because I'm fucking him.

The uneasy silence stretches on before the conversation resumes. She shoots me a glare, and I know her hatred stems from thinking Damiano is hers.

I keep my expression neutral, ignoring her as I take another bite of my food. She is sadly mistaken. Damiano is *mine*, and I will get her back for that little stunt she pulled.

With Damiano off handling whatever situation pulled him away, the other brothers quietly excused themselves without much explanation. Only Nikolai had the decency to let me know they'd be back later tonight, offering to have someone take me home or stay here. I told him I'd hang out in my room, and with a nod, he strode off toward the Volkov wing.

As evening settles over the estate, more men arrive, filling the space with noise and movement. I try to distract myself with TV, but the restlessness creeping in makes it impossible to sit still.

I crack open my door and listen, straining to track the noise. When the voices start to fade, I slip out, treading lightly down the stairs and rounding the corner. Maybe Dom is back. If not, I'll find Nikolai.

It's getting dark, and Damiano has been gone all day. I'm antsy to see him, and I want to know what he's been doing. I hurry down the long corridor, but the noise of laughter and conversation grows louder.

"Hey!" someone shouts from behind.

I ignore the voice and keep walking, my steps quickening as I try to put distance between myself and whoever it is.

"We share," another voice chimes in.

I'm jerked back and slammed against the wall. A body presses into mine, trapping me in place.

"I was calling you," the man drawls, his breath fanning along my hair. His hands travel up my sides, intrusive and unwelcome.

"And I was ignoring you," I bite out, keeping my head turned to the side.

Another girl, Ruby, walks up, aiming a flirtatious grin at the group of men.

"Check her neck, Bobby," she says casually, wrapping herself around one of the other guys like it's a game she's used to playing.

He leans away, settling on my neck. The marking holds him captive as he studies it, and the second he grasps who put it there, his body tenses, and he pulls away.

A quiet shift in the air follows as he pivots and walks off, the rest of the group following as if nothing happened. As Ruby passes, she throws me a quick wink—a silent reassurance that she's on my side. I exhale slowly, mouthing a grateful *thank you* as they disappear from sight.

Relief washes over me, but it's fleeting. More men will come, and I know I can't keep slipping away unnoticed. My best chance at avoiding situations like that is to stay busy or near the Volkov brothers.

I talk one of the kitchen staff into letting me help, and she hands me a bowl of strawberries to slice for one of the alcoholic beverages. I keep my back turned from the gathering, concentrating on cutting.

Numerous times, I hear footsteps begin to approach me, only to be redirected by one of the guards.

It's almost like moths drawn to a flame.

Someone moves in, and I sense a hand reaching out for me.

"Touch her, and I'll snap your neck."

I don't even need to turn to know it's Dante. The man jerks back, his eyes widening as he takes a step away, raising his arms in surrender.

"Sorry, Mr. Volkov. I didn't know she was yours." Then he hurries off.

Dante leans against the counter next to me, facing the crowd, his knuckles whitening as he grips the edge.

"Thank you," I say, looking down at his broken hand. "Does it hurt?"

He's silent, then his head turns. "Not as bad as other things."

I don't grasp his meaning, but as we stare at each other, I feel like he's pleading with me to understand.

He straightens, smoothing his hand down his tie. "When the opportunity arises, I'm going to fuck you again."

The promise of his words hangs in the air, making my entire body stiffen. It's not a matter of *if*—it's a matter of *when*. Then he strides away.

I glance over my shoulder, watching him walk off—only to find Em observing the exchange with a questioning expression. Ignoring it, I turn back and continue slicing the strawberries.

When I finish, I'm told there's nothing more for me to help with. As I step out of the kitchen, men from all around the room take me in. I walk straight to Nikolai, who's deep in conversation with a group.

I run my fingertips along his back in acknowledgment, and his smile lets me know he doesn't mind me staying.

The girls around me shift as if following an unspoken script. Most have already paired off, slipping easily into the waiting arms of men. One by one, they disappear into the shadows, led away with a confident grip on their wrists. When they return, their faces are smooth, their smiles carefully arranged. And the cycle continues—a man claims them, leads them away, and before long, another does the same.

I try to count how many times it happens—how many times the same girls disappear, only to return later, just to be taken away again by someone new. The number rises too quickly, slipping beyond anything I can keep track of. But really, what's the point? I can't stop it. I can't stop them from being led away and brought back over and over. And honestly, I still don't understand why Damiano insists on keeping me to himself. I'm supposed to be one of the girls being used just as they are.

The room is busy, and the first couple times men walk by, they brush against my ass. I chalk it up to an accident until one hand almost makes it up the back of my dress. When I turn to look, he winks at me and keeps walking. My discomfort builds, growing stronger with each passing glance. When Nikolai starts to leave one group, I reach out and grab his hand.

"You're not leaving me with these freaks." I tighten my grip.

He gives me a reassuring squeeze, guiding me along with him.

For the next hour, I stay glued to his side, his presence the only thing keeping the unease at bay. I notice that Lacy, the girl Nikolai seems to favor, isn't here tonight. I wonder if he intentionally keeps her away on nights like this. Though she's absent, her friend Ariel has stepped into the protective *that's my man* role over Nikolai in her place, glaring at me since I approached him.

I start to dwell on it, but arms wrap around my waist, firmly pulling me against a solid chest. The sudden contact jolts through me, and strong fingers cradle my jaw, tilting my face toward him with a controlled possessiveness.

Damiano.

His mouth claims mine, the kiss searing and unapologetic, as if making up for the hours spent apart. The frustration I'd been holding onto over the tattoo vanishes, drowned by the sheer relief of his touch.

"Thanks," he murmurs, pulling back just enough for the word to slip out.

For a moment, I'm confused—until Nikolai's hand slips from mine and he steps away. I hadn't even realized I was still holding on to him.

Guests continue to stare, but with Dom here, their attention doesn't faze me. His presence ignites a newfound boldness because with him by my side, I feel untouchable. Turning in his embrace, I drape my forearms over his shoulders, letting my body sink into the comfort he offers. My muscles loosen, finally relaxing for the first time in what feels like hours.

"Busy day?" I ask, keeping my tone light.

"It's about to get even busier," he says, brushing his lips against mine again.

"Why's that?" I tilt my head, gazing up at him.

He leans closer, his mouth grazing the shell of my ear as he murmurs, "Because I'm going to tie you to our bed and have my way with you."

"Mmm," I hum, locking eyes with him. "Sooner rather than later, I hope."

A low laugh vibrates against me as his grip on my waist tightens. "You'll wish you hadn't said that, baby."

"Maybe," I reply. "But right now… you're coming with me."

"Oh yeah? And where are we going?"

I turn and tug him, urging him to follow. "You'll see."

He shrugs and falls in step behind me, his quiet confidence matching my determined stride. We weave through the crowded house, their chatter fading into the background as we climb the stairs. I lead him straight to Trixie's room and push the door open.

It remains untouched since the cleaners came through this morning, the bed perfectly made, pillows meticulously arranged. I turn back to Damiano, catching the way his smirk deepens as he watches me, intrigued.

"Get on the bed," I command.

His brow arches, eyes flicking around the room with curiosity. He doesn't argue, just makes his way to the bed, lowering himself onto the edge.

I step closer, jerking my chin toward the headboard. "Move back and lie down."

He obliges, leaning into the pillows with his arms tucked behind his head.

I slip out of my clothes, letting each piece fall into a heap at my feet. Kneeling onto the bed, my eyes lock onto his as I crawl forward, taking my time, heightening the anticipation with every inch I close between us until I'm straddling him.

My hands slide to the buttons on his shirt, working them loose one by one, then shift to the buckle of his pants, freeing his hard cock.

He follows my every move, but there's a trace of humor in his expression.

"Do I even want to know why we're in here?" he quips.

"Isn't it obvious?"

I wrap my fingers around him, stroking slowly at first, savoring the way his breath hitches under my touch. Without breaking eye contact, I position myself over him and sink down, a low, guttural moan slipping free as the sheer size of him stretches and fills me. My head tilts back, my eyes fluttering shut as I let the sensation consume me.

I find my rhythm, rolling my hips in slow circles, taking in every inch of him. He clamps onto my waist, guiding me. The room is charged, my panting mixing with his low groans.

When the door creaks open, it doesn't deter me—it fuels me. My pace quickens, the thrill of being caught only heightening the sensations. She wanted to fuck around, now she gets to find out.

"You cunt!" Trixie's furious shriek cuts through the air.

I glance back over my shoulder, rolling my eyes dramatically as I moan his name.

"Damiano," I groan as I pull him upright by his open shirt, his chest glistening with sweat.

His hand slaps down on my ass at the same time her horrified gasp rings out, and it's just as satisfying as her walking in to find me having sex in her bed. It's even more satisfying when she fully registers *who* is beneath me. Her eyes go wide, her jaw slack with shock as if her world has just shattered.

I keep my gaze locked on hers as I ride him—faster now—taking him deeper with each roll of my hips. He groans into my neck, his fingers digging into my ass as we both teeter on the edge.

A cry escapes me as he shudders beneath me, his release following mine. He falls back into the pillows, spent, while I slowly lift off him, deliberately angling my pussy toward her. I make sure she sees his semen slipping from me as I lean down to kiss him.

I glance toward the doorway where Trixie stands frozen, her face a volatile mix of rage and disbelief. I scoot myself across her bedding, then climb off, grabbing the edge of her perfectly folded comforter and wipe myself clean with it.

I smirk, smoothing the soiled fabric back as if nothing had happened.

"Oops." My voice drips with mock innocence. "Hope you don't mind."

Her silence is deafening, but the fury in her eyes is glorious. Her mouth remains slightly agape, incapable of a response as Damiano's low chuckle rumbles behind me. He rises from the bed, buttoning his shirt lazily as I slip my dress back into place before he slings an arm over my shoulder.

Together, we walk past her, my posture confident, a quiet triumph coursing through me.

"Oh, and Trixie, at least now you can honestly say that Damiano was fucked in your bed."

Chapter

THIRTY-TWO

Rainey

Damiano is spoiling me—so much so that I need to be near him constantly. I'm so accustomed to his presence that being apart from him is unsettling. This morning, he kissed me, murmured that he'd return after he took care of some stuff, and disappeared. But hours have passed, morning fading into afternoon, and now evening creeps in with no sign of him.

Every conversation at the main house revolves around the poker party happening tonight. The endless chatter leaves no doubt about where he is; I just don't understand why he didn't invite me to go along. Since he created this needy monster in me, he can deal with me hunting him down.

I make my way toward the front. The only way I know how to get to the secluded gathering spot is by following the route the van took the two times I've been out there. Something tells me that's where he'll be.

I wish he would work on communication, because this whole secretive shit is irritating the fuck out of me.

As I stride down the front steps, two guards step in front of me.

"Either move or you can deal with Damiano."

They look at each other, then part so I can pass.

As I make my way down what feels like a never-ending road, I'm thankful I decided to wear pants and boots—walking this in heels would have already given me blisters.

I hear what sounds like an ATV approaching and turn, hoping it's Dom, but this one is dark red. Marko slows to a stop next to me, leaning over in the seat.

"Need a lift?"

"Where are you headed?"

"Wherever you're needing to go," he replies easily.

I peer in the direction I was going, and all I see is road. "Can you take me to wherever the auction was?"

"Hop in. That's where I was headed."

I don't know if that was actually his destination, but it is now. If it were any of the other guards, I probably would have declined, but if I'm reading the signs correctly, this is Tess's "man," and he's always with Dom, Nikolai, or Silvano, which makes me think he can be trusted for a short ride.

He doesn't speak the entire way, and I'm glad because I don't want to make small talk. Though I always hear Tess and him laughing when they're in her room, so I assume he's quite funny.

We reach the house much faster than I could have on foot. I also might have ended up lost since the road veered off in two directions, and I would have taken the wrong one.

He parks by the front steps, and we both climb out. Two guards stand at attention at the bottom of the stairs leading to the front door. I meet their cold gazes, my heart thudding in my chest, but I'm determined to see him—and if I have to make a huge scene to do so, then I will.

"Damiano sent for me," I say firmly, willing my voice not to waver.

They look back at Marko, who nods as he approaches, and they step aside, granting me entry.

Coming through the front entrance is strange—every other time I've been here, it was through the back garage, shuffled discreetly down the corridors into one of their infamous "fun" rooms.

This is an entirely different experience.

The house is eerily quiet, the kind of silence that seems alive— watching, waiting. The wood floors are polished, without even a single scuff or smudge. Intricate woodwork lines the walls, and every surface gleams under the soft glow of well-placed lighting. It should feel warm, inviting even, but instead, it's hollow—like the soul of it has been stripped away.

My ears strain for any sound, and when I hear nothing, I head toward the stairs, descending into the belly of the house. The stillness presses in from all sides, amplifying each footstep. The luxurious surroundings make it all the more unnerving, offering no hint of life.

Workers move through the large casino room, men carrying crates of drinks, food, and decorations. I'm so out of place. I just stand here, taking it all in.

"Excuse me." I reach out slightly, signaling to the man carrying bottles of liquor.

He pauses and smiles when he sees me, then nods toward a hall at the end of the room. "Head straight back, through the double doors. He's down there."

I watch him go, still staring long after he's gone. He knew I was here for Damiano? So he also knows who I am.

That's kind of cool.

I follow the corridor he gestured to, relieved my instincts were right about finding him here. If he hadn't been, my brain would have conjured up all kinds of scenarios of him with one of the other girls. Now I want to yell at him just for that thought even creeping in, since he didn't tell me what he was doing.

I want no part of the activities that go on in this basement, so I'll be quick. I'll figure out when he's coming home and try to lure him back with me.

Faint voices reach me, drifting like whispers in the wind. I'm starting to second-guess myself. I don't think any of them will appreciate me interrupting, but you know what? Communication. If it's a problem, he needs to say so, and I've already made it this far.

Finally, I reach my destination, hovering over the handle briefly before thinking, *fuck it*, and pushing it open. The faint murmurs swell into a low hum of conversation, filling the area beyond.

My breath catches in my throat as I sweep over the room. The Volkov men are gathered, intimidating as always. But that's not what sends my stomach plummeting into a tailspin.

It's Jules. *My Jules*. My best friend.

Every pair of eyes shifts toward me as I take in the scene.

"That's not going to fucking happen," I say firmly, adding a touch of colorful language to the same words Damiano used with the man who paid for private time with me from the *Round Room*.

I position myself between Jules and the others. They should be glad Dom's gun isn't within arm's reach of me this time because I'd just start shooting.

"Baby, come here." Dom extends his hand toward me.

"She's a lesbian," I snap, glaring at him. "You can't be serious."

He takes a cautious step forward. "We're just talking. Come here so we can talk."

"Your next steps better involve grabbing your damn keys to take Jules out of here." I narrow my eyes at him.

A light touch rests on my shoulder, breaking my focus.

"Hey," Jules says softly, her voice calm as she tries to pull my attention back.

I keep my glare locked on him, then let her guide me. She turns me toward her and wraps her arms around me in a warm embrace. I pause, a dozen questions swirling in my mind—how she ended up here, what happened—but I don't ask. Instead, I squeeze her tightly, letting the silent comfort between us speak for itself.

"Are you okay?" she whispers.

"Yeah," I whisper back, though the word rings empty.

I don't know what to tell her. What to make of this situation.

When she releases me, she takes in my appearance and smiles. "You're so goddamn beautiful."

I want to return the smile, but I can't. "We need to go."

"Why don't we go for a walk so we can talk?" she suggests. There's something almost apologetic in her expression, and it stirs a pang in my chest.

"That's a good idea." I extend my hand to Damiano. "Give me your keys."

He shakes his head. "You're not leaving."

I want to haul off and hit all of them. Maybe if I wind my arm back far enough, I can get each of them in one swing.

"Come on," Jules coaxes, trying to steer my attention back to her.

"We can't just go for a walk. We are prisoners."

"Sure we can," she replies confidently.

"Niki, we need to debrief," Dante states.

Niki? Why did he call her Niki? They must have her confused with someone else.

Relief washes over me. This is just a misunderstanding. We can sort this all out, and they can take Jules out of here. Maybe I can talk Damiano into giving her some money so she can get out of that dumpy apartment and go somewhere safe.

My attention shifts to Dante, who suddenly looks a little uneasy. Then I glance back at Jules. Then back at Dante.

She has his nose.

Why does Jules have Dante's perfect nose?

I scan each brother and Jules. Then back to Nikolai. Then back to Jules. My stomach drops.

They're practically identical. The same sharp features, the same piercing gaze, the same flawless face— Valentina's face.

Back and forth, my eyes flick between the two of them, the realization settling over me.

I raise a finger, pointing at Nikolai, then at Jules, and back again. The words won't come, but my feet take a step back as the truth hits me square in the chest.

"My real name is Nikita Volkov," she states, taking a step closer and reaching out as if to steady the ground beneath us.

My mouth falls open, and I look between her and Nikolai, my brain scrambling to make sense of it.

"Twins," Damiano says, clearing up the confusion.

"Why the hell do I think your name is Jules?" I demand, my voice rising as I stare at her, waiting for an explanation.

She looks to Damiano, and he meets her gaze, but the silence between them stretches on. Not a single word is exchanged.

"Screw all of you," I snap, spinning on my heel and heading for the door.

"Baby, wait," Dom calls after me, his voice pleading.

"Let me," Jules—no, Nikita—says.

But I don't stop. My feet move faster than I thought possible, driven by anger. The gravel crunches beneath my boots as I storm away, not caring where I'm headed—just that I need to get out.

Damiano's house. My house. I don't even know anymore.

Everything is just an *illusion*.

"Rainey! Wait!" Her voice follows me, urgent and desperate, but I block it out.

I keep moving, my legs burning with the effort. She's not the Jules I knew. Not the best friend I trusted. She's someone else entirely, and right now, I can't stand the sight of her.

"Please! Just stop!" she yells again, her footsteps pounding behind me.

I whirl around, my fury spilling over. "What do you want from me?" I shout, my voice shaking with rage. "What could you possibly say to explain this? Because right now, it feels like my best friend—the only person who kept me sane, who was my safe place—inserted herself into my life on purpose just to set me up to be brought here."

She stops a few feet away, her face crumpling with emotion. "I will explain everything to you. I just need you to be willing to listen."

"Listen?" I scoff. "Do you even realize what you've done? Was any of it real? Were you real? Or was this all just some game to you? To your brother?" My words come out fast, hot, and harsh.

"It was real. All of it was real. You were my best friend. You still are. But my brother… he—he wanted you."

Her words hit me like a slap, the admission a fresh wound. My laugh is bitter and humorless. "Your brother?" I sneer. "That's real fresh. Were you aware that I was dragged here against my will to be a whore?"

She shakes her head. "He's an idiot. You were never brought here to be a whore."

My eyes widen with fury. "I was put up for auction! No—correction. I never even got the opportunity to be bid on like the worthless nobody that I am. I got to be your brother's birthday fuck! He took my virginity in front of a room full of people!"

She looks almost angry, and her next words punch the wind right out of my lungs. "And you took his! In front of the same people."

I stare at her, my mind reeling, trying to make sense of what she just said. I must have misheard. Surely, I misheard.

"Excuse me?" I brace myself against the tree beside me.

Her expression remains the same. "He was a virgin too, Rainey. Have you ever even asked about his past? About his trauma? Why do you think he never attends the auctions? Why do you think half the staff is furious that he went to his first-ever one for you? He's off-limits. He doesn't let people touch him—especially not women. He's a recluse who keeps to himself. Hell, he doesn't even let people in his house most of the time."

I think back to Valentina's slip—she had mentioned six sons before correcting herself, saying she had five sons who like sex.

No. It can't be.

He was so good.

"You're perfect for him," she continues, her voice softening. "And yeah, you can be mad that we lied, but from where I stand, this is a better life than what you were living, and my brother wanted you so badly that he set an entire plan in motion to make it happen. He might not always go about things the right way, but his heart is in the right place."

Bitterness creeps into my tone. "And when he decides he's had enough? Or wants something different? What then? Do you all just let me go? Or I end up six feet in the ground?"

Her gaze hardens. "He will never want something different. Do you have any idea how unsure we were that he'd even go through with having sex with you? But from what I hear, he's doing just fine."

My eyes widen, the heat creeping up my neck as memories flood back. Fine? He's incredible. If he was a virgin, he's nothing short of a natural.

"Well, I have to debrief. An explanation is part of it. Will you come back with me?" Her tone is hopeful, though her posture says she's bracing for rejection.

I hesitate, weighing my options. Part of me wants to say no, but I'm happy to see a familiar face, and despite myself, I'm happy it's her.

"When I first got here, after the auction, I had to stand naked in front of everyone. I was attacked by another man, and Damiano killed him on top of me. I was brought back to his house and fell asleep to the smell of you on his pillow. It was comforting. I never questioned why he would smell the same as you, but now it's obnoxiously clear. You all smell similar, actually. I can't believe I never pieced together you were their sister."

Just as I'm sure mom and I smelled similar—like stale cigarettes from the cartons she smoked each day inside our trailer.

"I still want to be best friends. I'll do anything to earn your trust again, Rainey."

I stare at her, not even sure where to begin to mend our friendship. "What do I call you?"

"If Jules is what you're comfortable with, that's fine. I prefer Niki, but for you, Jules is fine."

"Are you actually a lesbian?"

Her smile widens, teasing but genuine. "I go both ways but prefer women." She reaches out and tugs on my arm. "Come on. I have to do this with a bunch of testosterone-riddled men and don't want to be alone. They'll all be on their best behavior with you around since they all have fat crushes on you." She links her arm with mine and starts pulling me back.

Why are none of them married?" I ask the question I've wondered since I got here.

"You and Dom are to be married."

I lift my brows. "I don't see a ring."

"He can't leave the property. You'll have a ring. Ma tried to give him one of her rings, and he said he didn't want her leftovers. As for my other brothers—Nikolai and Lacy are kinda seeing each other, I guess. Gio sleeps with whoever is available when he is. Andrei has like four different girls that he rotates through or just brings them all back to his room. Silvano will sleep with whatever girl was tested most recently, and her results were clean. And Dante is practically exclusive with Em."

I turn my head toward her in surprise. "Why be exclusive if you plan on cheating?"

"They wouldn't. Hence, nobody being exclusive except you and Dom."

"But you just said Dante and Em are exclusive," I say, confused.

She smiles. "I said practically. Dante hasn't slept with anyone besides Em for a couple of years. His house is being built on the other side of our parents' house. He'll probably have Em move in with him."

I want to laugh. I want to be descriptive when I say that him sleeping with only Em is not true at all—that I personally know just how untrue that statement is because Dante's big-ass cock fucked me in the *Round Room* and practically promised he's going to fuck me again. But I'm not going to stir up trouble. And I like Em. I definitely don't want her to know he basically cheated on her with me. I may have been chained to the wall with no escape, but I wanted him every bit as much as he wanted me.

"What would happen if Dante found out she slept with someone else?"

She shrugs. "It's different being one of the women working. You do as you're told. Ultimately, the man having sex with the woman is responsible for any fallout that may come from the interaction. Whatever man is bold enough to sleep with Em will face whatever punishment Dante deems appropriate if he has a problem with it."

"And if Em initiated it with someone else?"

"Doesn't matter. The outcome would be the same. The man would deal with the consequences of going through with it. She's a worker. She will be innocent of all wrongdoing."

I shake my head, pushing away my thoughts.

Stay in your own lane, Rainey Lane.

We enter the same room as before. The men are gathered around the large table, their eyes flicking toward us the moment we step in. Damiano stands when he sees me, but he doesn't move any closer.

I walk toward him, stopping just a couple of feet away, my eyes narrowing as I stare at him. "You were a virgin?"

"I was."

"Why me?" I ask, searching his face.

His answer is simple. "Because I couldn't stay away."

"Why did you force us both to lose our virginities in front of all those people?"

"To send a message that you are mine and I am yours."

"And you ripped my butt open, saying any hole that wasn't claimed would be fair game to anyone else. But you wouldn't have let someone else near me, so why did you do that?" I ask pointedly.

"I'd never been inside either hole. I wanted to feel yours."

"And?" I'm not sure what I'm expecting him to say, but I wait for his response.

"And it was incredible."

I chew on the inside of my cheek, mulling over his words. It was embarrassing, but he's right—it did feel incredible.

"Fine."

Stepping toward him, I close the distance.

He sits back down, his gaze locked on me, watching intently as I approach. He holds his arms out slightly—an open invitation, waiting for me to settle.

I ease into his lap, and when I do, his arms wrap tightly around me, pulling me flush against his chest as he exhales into the back of my neck.

Everyone seems to want to focus on me, so I glance around the table. "What? I thought we wanted Niki's account of everything. No need to gawk."

At that, everyone turns their attention back to her.

"I want to start by saying that all of it was worth it to me because my brother got you." She stares directly at me as she smiles, her beautiful… Nikolai smile.

"And getting to know you, seeing your struggles firsthand—even though you never wanted to talk about them—you became my best friend. Truly. And if Dom decided you weren't what he wanted after all, I was going to fight every other brother of mine to make you mine."

I'm not sure how to respond. That confession settles over me, sending a warm, fuzzy sensation through me.

"It's rare when my brother talks. It's even rarer for him to ask for something. And in the twenty-seven years I've known him, he's never—not once—asked me for anything. So when he came to me and asked for help, I didn't even question it. I didn't care what he needed me to do. I would have done anything."

I notice when she looks back at him, and the quiet way he acknowledges her.

"The original plan," she explains, turning her attention back to me, "was for me to befriend you. Then I'd introduce you to my brother. Simple enough, right?" Her tone grows wry, as if recalling how naïve that initial plan had been. "But while hanging out at that shithole of a bar where you worked, I realized there was more going on. The drug dealers from my apartment complex used to hang out there too. That's when Dom asked me to figure out if they were getting their supply from Cristiano.

"I didn't realize how easy it would be to confirm Cristiano's involvement. That part was a piece of cake. You, on the other hand, were the hard part. Befriending you wasn't as simple as I thought it'd be. And when your home life got worse and you refused to move out, you weren't exactly in a position where meeting a man, any man, was going to go well. That's when Dom stepped in. And, well, everything after that is history.

"Cristiano has been circling closer, somehow staying undetected. Sightings have popped up here and there, but nothing solid. Most nights, when I was at the bar, the men would brag about stupid shit, but after a few too many beers, their lips would loosen. That's when I got confirmation—Cristiano's been supplying drugs through the city. The guys from my apartment? They were getting their stash directly from the warehouse where the shootout happened.

"Word got out that I was asking questions. I got home after a fourteen-hour drive, completely dead on my feet, and that's when they jumped me. I was thrown in the back of a car. I pretended to be unconscious, and when they stopped, I managed to get free— but my phone was left behind in the car. That's why it pinged at the warehouse.

"I had to go into hiding after that. Ricky Moretti took me in. Apparently, having Damiano Volkov as a brother means people think twice about messing with you."

Her amusement is unmistakable. "He welcomed me—well, sort of. More like he strong-armed Papa into an alliance, claiming he wouldn't let me go otherwise. Pa wasn't exactly thrilled. He told Ricky no deal, so Ricky said he'd torture me." She smirks, the edge in her voice almost playful. "Spoiler: they didn't do shit. Obviously. Otherwise, I wouldn't be sitting here."

Her smile widens, her tone carrying a note of triumph. "Pa threatened to send Dom after them if they didn't let me go. And here I am. Mission accomplished."

She leans back, her beautiful smile as radiant as ever.

WHEN THE POKER PARTY BEGINS, EVERYONE SHUFFLES OUT, LEAVING Dom and me alone. I stay seated, turning toward him and wrapping my arms around his shoulders as I cross my legs.

"You're not very good at this relationship stuff," I remark, lifting my brows.

"I know. I'm trying, though."

"Why would you have me brought in as a whore?" I keep my voice light but pointed.

His head falls back, and he lets out a long, exaggerated sigh, like he's been through this conversation in his head more than once. "To keep you pliant, I suppose."

I blink at him, incredulous. "I was literally offering myself to you on the bus."

"Yeah," he acknowledges. "But I had a plan in motion, and I didn't want to deviate."

"That's got to be one of the dumbest things I've ever heard."

He dips his chin in a lazy nod. "Yep."

"So, what's next? Do we have to get married and, as part of the vows, sacrifice a virgin or something?"

He chuckles, the sound deep and genuine. "We already gave up our virginities, so I think that's all the sacrifice we need to offer up."

"Good." I comb my fingers through his hair. "I'm glad I didn't know how good sex felt. I would have totally slept with the man who got my purse back and the guy on the bus." I wink.

His lips brush against mine softly. "What about the man who tried to buy your dinner at the café? The one you wouldn't give your number to—even after you ruined his burger by piling fourteen inches of fries on top of it."

I smile at him, confused, then my expression falls flat as realization dawns. My mouth drops open, and I smack his shoulder. He laughs, pulling me in for another kiss.

When he pulls away, I shake my head. "So, do you come here often?" I echo his own words from that night.

His grin widens as he captures my lips again. "You totally would have slept with that guy. He was smooth."

I nod. "I would have fucked him on the stool, on the floor, on the bar, on the sidewalk—anywhere he wanted."

"You should show me all the ways you would have had sex with him."

I sigh playfully. "I don't know about that. I might have to worry about your dick."

He tightens his arms around me, a teasing glint in his eyes. "Worry? There's nothing to worry about with it. He's perfectly healthy."

"Is he? He was in my butt—he's super dirty now," I tease, pinching his side lightly.

He nips at my jaw. "Mmm, we haven't done that in a while. It sounds fun."

"I'm down."

We settle into a quiet, comfortable moment, the distant sound of laughter drifting in from just beyond the door.

"So… we're confined to the property. Is this, like, forever? Or…?"

"For now," he replies.

I wrinkle my nose. "That's such a lame answer."

He sighs softly. "Sorry. It's all I've got for now. Wanna go gamble? Or…" His voice drops suggestively. "Do butt stuff?"

I laugh as I stand and take his hands, pulling him to his feet. "Butt fuck," I confirm, letting him lead me away.

Chapter
THIRTY-THREE

Damiano

I gave Dante three extra days to come up with a solution for Mat-thews. Now, I want answers.

When I walk into his office, he doesn't look surprised—just lifts his gaze from the screen in front of him. He knew I'd be back. He knows exactly why I'm here.

Without waiting for an invitation, I drop into the chair across from him, leaning back and crossing my arms.

He doesn't waste time with pleasantries. Instead, he turns his monitor toward me so I can see the large sum of numbers on the screen.

"And that is?" I ask, uninterested.

"How much Trixie makes us."

I scoff. "I don't care how much she makes us. I'm not here about her." But he already knows that.

He exhales, running a hand through his hair, leaning back in his chair. "What's your plan?"

"That's what I'm here to figure out." My fingers drum against the armrest as I consider my next course of action. "I don't want Rainey thinking for even a second that I'd touch someone like Trixie. But more than that… I don't like people using my house like it's some damn brothel."

He leans forward to rest his elbows on the desk. "So, you want her out?"

I pause, letting the thought settle. "Yes. But you know what I want more right now."

He nods, lips pressing into a thin line.

"Did you talk to him yet?"

"No," he replies. "I'm leaving it up to your discretion. My advice? Let him explain himself. But if you need him for closure, I support you."

"Thanks."

Silence lingers between us as I weigh my options. I reach across the desk, pick up Dante's phone, and dial Matthews.

"Hey, come to my office," I say. Matthews agrees immediately, and I hang up.

Nobody can tell our voices apart over the phone. If I had called him myself, he might've second-guessed it. But Dante's office phone? He'd never question that.

I fire off a quick text to Silvano and Marko, instructing them to wait just outside. If Matthews tries to leave, they're not to let him.

Minutes later, a knock echoes through the room.

"Come in," Dante calls.

Matthews enters, and his relaxed expression vanishes as soon as he sees me sitting there. His brows lift as uncertainty flashes across his face.

"Sit." Dante nods to the chair beside me.

He falters, then moves toward it, his steps cautious. "Everything good, boss?" He flicks his gaze between the two of us.

I shake my head. "No. Not at all."

Reaching for my phone, I place it on the desk in front of him, angling it so he can see the footage playing. His own face stares back at him—him and Trixie, tangled together, in my house.

His eyes widen. Hands lifting in surrender, he stammers, "We had permission to be there."

"And who exactly gave you permission to be in my house?" My voice is even, but there's no mistaking the edge beneath it.

"Trixie said you did."

I lift a brow. "Trixie told you that you had permission to have sex in my house? The house no one is allowed in?"

He shakes his head quickly. "I—I don't know. She kept teasing me with sex, then never putting out, and when she finally said she would, she told me to meet her at your place because…" He swallows hard. "She said you wanted to watch or some shit."

The words leave his mouth, and silence settles over the room as he realizes just how far-fetched it sounds.

I lean forward. "Do I strike you as the kind of man who watches a worker get railed by a front gate security guard?"

He opens his mouth, but nothing comes out.

I continue. "You don't even work inside the house, and yet you thought you'd be permitted inside my personal home? While my girlfriend was there? Alone?"

His panicked gaze shifts to Dante, searching for an ally. But Dante just crosses his arms and stares, offering him nothing.

Matthews exhales, shoulders sagging. "I never questioned it. I just wanted to fuck her."

I shake my head slowly. "What should happen to you?"

His face drains of color, like he hadn't considered that there would be consequences.

"I—uh…" He wipes the sweat from his hairline. "I should have to pay for her services?"

A dry chuckle escapes me. "You went to my house. You had sex with Trixie in my house. And you think all that should happen is you pay for something that was already offered to you for free?"

I observe as realization sets in. He knows he's done.

"I—I have a kid on the way," he blurts out, desperation creeping into his voice.

I tilt my head slightly, unimpressed. "Congratulations?" My tone is flat, making sure he knows I don't really care.

"Damiano, please," he chokes out. "I swear, I would never intentionally cross a line. I really thought we had permission."

I lean back in my chair, letting him squirm as the silence stretches. Finally, I speak. "I came back right after. How was this plan supposed to work if you thought you were there for me to watch? You left out the back afterward. If you thought you were allowed there, why didn't you come say hello?"

His mouth opens, then closes. He looks like he's grasping for an answer but coming up empty.

"I—I don't know. I really don't want any problems. I'm sorry. That's all I can say. I'm really fucking sorry."

I arch a brow. "You don't want problems, but you had sex with Trixie in my house, snuck out the back as I was walking in—all while you have a pregnant wife at home?" I shake my head. "That about sum it up?"

His Adam's apple bobs as he swallows. "I'm sorry."

I let his words hang in the air. "So this is the final version of the story? This is your last chance to come clean."

His lips part, hesitation flickering across his face, but then he nods. "Yes."

I stand and stride toward the door. As I step out, Silvano and Marko both straighten from where they're leaning against the wall.

"Go get Trixie," I tell Silvano then turn to Marko. "Get a sedative ready. When you get back, come inside. When I give you the signal, sedate him."

Marko nods once in understanding and disappears down the hall.

I reenter the office, but this time, instead of sitting, I move to the other side of Dante's desk and lean against the desk behind him, my arms crossed as I stare down at Matthews.

"Am I going to lose my job?" he asks.

I don't answer. He's worried about losing his job when he should be asking if he's going to walk out of here alive.

A knock sounds at the door.

"Come in," I say, not taking my eyes off him.

Silvano enters with Trixie right behind him, seeming content until she sees Matthews sitting here.

"Come in," I repeat.

Silvano remains by the door, while Marko stands a couple of steps behind Matthews. Trixie stands toward the back, shifting uncomfortably.

"You told me you were assaulted. Was he the one who did it?"

Her eyes dart between me and Matthews, eventually settling on me. "I—I don't know...I didn't see who it was."

I tilt my head. "Do you want to try that again?"

Panic flickers across her face as she realizes I'm not playing. She glances at Dante, but he looks just as irritated.

"He's been harassing me," she says quickly, latching onto a new story. "I didn't want to complain, but I started to worry he was going to sneak into my room—"

"What the fuck! You bitch." Matthews snaps, moving to stand, but Marko grips his shoulder, shoving him back down.

Trixie's voice wavers, but she keeps going. "I went to your house to talk to you about it. I saw him following me. When I got inside, only Rainey was there. We talked briefly, and then Matthews came in. I didn't want her in any danger, and then he at-tacked me."

"What the fuck, Trixie?" Matthews growls, gaping at her.

I stare at her pointedly, making it clear I find her just as guilty as him, keeping my tone void of emotion. "You're the one who makes us money. One of you is going to die for what you both did." I let the words settle before giving her the choice. "You can decide. Do you want to die, or should it be him?"

"Oh, fuck no!" Matthews shouts, struggling against Mar-ko's hold.

"Him," Trixie blurts, pointing at him. "I didn't do anything."

"You fucking bitch!" Matthews spits as he pushes up from the chair—just as I nod to Marko.

The needle pierces his neck, and his hand flies up, clutching the spot, realization setting in too late.

I push off the desk and step forward, watching as his body sways. "See you downstairs," I tell him as his eyelids flutter and his body slumps.

Silvano and Marko move in, lifting him between them and hauling him out.

I turn back to Trixie, who stands frozen in place. "You being a slimy person just signed his death certificate," I tell her. "I hope it was worth it."

Without another glance, I stride out of the room.

MATTHEWS IS TIED TO A CHAIR IN FRONT OF ME, HIS BODY SLUMPED forward as he starts to stir. I sit across from him, forearms resting on my thighs, watching as his head lolls side to side. A low groan escapes him as his eyes flutter open, blinking sluggishly as he fights off the effects of the sedative. His gaze finally locks onto mine, and the realization of where he is immediately kicks in, waking him fully.

"Damiano, I have a son on the way." His voice is hoarse, thick with desperation.

I shrug, unmoved. "You didn't care about your son when you were chasing tail to my doorstep."

Regret flashes in his eyes. "No, and I apologize."

His breathing grows uneven, panic settling in. "Please! I'll do anything. Anything you want."

I lean back, leveling him with a cold stare. "I've spent so much time trying to earn Rainey's affection. She was mistakenly taken to the *Round Room* when she wasn't supposed to be. It terrified her. And she was purchased—my girlfriend was purchased. I happened to be walking by at the exact moment it happened. I'm still cleaning up the aftermath." I shake my head. "You added to the hardship."

His shoulders shake, his eyes growing glossy with unshed tears. "I never meant to cause problems. I swear, I'll do anything to fix this."

Even if I considered Dante's input, it still wouldn't change the outcome today. Rainey was devastated, and for that alone, I shake my head at him.

He swallows hard. "Are you going to torture me?"

"You've never been an issue," I admit. "You've been loyal for two years. So, I'll let you decide how it ends."

A choked sound leaves him as tears spill down his face. His throat bobs as he struggles to speak, then he gives a single nod. "Bullet." His voice cracks.

I hold his gaze, then nod.

Standing abruptly, I reach for my gun. He doesn't even have time to process it before I press the barrel to his forehead and pull the trigger.

The shot rings out, and his body slumps, head falling back, his lifeless eyes still wide with shock.

Actions have consequences.

And Matthews just learned that the hard way.

Chapter

THIRTY-FOUR

Rainey

The weekly parties are starting to annoy me. I'm tired of watching the girls being used, tired of the empty conversations where I ask Tess if she's okay, only for her to seem genuinely annoyed by the question. She always brushes it off with the same dismissive response: "It's all part of it," before carrying on like none of it bothers her. But it bothers me.

Thankfully, our house is far enough away from the main house that most of the time, I can pretend they're not happening. Dom and I usually stay home, wrapped up in our own little world, while everyone else does whatever it is that they do. On nights when Dom is working, Niki comes over to keep me company.

If there's one thing all the Volkovs seem to have in common, it's their relentless secrecy. None of them give anything away—not without a fight. I've learned not to ask questions about what

Dom does when he's away, and I never press for details. Every now and then, if he seems particularly tense, I'll try a casual "Rough day?" His responses are always clipped, half-hearted at best, as if he doesn't have the energy to unpack it—or doesn't want to.

Tonight, the evidence of his "rough day" is impossible to miss. When he walks in, he's clearly tried to clean himself up, but there's still blood streaked across his clothes. It's never his own, but I still always subtly look over every inch of him to make sure he's not injured.

Niki and I both freeze, our conversation forgotten as we watch him kick off his boots by the door.

"Rough day?" I ask, keeping my voice light.

"It was fine," he says curtly, already heading toward the bedroom.

"Did you not want a kiss?" I call after him.

He walks back, leans over the couch, and presses his lips to mine. Without another word, he turns and walks away.

I glance at Niki, whose wide eyes match my own. "Is that how fucking annoying I sounded the entire time we used to hang out?" she whispers.

"Yep."

She smirks and nudges me with her elbow. "You weren't any better."

"Yep," I let out a laugh.

We both turn our attention to the front window as Nikolai makes his way up the porch stairs.

"Oh goodie, your wannabe boyfriend is here now," she mocks playfully.

I raise a brow at her, confused by the comment, but offer Nikolai a smile as he walks in.

"What's up, troublemakers?" he greets, plopping down between us.

"We were talking about you," Niki says casually, not missing a beat.

"Why?"

"I was just telling Rainey how hairy your butt is."

He flashes a wide, shameless grin, nodding in mock approval. "Nice."

Niki smirks. "So why are you here? We were having a girls-only chat."

"Dante says we're all required to show up at the party tonight," Nikolai replies, reclining against the couch.

"Fun," she says dryly. She stands, brushing off her pants and holding a hand out to me. "Let's go to the spa. If we have to go, we might as well look good."

NIKI PRACTICALLY DRAGS ME DOWN THE HALLWAY AFTER WE FINISH getting pampered. When we step into her room, she heads straight to the closet, rifling through a sea of dresses.

"I have just the thing." She pulls out a red, sparkly number that practically glows under the light. The fabric is tight, with a deep neckline that dips scandalously low and two thin straps meant to hold it together on my shoulders. The chest area is loose and draped just enough to give it a hint of elegance despite its daring cut.

"You can't wear a bra with this," she adds matter-of-factly. "But trust me, your boobs will look so incredible, you won't care."

She wasn't wrong. I shimmy into the dress, and when I glance in the mirror, I can't stop staring. It molds to my body, emphasizing every dip and curve in the most flattering way.

"I told you." She winks, already pulling out her phone. "I'm texting Dom to bring you some heels."

As she taps away on her screen, she crosses the room to pick out a pair of earrings. "Want to borrow a pair?"

"My ears aren't pierced, actually," I admit casually.

She looks up at me, blinking in disbelief. "Wait… like, for real?"

I nod.

She sets her phone down and walks over, moving my hair to the side to check for herself. "Holy shit, I thought you were joking."

A knock echoes through the room. Niki strides over to open the door, and Damiano steps in, holding my heels by their straps. The second he sees me, he stops, his eyes scanning me from head to toe.

I do the exact same to him. He's fucking stunning.

His black suit is perfectly tailored—so much so that I don't even want him going anywhere other women's eyeballs will be.

"Take it off," I say after we stare at each other for what feels like forever.

He arches a brow, momentarily confused, and I point a finger at him, motioning up and down his body. "You look too good. I'm going to suck on every inch of you. Take the suit off."

He winks, then walks toward me, holding the heels out.

"Lame," I mutter, snatching them from him. Turning away, I stride back to the bench at the end of Niki's bed and slip them on, fastening the straps. When I stand, I catch her giving him a once-over.

"You could've at least worn a tie to match her dress," Niki teases.

He looks down at his tie, then meets her gaze, shrugs, and extends his hand to me.

I approach, wrapping my arms around him. "Can we just go home? I'll act injured, and you can carry me out, and we can go hump or something. Really, I'm down for whatever if you get me out of here."

He kisses the tip of my nose. "No." Then turns, pulling me along.

We descend the stairs together, Niki leading the way. We walk farther to get to the location where the house is packed—a swirl of laughter, music, and conversation reverberating through the walls. As we move along the large corridor, I dread every step that brings us closer to the gathering.

The women are provocatively stunning in outfits that barely cover their bodies, and guilt creeps in for being spared from the things they'll be subjected to tonight.

On the outskirts of the party, some men press women against the walls, taking them fast and hard, indifferent to who's watching. Others are led away, disappearing behind closed doors. A few women settle onto men's laps, their voices carrying over the music as they lean in close, while others cling to groups of men, their bodies on display as hands drift over bare skin. The attention is eagerly absorbed, each interaction feeding the hedonistic pulse of the room.

The intensity of it all is too much, too fast, and I'm sure I'm going to vomit. The overwhelming noise, the suffocating crowd—it all presses down on me. Desperate for something to ground myself, I grab a champagne flute from a passing tray and down the entire thing in one go.

Damiano's gaze tracks my every move.

Setting the empty glass on another tray, I wrinkle my nose. "I hate these stupid parties."

His laughter is low and rich, keeping a steady touch on the small of my back, guiding me forward as we navigate the crowd.

We can barely take a few steps without someone stopping him to talk. I watch the way he handles it. He doesn't enjoy these parties either; I can see it in the subtle tension in his jaw, the way he never even tries to smile. Yet he moves through the conversations with ease.

I can't help but marvel at him—the way his mouth moves when he talks, the way his perfect teeth fit in his perfect mouth.

It's ridiculous how captivated I am by something as simple as him speaking.

A man joins the group we're standing with, and lo and behold, Trixie is on his arm. She giggles at everything he says, clinging to him as if he hung the moon. It's almost comical how convinced he is that she's madly in love with him. I can practically see the hearts bulging out of his eyes.

And Trixie? Her heart eyes are all for Damiano. Every time he's talking, she looks at him like he's the only man in the room.

But as I watch her fawn over him, all I can think about is how his cock was in me just hours ago—and how, after this, it will be again. The thought fills me with a twisted satisfaction that warms me more than the champagne.

I keep drinking, flute after flute, just trying to get through the night. By the time I'm more drunk than buzzed, the party starts to become a little more tolerable—or maybe I've just stopped caring.

I look around at the people here and find it weird how most of these men are attractive, yet they're as slimy as they come.

"Let's leave," I whisper.

He looks down at me, and without giving him a chance to tell me no, I add, "Or go somewhere private. I want you to finger me or something."

He smiles and leans in to kiss me.

"I'll do anything you want as soon as we get home," he murmurs in my ear.

I grin up at him. "I'll be drenched by then if you keep standing here looking so mouthwatering."

He winks and spanks my butt.

Letting out a sigh, I scan the room again. They should sage this house. Most of these men ooze evil.

"I need to pee," I tell him.

He kisses me softly. "Okay, baby."

In the bathroom, I delay leaving far longer than necessary, partly because the room won't stop spinning but mostly because I don't want to go back out there. The men here are sleazeballs, every one of them. And every time I come to something like this, I'm reminded that it's Dom's family behind it all. They're no different. Just as complicit.

I brace myself against the wall, debating how much longer I can hide, when a knock startles me. With a sigh, I straighten up, steadying myself.

Trixie stands in the doorway, her eyes narrowing as she levels me with a dirty look.

I meet her glare with one of my own. When she doesn't move, I roll my eyes and step toward her. If she chooses to block my way, fine. We'll see who ends up on the ground—her, me, or both of us. At this point, I don't care.

"Your weird little friend was requesting you out back," she says, sounding utterly annoyed.

I pause, cocking an eyebrow. My voice is flat, matching her attitude. "Who?"

She shrugs dramatically. "I don't know her name. The one glued to your nipple," she sneers, rolling her eyes as she saunters past me. She doesn't miss the chance to shoulder-check me on her way out.

It makes me stumble back into the doorway, the room spinning even more than it already was.

"Bitch," I mutter as annoyance flares.

I head toward the back door, letting the cool night air brush against my skin as I step outside. It feels good, soothing against the suffocating heat and noise from inside. Even better, it cuts through the haze from all the champagne I downed.

Hanging onto the rail for balance, I descend the patio stairs, scanning the darkened yard. I assume the "friend" Trixie mentioned must be Tess. My suspicions are confirmed when I spot her rounding the corner, her face lighting up when she sees me.

"Were you looking for me?"

She stops a few feet away, her expression shifting to one of confusion. "I was told *you* were looking for me."

I glance around the shadowed yard, thinking I heard something. "Weird. Who told you that?"

"Trixie," she replies, her tone edged with suspicion. "Are you drunk?"

"It's the only way I can even stomach these stupid things," I admit with a groan.

She shakes her head. "You, my darling, picked the wrong career. Why don't we get you inside so you can sit down? Maybe Damiano should take you home."

"Yeah," I agree, secretly hoping my tipsy state will convince him to call it a night and get me out of here.

She scans the yard. "I wonder why Trixie sent us both looking for each other?"

Rolling my eyes, I reach for her. "Because she's an idiot."

Together, we turn toward the house, only to stop dead in our tracks.

Five figures step out of the shadows by the stairs, their presence looming, unmistakably threatening.

"Well, well, isn't it a beautiful evening, ladies?" one of them says, his deep voice carrying a sinister edge.

"Sure is," I reply, my tone clipped as I move to step around them.

The man in front reaches out, clamping around my arm. "Not so fast, slut," he growls, his lips curling into a wicked sneer. "We heard two bitches were looking for some cock."

"Get on your knees. Both of you," the tallest man commands.

Tess immediately drops to the ground, her compliance automatic. I, on the other hand, stand frozen, my body refusing to move.

"Damiano is waiting for us." I straighten my shoulders and lift my chin.

They smirk, moving to their belts. One of the men steps toward Tess, unzipping his pants and pulling himself free. He presses forward into her face, and she opens her mouth to take him in.

"Fuck," I whisper, panic surging as I glance toward the house, desperately weighing my chances.

I decide to run, bolting to the side in an attempt to dodge them, but a foot juts out, and I go down hard. Pain shoots through my hands and knees as they slam against the concrete, blood smearing beneath me.

"I'm Damiano's," I gasp, forcing my voice louder.

A rough hand yanks me upright by my hair, pain ripping a cry from my lips. I claw at his wrist, my nails digging into his flesh as I twist and thrash, but his grip remains firm.

"You think that means something to me?" he taunts, his breath hot against my face as his arm coils around my waist.

Revulsion floods my system as his erection presses against me, and I rear back, driving my elbow into his ribs. He grunts, his arm tightening painfully, then he shoves me toward the iron patio table.

My palms slap against the cool surface, stinging from the impact. As I push myself upright, my arm is grabbed, and I'm jerked around.

"Don't touch me!" I scream, shoving at him. He stares down at the angry welts along his chest, then starts laughing, the sound cruel and mocking.

He swings out, the backhand snapping my head to the side. Stars burst in my vision, but even as I stagger, I lash out, my fists swinging blindly.

"Let me go!" I twist in their hold, another strike landing on my stomach and knocking the air from my lungs as I fold over.

"You're making this worse for yourself," one growls, grabbing my wrist to pull me in. I yank free, clawing at his face, leaving bloody streaks that earn me a shouted curse.

"Hold her down!" another barks.

Chairs from the table are kicked aside. The metal clatters loudly, a sound that rings in my ears as my heart thunders. My body aches, scalp burning from the pull of my hair, but I refuse to stop fighting.

I'm dragged onto my back, splayed across the table with my arms pinned above me.

My chest heaves as I glare at the man looming over me, his smirk filled with sadistic glee as he slams his palm into my temple. My vision blackens as my dress is yanked down, my breasts spilling free. My brain tells my body to cover itself, but my body remains limp.

A guttural groan follows. "Perfect tits," one mutters, swinging down, striking me hard across my chest.

I yelp at the sting, pain radiating through me, but it only spurs him on, and he does it again. My struggles intensify, my legs kicking wildly, but they hold me firm. Rough hands grab and squeeze, alternating between kneading and slapping as another man lowers his mouth to my nipple, biting and sucking with agonizing force.

I scream with everything in me. Even when the heavy hand smashes down over my mouth, the impact jarring my jaw as pain shoots through my face, I still scream.

Blood pools on my tongue, the coppery taste thick and nauseating. But even with the pain, even as my drunken body and brain struggle to communicate with each other, I don't stop fighting. My nails dig into anything they can, my legs lash out, and I thrash until my muscles ache.

None of it seems to matter.

None of it compares to the horror of what comes next.

My panties are torn away, and my fear heightens to an all-time high. I kick my legs frantically, desperate to break free, but there are too many hands—strong hands gripping my thighs and ankles, forcing me open.

I convince myself that the sound of the buckle unfastening and the zipper lowering *isn't real.* Even as a body forces its way between my legs, I tell myself *this isn't real.*

The rape begins, and my mind fights to escape, slipping somewhere far away as my body is pinned and violated.

I struggle to focus, to sober myself enough to keep fighting, but my face throbs from the blows. My nose, jaw, and lip sting, the open wounds burning. I try not to feel. Not the intrusion, not the pain, not the humiliation.

"Fuuuck," one of them groans, his voice thick with depravity. "She's as good as promised."

Every part of me is being assaulted—my breasts, my core, my face as it's hit with a penis, my heel being pulled off, and my foot is being rubbed against another man.

Fingers jam down my throat, triggering my gag reflex as my eyes burn. I twist to the side, retching violently.

Laughter surrounds me, loud and merciless. Hands seize me, yanking me off the table only to slam me back down on my stomach. A cock forces its way into my mouth, so deep the gagging turns to heaving. My body convulses, but the strikes come faster— fists, slaps, blows from every direction. One lands hard enough to rip me from consciousness.

Darkness.

I resurface to blinding pain. A sharp thrust into my butt tears through me, my vision tunneling as I choke on a scream. A heavy hand cracks against my skin. Again. And again. And again.

My hair is ripped back so hard my neck strains, and I wish my neck would break. A hand clamps around my throat, squeezing until my face tingles, and I wish he'd finish it. Squeeze harder. End it. Anything to make it stop.

I'm yanked upright, dragged off the table, and shoved to the ground. My bloodied knees slam against the cement, the sting barely registering against the all-consuming agony. A scream rips from my throat as fabric—maybe a tie—is shoved into my mouth. Another piece wraps tightly around my head, gagging me completely.

My arms are wrenched behind my back, my wrists bound with another tie. I thrash, my muffled cries breaking through the gag as tears stream down my face. But my efforts are futile; he holds me down with cruel strength, slamming into me while my body aches with every thrust. Each time they withdraw, I falsely believe it's over.

I'm jerked upright, shoved forward onto the chest of another man, my head spinning, the world tilting dangerously. My body no longer feels like my own—until I sense another presence behind me.

My panic turns to icy dread as he presses against my back entrance. *Not both at the same time. God, not two.* A sob catches in my throat, the fabric gag muffling it as my head is yanked back. My vision blurs, and I stare up at the night sky, wishing—praying—that my soul could escape this body and float away with the stars.

The world fades in and out, my mind clinging desperately to one thought: Damiano. His smile, the way he holds me, the way he looks at me as if I'm his entire world.

But I know, deep down, that he'll never look at me the same again.

Over and over, I'm tossed around like a rag doll. One man forces himself inside me while another takes me from behind. When they're finished, I'm handed off like an object, my body barely able to keep up with the cycle of brutality and pain.

My face is shoved into the grass, the cold blades scraping against me as the assault continues. Voices blur in the background—laughing, murmurs, jeers—but none of it makes sense. The world around me becomes distant, a muffled haze.

I lose track of how many turns they take, how many times I'm spanked and hit, my mind retreating to escape the searing pain and the unrelenting horror of it all. Blood pools from too many places to count, and I just want it to end—for death to release me from this nightmare.

Eventually, the assault slows. Whether because they've decided they've had enough or because their flaccid cocks can no longer work, I don't know. I'm shoved off the man below me, falling on my shoulder as I groan in pain.

"Fucking slut." One of the men spits on me.

Two more stand over me, finishing on my face, hair, and chest, their mocking laughter echoing in my ears as they zip up their pants.

The gag is ripped from my mouth, leaving my lips raw and throbbing. I barely catch my breath as two of them roughly haul me to my feet, their bruising grips digging into my arms. They yank my dress back over me with careless, jerking motions, leaving it twisted and disheveled. My heel is put back on, but they don't even bother fastening the strap. Without a moment's pause, I'm shoved forward, their actions as cold and indifferent as the entirety of the rape.

"Walk," one barks.

My legs tremble violently as I stumble up the back patio stairs. Every step is a struggle, but somehow, I manage. I can feel how swollen my face is. Actually, every part of me.

Tess and one of the men are waiting at the top when she reaches for my hand.

Together, we move forward, but my mind lingers behind, shattered and broken.

The house is still alive with music and laughter, completely oblivious to the nightmare that just unfolded outside. My gaze shifts to Tess, and I realize with a pang that she's untouched—no injuries, no marks. She's so used to this, to the violence and assault, that she complied immediately, sparing herself from harm.

The men trail behind us, one slapping my butt as he walks by. But then, a sudden silence falls, broken only by a loud, "Oh, fuck!" followed by the thunder of footsteps.

"Get her out of here," Dante bellows.

Two women carrying trays of alcohol immediately set them down, hurrying toward me.

"Don't fucking touch me!" I snap, jerking away before they can reach me.

Damiano steps forward, his voice calm. "Baby, you're gonna go shower."

Valentina and Niki rush over, their eyes wide as they take in my appearance. Horror flickers across their faces, their gazes darting over the mess of me—my torn dress, bruises, and blood.

"I'm not leaving." My voice wavers, but my resolve doesn't. "This is what we're here for, right? I just had five dicks inside me—I can handle as many as I need to."

A collective gasp ripples through the room, but Damiano remains composed. His attention shifts to the men. "You were just with her outside?"

The men exchange glances, one of them smirking. "Yeah. We were just getting acquainted with the new tail."

"And you?" His gaze locks on the next man.

"Yeah, had her a couple times," the man says confidently. "She gets tighter the more you fuck her. Plenty more miles you can put on her if you wanna have a go."

Damiano's face remains expressionless, but there's a danger-ous stillness to him now. "Who else was out there?"

The shorter man—the one who came on my neck—grins smugly. "These two sluts and us."

Damiano nods slowly, his gaze sweeping over the men. "What do you make of the tattoo on her neck?"

The men glance at each other, their confusion apparent.

"Which one of you is Damiano?" he asks.

Again, their brows furrow in confusion.

Damiano's hands slide into his pockets, and he rocks back on his heels. "Well, here's the thing. The name on her neck… it belongs to me."

His words hang in the air, and these men don't seem to comprehend what they've done. So much so that the shorter one breaks the silence with a lighthearted laugh. "Her body's like a billboard for that sweet pussy and tight ass."

Damiano's gaze darkens, but his voice remains calm. "Get her showered," he says, turning to Valentina and Niki.

Valentina steps forward, her hand outstretched toward me.

I yank my arm back. "My body is here to be used, isn't it? I don't think five men's semen all over me will bother any of the others who'll rape me tonight." My glare cuts through the silence, daring anyone to contradict me.

Damiano's calm facade cracks ever so slightly, his jaw tightening. "Get her out of here," he repeats, this time with more steel in his tone.

"Come on, sweetheart," Valentina says gently as she tries to take my arm again.

I start to pull away, but Nikolai steps in, positioning his face right in front of mine. "These parties suck. Yeah." He nods, trying to get a reaction out of me. "You're bleeding. I'm going to bring you with me so we can get you cleaned up." He searches my eyes to see if his words are getting through.

I just stare at him, my mind completely blank. I don't know what to do.

"I'm going to take your hand, okay?"

He reaches out slowly, gently taking my wrist. Noticing the damage to my palms, he settles for cupping the back of my hand as he wraps his arm around my waist.

"We need to clean you up. Plus, you hate these things. Let's wash off the makeup and get you into some comfy pajamas, okay?"

His tone is soothing as he meets my gaze and nods again, his expression steady, almost reassuring.

The fight drains out of me, replaced by a hollow numbness. I stop resisting, letting him guide me away.

As Valentina begins to undress me, I hear a gasp from Niki. Nikolai covers his mouth, stifling his reaction.

I don't need to look down to know the state of my body; I can feel it—every mark, every bruise, every bite.

By the time I step into the shower, the shock has fully consumed me. I stand motionless as scalding water pours over me.

"Jesus… how many times did they—"

Valentina whirls on Nikolai, cutting him off. "Shut up."

"Sorry." Then he hesitates, adding, "It's just… I've never seen that much semen."

Niki steps into the shower fully clothed, picking up the hand-held sprayer. She adjusts the stream and sprays me down gently.

"Is that grass?" Nikolai asks.

"Ay yi yi, son," Valentina huffs. "Go watch *Blue's Clues* if you can't piece this together."

"We need a doctor. There's blood coming out of her bottom," Niki says, kneeling behind me as she looks at Valentina.

"Are you sure it's not her—" Nikolai begins, but Niki cuts him off.

"Does it really matter? She's bleeding."

"I already called one," Valentina says, standing at the edge of the shower with a towel held open.

The water swirling at my feet turns red as I stare down, distant and detached, as though this isn't my body. It's foreign—dirty, broken. No longer mine.

"Doc's here," Nikolai announces from the doorway.

"No," Valentina snaps. "Tell him to send Dr. Petra."

"He's already here," Nikolai says cautiously.

Valentina's glare hardens. "She was just assaulted by men. Another man is not touching her. Get Petra here. Now."

"Yes, Ma," he murmurs, retreating quickly.

Niki washes my hair and body with a tenderness that makes my heart ache. Each careful stroke seems like a lie, a kindness I don't deserve. I stand here, numb, the hot water tracing paths down skin that isn't mine anymore. It belongs to the hands that defiled it. It belongs to *them*. Not me. Not Damiano.

I squeeze my eyes shut, willing myself to disappear, but I can still feel them. The filth of their touch is carved into me, deeper than soap can reach. No amount of scrubbing will make me clean again. I am ruined. Worthless. Tarnished in a way that can never be undone.

I was Damiano's. This body was his. Now, it's disgusting. This useless tattoo on my neck did nothing. It didn't keep men off me. It didn't even almost deter them. I should cut it off.

I hope the sight of me—of what's left of me—is enough to make Damiano sick. Maybe he'll put a bullet between my eyes and end this miserable excuse of an existence. Or maybe, next time, I can be raped by the entire party. That would surely make the Volkov family money.

All these girls using their bodies to make this family rich. And all we get out of it is a broken soul.

When she finishes, she shuts off the water and takes the towel from Valentina, wrapping it lightly around me.

I'm led to the bed, my gaze falling on the nightstand. There's a framed photo of the entire Volkov family, and my eyes immediately find Damiano, his handsome face bringing tears to my own. The picture next to it is of Valentina and Lorenzo. This must be their room.

"Get on the bed, sweetheart," Valentina says softly, pulling back the covers.

My chest squeezes a little tighter as my body complies, climbing in on her side of the bed—the same side that is Damiano's in our bed.

No longer *our* bed.

Just *his* bed.

My mind disconnects, unable to process the world around me. The voices blur into a muffled hum, though Valentina's sharp tone cuts through the fog.

"Just sedate her, for God's sake."

Through the haze, I catch glimpses of Nikolai and Niki standing nearby—their worried faces swimming in and out of focus—and then everything fades to black.

Chapter

THIRTY-FIVE

Damiano

I head to the basement, my boots striking hard against the cement stairs, each step reverberating through the cold, lifeless space below. When I work, I compartmentalize—I have to. But this time, it's different. This time, it's personal. My woman was hurt, and the small flicker of light that I'd fought to keep alive in her—the part of her that could still believe in something better—is gone. I saw it in her dead, vacant eyes. The life she'd barely been holding onto was ripped away, leaving only emptiness behind.

The room is massive, with bare gray cement walls that stretch high, exuding an unwelcoming presence. No windows break the expanse, sealing it off completely from the outside world. Industrial lights hum overhead, casting a harsh glow that illuminates every detail, leaving no shadows to hide in.

At the far end, three chambers stand against the cement back-drop. Each chamber is oversized, with wide, reinforced doors that make it easy to move in equipment—or bodies—with ease.

Inside, three of the walls are painted a muted, somber gray, blending with the sterile surroundings. The fourth wall, however-er, is a floor-to-ceiling shield of highly advanced glass, capable of being manipulated to serve different purposes. From the outside, it can appear as a transparent window, offering an unobstructed view of everything within. Alternatively, it can be transformed to look like a mirror, reflecting the room back at its occupant, or even masked entirely to resemble another gray wall.

The person inside can see nothing unless I want them to—trapped within the limits of what I allow—while anyone standing on the other side sees everything, as if the glass were completely clear. These chambers are built for control, ensuring every inch of fear and vulnerability is laid bare.

The five men are lined up in the center of the room, each tied securely to a chair. They can't move, every muscle rendered useless, but their eyes are open. They're aware. They feel every-thing. That's the beauty of the drug: complete paralysis, but full consciousness. It's perfect for situations like this.

Four of my men line the side of the room. Silvano stands apart at the end of the row, positioned slightly ahead, a calculated placement that keeps him between the TV and the others while still offering them a clear view.

Andrei is seated at the computer hub near the room's center as he prepares the footage. As I approach, he rises from the roll-ing chair, grabbing his tablet. The footage flickers to life on the large TV.

I stride forward, stopping beside the hub and the line of men, positioning myself where they can see both the TV and feel the weight of my presence.

I remove my suit coat and tie, draping them over the back of the chair Andrei just got out of, then unfasten the top couple of buttons of my shirt. Crossing my arms over my chest, I jerk my chin toward the screen. "Play it."

Andrei nods and presses the button.

The footage begins, crystal clear, as if we were standing right there. I already know what's coming. I've seen this kind of thing, I've felt it myself, but watching it now, knowing it's Rainey's rape, it's a different kind of fury.

Rainey tries to stay composed, but her eyes betray her as they flick between the house and the men blocking her way back. She tells them I'm waiting for her. She tells them she's mine. But they don't listen. They didn't want to listen. Typically, when my name is mentioned, people tremble. But not these men.

There's a reason she was out there, alone and vulnerable. Someone set her up. These men hurt her.

Silvano's hand comes up to cover his mouth as the screen shows them tearing into her. They assault every inch of her with such brutality, leaving no part of her untouched.

As she's shoved off the body of one man, she's hit—punched in the stomach, forcing her to bend over in pain. Then she's struck across the face as they laugh, only to be shoved onto another man.

I notice the exact moment the fight leaves her. The light in her eyes extinguishes as she stops struggling and stares blankly at the sky, her body going limp even as they take her again and again.

One man finishes and shoves Tess to the side like she's nothing. She stays where she's told, her head bowed, her body shaking. He strides over to the pile already hurting Rainey, shoves the man that's behind her to the side, takes his position, and kneels behind her, forcing himself inside her. His hands grip her throat, squeezing until her face turns purple. Her eyes close—not in pain but in surrender. Like she's hoping he takes it too far, for too long, and accidentally kills her.

The silence is broken only by the sound of the video playing. Every second of this is burned into my memory, and I know each of these men will beg for death by the time I'm done with them.

And they won't get it. Not quickly. Not mercifully. They'll suffer for her. For every piece of her they stole.

And when I'm done, there will be nothing left of them but ash.

"Play it again," I command as the video ends.

Andrei's wide-eyed stare lingers on me, not just in hesitation but because he doesn't want to see the heinous assault again. But I don't care. This happened to Rainey. This is the way she was abused under our roof. Under our protection.

"I said play it again," I bark, my voice echoing off the walls.

He lets out a sigh, and the video restarts. My eyes stay locked on the screen, taking in every detail, every movement, noting what each of them did. I don't miss a single thing.

As soon as the first man steps between her legs, positioning himself, I have the details I need to begin.

"Start it over."

Andrei obeys, restarting the footage. This time, I count aloud every single time Rainey told them she was mine, every time she begged them to stop, hammering home their mistakes.

When the video reaches the same point again—the man positioning himself between her legs—I tell Andrei to pause it once more.

I shift my focus to the men tied to the chairs, their eyes darting wildly, panic etched across their faces. I step up to the one who went first, the one who dared to violate what's mine.

"*Like that means something to me.*" I meet his eyes. "Does that mean something to you now?" My gaze locks with his. "*I'm* Damiano. Everything she said is true. She *is* mine. And I *was* waiting for her."

I turn to my men. "I want him." I point at the bastard.

His eyes widen in terror as my men move in, untying his re-strained body. He's too sedated to fight back as they drag him toward the first chamber. His friends watch, helpless and horrified, knowing their time will come.

"Andrei, push the feed into that room," I instruct.

Andrei nods, already working. He doesn't need further explanation. Our family knows how I operate—we've always been on the same page without needing to spell it out.

He hands me his tablet, and I skim the man's file. Married. Two kids at home. Seven illegitimate children from the women he's raped. A pattern. No one else will suffer because of him.

But that doesn't mean I can't mess with his head before I kill him.

"Remove his clothes."

My men waste no time cutting away his clothing piece by piece, leaving him exposed.

Breaking them always starts with the mind. Pain alone doesn't do it; they stop comprehending once agony takes over. But fear? Fear eats them alive.

"I would've assumed your wife was forced into marrying you, but it seems she did it willingly," I say, my voice remaining calm. "She was also complicit in the rape of a minor. When the cops asked her about your whereabouts that night, she lied *for* you. My men are on their way to your house right now," I continue. "They have the footage we just watched, and they'll reenact every detail of what you did to my girlfriend. Every. Single. Thing."

Tears leak from his eyes, drifting down to his hair as he stares up at the ceiling. The truth is, she won't be touched, though. She will, however, spend forever thinking he ran off with another woman. She'll never know what really happened to him.

"And here's the best part," I add. "The child your wife is carrying? It's not yours. It belongs to your buddy over there." I nod toward the man sitting at the end of the line—the one who joined the assault late.

The realization hits him like a freight train, and his eyes attempt to turn toward the man I've singled out, but he can't quite see him. I step closer, gripping his jaw and forcing his face in the right direction until their gazes lock.

"Say hi, Daddy," I taunt, lifting my hand in a mocking wave toward the man outside.

"But surely," I continue, "you didn't expect her to stay faithful to you, did you? Not when you've never been faithful to her."

As I speak, I begin prepping. The floor is designed with a drain in the center to make cleaning messes easier. Everyone shits themselves. It's inevitable. It also makes cleaning blood and other bodily fluids easier.

Marko wheels in the new contraption I recently got, its purpose unmistakable.

"You ever had anal?" I ask, adjusting a few dials.

His eyes widen further, his breathing ragged.

"Relax," I say, my voice devoid of emotion. "I'm not going to touch you. This machine will handle it."

The screens are designed to blend seamlessly into the walls, nearly invisible when not in use. I activate the one directly in front of him, adjusting it to ensure he has a direct view. With a press of a button, the footage plays again, the horrifying scenes broadcast directly to him and the remaining men just outside.

"Flip him over."

Marko and Silvano step forward, hauling him to the edge of the metal table and bending him over it. I secure his wrists with handcuffs, ensuring his body stays exactly where I want it.

"This machine will do to you what you did to my girlfriend until you figure out how to stop it yourself." I attach the oversized dildo to the device. "The speed? That's controlled by your own heart rate. The more you panic, the faster it goes."

Satisfied with the setup, I flip the switch. The machine hums to life as it begins its work. Without sparing him another glance, I step out of the chamber, Marko and Silvano trailing behind me.

Back in the main room, I head straight to the remaining men, stopping in front of the one who assaulted both women.

"Him." I point.

His eyes widen, sheer terror etched into every line of his face. Marko and Silvano close in, swiftly untying him from the chair and dragging him toward the middle chamber.

"Cut his clothes off." I give the instruction as I turn and leave.

I step back into the chamber with the first man. His body is drenched in sweat, but he still remains unable to move. The machine is moving so violently now that blood is dripping onto the floor beneath him. He's silent, unable to make a sound, but the sheer agony in his expression speaks volumes.

I switch off the machine, pulling it back slightly as I grab a pair of gloves from the nearby cart. I remove the dildo from the device, place it on a sterilized metal table, and replace it with an even larger one. I prepare it the same way—lubing it up and positioning it exactly where I want it—then flip the machine back on. It resumes immediately at the same relentless pace, matching the rapid rhythm of his panicked heartbeat.

At least now he knows how fast Rainey's heart was racing as multiple men violated her, helpless and unable to move.

I carry the soiled dildo back to the other chamber, where the second man waits, naked and restrained in a chair resembling one you'd find in a dentist's office. The chair is raised, positioning him upright, vulnerable, and fully exposed. Holding up the dildo, I make sure he sees it—the white now stained with blood and filth.

"He needed something bigger," I say, letting my words settle as I watch the tears streak down his face.

I smirk at his helplessness. "Relax. This isn't going where you think it is." My tone drips with cruel amusement. "You can suck on it instead."

Gripping his jaw, I force it open, ignoring his muffled protests as his eyes widen in panic. I shove the dildo into his mouth, pressing it against the back of his throat. His body convulses in reflex, gagging and struggling, but there's no escape.

When I finally pull it out, a thick string of saliva trails after it, dripping down his chin and onto his chest. His breath comes in sharp gasps as his body heaves.

I roll a small stand in, its wheels squeaking faintly against the floor. From the shelves beneath, I begin pulling out items—tools, devices, and implements that each have a purpose.

"If you can manage to get a boner right now." I glance over my shoulder. "I'll let you leave." I know as well as he does that it's impossible.

His eyes stay locked on mine, wide with panic, as I plug in a blender. Slowly, I prepare a metal tray with an assortment of tools, the faint clinks of metal against metal slicing through the silence. Nearby, I set up the feeding tube. The bag hangs from a pole, the attached tubing ready to deliver the contents I'm about to prepare.

Pulling the tray closer, I grab the tablet and change the footage displayed on the screen. The video rewinds to when he pushed the other man aside and assaulted Rainey. I press play, pointing to the screen as the scene unfolds.

"Where you put your dick…is *mine*. She didn't give you permission to touch her body."

The footage loops again as I grab a large pair of scissors. His gaze darts between the screen and me, his breathing shallow and rapid as realization dawns. The moment my hand clamps down on him, his body stiffens, though the paralytic renders him powerless to fight back.

The snip is slow and excruciating. Blood pools on the floor as his face drains of color. His attempts to speak come out as garbled slurs, the paralytic dulling his ability to form words.

"You forced this into my girlfriend." I hold up his severed penis, letting the gravity of it being gone settle over him. "So now, I'm going to force the same penis into your stomach."

His eyes widen in sheer terror, his breath hitching as he processes my words. Without breaking eye contact, I toss the severed flesh into the blender and turn it on. A sickening whir fills the room, wet and mechanical. His face pales further, his head lolling slightly as he passes out.

"Pathetic," I mutter under my breath as his body goes limp. I glance at Silvano and Marko, rolling my eyes as I sigh.

Marko snorts softly, and Silvano shakes his head, his expression impassive but faintly amused.

I pour the liquefied remains into the feeding bag, sealing it tightly, then hanging it on the stand. The attached tubing is prepped, and I guide it through his nose and down into his stomach.

"Wake him up," I demand. Silvano steps forward with a vial of ammonia, waving it under the man's nose until his eyes snap open again.

"You missed the main event," I say, my voice flat. "But don't worry—you'll experience it firsthand."

Securing the tube in place, I release the clamp, allowing gravity to pull the thick liquid into him. His eyes bulge, watering as he struggles against the inevitable, but he's powerless to stop it. I stand back, watching dispassionately as the bag slowly empties, the contents disappearing into him.

The sound of a crash from the next room draws my attention, but I smile coldly, turning back to him. "Looks like your buddy is regaining body function too."

The hours blur together as I move between the rooms, my focus unwavering despite the fatigue creeping in. Andrei isn't used to my side of work and is the first to leave, muttering something about needing air. Silvano sticks around longer but eventually leaves when Dante calls him away to handle other matters.

My other men? They've made themselves comfortable, sitting at a table off to the side, watching me work while devouring a few pizzas they had delivered.

I no longer keep them fully paralyzed. Their bodies remain immobile, but I savor the screams and the pathetic insults that spill from their mouths. It's even better when they have the audacity to gloat about what they did to Rainey—it only gives me reason to drag out their suffering. The more they talk, the slower I make it.

The second man broke quickly, pleading for forgiveness, but after twenty-three hours, I was done with him. His throat met the edge of my blade, and his lifeless body was dragged to the crematorium. I didn't even bother cleaning. The third man was hauled in, the blood and stench of his predecessor still saturating the room.

The claw marks she left on him are a stain he has no right to wear. I press the cheese grater against his flesh, dragging it over his skin with slow strokes, stripping away every trace of her touch. He doesn't deserve her marks. They're too good for him.

Fifty-two hours pass, a blur of blood, pain, and vengeance. Three of the men who hurt Rainey have felt my wrath. Two are dead. One clings to life by a thread. The last two remain un-touched—for now.

I've been awake too long. My vision blurs, my body heavy with exhaustion. Even I have limits.

The main chamber reverberates with the tortured screams of the man still being punished by the machine, his agony filling the air.

I turn to my men, my body and brain tired. "Watch the others. No one moves unless I say so."

They nod, and I leave, heading to my private office. It's sparse, free of distractions. A simple couch rests against one wall, and monitors line the opposite, displaying live color feeds from each chamber. The far wall is a one-way mirror, seamlessly integrated into the design, giving me a full view of everything on the other side while remaining unseen.

I sink onto the couch, my body finally relenting as I let my head fall back against the cushions. On the monitors, the two untouched men are still tied to their chairs, fear etched into their faces as they listen to the screams from the other room.

Sleep takes me quickly, exhaustion dragging me under.

Chapter

THIRTY-SIX

Rainey

I remained under sedation for two days.

Whether it was an act of kindness to let my body start heal-ing, a chance to rest my fractured mind, or simply a method to keep me in line, I can't say. But when I finally wake, reality slams into me, bringing with it a flood of emotions: sadness, disgust, pain—mostly rage.

I take myself in, noting the bandages crisscrossing my knees and hands, the swollen tenderness of my lip. The sight of the wrappings fuels a fresh surge of fury. I tear them off, ignoring the sting of adhesive.

We're all whores. I was stupid to think I was any different.

Despite the aches that rattle through my body, I push myself out of bed and leave Valentina's room, heading straight for the girls' quarters.

I'm raw in my most sensitive areas, and I have never felt something so horrible in my entire life. Every ache and burn is a reminder of what was done to me and the gruesome nature of the rape.

My room remains untouched, frozen in time like nothing happened. But everything has.

As soon as the door shuts, the dam breaks. A sob rips from my throat, and I crumble, my knees hitting the carpet with a dull thud.

I'm desperate to rid myself of the feeling—their hands, their breath, their bodies invading mine. The phantom sensation lingers, clinging to me and refusing to fade. I squeeze my eyes shut, but the darkness offers no escape. It only amplifies the memories, trapping me in an endless loop.

I want to peel my skin off. Scrub away every last trace of them. Erase it all. My nails dig into my arms, pressing deep, leaving behind fresh, bloody trails—but I don't care. It's not enough. It will never be enough.

I shove myself up, lurching toward the bathroom, barely making it before I'm on my knees again, dry heaving until my ribs ache. Nothing comes up, just gasping, choking sobs that shake me to my core until I feel like I might splinter apart.

I stumble to my closet, ripping my clothes away in a frenzy to get them off.

I can't stand it. I can't stand the thought of them.

I slide down the wall, curling into myself. My knees bend in, arms wrapping around them like they might somehow hold me together. But they don't. The weight inside me is unbearable, crushing my lungs, making it impossible to breathe.

The waterworks begin again, my body shaking uncontrollably. The sound is ugly, echoing off the walls. Another follows, then another, until there's no stopping them.

Tears spill hot and fast, soaking my arms as I press my face into them, trying to muffle the choked cries. But there's no muffling this. No containing it. It's been festering, suffocating me, and now it's all breaking free.

I tuck into myself as much as I can manage, as if I can disappear.

Time slips away.

I cry until my voice is hoarse, until I'm too weak to shake anymore, until the only thing left are the silent tears slipping down my face, soaking into the floor beneath me. Until I'm empty. Until I'm just done.

And then I lay there, curled up, letting darkness close in around me.

And Damiano? I thought he might at least come to check on me, to see how I'm holding up. But he hasn't. He's been absent, silent, as if I don't exist. As if I'm already gone. Maybe, to him, I am. Maybe he's holed up in his house, locked away with orders to keep me from getting anywhere near him. He's made up his mind. He's done with me, but he's too much of a coward to tell me.

I remain in place until my body aches and the carpet makes it clear it has no intentions of swallowing me whole.

I move on autopilot, forcing myself upright despite the stiffness weighing down my limbs.

I refuse to think. My mind is blank, hollow, detached from the girl who was crying on the floor minutes ago. That girl is gone. And I refuse to let those pieces of shit be the last thing that was inside me.

I slip on the first dress I find and leave.

My legs carry me forward before I even realize I'm moving. Down the hall. Through the house. My footsteps are steady, my pace quick, but my head feels light. Distant. My mind lags behind, unwilling to catch up.

By the time I reach the Volkov meeting room, my breathing is even, controlled. The doors are shut, a solid barrier between me and whatever conversation is happening inside.

They're in there.

Damiano might be in there.

I'll confront him. I'll tell him I don't care that he no longer wants me, even though that's a lie. But he doesn't need to know that. I'm on my own now. And I doubt they'll let me go. Obviously, they won't let me go. This is why we're here.

I push it open and quickly find that Damiano is nowhere in sight—just the other five brothers and a couple of the guards, Marko and Ricco among them. Everyone stares as I enter, and I try to keep it together. I know I look like a mess, and as their gazes trail down my body, I realize I never even tried to wash the blood off my arms.

I stare at Dante for a long time, wishing someone would say something, but no one does.

"I need to talk to you," I finally say.

A throat clears, and Silvano speaks. "We are all here for you, Rainey. We will help in any way you need. You can talk to all of us."

"I didn't ask to talk to all of you, did I?" I bite out. "I want to talk to you." I turn my attention back to Dante.

He sets the papers on the table, scoots his chair back, and walks toward me, gesturing for me to go first. I step out, and he closes the door behind us.

"Can we talk in your office?" I ask, and he nods, then leads the way.

He motions for me to enter first. I step inside and lower my dress as he shuts the door. When he turns, he stops and watches me.

"Rainey, stop."

"I feel them on me. It's all I can feel—their disgusting hands, their disgusting mouths, their words, and their cocks fucking me. It's all my mind can think about. I can't live like this, Dante." Tears stream down my face. "I just want someone I love to replace their touch."

He strides across the room with purpose, gripping my hips as he lifts me effortlessly. My legs wrap around his waist, and as our mouths collide, everything else fades. His lips claim mine with a need that shatters any doubts I may have had.

He places me on his desk and my hands slip between us to undo the buttons of his shirt. As the fabric parts, heat radiates from him, my palms gliding over the defined ridges of his chest. My tongue follows, tracing each contour, drinking in the scent of him—rich, masculine, addictive.

I fumble with his belt, shaking slightly as I free him, my fingers wrapping around his girth. I never got to see him, only felt him, his size, and now, seeing and touching him confirms what my body already remembers.

He tilts my chin back, and our mouths crash together again, tongues tangling as he presses against me. He pushes me onto my back, his lips trailing down my neck, over my collarbone, until he lowers himself between my legs.

For a brief second, doubt flickers. Is he really going to—? But he doesn't hesitate. His mouth finds me, and the moment his tongue strokes over me, my back arches off the desk. He isn't grossed out by me. No, he's worshiping me—proving it with every slow flick of his tongue as he feasts on me like I'm the only thing he's ever wanted.

A moan rips free, my fingers tangling in his hair as I try to pull him impossibly closer. He doesn't stop until pleasure crashes over me, until I'm trembling beneath him, gasping his name.

His lips travel back up, trailing over my stomach and pausing at each breast to tease me with soft, tentative kisses. He seems unbothered by the bloodied bite marks left there before moving up my throat. By the time his mouth finds mine again, I'm dizzy with need.

I feel him at my entrance, his tip nudging against me. "I need to sit up," I whisper.

Confusion crosses his face, but he says nothing. He reaches out, sliding his hand behind my back to help me up. I shift closer to the edge of the desk, parting my legs wider, my gaze locked on his. "I need to watch."

Something dark and heated flashes in his eyes, but he nods, dragging himself along my slick folds, then positioning at my entrance again. Slowly, he presses in, and I let out a soft, breathless moan.

It feels good. Really good. Then a flashback rushes in—the groaning of *how good I felt*. My eyes flutter, but his hand grips my jaw, anchoring me in place, forcing me to stay with him. "Watch me. Just me."

I nod, battling to stay present, to not let my thoughts intrude on this. Because right now, it's just him. Just us.

He's gentle. More gentle than anyone has ever been with me during sex. I like it rough. But right now, this is exactly how I need it.

He keeps me here—entirely present. His hands don't roam, don't claim. They just hold me. His forehead presses lightly to mine, our breaths mingling, our gazes locked, as if he's afraid to look away, afraid I might slip somewhere he can't reach me.

I won't. He won't let me.

He moves with slow, measured care, his body easing into mine softly, rewriting over the assault with something special. Each slow push, each gentle pull, is a promise. He won't hurt me. He won't rush me. He won't take anything I don't willingly give.

My fingers dig into his back, holding him, giving him my trust. His muscles flex beneath my fingertips, controlled and restrained, his pace unwavering as he stays right here with me. Letting me feel. Letting me remember that this is what it's supposed to be.

Safe. Consensual.

His thumb strokes along my cheek, his lips brushing mine. He offers himself to me, letting me take whatever I need. His hips rock forward in a slow, deep glide, his breath catching as I pull him closer, my body responding not from fear or force, but from how good he's making me feel.

He's not them. He'll never be them.

With every tender thrust, every whispered reassurance against my mouth, he erases the ghosts with his patience.

Wrapping one arm around his neck and bracing my other hand against his desk, I move against him with growing urgency. My legs tighten around his waist as my hips glide over him, needing more. Our panting mingles, as our rhythm turns desperate, frantic—until our orgasms erupt, pulling us under together.

When he pulls out, he does it slowly, as if savoring every second. My body is still pulsing from the intensity, but he's still hard, thrumming with restrained desire

I chew on my lip, and he leans in, brushing a soft kiss against my mouth. "What's on your mind?" he murmurs, his voice lower now.

I hesitate. "Are you comfortable with… anal?"

"Sure."

I don't even know how to say it. I don't want to admit that they did that to me. But I don't need to explain. He understands. His hands slide around my waist, and he lifts me off the desk, setting me on my feet, turning me and bending me over. My palms flatten against the cool surface as I watch him open a drawer and pull something out.

Lube.

The sight of it makes me relax. He pours some into his hand, coating himself with slow, measured strokes before tossing the bottle aside. I spread my legs wider, inviting him in, needing to feel him.

When he leans into me, he tightens around my hips.

A slow push, stretching, filling—and then we both groan at the same time.

His arms wrap around me, pulling me upright against his chest, his warmth blanketing me as he locks me in place. He finds my breasts, cupping, kneading, teasing, each movement in sync with the steady thrust of his hips.

I let my head fall back against his shoulder, my fingers finding his and interlocking, holding onto him as he moves inside me, making us both feel good.

Then his hand slides lower, dipping between my legs, finding my clit.

A broken moan escapes me as he circles it, rubbing in slow, teasing strokes while still driving into me from behind. The combination is devastating, a slow build of pressure coiling deep.

His breath is hot against my ear. "Let go."

His voice alone is enough to unravel me. Every muscle clenches as my release spills onto him, and he keeps stroking me through it. I shudder in his arms, gasping his name.

He holds me there, letting me come down, his own movements growing erratic as he groans, his grip on me tightening as he finds his own release.

For a moment, neither of us stirs. Only heavy breathing and the quiet hum of satisfaction settle between us.

"We need to scoot to the right just a couple steps," he says, and I turn to look up at him. "Tissues." He points to the box just out of reach.

I smile and move with him as he grabs the box. "Ready?" he asks.

We each take a couple, and he slowly pulls out.

We silently clean ourselves, and he fastens his pants back up.

"That felt good. Thank you." I glance up at him, then toss the tissues in the trash. Taking a couple more, I try to wipe off any extra wetness that might be left behind.

"Are you comfortable?" he asks, and I wonder if he's asking if I have any regrets. He points to the soiled tissue, and I nod, tossing it in the trash.

"If you're not, I will lick every bit of that out of you."

I stare at him, searching his eyes, trying to keep the tears at bay—but they escape, and before I know it, I burst into sobs. I don't know why he's being so nice to me. First Valentina and Nikita, and now him. I'm a nobody. My body is ruined forever, yet he just had sex with it like he wasn't disgusted, and now he's offering to lick his own semen out of me just to make sure I'm comfortable.

He grabs me by the back of the neck and pulls me to him. My arms wrap around him so tightly as I hysterically cry. He lifts me, carrying me to the couch and settling me on his lap.

He holds me until silence eventually blankets us, his hand softly running up and down my back.

"I'm sorry," I murmur, letting those be the first words to him once I finally find my voice.

"You never need to apologize to me. Not ever."

I nod, keeping my face tucked against his neck.

"Trauma and PTSD can eat you alive. We have a therapist who comes twice a week. We all see her. Can I have her come talk to you? I can stay with you, or I can leave you alone. I think it would be helpful."

How do I even begin to talk to someone about what happened? And why would I? Do all the girls meet with the therapist? Maybe that's how they get by.

"Just think about it, okay?"

I sit up and stare at him. "I'm so tired. I want to sleep without the nightmares."

"I can give you something that will help you sleep," he offers.

"Please."

"If you're okay with it, I'd like to take you back to my room. Just to sleep," he adds quickly.

I nod, and he smiles. "Okay, get dressed."

By the time he leads me through parts of the house I never even knew existed, the medicine has already started to take effect, my body growing heavy with drowsiness.

When we reach his suite, I sit on the edge of the bed, my eyelids drooping. He disappears and returns, kneeling in front of me as he helps me out of my dress. He slips a T-shirt over my head then eases me under the covers, making sure I'm settled.

Chapter
THIRTY-SEVEN

Rainey

I blink awake, my eyes adjusting to the dark. Arms are wrapped securely around me, and it takes me a second to figure out if it's Damiano or Dante. It's Dante. I'm still in his room. How long was I out?

I'm relieved I didn't wake up alone. That's the last thing I want right now. It's in the quiet solitude that my thoughts are the worst.

The effects of the drug still linger, leaving me sluggish with exhaustion. As I close my eyes, Dante's phone beeps on the nightstand. The screen stays lit, casting a faint glow in the darkened room, but he doesn't stir.

"Dante?" I whisper, but still nothing.

It's been months since I've used a phone. I've thought of a million things I'd do if I ever got my hands on one—the first being calling the cops, and then Jules. But now, I'm feet away from one, and all I want to know is if he's talked to Damiano.

I shift away from him, scooting across the bed carefully to avoid waking him. He's still sound asleep.

When I pick up his phone, the text he received *is* from Damiano. My heart squeezes, and my fingers shake as I slide his screen open and pull up the messages. All it says is "2."

I scroll up through the last couple of days to see what's been said—if I've been mentioned.

Dante:

She's in bad shape. She was given a sedative. Petra is doing a full examination on her.

Dante:

Give me an update.

Dante:

Rainey is awake. We need to talk.

Damiano:

Busy. Get Nikolai if you can't be bothered.

Dante:

I've got her.

Dante:

It's been five days. How many left?

Damiano:

2

I stare at the conversation, unable to believe he couldn't even take two seconds to come see me. He's too busy to check if I'm still alive. Those rapists probably didn't even get in trouble for what they did.

I exit the messaging app and open his photos. This is wrong on so many levels, but I don't care.

Scrolling through, I find random pictures—vehicles, distant shots of men, documents—everything seems tied to business. Then, mixed among them, I spot photos of him with his brothers. Him with his parents. Even a few with Em.

But what I wasn't expecting… were the ones of me.

One photo stops me cold. Nikita took this. It was one of the days we hung out by her pool—she had let me borrow a swimsuit, and we spent the afternoon lounging. I remember this. I was sitting on a beach chair under an umbrella, my head tilted back, caught mid-laugh.

Why would he have this picture?

When he stirs, I lock his phone, place it back on the nightstand, and crawl back into bed.

When I wake in the morning, he's gone. Of course, he's gone. I replay the text messages, thinking about the photo he has of me—one taken before I was ever here—and wonder what it all means.

I lift my hands, noticing the bandages wrapped around my palms again, along with the ones tracing the lengths of my forearms where I tried to skin myself.

"I have breakfast if you're hungry," a voice says.

I sit up and turn toward the windows.

Dante sits at a table, going over papers beside his laptop, a plate of food in front of him. He gestures to the chair across from him.

"Come eat."

I get out of bed and stand, making sure my legs will work with me. They do. When I sit down, he pulls the lid off a plate of food, then sets his work aside and eats with me.

"Does it look bad?" I ask after noticing he's been staring at me since I sat down.

He wipes his mouth and shakes his head. "Nothing could dull how beautiful you are."

I look up at him, trying to figure out if he actually means that or if those are just the nice words he says to everyone. I can't tell. He seems sincere, but I don't have the brain capacity to analyze it.

"I have to leave for the day." He sets a pill on the table in front of me. "You can sleep if you'd like."

"Yeah. Thanks." I pick it up and take it, already wanting sleep to come back.

I take another bite of my eggs and stand. He watches as I walk to the bed. I don't even remember how I got out of my dress—or where it is now.

"Stay. Please." He rises and walks toward me.

"I don't want to intrude."

"I'll be gone most of the day. It's no intrusion." He steps closer until he's right in front of me, then wraps his arms around me. I sink into him, returning the embrace.

We stay like that until his phone rings. He releases me, tells me to climb back into bed, and I do. A soft kiss lands on my forehead, and he lingers, staring down at me before leaning in again, pressing another kiss to the same spot. Then, without another word, he strides out.

When I wake, I'm alone, and nightfall has set in.

I stand and notice a silk nightgown laid out for me, along with matching panties.

I slip them on, relieved that both fit and cover me. Sliding into the matching robe, I leave without even bothering to tie it.

Maybe Damiano doesn't want to be near me after what happened at the party. Perhaps he blames me, sees me as ruined—something tainted.

If that's how he feels, I deserve to hear it from him, not endure this quiet disregard. Avoiding me is cowardly, and I won't allow it to continue.

Determined, I slide on my slippers and make my way back through the house. I don't even remember how I got here, but I'll find my way back and demand someone bring me to him.

The house is quiet; all the girls are most likely at an event. Faint voices drift from the living room, and as I approach, I see Nikolai talking with two guards.

Their conversation comes to an abrupt stop when they notice me.

"Where's Damiano?"

Nikolai appears surprised to see me, but he responds. "Working."

"Working where?"

"Here," he replies.

"I want to see him."

He briefly meets the guards' eyes then shrugs, rising to his feet. "You squeamish around blood?"

"No."

"Good. Come on."

I fall into step behind him as he navigates the massive house. The hallways stretch endlessly, and the muted sounds of our footsteps echo softly, amplifying the stillness in this section of the house.

We turn corner after corner, passing closed doors one after another. Finally, the corridor opens up, and we step into a giant, high-ceilinged library.

Bookshelves stretch from floor to ceiling, crammed with leather-bound tomes that look as old as time itself. The scent of aged paper and polished wood fills the space, warm and oddly comforting.

Nikolai walks purposefully. At first, I think he's messing with me when he turns down an aisle and walks to the far end. But then, he places a hand against one of the shelves, and with a soft click, the heavy bookshelf swings inward, revealing a concealed entryway seamlessly hidden within the wall.

The air changes as we step through the hidden doorway. The narrow staircase spirals downward, and with each step, the temperature noticeably drops. It feels oppressive down here—dark, despite the sterile, artificial light illuminating the path. The bare walls and narrow steps add to the suffocating sensation, and I reach out, gripping the back of Nikolai's jacket as we descend.

Then I hear it—yelling. Faint at first, muffled by the distance, but it grows louder with each step we take.

The staircase opens into an underground area, its gray cement walls towering above us. It feels cold, not just in temperature but in atmosphere. There's no sign of natural light, no windows, just an unshakable sense of foreboding that settles over me.

At the far end of the room, I see Damiano in an enclosed space. I should feel sick at the sight in front of me—the glass rooms filled with scenes of horror. But all I can focus on is the footage playing on the screens, both inside the room and on a monitor just outside where I stand. My assault is being replayed in brutal, graphic detail.

One of the guards glances at the screen, his face paling. He mutters, "Holy fuck," as he turns away, unable to stomach what he's seeing. *No shit, my guy. I didn't enjoy it when it happened.* Nikolai doesn't even look at the footage.

I turn and stare up at him as he gazes blankly into the room where Damiano is.

"Why won't you look?" I ask curiously.

"I've seen it," he says, his eyes remaining fixed ahead.

I nod, then turn back to where Damiano is. A dark flicker of satisfaction stirs within me. Inside, the man who kept assaulting me from behind is now bent over a table himself, completely naked and at Damiano's mercy.

Damiano sets up a machine behind the man. His screams echo faintly through the glass, and I feel a twisted sense of justice rather than fear.

"This is the same size as my cock," Damiano snarls. "Now you'll know what it feels like."

The sheer hatred in his tone makes my knees threaten to buckle. I watch as the man begins to plead, but his cries are drowned out by the screen replaying my assault. The footage loops, cutting to the exact moment he tore into me. He's sure acting like a little bitch now that he's the one being assaulted.

Damiano hits a button, and the machine roars to life. The object plunges into the man with such force that he jerks upright on the table, a guttural scream tearing from his throat.

Tears blur my vision as I storm toward the door. I shove it open so hard it slams against the wall, my rage bursting forth.

Damiano's head snaps toward me, his eyes wide with surprise. I march straight to the table, ignoring the man's pathetic cries. Grabbing a fistful of his hair, I yank his head up, forcing him to look at me. Tears streak his face, mixing with the sweat dripping from his brow.

"Does it feel good?!" I yell, my voice trembling with fury. "Does it feel good when something is shoved in your ass?!" My grip tightens as I lean closer. "The only difference here is you don't have five repulsive, sweaty men taking turns. But hey—looks like the blood dripping from your ass is making it easier for the machine to do its job."

I let go, his head dropping back onto the table with a thud as he squirms and sobs. I glance at Damiano, my voice cutting through the man's cries. "He fucked me a lot harder than that."

Damiano's jaw flexes, his eyes locked on mine as he turns a dial. The machine speeds up, its movements brutal, and the man's screams rise to a deafening pitch.

"Stop it," I say, my voice quieter.

He reaches for the dial, the machine slowing to a stop.

I walk to the table, bringing my face close to his. "How many times did I tell you I belonged to Damiano? How many times did you ignore it? What did you think would happen if you raped his girlfriend?

My voice drops as I fight to keep myself calm, unwilling to let him see how much they broke me. "I hope you enjoyed taking what wasn't yours. Because my body will be the last you ever touch, you piece of shit."

I spit in his face, straighten, and walk out.

Anger radiates through me as I pace the room. My thoughts churn with all the ways I want to personally hurt the men who hurt me. I stop abruptly in front of the next room, staring through the wall of glass.

I lock onto the man inside. He's strapped to a chair, unable to look away from the screen displaying my assault. My stomach twists at the memory of how he slapped my boobs, sucked, and bit me. My eyes stay fixed on the monitor, on the cruel evidence playing out before us.

Damiano's voice cuts in behind me. "Take her back to my house and stay with her until I get back," he orders Nikolai.

Still staring at the screen, my voice comes out detached. "Why'd you cut off his nipples?"

He approaches, standing beside me as he stares into the same room. He's silent for a long time, eventually saying, "Because of the way he assaulted yours." His tone is void of emotion.

"What did you do with them?" I ask, the words leaving my lips before I fully register them.

"I made him eat them."

I nod faintly, not fully comprehending his words. My attention remains fixed on the screen, unable to recall this part of the assault. "There were five of them," I say softly, my voice cracking. "Not just these two. Five men raped me."

Tears leak down my face.

"The other three are dead."

I stare up at him, tears streaming faster than I can stop them. I shouldn't feel this way. I shouldn't be happy about this. I shouldn't want this for them. But I am. I'm selfishly happy that justice was served to the men who assaulted me—and Tess.

"Is this where you've been?"

"Yes."

"And your job is, like, killing people?"

I've always known he was dangerous. He radiates it. So I'm not even surprised by this.

"Yes."

"Do you want me to go back to your house?" I ask, biting the inside of my cheek nervously.

His brows knit together in confusion, and he steps forward, closing the space between us. His hand cups my cheek, his thumb brushing away a tear as his eyes bore into mine.

"I love you, Rainey. I loved you yesterday, I love you today, and I'll love you tomorrow. What happened to you isn't your fault."

I stare up at him, his words stitching together the pieces of my heart that were falling apart. I nod, my gaze drifting to the rooms behind him.

"It just feels like you're avoiding me," I murmur.

He shakes his head, pulling me into his arms. "I'm so angry," he whispers into my hair.

"Me too," I admit, tears spilling freely as I cling to him.

"There's nothing I could do to any of them that would ever be enough, and I hate it."

"You leaving me alone right now makes me feel worse," I confess.

He rests his cheek against the top of my head, holding me tightly. "I'll finish this," he promises.

When he leans back, he kisses me, soft but firm.

When we finally pull apart, he peers over my shoulder at Nikolai. "Take her home."

Nikolai nods, and Damiano kisses me one more time before I turn and walk away.

Chapter
THIRTY-EIGHT

Rainey

Damiano leans against the bathroom doorframe, hands shoved in his pockets, watching me. My eyes catch his in the mirror, and I smile, taking in just how handsome he is.

It's been three weeks. Three weeks since the assault. Three weeks of battling the remnants left behind while trying to wrap my head around the fact that he still wants me.

He hasn't gone back to work since the night Nikolai took me down to the basement, to the truth of what Damiano does when he leaves here. I understand now why he comes home quiet and distant, why he doesn't want to talk, and why his responses about his day are always vague.

Through all of this, his devotion to me hasn't wavered. If anything, he's more attentive than ever. I've come to crave the way his constant presence keeps me sane, the way he holds me when the nightmares drag me under and stays in bed with me until I wake.

I don't know if he does it to make sure I never wake up questioning whether today is the day he realizes he doesn't want me anymore, or if it's unintentional. But every time I wake and he's still there, I feel instantly comforted.

Dante kept pushing me to talk to their therapist, and eventually, I agreed.

Dr. Winn is wonderful. She's even praised me for getting Damiano to attend three sessions with me—couples therapy to help us move forward. In those sessions, I admitted that sometimes I feel undeserving of him, that when we have sex, I can't shake the feeling that I'm getting filth on him somehow.

We've talked through it, working together to find solutions that help me cope and move past those thoughts.

Maybe it's wrong, but knowing those men, those monsters, were tortured brings me a dark sort of peace. It feels like closure, a guarantee they'll never hurt anyone else the way they hurt me. That much, at least, is certain.

The memories, though, remain a fractured mess. I can't piece them together during the day, but at night, in my dreams, each of those men is still alive, coming back for an encore.

Dr. Winn had been given permission to disclose Damiano's medical history, and when she did, it changed the way I saw everything about him—not in a fearful way, not in a way that unsettled me, but in a way that made me understand.

He had suffered a traumatic brain injury as a child—one severe enough to damage the part of his brain responsible for processing emotions. They'd run tests on him, studies that should have shown at least some level of activity in those regions. But there was nothing. No spark. No flicker of empathy, guilt, fear, or attachment. The parts of the brain that made someone human—

the ability to love, to care, to hesitate before taking a life—were essentially dead inside him.

Even with his family, the people he had grown up with, the ones who had raised him, his brain didn't feel anything. No warmth, no love, no grief at the thought of losing them. He had a loyalty to them, yes—a deep, unwavering sense of duty to protect them, to uphold the name and the empire they had built. But that loyalty wasn't tied to emotion. It was ingrained, logical, a responsibility rather than a connection. If one of them were killed, he wouldn't grieve. He wouldn't feel devastation or loss. He wouldn't feel anything at all. He would just… be.

And yet, something had happened that shouldn't have been possible. A *phenomenon*, Dr. Winn had called it. Because when it came to me, Damiano's brain—those parts that were supposed to be dormant—lit up.

I wasn't just someone he cared about. I was the only thing in his world that registered. The only thing that made him feel anything at all. They had tested it repeatedly, and every time, the results were the same. In a mind that otherwise existed in cold calculation, I was the one and only exception.

It wasn't love the way most people understood it. Damiano didn't process emotions like an average person. He never had, and he never would. He didn't differentiate between affection and possession. He didn't understand the concept of letting go. In his mind, I wasn't just someone he wanted—I was someone who belonged to him in a way that was absolute. I was his, and he was mine, and nothing in this world could change that.

Dr. Winn had told me this to help me understand. *He will never leave me.* Not because he has to stay. Not because he feels obligated. But because, to him, I am the only thing in existence that matters.

I had been afraid that after what happened to me, he would decide he didn't want me anymore—that he would see me as used and tainted. But that was never something his brain was capable of processing. She explained that he didn't have the capacity to dwell on the past. Now that my rapists were dead, his mind had closed that chapter entirely. It wouldn't resurface, wouldn't linger—unless I was the one to bring it up.

She had also clarified that this wasn't the case for everything. The way his brain functioned depended on whether a situation had a definitive resolution. If there was a solution that closed the loop, like eliminating a threat, he could move on as though it had never happened. But if any part of it remained unresolved, if there was even one loose thread, his mind would fixate on it as a whole, unable to let go until it was fully dealt with. His thoughts didn't break things into pieces or process them gradually.

Cristiano.

Knowing about his medical condition makes so much sense— sense of things I didn't even realize I was curious about. But it also makes me want to rub it in Trixie's face that she doesn't have a snowball's chance in hell with him. And that feels really fuck- ing good.

Damiano pushes himself off the wall, pulling me from my thoughts. His expression is intense as he walks toward me.

"What?" I ask, setting the brush down on the vanity and swiv- eling on the bench to face him fully.

"New girls were brought in." His hands slide out of his pock- ets as he steps closer, leaning against the counter next to me. "Two, actually. And one of them is claiming she was one of Cristiano Fierro's captives."

My eyes widen. "Isn't this good news?"

"Possibly."

"Possibly… but?" I wait for him to give the but I know is coming.

"But something feels… off."

"Off?" I repeat, narrowing my eyes.

"She's too clean. Too calm. She didn't act like the others we've rescued. No shaking, no crying. She looked around like she was studying the place, not like she was relieved to be out of hell."

A laugh slips out before I can stop it. He stares down at me, waiting for an explanation.

"You said the *others you've rescued*. It's just a funny word to use."

"How so?"

"Are you serious? Your family doesn't *rescue* women. You enslave them and force them to use their bodies in vile ways."

He narrows his eyes briefly, then shifts back to indifference.

Choosing to move past the obvious truth bomb I dropped on him, I continue, "So, you think she's a spy?"

"That's exactly what I think." He straightens. "I need you to spend time with her, talk to her, and see if she reveals anything suspicious. When you're required to work, you'll be the first one escorted out to me. We can't risk keeping her here long-term if she's working for Cristiano."

I cross my arms, fixing him with a pointed look. "For starters, that sounds a lot like I'm moving back into my old room. And secondly, I have no idea how to get someone to reveal anything."

"You're not interrogating her. You're connecting with her. It's different."

"How is that different?"

"You…" He hesitates, visibly searching for the right words. "You understand the darker realities of…"

"Just say it." I cut him off. "You mean I know what it's like to be raped. So you think I can connect with her by reminding her we're stuck here, having men use our bodies in every deranged way possible to satisfy themselves."

"Baby, I would never—"

"You would never what? You want to make it seem like less than that? Go ahead. You just seemed to be struggling with words, so I figured I'd help you out." I push past him, storming back into the bedroom.

"Fine. Yes, you were raped in the most brutal, unimaginable way. It was the worst kind of violation. The women here—they know what they're getting into. They choose how many men they can handle, and those who can't handle more than one are only given one. But you? You were never meant to be with anyone but me. What happened to you was beyond messed up.

"But that's exactly why you're the most qualified to talk to someone new and scared. Because you've endured the unimaginable, and yet you're still here. You still smile, still laugh, and that strength is what someone like her needs to see."

"You never answered me. Am I moving back into my old room?"

"Not permanently."

"Not permanently," I repeat, my stomach twisting as I wait for him to laugh or tell me he's joking. But nothing else comes. "What's the big deal with you guys and Cristiano? Why can't you just make up and quit trying to kill each other?"

"Cristiano is out for blood. There's no reasoning with him or talking him down."

"What would be the purpose of planting a spy? To learn secrets? To map out the house or operations so he can ambush us?" The whole idea of someone pretending to be a sex worker just to infiltrate the house doesn't make sense to me.

His eyebrows lift slightly, and he nods. "That's exactly why."

I can't bring myself to tell him how much I dread going back to the main house—that the thought of sleeping alone terrifies me or that I can't shake the fear of someone sneaking into my room at night to hurt me. Instead, I force myself to agree. "I'll help however I can."

He steps closer, looping one arm around my neck and pulling me into his chest. I let my hands settle around his waist, leaning into the comfort he offers.

"What if someone comes into my room?" I ask after a long pause.

"Then I'll kill them."

This doesn't feel like a safe enough answer for me. "Will there be cameras? What if I can't see them?"

I feel his body rise with laughter, and I tilt my head back to frown up at him. "What?"

"We don't need cameras, and you won't need to see them. If someone comes into your room, I will kill them right then and there."

"Like you plan on being there?" Hope blooms, but I don't want to let myself get too excited in case I'm misunderstanding.

"Of course I plan on sleeping with you." He pulls me back to him. "We get to act like enemies during the day, and at night, I get to sneak into your room and ravage you senseless."

"Why are we being sneaky?"

He slaps my butt playfully and kisses my temple as he releases me. "So she thinks one of the *scary* Volkov brothers is hurting you."

"What if she really is one of Cristiano's captives? What if she's just… traumatized?"

"That's what I need you to figure out. If she's innocent, she stays. If she's a spy… I'll deal with it."

I swallow hard, knowing exactly what it means when he *deals with it.*

Chapter
THIRTY-NINE

Damiano drives me back to the house, back to my old… new role as a worker. The transition is strange, as if I'm stepping into a past version of myself, and it's hard to mentally place myself there, especially since I've worked so hard to move on from what happened to me.

I learn that some of the other girls in the house have been brought in on the plan to determine whether *Anya* is genuinely one of Cristiano's former captives or if she's been planted as a spy. Their task is to feed her false information, mislead her, and watch her reactions. If she slips up or tries to report back, they'll catch her—though I doubt a spy of Cristiano's would be foolish enough to fall for something so simple.

The lies they spin are designed to provoke her, to see if she can be rattled. Yet as I hear some of the things they're telling her,

I wonder if she truly is a former captive—will she regret escaping one hell only to land in another? Whether she's a spy or a victim, the reality remains the same: she fled one mafia group only to end up in the clutches of another. And here, like the rest, she'll be put to work. She certainly meets their standards for a sex worker and will be paraded around at events, served up on a platter. I half wish, for her sake, that she didn't, so she could be relegated to cleaning or catering duties.

Damiano showed me a picture of her. She's gorgeous. Thick, wavy black hair falls just past her shoulders, framing delicate features that make her appear younger than her twenty-four years. She's petite, just the way they like the girls, with a small chest and a perky butt.

Her first day unfolds like mine once did, a carefully orchestrated performance meant to terrify her and the other new girl. The house whispers threats, painting a vivid picture of the horrors awaiting them. They're told they'll be used and abused, that the only way to avoid constant mistreatment is to catch the attention of one of the Volkov men.

They mention how three of them are currently "entangled" with three of the girls, but certain girls have already claimed which brother they want and will do anything to keep the others away. Then they bring up Damiano—the *crazy* brother—saying he's obsessed with one of the new girls and possessive to the point of insanity. That he goes mad at the thought of another man touching her, and even though she never sleeps with anyone else, he spirals into blind rages and takes it out on her at night when everyone goes to bed.

I let out a long, exaggerated sigh as Damiano parks, wanting him to know I'm not thrilled about this. He flips his center console up and rests his arm across the back of the seat, tugging on a lock of my hair. "Scoot over here."

I cross my arms and stare out my window.

He pokes my side. "I'm gonna put my finger in your butt if you don't get over here."

I push my pouty lip out as I move closer, and he smiles, leaning in and pulling it between his teeth. "Are you throwing a fit?"

I nod, pinching my eyebrows together.

"Mmm." He brushes his mouth over mine. Each stroke is slow, drawing me in deeper as he weaves through my hair. The world outside the truck fades away, leaving only the warmth of his body against mine. My fingers trail up his chest, debating whether making the first move would tempt him into having sex with me before we go inside.

A sharp whistle cuts through the moment, followed by laughter and low catcalls. We both pull away, turning to see Ricco and three other guards standing nearby, watching us with amused expressions.

"Don't stop on our account," Ricco calls.

I flip him off, and his laughter only intensifies.

Dante strides across the driveway, having seen us too, but he doesn't make any sort of acknowledgment. He just keeps walking.

"Ready?" Damiano asks.

"Nope."

I watch him climb out and then flop myself back across the seats, my arms resting above my head.

His hands glide behind my knees, pulling me across the seat until I'm perched on the edge. As I sit up, I wrap around his neck, and he lifts me from the truck. I circle my legs around his waist, holding him close, not quite ready to go inside.

I hook a finger under the collar of his T-shirt, tugging it to the side as I bite down and suck. I work my way up, kissing his neck and then sucking again just under his ear. He presses me against the truck, letting me mark him. Once I've left a deep purple hickey, I smile wide. "In case you forget about me."

"Yeah, okay," he says sarcastically, as if forgetting about me would never happen.

When we enter my room, I flop down on the bed, letting my face fall into the comforter. All I want to do is scream.

He stands behind me, his palms clapping down on my butt as he drumrolls on each cheek. Then climbs onto the bed, straddling me as he lays flush against my back. His lips trail kisses along my shoulder, working their way up to my ear.

"I want you to know, I really appreciate your willingness to do this. And I'm kind of looking forward to seeing this sexy body in one of your little dresses."

I grind my butt up toward him, aware of just how much he likes the thought of me in my skimpy dresses. He pushes back into me, a subtle groan escaping.

"You don't get this right now." I lift up until he rolls over.

"I thought we could have *goodbye-for-now* sex."

He seems hopeful but denying him is more satisfying than I expected.

"Nope." I slide off the bed. "Off you go, random man. Get out of my room." I point to the door.

He stands, wrapping me in a hug again. "Random man? That's not nice." He kisses my forehead. "Do you always let random men lick your butt when you wake up?"

"Do *you* always let random girls lick your butt when *they* first wake up?" I retort.

"Only my future wife."

I shrug. "If we were future anything, we wouldn't be apart."

He pecks me on the lips. "Okay, wife. How about we grab some thread and stitch our hands together?"

"That could work, but I think I'd rather have my hand stitched to your dick."

"Oh, that sounds delightful," he quips.

I smile and give his stomach a playful slap.

"Anya is in the room right here," he jerks his chin toward the wall the head of my bed sits against. "She'll be able to hear everything that happens in here… at night."

I nod in understanding. Basically, I need to stay on track because a slip-up in here, one Anya overhears, could ruin the whole plan.

Unfortunately, I slip into my old role seamlessly.

Back in my scant attire, in my old room, in my old spot, I lean against the window frame, staring out into the backyard toward the direction of our house. I just wish I could see Damiano. It's only been a couple of hours, yet it drags on as if weeks have passed.

The timing, however, couldn't be more perfect. I spot Anya—or at least a girl who resembles the photo Damiano showed me—sitting on a bench in the garden, staring blankly at the roses. Her dark hair is pulled into a loose ponytail, and she appears lost in thought.

"Mind if I join you?" I ask, approaching her cautiously.

She startles, turning toward me. She's quiet for so long that I take it as her hoping I'll just turn around and walk away. But I stand my ground. When she realizes I'll just wait here all day if I have to, she finally speaks. "No need. The rest of the girls already tried to scare me," she says flatly.

"I'm not here to try to scare you."

"So you're also not here to threaten that if I go near any of the Volkovs, you'll poison me?"

I pinch my lips into a thin line wondering which girl made those claims. "I don't need to threaten you. If they want you, they take you. You won't stop it. None of the girls here will stop it. It's the way it is."

"Maybe. But from what I hear, they're all spoken for. So getting their attention is a sure way to end up dead. Used by them, killed by jealousy. So which one of them are you here to stake your claim on?"

I raise my brow.

She scoffs, staring up at me. "Oh, come on. I have eyes." She looks me up and down. "You're *obviously* one of theirs."

I know this is part of the game, but the way she talks about them—insinuating they're slimy—rubs me the wrong way. It's almost like a sense of protection kicks in, as if I'm allowed to think that about them, but no one else can.

I briefly contemplate leaving but walk to the bench and settle in next to her, straightening my legs out in front of me. Lacing my fingers together, I rest my hands between my thighs. I follow her line of sight and take in the garden. It's beautiful out here.

I take a deep breath and let it out. "I'm Rainey."

I almost want to laugh when her head whips in my direction, and she gapes. I see the stories of Damiano's reputation have preceded him, but I keep my face neutral, staring absentmindedly ahead.

And with that, she seems to relax, as if she stands in solidarity with me, knowing how bad *I* have it here and how bad she had it there.

"Anya."

She keeps her attention on me, and I finally turn to meet her gaze.

"I'm Anya," she says again, this time as an actual introduction.

"Hi, Anya." I offer her a soft smile. "How are you holding up?"

"It doesn't really matter, right?"

I shake my head. "No, it doesn't. But sometimes, having someone ask something so simple and giving you the chance to release your fears helps."

She takes me in, as if she believes I, of all people, understand her struggles. "Better than I thought I would be, considering."

I tilt my head. "Considering?"

"Everything I've been through. I'm just… glad to be out of there."

I study her closely, trying to read between the lines of her words. "I can't imagine what it was like," I say genuinely. "I've been here for a while now, and if you prefer taking your chances in this place over staying with Cristiano, I think it speaks volumes about how bad it must have been."

Even suggesting that any of the brothers are bad makes me feel gross. *But they are, aren't they?* They sleep with girls who were brought here against their will, yet every one of those girls is more than eager when called away by them.

Her eyes flicker to mine, a hint of vulnerability breaking through her guarded expression. "Pathetic, right?"

I shake my head. "Not at all. You chose the best of two evils, I suppose."

She doesn't say anything.

"Can I ask? If you got free, why would you come to another mafia house? Why not go be free?"

She sucks in a breath and holds it, then releases it, shaking her head. "I can never be free. I was sold to Cristiano when I was only thirteen. I don't have family, money, or anywhere to go. I can't take care of myself. One of Cristiano's housekeepers, Fedora, was the most motherly person I've ever had. She was the one who took care of me. She cleaned me up after…you know. And when things started to get really bad, she told me I had to escape and find the Volkovs."

"Is there any part of you that regrets coming here?"

She actually seems to consider it. I don't know much about Cristiano other than how badly the Volkovs want him dead. That might also explain why Damiano isn't supposed to leave the property. Not that he ever really needs to. There's enough here to keep him occupied, no real reason to go out. But I know firsthand how suffocating it is to be trapped, like every day you're running on limited air. The moment you get past the gates, your lungs expand, and freedom rushes in.

I always assumed all the Volkovs were hunted by Cristiano just as fiercely as they hunt him, but it seems Damiano is the one they're all trying to protect. I don't understand why. Maybe he killed one of Cristiano's men. But if Cristiano's hatred for Damiano is as intense as everyone suggests, I can't even imagine what it would be like for Damiano's *girlfriend.*

She shakes her head slowly. "No."

"Even though you'll be doing the same kind of work?"

She rubs her hands over her thighs before lacing her fingers together. "I've been having sex since I was young. At first, it felt awful. But eventually, you go numb to it. You get used to it. And then… you start craving it. Just sex. I like sex. I enjoy how it feels. Rough sex, I can handle. But being beaten during it—I don't like that. And from what I've heard, that won't happen here."

I tense at her words. Because we aren't supposed to be severely hurt during sex here. Or maybe we are. When I was beaten during my rape, the horror etched across everyone's faces made me think it wasn't supposed to happen. I wonder if that's the life Anya has been living since she was thirteen.

"Do you have family?" she asks.

I scoff, though there's no humor in it. Family is supposed to mean something, but to me, it means nothing. "A mom. She traded me for her debt."

She blinks rapidly, processing. "Oh wow. That's fucked."

"Yeah. It was."

We sit in silence as the sun sinks lower, nearly swallowed by the horizon.

"We have to head back. We'll be expected in our rooms soon."

She nods and falls into step beside me as we return to the house.

Climbing the back steps, I catch a glimpse of the Volkov family at the dinner table. My chest tightens when I see Damiano. I love this man so much it hurts. Every part of me wants to go in, kiss him, and wrap my arms around him. But I don't get to.

"Are you okay?" she asks as I stare through the window, lost in thought.

That reaction works in my favor, as it appears I'm nervous to go into the house just by seeing him. I blink rapidly, forcing a pained smile as I pretend I'm fine. "Yeah, come on."

We step inside, moving quickly to avoid drawing attention, but Damiano halts us.

"Stop."

From my periphery, I catch her flinch beside me. We turn toward him, waiting.

"Why were you outside? Who was with you?"

I pause before answering. "Just me and Anya, sir."

"Get to your rooms." He dismisses us.

He's good. Really good. Because his coldness is actually hurting my feelings.

"Yes, sir," I say, glancing around the table.

Nikolai's smile finds me—his usual perfect smile. I take it as his way of telling me it's going to be okay, that I've got this. Like he's encouraging me.

"What was that?" Damiano bellows.

Anya flinches slightly, and even I'm not sure what he's referring to.

"What was what?" Dante asks, his fork hovering midair with a bite of steak.

"Why did you smile at her like that?" Damiano demands as he glares at Nikolai.

"Can I not smile at the pets?"

Damiano pushes back from the table abruptly. "Where have you been?" he barks at Nikolai.

"Relax. I wasn't with Rainey." He raises his hands in surrender.

When his head whips toward me, fury etched across his face, Anya tenses even more. He stalks forward so fast I barely have time to react as his hand clamps around my arm, yanking me toward him. His face hovers inches from mine, his rage unmistakable.

"Did you sleep with my brother?"

I don't have to fake being caught off guard. I want to look at Dante for help on how to respond, but I realize none of this is real. He isn't actually accusing me of sleeping with his brother.

I shake my head, carefully wording my response. "No, sir. I didn't sleep with *Nikolai*."

He pulls me even closer, roughly running his hand under my dress, making a show of checking for wetness. Though he never actually touches beneath my panties, she doesn't know that.

I wince, turning my head toward her and squeezing my eyes shut until he finally lets go. "Good," he says, smoothing his tie. "Get to your room."

"Yes, sir," I say with a nod, grabbing her hand and pulling her away as fast as possible.

Neither of us speaks on the way back.

At the top landing, Marko and Tess slip away together, giggling, completely unaware of us. Anya watches them, her grip tightening slightly around my hand.

When we reach her door, I stop. "Get ready for bed, then come back out. Valentina will be by with details for tomorrow."

I don't wait for a response. Instead, I turn and head to my room, lifting a hand as if to wipe away a tear.

I'd better get some damn good sex for this incredible performance I'm putting on.

For thirty minutes, I sit in my room. I turn on the TV so I don't have to listen to Marko hump the shit out of Tess, because right now, my jealousy can't stand it.

When Valentina strides down the hall, summoning us, I step out and find Trixie smirking at me as if she's privy to some secret I'm not. Annoyed, I tear my gaze away and focus on Valentina.

With a bright smile, she claps her hands. "Ladies, rest up. Tomorrow evening, we have an event at the *Fun House*, and I expect nothing less than perfection."

"Valentina," Ruby speaks up, "with us working tomorrow, are any of us to expect visitors in the night?"

The implication is clear. We all know the guards often take their breaks in the middle of the night—and just as often, those breaks lead them straight to one of the beds on this floor.

Valentina's response is immediate. "You can all sleep peacefully. There will be no visitors. I need every single one of you at your best for tomorrow's event." She pauses, letting the message settle. "Now, off you go!"

The girls drift away, their doors closing one by one, the soft snick of locks echoing through the hall. As I turn to my own room, my gaze snags on Anya. She stands a few feet away, staring at me with a pained expression.

I offer her a small smile, and she returns the faintest one before stepping inside and closing herself away. I pause, noticing her shadow still visible beneath the door. It's easy to imagine her standing there, her back against the wood as if bracing herself.

If I relied on gut alone, I'd believe she really is one of Cristiano's former captives. Every instinct I have screams it's true. But Damiano won't act on instinct—he needs proof.

I'M JOLTED AWAKE BY THE YANK OF MY BLANKETS AND A SLAP AGAINST my ass. Terror grips me instantly, my sleep-fogged mind scrambling to make sense of what's happening. *How many are here?* The scream of "No!" bursts from my lips before I can stop it, and my legs thrash wildly as I fight to protect myself. Not again.

The faint glow of the nightlight flickers on, and Damiano's familiar frame comes into focus as he climbs onto the bed, straddling my lap and pinning my arms at my sides.

"You can't be here!" I hiss, still shaking with leftover panic. "Your mom said nobody's allowed in our rooms tonight."

"Nobody knows I'm here," he replies, "and you're not going to tell anyone."

"Damiano, get out!" I snap, twisting beneath him.

He releases my hands, and his lips crash against mine. My breath hitches as the familiar taste of him floods my senses. I breathe him in. *I'm safe. It's Damiano. I'm safe.* The thought loops in my mind, soothing the remnants of fear.

"I didn't mean to scare you. I wasn't thinking."

"It's fine." But adrenaline still pulses through me.

"Take off your clothes."

"She's probably asleep," I whisper.

"She's not," he shakes his head. "Take off your clothes. Now." He grows louder and more commanding.

"No!" I shove at his chest. "Get out!"

His grin widens as he climbs off the bed, lifting me with him as our lips meet again. I wrap my legs around his waist, holding onto him as the kiss deepens.

The crash of the lamp shattering against the wall jolts me. A scream rips from my throat and I squeeze him harder. The sudden darkness disorients me, my wide eyes struggling to adjust, to make sense of what just happened.

"What was that?!" I blurt, disbelief woven into my words.

"Theatrics."

He sets me on the edge of the bed, tugging at the hem of my top.

"Get off me!" I yell, crawling toward the other side of the bed.

He's quicker. His hand snatches my ankle, yanking me back and sending a thrill racing through me.

And then, we put on the show of a lifetime.

She hears exactly what we want her to—my screams and the sound of a struggle. To Anya, it must seem like I'm fighting off an assault.

In reality, it's Damiano with me, gripping my wrists as he pins me to the bed. Our bodies move in a chaotic rhythm, rough and unrestrained. I love every second of it. But Anya doesn't know that. What she hears—my gasps, muffled protests, and Damiano's deep, guttural growls—paints a much darker picture. She has no idea this is exactly what I crave.

The walls in this house are not soundproof, and that is no accident. Every noise carries, reverberating through the space. Some rooms are even connected by locked adjoining doors, mine and Anya's among them. We have been told they will remain locked, but the thin barrier between us might as well not exist.

Her light turns on, shadows pacing beneath the threshold as she walks back and forth. Is she trying to block out the sounds? Or straining to hear every detail? Either way, the tension radiating from her room is undeniable, seeping through the cracks beneath the door.

Chapter

FORTY

Rainey

I wake to the covers shifting and roll over to see Damiano moving quietly. My brows knit as I watch, silently questioning what he's doing.

"Gotta get out of here," he whispers. "The women are already waking up."

I pout, pushing out my bottom lip. He smirks as he playfully pulls it between his teeth, then releases it and begins dressing.

"Don't get off on this side," he murmurs. "I'll send someone to clean up the lamp mess."

He kisses me once more before straightening.

"I'm gonna get off on this side just so my foot gets cut and you have to take care of me," I tease, sliding toward the edge of the bed.

He swats my bare ass. "Don't you dare."

I toss a grin over my shoulder, adding a wink as I head into the bathroom. His low, rich laughter trails behind me as I close the door.

By the time I make it downstairs, the house is alive with chatter. In the dining room, the long table is already filled with girls helping themselves to the spread of food at the center.

Em beams as I approach. "I had such a good night's sleep. It was refreshing not to worry about the guards dropping by for their 'breaks.'"

Her comment sparks a ripple of agreement, a collective sigh of relief as the girls echo their appreciation for an undisturbed night. She's clearly in the loop. A guard would never go to her room for one of those so-called "breaks." If anyone even tried, I'm certain Dante would kill them without a second thought.

Guilt settles in as I watch her with the others. She was kind to us from the start, never boastful, never possessive over Dante. Yet we all just know he's hers. And he never tried to be with anyone else.

Her only role seems to be staying at the house for Dante's convenience—and he takes full advantage of it. But I took advantage of him. I knew he wanted to fuck me again. For whatever reason, he still does. I don't understand it, and he knows as well as I do that if Damiano ever finds out, we'll both probably be killed. But I didn't care when I went to him. I wanted Damiano, and he wasn't there. I was desperate for someone familiar, and Dante was it.

I didn't think about Em at the time, but now I know. If the roles were reversed—if someone slept with Damiano, knowing we were practically together, just to make themselves feel better—I'd be devastated.

I'm a horrible person.

I turn away, unwilling to watch her any longer. Dante and I don't need to say a word to know we're taking this secret to the grave. But if she looks me in the eyes, I'm afraid she'll see the guilt written all over my face.

I'm almost certain that during the nights I stayed with Dante, lost in a drug-induced haze, we had sex more than once. I thought they were just vivid wet dreams, but every time I got up to use the bathroom, there was semen in me. And he was the only one in bed with me. We were both always naked, our clothes tangled somewhere in the sheets.

And if it wasn't a dream, then one of those nights, I climbed on top of him while he was sleeping, rode him reverse cowgirl, and screamed through my orgasm.

Whether it was real or not, I didn't care at the time. I was convinced Damiano was done with me. Only to find out later that while I was in Dante's bed, he was torturing the men who raped me.

All while I was fucking his brother.

God, I suck.

As I reach to scoop eggs onto my plate, I catch Anya staring at the marks on my wrists, evidence of where Damiano tied me to the bed as he went down on me. Her wide eyes linger before shifting to mine, then she quickly focuses back on her plate as I take my seat.

Valentina strides in, flawless as ever. "Good morning, ladies," she greets with a wide smile, her gaze sweeping over us. "How did everyone sleep?"

The chorus of positive responses pleases her, and her smile grows. "Wonderful. Nobody had any visitors in their rooms, correct?" She searches for any sign of discomfort or complaint.

Everyone shakes their head, but Anya's stare burns into me.

"Anya," Valentina says. "How was your second night?"

I keep my eyes locked on her. She appears to be deciding whether to speak up about what she heard. The room hangs in silence for a long moment, but she finally answers, "Fine."

Valentina studies her, head tilting slightly. "You look exhaust-
ed," she says, her tone laced with concern. "Once you're settled in,
I think you'll sleep easier."

Anya glances at me again before turning back to Valentina.
"Thank you," she murmurs.

After breakfast, I head down the hallway, but Anya catches up
to me. "Why didn't you say anything?" she blurts out.

"About?" I reply coolly, not breaking stride.

"You know what," she insists. "I heard what happened to you
last night. I know it was Damiano."

I stop abruptly, turning on my heel, and she nearly collides
with me. "Keep your mouth shut if you want to survive here," I
say evenly, my tone laced with quiet authority.

Her eyes widen, but I continue before she can respond. "Do
you want to know which Volkov brother you *don't* want wanting
you? Damiano Volkov. Do you want to know which brother wants
me? Damiano Volkov. He tortures and murders—that's his job.
You cross him, and he will slit your throat and fuck *me* on your
corpse. So mind your own business. You didn't hear anything last
night. You won't hear anything tonight or any other night. Are we
understood?"

Her face pales, and she swallows hard, giving a small nod.

"Good." I spin on my heel to leave, but her voice stops me.

"Let me help you."

I glance over my shoulder, arching a brow. "Oh yeah? And
how are you going to do that?"

She falters, her mouth opening as if to speak, but the words
catch in her throat. After a long pause, she swallows them
back down.

"That's what I thought," I say, turning away.

MEN ARRIVE EARLY FOR A MEETING WITH THE VOLKOVS, THEIR PRESENCE immediately stirring excitement among the girls. They gather near the front door, eager for a chance to catch the men's attention. As soon as the first group steps inside, the air fills with giggles and shameless flirtation. It doesn't take long before three girls are chosen, their victorious smiles bright as they stroll off with the men, leaving the others by the door casting envious glances their way.

"Why are they so eager?" Anya asks.

"Because they won't have to go to the *Fun House* tonight," Lacy replies matter-of-factly, barely glancing at her as she speaks.

Anya's brows furrow. "What's the *Fun House*?"

"Not anything fun," I interject, keeping my tone flat.

THE LIVING ROOM FILLS WITH QUIET CONVERSATION AS THE GIRLS working tonight lounge on the couches, waiting for Valentina to give us instructions. She walks in and stops at the center of the room.

"Ladies," she begins, smoothing the fabric of her perfectly tailored dress, "tonight is a collar night. The men will be playing poker, but the *Round Room* will be available." Her gaze sweeps across the room. "You'll all be wearing the required attire. It's always a crowd favorite."

I still remember the last *Round Room* fiasco. I tried to shoot Damiano, and Trixie bashed my skull in. *Fucking bitch.* I glance over at her and can't help the disgust I feel for her.

"Like always," Valentina continues, "the wardrobe will be placed on the working girls' doors, and you'll be expected to be ready on time."

The sound of footsteps draws everyone's attention to the doorway just as Damiano strides in. His presence shifts the energy in the room instantly. Valentina's face lights up with an overly sweet smile as she greets him. "Hi, dear, is everything okay?"

I've come to see another side of her. Beneath her composed and commanding exterior, she loves her children deeply, especially Damiano. I wonder if people favor him partly out of fear. However, Valentina's love, or at least her generosity, extends to those her children care about. From the beginning, she has been kind to me. She welcomed me without hesitation and has looked out for me ever since Damiano 'claimed' me.

He doesn't bother acknowledging his mother's greeting. The moment he enters, he locks onto me, and his intensity makes my heart leap. I try to act indifferent, but my entire body hums with excitement. My hands shift awkwardly beneath me as I sit beside Anya, doing my best to appear unaffected while also trying to seem nervous.

Her hand slides to my wrist, subtly holding it. Guilt pricks at me for deceiving her, but she could be deceiving all of us.

He sits on the ottoman directly in front of me, blocking my view of the TV—even though I wasn't watching.

"You're in the way," I say, trying to sound indifferent even as my pulse quickens.

"Get up," he orders.

I meet his gaze, arching a brow. "Excuse me?"

"She's working tonight, son," Valentina interjects.

"I'll keep her busy until then," he replies, clapping his palms against my legs. "Let's go."

"I have to get ready for tonight."

"And I want to have sex."

I glance around the room, noting all the eyes on me. "Can you just come by later?" I whisper.

"No. Get up," he repeats.

"No," I try to say more firmly.

He grips the backs of my calves, and suddenly, I'm staring up at the ceiling as he begins undoing his belt. My mouth falls open. I can't believe he would even try to make a show of this right now. But he would. He absolutely would fuck me in front of everyone and not care at all.

"Okay, fine, geez," I say, pulling myself back into a sitting position.

He stands, clamps a hand around my arm, and jerks me to my feet.

A brief hint of annoyance crosses Valentina's face. "She'd better not come back too tired to work."

Damiano glances over his shoulder at her. "She'll come back however I send her back."

The murmurs from the other girls fade into the background as he drags me from the room.

"Where is he taking her?" Anya's voice rings out behind me.

"He takes her back to his house so nobody can hear what he does to her," someone mutters.

I can't make out who said it, but it's the last thing I hear as we exit through the back door.

By the time we return to his house, I'm leaping into his arms, wrapping myself around him and squeezing tight. "Are we done with this bullshit yet?" I murmur against his lips.

"Not yet, baby."

I pull back slightly, pouting. "Let's skip the party tonight, stay in, watch movies, and cuddle."

He sets me down gently. "What's your read on her so far?"

I pause, letting my thoughts sift through the moments I've shared with Anya. She seems shattered, fragile in ways I recognize too well. Then I remember the way she reached out to me earlier, as though she truly believed Damiano was hurting me.

"I don't think she's a spy," I say finally. "She's just… broken. Like the rest of us."

His jaw tightens and his features harden. Finally, he nods. "Okay. But keep an eye on her, just in case."

I cross my arms, staring at him pointedly. "You don't have to be so suspicious of everyone, you know."

"I can't afford not to be."

"What if I'm a spy?" I tease, my lips curving into a mischievous smile. "You let me into your bed."

"I watched you for a year. If you were, I'd have figured it out by now. And if you were a spy, I think you would've changed sides once I bedded you." He reaches out, grabbing the front of my dress and pulling me back toward him.

"Pretty sure you were just as clueless as I was when it came to sex," I counter, poking his chest.

He presses his lips to mine. "We managed just fine."

The hours pass in a warm haze of laughter and teasing. We stay tangled in bed, arguing over the most pointless things—like who was more clueless during our first time or why he thought it was a good idea to have our first sexual encounter in front of others when we barely knew what we were doing. He jokes that immediately after putting his dick inside me, he regretted choosing the auction for our first time since he thought for sure he was going to come right away because it felt so good.

He swings his legs over the edge of the bed, running a hand through his hair as he stands. He reaches back and taps my leg. "Get up."

I groan, burrowing deeper into the blankets. "No. I want to cuddle."

He exhales through his nose. "Okay."

The next thing I know, he climbs back onto the bed—but instead of lying down beside me, he moves swiftly, flipping me onto my stomach. His arm snakes around my neck, pressing just enough to make my body tense in confusion.

I try to turn back, but his grip tightens slightly. "What are you doing, babe?"

"If someone attacks you from behind and locks you in a choke-hold, you need to know how to get out of it." His voice is calm and controlled. "If you don't, they could render you unconscious. Or worse, kill you."

A chill moves down my spine, my body instantly more aware of the position I'm in.

"You feel that?" he asks, pressing just a little more against my throat before easing off. "They don't even have to be that strong. If they cut off blood flow, you'll be out in seconds. But there's a way out."

I shift, testing his hold, but he keeps me locked in place.

"First, don't panic," he instructs. "If you freak out, you'll burn through oxygen faster, and they'll have an easier time taking you down. Now, bring your hands up and grip my forearm. Tight."

I do as he says, wrapping my fingers around his arm.

"Good. Now turn your chin toward the crook of my elbow—never toward their hand, or you'll tighten the choke on yourself."

I shift my head as he instructed, feeling the slight difference in pressure.

"Now, drop your weight."

I go limp, and his hold adjusts slightly.

"That's it. If someone grabs you like this, they expect you to struggle up, not down. Drop fast, make yourself dead weight. It'll throw them off balance."

His voice remains steady, guiding me through the next steps.

"Now, as soon as you feel them shift, move fast. Slam your elbow into their ribs or stomach—aim for soft tissue. If you can, reach back and claw at their face or dig your nails into their fore-arm. Anything to make them loosen their grip."

I follow his instructions, jabbing my elbow back, and he grunts softly in approval.

"Now pivot—turn toward me."

I twist, slipping from his grip, and stumble back onto my knees, breathing hard.

He smirks. "Not bad. Now get up."

I push myself to my feet, and he moves to stand in front of me.

"There are a few key spots that do the most damage," he says, lifting his hand to tap my forehead lightly. "First, the face. Eyes, nose, throat. Gouge, strike, or crush." His fingers trail lower, tapping the center of my chest. "Sternum—drive your palm into it hard enough, and it'll knock the wind out of them."

He steps back and motions to my leg. "Knees. A well-placed kick can buckle them completely. And if they're a guy?" He smirks. "I don't need to tell you where to aim."

"Let me try." I reach between his legs, and he steps back, laughing.

"Let's not."

He suddenly lunges, and I barely react before his fingers press into my side.

"Ribs," he adds, stepping back again. "A sharp elbow strike here can break them. And if they're grabbing you, don't forget the wrist. Twist against their thumb—it's the weakest point of their grip."

I exhale, absorbing everything. "Why do I need to know this when you can just protect me?"

"I will always protect you. But you need to know how to protect yourself."

I lift my brows. "Do you think about this often?"

He shrugs. "I think about how to keep you safe."

His words settle over me, something warm blooming in my chest.

"Because you looove me," I drawl.

"Yes."

"Because you wanna marry me." I grab his wrist and step into him.

"I will."

"Because you wanna have babies with me." I press my chest to his.

"At least five." He bends down and kisses me. "Now, let's see if you remember anything I just showed you."

I groan. "Can't we just go back to cuddling?"

His smirk widens. "Tonight."

He continues showing me different scenarios where I could end up in a hairy situation and how I can get myself out of them. Eventually, though, the time comes when I have to get up and prepare for the night.

Dread settles in my stomach as I think about the leather bondage outfit waiting for me.

Damiano drives us back, his hand resting on my thigh the entire way. When we arrive, he peels away to talk to his brothers, leaving me to head to my room alone.

The leather outfit hangs on my door, just as I knew it would be. As I approach, I realize none of the other doors have one. It almost seems like a sick joke that I'll be going to the *Round Room* alone, but I know that's not the case. Everyone else is probably just already dressed and ready to go.

The tight straps and revealing cuts have become second nature by now, but they still make my skin crawl. Tonight feels different, though. Knowing Damiano is the only man who will touch me softens the blow, even if just a little.

I slip into the outfit, carefully adjusting the straps to make sure everything that should be covered is concealed beneath the thin, unforgiving leather. My hair is pulled into a high ponytail, as we were all required to do, and I trace my fingers over my neck tattoo.

Anya has either never noticed it, never paid attention, or never wanted to ask. But tonight, it's unmistakable.

By the time I'm done, the reflection staring back at me is one I've learned to accept, even if I don't recognize her some days.

Stepping into the hallway, the other girls are already lined up, their faces carefully blank. Valentina strides toward us, assessing each girl.

She stops in front of me, trailing up and down my body. "How rough was he?" she asks, her tone light but carrying an edge that suggests she already knows the answer.

Her act is impeccable.

I keep my eyes trained forward, my face blank. "He didn't do anything I couldn't handle."

I catch Anya staring at me. I can tell she doesn't believe me, but she stays silent.

Valentina watches me for a beat longer. "Good," she says, her red lips curling into a faint smile. "We've already had four guests inquire about you. If we can manage to keep that son of mine occupied, we'll slip you into a private room for some fun."

Anya hangs on to every word exchanged in this house. Without waiting for a response, Valentina turns on her heel and heads toward the stairs, her long dress sweeping the floor as she moves.

We follow in silence, our high heels clacking against the floor. As Tess and I pass Anya, she steps in line behind us.

Tess leans in, speaking just loud enough for Anya to hear. "Really though, how rough was he?"

I let out a theatrical sigh and exaggerate my walk, making sure Anya notices the slight stiffness in my stride. "Really rough." I glance at Tess with a mock grimace.

Tess stares at me sympathetically. "Did you put numbing cream on before you got dressed?"

"Of course. But it still feels like he's in both holes."

Tess's brows knit together as she stares at me. Anya's subtle reaction lets me know the plan is working.

She's listening, absorbing everything.

Chapter
FORTY-ONE

Rainey

We're shuffled into the large house in small groups, the girls splitting off in different directions. Some are sent to the *Round Room*, handcuffs fastened behind their backs before they are chained to the walls, while others are directed to the kitchen to prepare drinks. When it's my turn, a tray is shoved into my hands, and I find myself standing alongside Anya and three other girls. The man barking orders doesn't spare us a glance as he commands, "Walk around and serve. Don't stop until your tray is empty."

I balance the drinks as we step into the casino room. It's more intimidating with all the men around. When it was just me down here with the workers, it wasn't nearly as daunting.

Girls I've never seen before walk in with guards and are shuffled down a hall to an area I've never been. It has me questioning if there are workers being held in other houses too, and how they decide who lives in the actual Volkov house and who is placed somewhere else.

I don't even want to ask Damiano how all this works since it will just end up pissing me off. I'm stuck in this life now and don't need to be mad while I'm living it.

Tonight, I notice this event is different—there are women among the guests too, all dressed in elegant cocktail gowns with flawless hair and makeup. It strikes me as odd since most of the men here will sleep with the girls. Then it dawns on me. What if the women want to sleep with them too? Would they be required to do that?

Thick cigar smoke saturates the air, burning my eyes and coating my throat. A live band plays in the background, their music a seductive undercurrent to the debauchery unfolding all around. Some guests lounge near the stage, their attention split between the melody and the heated kisses they exchange, their hands wandering without shame.

The room itself is expansive, illuminated by the warm glow of chandeliers. Men sit in high-backed chairs, fixated on the stacks of chips and cash piled in front of them.

As we weave through the room, offering drinks, the men leer and make crude remarks. I wonder how much trouble I'd get in if I were to smash my tray over their heads.

"Two hundred thousand," a man calls, tossing a stack of chips onto the table. Another laughs, matching the bet. The stakes are absurdly high, the atmosphere pulsing with greed and arrogance, and I find them absolutely pathetic. All this money, and they have to get pussy from girls who can't freely consent.

I slip back to the kitchen to refill my tray, setting it on the counter as Anya appears beside me. "Who's the man sitting next to Damiano?"

Peeking into the casino, I spot Damiano at his table, exuding his usual confidence. "Silvano Volkov," I whisper.

"Does he have a girl?"

"I'm not sure," I admit. "He doesn't talk much. Mostly just to his brothers."

She nods, picking up her refilled tray. "Does he…you know… have sex with us? Not you—I mean, I know you're Damiano's… Not that you're his…"

I smile softly, amused by her flustered rambling. "Why don't I find out if Silvano is involved with anyone?"

Her cheeks turn a deep shade of pink as she quickly shakes her head. "Oh no, it's fine. Really."

I give her a knowing look but don't press further, turning back toward the smoky chaos of the casino.

As I make my way around the tables, a man calls out to me, "Pick that up for me, sweetheart," letting a napkin fall deliberately to the floor.

Suppressing the urge to roll my eyes, I crouch to retrieve it. Just as I rise, he leans forward, his face abruptly invading my space. He grips the strap covering my breasts, yanks it down, and shoves his face between them.

"What the fuck!" I gasp, stumbling back.

Before I can fully react, Damiano is out of his chair, his expression dark and furious. He yanks the man from his seat by the collar, the force causing the table to rattle.

My tray is removed from my hands, and another pair of arms reach around me, quickly adjusting the leather strap back into place. I turn to see Dante, his anger unmistakable. He pulls me back as Damiano's fist collides with the man's nose, knocking him backward with a resounding crash.

I try to push forward, but Dante holds me tighter.

"Don't intervene," he warns.

"I want to punch that bastard too!" I snarl as I attempt to pull away again.

The room falls silent as everyone watches, with no one trying to help or stop it. When Damiano straightens, he spins, reaching out and gripping my wrist as he drags me away.

The door to the kitchen swings shut behind us, and the sudden quiet is jarring. I barely have time to process it before I'm pushed against the stainless steel table.

"Damiano," I start, but he forces my chest flat against the cold surface.

The sound of his loosened belt hitting the edge is the only warning I get before he slams into me. My palms press flat on either side of me as I try to lift myself. He wraps my ponytail around his fist, tugging hard, while his other hand bears down on my lower back, keeping me trapped.

He takes me fast, his hips driving into me over and over, each thrust more forceful than the last. The raw sounds of his grunts fill the room, blending with the muffled clinking of glasses and distant murmurs.

The girls move around us, but no one says a word. This isn't the first time something like this has happened, and it won't be the last.

The door swings open, and Anya steps inside. I can tell just from her expression that she came to find me. Surprise—she found me. She freezes, her knuckles whitening around the tray, and I squeeze my eyes closed, wincing at the pain from how deep he's penetrating.

"Quit gawking and get to work," someone snaps from behind her.

She nearly drops the tray, quickly scurrying past us.

The same woman mutters to her, "You'll get used to it. That'll be you soon enough."

The whimper I've been fighting to keep down escapes when his rhythm shifts, his hips hammering harder, and my insides ache. He's furious—furious that another man dared to touch me—and now he's pouring every ounce of that rage into me.

More women come and go, the sound of their footsteps and whispered exchanges filling the kitchen. Some steal quick glances in our direction, while others keep their eyes averted, as though pretending nothing is happening will make it true.

Finally, his movements slow, and he stills, finding his release. I exhale a shaky breath, thankful it's finally over because that fucking hurt. My muscles slowly unclench, no longer forced to brace against his relentless thrusts.

"Clean yourself up," he orders, abruptly pulling out. He's cold and detached as he takes a step back and begins fastening his pants.

For a moment, I stay there, bent over the table, trying to gather myself. I push upright, glancing down at my outfit to ensure all the leather straps are still in place.

He waits more patiently than I would have expected, and when I stride toward him, he walks out ahead of me. I follow behind, still acutely aware of every step I take.

Back in the casino, he moves as if nothing happened, returning to his seat at the poker table. I walk toward where my tray is, but he clamps onto my wrist and pulls me onto his lap.

The men around the table don't even blink, their attention fixed on the cards and chips in front of them.

Damiano's arm loops around my waist, holding me securely as he continues to play. His other hand occasionally taps the table or flips his cards. Between turns, he kisses my shoulder, nipping gently at my skin.

The night stretches on endlessly as the men at the tables come and go, some disappearing for an hour or two to the Round Room at the far end of the house, only to return later with flushed faces and loosened ties.

Despite my attempts to follow along, I'm not catching on to the game, so I end up watching the players more than the cards, noticing how unnerved the others seem by Damiano. I wonder how much people know about what he does—maybe it's common knowledge that he murders people? Maybe all these people in here are murderers, and the only thing that sets him apart from the rest is that he has a brain trauma that makes him a psycho.

I also notice he's really good at reading people, even when he doesn't appear to be paying attention. It's quite fascinating, especially since his pile of chips continues to grow steadily while the tension among the men escalates with each passing hand.

I stay perched on his lap, my body stiff as I do my best to fade into the background. He occasionally pulls me from my thoughts, idly tracing patterns along my waist. I try to keep my sigh unnoticed as I glance around, attempting to distract myself.

Anya is across the room, approaching a man in a gray suit and giving him a drink. But it's not just the drink that draws my focus. Subtly, she slips him a folded piece of paper as the glass is exchanged. The man nods faintly, tucking the paper into his pocket before turning back to the table.

I shift my focus to Damiano, sliding my arm around his shoulders and leaning in to feign intimacy. "Anya just passed something to the man in the gray suit. He put it in his pocket."

He keeps his attention on his cards, tapping the table. "Let me know if he moves."

I nod, keeping my arms draped around his neck as I nuzzle closer, brushing soft kisses behind his ear while staying locked on the man in gray. Anya disappears toward the bar, and the man begins to shift, glancing around before gathering his chips.

"He's collecting his stuff."

Damiano exhales, scanning the room before raising a hand to summon a man who approaches immediately. Turning back to me, he says calmly, "Get his attention and do whatever it takes to retrieve the paper."

I stare at him, stunned. "No one's going to let me near them with you sitting here, especially not after that massive shitshow you pulled earlier."

His lips curl into a smirk. "I'm leaving… with Melanie."

My mouth falls open, a protest forming on my tongue, but before I can speak, he cuts me off with a quick kiss. "Perfect. Keep that scowl, and you'll be well on your way to being believable."

Before I can respond, he lifts me from his lap and stands, slapping my butt lightly to signal that I should get moving. "Don't lose my money," he says, directing the comment to the man now sliding into his seat and gathering his cards.

I gape after him as he strides over to Melanie. She lights up as he approaches, giggling when he whispers something in her ear. She clings to his arm as they leave, her face a picture of smug satisfaction.

The man in gray notices, his gaze flicking between me and the retreating pair. I hold my shocked expression until they disappear, then angrily stride away, settling onto a high-top chair near the pool tables.

"That's rough," someone drawls.

Gray Suit approaches, and I flash him a coy smile. "Only if the night ends with me alone."

His grin widens, his interest piqued. "I can make sure it doesn't."

"Maybe you should," I murmur, letting my tone dip just enough to sound inviting as I reach for him.

I shift slightly, perching myself on the edge of the chair and parting my legs just enough to draw him closer. His breath hitches, a low groan escaping as his lips curl into something darker, something predatory. His hands slide up my thighs, and he steps into the space between us, his body crowding mine. Just where I want him.

He brushes against my neck, placing a wet kiss on my skin. My stomach turns, but I keep my composure, letting my fingers slide to the front of his pants. Unimpressed doesn't begin to cover it, but I continue playing along, running my palm along the short length of his dick through the fabric. He groans as I squeeze enough to distract him, slipping my other into his pocket to retrieve the folded paper Anya passed him.

As he tilts his head, angling for a kiss, a deep, familiar voice interrupts. "Mind if I cut in?"

Nikolai stands there, his broad frame casting a shadow over Gray Suit. His hands rest casually in his pockets, but the air around him is anything but relaxed. Relief floods me, the tension in my body loosens.

The man hesitates, irritation flashing across his face, but Nikolai's presence leaves him with little choice. "No problem," he mutters, stepping back reluctantly.

I offer the man a sympathetic glance to keep up the act, then casually slip the paper into Nikolai's shirt pocket as he steps into the space the man vacated. My palm grazes his chest as if it's just part of the flirtation that comes with my job. He takes hold of me, pulling me from the chair, and leads me through the room. To the men watching, it's just another brother taking me somewhere private, and everyone knows what that means.

As we pass Gray Suit, he turns his head toward me and winks. I respond with a sweet, practiced smile, pretending to bask in the attention.

Before we stride down the hall toward the office, I peer casually over my shoulder one more time, noticing Gray Suit trailing a short distance behind us.

"He's following us," I murmur.

Nikolai pivots toward me. Without warning, he grabs my ass, hoisting me up. My back meets the wall as his lips crash against mine, the kiss deep and consuming. Instinct takes over as my legs wrap around his torso, my arms locking around his neck.

The man knows what he's doing.

When he pulls back to kiss my neck, I peek toward the end of the hallway, catching Gray Suit's expression darken as he turns on his heel and storms off.

"He's leaving," I manage.

Nikolai glances discreetly to confirm, then lowers me back to the ground. I spot Trixie at the other end of the hall, striding toward us with a smug grin plastered across her face, pleased to have witnessed the scene.

"Ready?" Nikolai asks, his tone even, as if nothing just happened.

I clear my throat, pushing off the wall. "Yep."

Once inside the large office, Nikolai pulls the folded paper from his pocket and passes it to Damiano. He takes it, his eyes flicking between the two of us.

"Everything good?" Damiano asks.

"It better be something good on that paper," I huff, crossing my arms. "Because I had to touch that guy's tiny dick, then deal with him being so mad that Nikolai interrupted him getting his rocks off, he decided to follow us. And then big-mouth Trixie caught us making out in the hall while Gray Suit stomped away like a baby." The words tumble out in a rush, my irritation spilling over.

Dante points from Nikolai to me. "You two made out?"

"Yes, Dante," I snap, emphasizing his name. He, of all people, shouldn't be passing judgment—not when he fucked me in the *Round Room,* starting a whole fiasco that put us both on the fast track to meet our maker.

Damiano ignores the exchange, unfolding the paper and skimming it. His brow furrows as he gives it to Dante.

"What the fuck is this?" Dante mutters, studying the cryptic text.

Nikolai steps forward, takes the paper to read it himself, and then passes it to me. I frown at the nonsensical string of letters:

GLL / NZML / TFIW; VEVILDM / ZIVNW

"What does it mean?" I ask, confused.

"It means Anya's definitely a spy," Damiano growls.

"We don't know what this translates to," Nikolai counters.

"We'll figure it out," he says coldly. "And when we do, *I'll deal with her.*"

Chills run through my body at his words. I know exactly what that means, but I'm not fully convinced she's a spy by choice. What if she's being coerced?

"Won't she know you're onto her when Gray Suit finds the message is gone? He's gonna know it was me."

"He won't make it past the gates," Damiano says flatly.

"What was the interaction between the two of them?" Nikolai asks.

"Nothing major," I reply, thinking back. "She gave him the piece of paper with a drink, and he slipped it into his pocket. No other indications they were even familiar with each other."

Nikolai nods, processing, before saying, "Go put your tray in the back and tell Anya a deal was struck—that you're going home with him for the night."

I blink at him, confused. "Why?"

"She seems to like you," he says with a shrug. "If he's trouble, she won't want you to go."

"Fine. But keep your brother's big-ass cock in his own pants." I point at Damiano's crotch before locking eyes with Nikolai. Turning to Melanie, I fix her with a pointed glare.

I head into the kitchen, balancing my empty tray as I weave through the busy space. The noise from the casino fades slightly, replaced by the clinking of glasses being washed. Setting my tray on the counter, I exhale heavily.

Anya is standing near the sink, wringing her hands.

"How late are we here?" she asks, stepping closer.

"I'm not sure. Probably another hour or so. See you later." I give her a quick wave as I start to leave.

Her brows furrow, and she moves in. "Where are you going?"

I roll my eyes, feigning indifference. "Apparently, a deal was made with the guy in the gray suit. I'm going home with him, and he's supposed to bring me back tomorrow."

Her face pales instantly. "What?"

I shrug, keeping my tone nonchalant. "Who knows? Damiano decided to take someone else to the back, and while he's been away, some other stupid deal was made."

"No!" she blurts out, loud enough to draw the attention of a few nearby girls. She steps in closer, her urgency unmistakable. "You can't go with him!"

I stare at her, confused. "I don't really have a choice. I do as I'm told."

"Rainey, I'm telling you, you can't go with him." She reaches out, grabbing my arm.

"I'll be punished if I don't."

Her voice quivers. "You'll be killed if you do."

"What do you know, Anya?"

She hesitates, her lips trembling as though she's deciding whether to speak. "Just…please. Don't go with him."

"See you tomorrow," I say, brushing her off and turning to leave.

"He's Cristiano's hitman," she blurts. "They want to take out Damiano."

I freeze mid-step, whipping around. "How do you know that?"

She doesn't say anything; she just stares.

"How do you know that, Anya?"

"Because… I was raped by Cristiano and his men daily. Because I was forced to let men fuck me in the meeting room for entertainment while they made deals. And that man? He's the hitman."

"What did you slip him?" I question.

She seems taken aback, her confusion turning into shock when she realizes I know she passed him something.

"A coded message. It said there are too many people here. It's not safe to attack."

"You're coming with me." I grab her arm and drag her out of the kitchen, leading her to the office and shoving open the door. Silvano has joined the group, but Melanie is gone. We stride in, and I shut the door behind me.

She locks onto Silvano immediately, and her cheeks flush.

Sighing, I turn to him. "Can you go—like, grab a drink or something?"

His brows knit together as confusion flashes across his face. The same confusion ripples through the others.

"She needs to talk, and she has a crush on Silvano. Him staring at her isn't going to make this happen any faster." The words tumble out before I can stop them, and as soon as I realize what I've said, I turn back to her, pressing my lips together in regret.

Her eyes are huge, and her face flushes even more.

"I'm so sorry. I didn't mean for it to come out like that."

"Perfect," Damiano cuts in. "Because he's had the hots for her since she got here. So either she explains what she's really doing here, and they can go have sex, or I put a bullet through her brain for being a spy, and he can have sex with her corpse for all I care." Damiano cocks his gun.

"Put your fucking gun down, you psycho. She's not a spy!" I snap, storming toward him and reaching to snatch it from his grip.

"Rainey, enough," Dante interjects.

I whip my head toward him and glare. "Shut the fuck up."

Damiano slams the gun onto the desk with a loud crack, and in the next instant, his hand twists into my ponytail. He jerks my head back as he stares down with a chilling intensity.

"Talk," he growls through clenched teeth, though I know the command isn't for me.

She immediately starts, and for the next hour, she spills everything she knows. Words tumble out of her in a panicked rush as she recounts every detail she overheard about the plan to kill Damiano. She explains that she hadn't expected to see Gray Suit here, but when she did, he threatened her life, demanding that she get Damiano alone—or else he would take her back to Cristiano and let him deal with her. She admits to slipping him the note, warning that there were too many people.

Damiano speaks with cold intent, "If I find out you're lying, I'll skin you alive."

Her eyes widen, fear flashing across her face, and she nods frantically, too terrified to do anything else.

The silence settles as everyone begins to disperse. Damiano takes my hand, leading me out of the house. I climb into his truck, and Silvano opens the back door for Anya. She slides in, scooting to the center, and he climbs in after her.

When we arrive, Damiano parks on the side of the house, and the four of us step out, walking inside together. As we ascend the stairs, the silence is broken by a loud smack to my ass.

I whip around to glare at him. "I'm tired. Make this quick."

He grins, shaking his head, and gestures toward my door. "Keep walking."

I roll my eyes and turn back down the hall. Anya approaches her own room, our gazes locking momentarily. Her lips twitch as if to suppress a small, nervous smile before she steps inside. Silvano follows her, the door closing softly behind them.

Chapter
FORTY-TWO

Rainey

The morning sun filters through the canopy of trees as Anya and I stroll along the stone path that winds through the estate's gardens. I tuck my hands into the pockets of my jacket, stealing a glance at her as she walks beside me. She seems lighter today, almost glowing.

"How was it?" I ask casually.

Her cheeks flush instantly. "It was… really good," she admits. "Incredible, actually."

"Oh? Do tell."

"The chemistry between us…" She lets out a soft laugh. "It was off the charts. I've never had so many orgasms in my life."

I smile, only able to speculate how it must have felt after being violated so many times a day. I'd never ask her if she was ever able to orgasm with any of the men who hurt her, or if last night was her first, but then again, I'm sure none of the men cared much about trying to satisfy the woman they assaulted.

"Well, perfect. I'm glad it was everything you hoped it would be."

Her grin widens, and she nods. "I really like him. He's… different. Gentle, even when he's not. It's like he actually sees me, you know?" She pauses, then looks at me thoughtfully. "I wish you could've caught the attention of one of the nicer brothers. Like Nikolai."

I scoff, rolling my eyes. "For *me*, any of the brothers are better than being forced to sleep with random men all day."

She stares at me as if she wants to ask whether I truly believe that but doesn't say anything.

We continue walking in silence until she turns back to me. "I'm not a spy. I know Damiano isn't convinced, but I'm not. And if I were, I would deserve to be skinned alive."

I agree with her statement. "Yes, you would deserve that if you were spying."

"I think—" she hesitates. "I think Damiano is actually in love with you. I see the way he looks at you. No matter what you're doing, he's always staring. And maybe he just doesn't know how to act, but maybe if you gave him a chance to be with you… he would act better… not so rough."

Her words alone are enough to set off a storm of butterflies inside me, yet I still can't even tell her the truth.

We walk back toward the house together. As we near the spot where the incident happened, I keep my gaze fixed straight ahead, refusing to even acknowledge the iron table. The memory is a raw wound I'd rather not pick at.

"Well, well, well," someone says.

We both turn to see Trixie sitting exactly where it happened, her posture relaxed, a smirk plastered on her lips.

"I must say," she drawls, dripping with malice, "Damiano kicking you to the curb has been the highlight of my existence. I guess that's what happens when you're such a tramp, coming out here to get fucked by a group of men, then moving right on to his brother."

I knew she was going to mention Nikolai and me kissing to Damiano. He told me right after she went to him. Nikolai walked in on it and asked her why she doesn't shut her fucking mouth. She didn't dare argue with him, and I wanted to kiss him all over again just for talking shit to her.

After my brain gets over the bitterness of her tattling, I realize what she said. My heart starts pounding rapidly, and it's as if all the pieces fall right into place.

"Excuse me?" I manage.

Trixie's grin widens with satisfaction. "Oh, I wasn't about to miss the show. You begged like a pathetic little bitch. It was honestly quite embarrassing." She stands, brushing off imaginary dust from her skirt. "I'm just disappointed they didn't fuck you up more."

My stomach twists, the ground beneath me unstable.

She was waiting outside the bathroom for me.

She's the one who said someone was looking for me out back.

My voice trembles with rage as the realization hits.

"You… you set me up to get raped?"

"Of course I set you up, dumbass," she sneers, flipping her hair over her shoulder. "Though I'll admit, I'm a little disappointed I could only find five men willing to fuck a slut. You did put on quite the performance, name-dropping Damiano to get out of it. How'd that work out for you?"

"Those men were tortured for what they did to me!"

I realize they didn't even know they were assaulting girls who didn't want it. They were under the impression we were willing.

"Oh, so sad," she mocks, pushing her lip out. "You could say thank you. Five sexy men fucking you is a thrill. You had all their attention until they were finished, shoved you away, and you realized all you're good for is men jacking off on your face."

My vision goes red, and I lunge at her, my fist connecting with her nose. She stumbles back, falling to the ground with a shriek. I'm on her in an instant, fists flying as I channel all the humiliation, anger, and pain into each punch.

"You fucking cunt!" I scream. I don't care about consequences or who might be watching. All I want is to destroy her, to make her pay for everything she's done.

She claws at me, her nails raking across my skin as she squeals and screams for help. But I don't stop. I can't stop. Every ounce of rage I've held in comes pouring out as I land blow after blow.

Suddenly, strong hands grab me, yanking me off her. I thrash against them, screaming for whoever it is to let me go, desperate to get back to Trixie and finish what I started.

"What's going on?!" Dante's voice booms across the patio as he, Nikolai, and Silvano come down the steps.

Dante sweeps over the scene, his expression darkening as he takes it in. "Call Dom," he orders, and Silvano quickly pulls out his phone.

"Let her go," Dante orders. The guards loosen their grip and take a step back.

As soon as I'm free, I lunge for Trixie, vengeance driving every muscle in my body—but Dante is faster. He catches me mid-motion, pulling me back.

"She set me up to get raped!" I shout, kicking my legs and clawing at Dante's arm.

"I would never!" Trixie shouts with false outrage.

"You just admitted it!" Anya cuts in, stepping closer.

Trixie turns on her. "Who even are you? Do you even belong here?"

"Watch your fucking mouth," Silvano bellows, pointing at her. Damiano strides into view, his face twisted with fury.

"If you want me to put her down, be prepared to hold her back," Dante warns, still holding me while I flail.

"What happened?" Damiano reaches out, grabbing my chin and holding it tightly as he scans my face.

"She's the reason I got raped!"

His reaction is immediate. He marches toward Trixie, his fist swinging back before connecting with her face in a brutal arc, sending her sprawling to the ground. Blood splatters across the patio as she crumples, her body landing motionless.

"Get her downstairs. Now!" he roars. A guard steps forward, grabbing Trixie's limp body and hauling her away without pause.

The adrenaline drains from me in a rush, and everything comes crashing down. Tears spill freely, my sobs shaking my entire body. Dante releases me, and Damiano is there, pulling me into a tight hold. His embrace feels unshakable, as though he's determined to absorb all of my pain.

"Anya, go inside," Dante says firmly.

She hesitates before walking away, her steps slow and reluctant. Dante, Nikolai, and Silvano linger, watching silently as Damiano holds me close.

"Have Andrei pull the footage from that night, following Trixie," Damiano says, his tone controlled but brimming with venom. "And everything that just happened."

Nikolai nods, already reaching for his phone to make the call.

IT'S CONFIRMED THAT TRIXIE SET UP MY ASSAULT. I KNOW DAMIANO is going to deal with her, and I want to be there.

"I can keep you preoccupied while Dom takes care of things," Dante whispers as I wait in the hall for Nikolai.

"Tempting. But no thanks."

"Ready?" Nikolai approaches, retying his damp hair into a bun, the smell of his body wash wafting toward us.

"Yep," I say, walking toward the library, hellbent on watching what happens to her. Nikolai falls into step beside me, not saying a word.

He brings me down below the house where Damiano works. He's talking with a group of men and turns when we enter, striding over to me and running his hands up and down my arms. There's no need to ask if I'm sure I want to be here. He knows I do.

I walk right up to the glass wall of the room where Trixie is being held, and my hatred begins to take over.

She looks toward the door as Damiano enters, appearing almost calm as he takes a seat across the table from her.

They stare at each other for a long moment before he asks, "Do you know where you are?"

She takes in the surroundings, then shakes her head.

"Do you remember what happened before you came down here?"

She hugs herself tighter, a flicker of nervousness crossing her face.

"Andrei pulled the footage. We heard what you told Rainey, and we also know what happened the night she was raped." The words hang in the air, and she meets his eyes, then lowers her head. "You chose Matthews' fate. Now, once again, we sit face to face because of your actions. What should happen to you?"

Her head lifts, and her expression shifts. "I'll do anything you want of me, Damiano. *Anything*." She places her hands on the table, letting the suggestion in her words linger.

Shrugging, he stands. "Take off your clothes."

She rises slowly, maintaining full focus on him as she undresses seductively. Once bare, she stands motionless, waiting for his next command.

"Put this on." He tosses a blindfold onto the table.

She glances down at it, then grins as she takes it and slips it on. "Bend over the table."

She obeys, adjusting her position. One of the men Dom had been speaking with earlier steps into the room, completely naked. He moves behind her, pressing a hand to her back. She parts her legs, ready, convinced that Dom is about to take her himself. Even as the man pushes into her, she groans Damiano's name.

"Is that okay?" Dom asks, his tone neutral.

She lets out a breathy, exaggerated moan. "Yes."

Without another word, Dom exits the room, and four more naked men walk in.

The two-way mirror adjusts, turning into a clear pane of glass. Damiano and I stand motionless, watching. The man behind her picks up his pace, yanking her head back by her hair. She becomes louder, completely lost in it—until the blindfold is ripped away.

For a single breath, confusion lingers. Then she locks onto us standing on the other side of the glass, and panic flashes across her face.

She fights as the men close in from all directions, forcing on her exactly what she had orchestrated for me. Funny enough, she's been with each of them countless times, yet now that it's against her will, she doesn't seem to want it as much.

When they finish, she's handcuffed and shoved back into the chair.

I enter the room first, Damiano following behind. "Guess we both looked pathetic fighting off five men." I shrug, settling across from her. "You will die today, Trixie. And I just want you to know, Damiano and I will go on to marry, have children, and live a long, happy life together while you rot in the dirt. I hope it was worth it."

Damiano stands beside me, glaring down at her. "How do you want it?" he asks me.

"I'd want her throat slit. But she can choose."

Trixie starts crying, pleading with Damiano, swearing she loves him.

He watches her for a moment before saying, "It's your lucky day. I don't want you dead after all. You'll be brought to my room, and you'll serve me." Then he turns and strides out.

As soon as the door closes, her tears vanish, and a smirk takes their place. "You bitch. I win."

"How can you smile after that?" I stare at her like she's actually lost her mind.

"You think that's the first time I've had sex with all five of them at once? You're the pathetic one here, don't forget that. And while I ride Damiano's cock tonight, I'll make sure someone pays you a visit."

Damiano strides into the room, his hand wrapping around her throat as he lifts her against the wall until her feet dangle above the floor. She kicks and thrashes as she realizes there's no escape.

I find myself also stunned by his unpredictability.

When she finally goes still, he holds her there a moment longer, then lets her fall lifelessly to the floor.

I expected to feel sad. Something. But I feel nothing at all.

When he turns back toward me, I lift a brow. "What was that about?" I'm not sure why he said she wasn't going to die, then he immediately came back in and killed her.

"Didn't want you to have any regrets. Figured she wouldn't be able to help herself with the threats."

I accept his answer and stand.

"Can we go home now?"

"Yeah," he says, holding his hand out to me.

Chapter
FORTY-THREE

Damiano

I am still learning how to deal with human emotions.

Other people's emotions.

Rainey's emotions.

She seemed fine when we left the basement, but then she suddenly projectile vomited in the hallway.

Dante and Silvano were down the hall and rushed over. Dante picked her up and carried her off to see the doctor.

I should check on her and make sure she's okay after what she witnessed, but she chose to be there. I have given her space, but the longer I stay away, the angrier I become. I'm angry at Trixie for setting up other men to touch what is mine and at Rainey for the way she consumes me.

I want to punish her, not for anything she has done, but for what she makes me *feel*. She has embedded herself in my veins, making it impossible to function without her. She is my oxygen, and the thought of losing her suffocates me. Even as I try to quiet my frustration, I feel an equally strong need to make her feel good.

Heading to the armory, I skim over the selection of cuffs until I find the pair I want—a set with a long chain between them, perfect for what I have planned. My next stop is the bedroom. The bed needs to be prepared. I drill the chain high into the top of the bedframe, making sure it is positioned so that, even in heels, her arms will stretch upward, leaving her entirely at my mercy.

I make my way to the wardrobe room where the girls' outfits are kept. Rows of garments hang neatly, categorized and pristine. I land on the leather set meant for the *Round Room*. It has been cleaned and rehung, waiting for tonight's use. I take it off the rack, draping it over my arm.

The house is silent when I step inside. The clock on the wall shows just past midnight, and everyone is already asleep. I assume she would be too, but something tells me she might have trouble sleeping after what she witnessed.

When I enter her room, she is sitting on the windowsill, gripping the edge on either side as if she had been waiting for me.

I move to my usual spot just inside, leaning casually against the wall where I've stood countless times. I drift over her, taking in her posture and searching for any sign of how she feels. She doesn't seem upset. If anything, she seems…ready.

"Well?" she asks.

"Well, what?"

"Are you going to fuck me?"

I push off the wall, locked on her. "Yes. But you might not like it."

Her lips twitch into the faintest smirk as she rises from the windowsill. "I'll be fine," she replies confidently, heading toward the bed.

I stop her with a single command. "We're going back to our place."

Her steps falter, and she glances up at me, curiosity crossing her face before she shrugs and slides into her slippers. I turn and leave the room, trusting her to follow, but she hesitates in the doorway, watching me.

"Walk," I order.

She holds my gaze as if trying to decipher my intentions.

"I said walk."

Finally, she moves past me toward the stairs, and I follow close behind.

When we reach the house, I lead her to the bedroom. The outfit I laid out catches her attention immediately. She stops in the doorway, brows pulling together as she takes in the leather straps and heels resting neatly on the bed. Then she turns to me, her expression questioning.

"Why this?"

"Because I said so," I reply, moving to the buttons of my shirt, undoing them slowly.

She rolls her eyes, grabs the hanger and shoes, then disappears into the bathroom.

When she steps out, my breath catches. She's intoxicating.

"At the end of the bed," I command. She sighs but moves to where I indicated. "Hands up."

She obeys, and the sight of her bound and exposed sends a rush through me.

"Comfortable?"

"Hardly," she mutters.

"Good."

I reach for the gag, slipping the ball between her teeth and fastening it securely behind her head. Her muffled protests excite me, her chest rising and falling rapidly as wide eyes lock onto mine. She's stunning like this.

From the bedside, I grab one of the leather whips. Soft enough not to cause real harm but firm enough to make her skin sting. I trail the strands down her back, watching her muscles tighten beneath the touch of leather. She turns her head, trying to see what I'm doing, and I bring it down lightly against her backside.

Her lashes flutter closed briefly, a flush creeping across her cheeks as she lets the sensation roll through her. I can tell she loves it—the way she leans into the next strike instead of pulling away, the small moan slipping past the gag, even as she feigns resistance.

I step closer, running my fingers over the area where the whip landed. Her skin is warm beneath my touch, heat blooming in its wake.

"You like that," I murmur.

Her response is a mix of a whimper and a gasp, body taut beneath the restraints. I pull back and strike again, a little harder this time. The leather meets her skin with a sharp crack, her muffled gasp filling the room as she shivers, caught between anticipation and surrender.

I let the whip fall away briefly, soothing the mark with my palm, tracing slow circles over her heated spot. A third strike lands, and her reaction is immediate—her back arches, breath catching behind the gag.

I alternate between the sting of the lash and the warmth of my hand, the contrast blending together, leaving her panting.

"You're perfect like this," I whisper, dragging the strands lightly down her side, teasing as she shivers under the contact. Finally, I toss it aside and grip her waist, pulling her closer, my fingers sinking into her soft curves.

From the drawer, I retrieve a sleek black vibrator and hold it up so she can see. Her eyes widen, head shaking as she tries to speak through the gag. When I step closer, she twists away, but I only smirk, trailing the cool, smooth surface along her collarbone, hovering near the swell of her breasts before moving lower.

A whimper slips past the gag as I take my time, running the toy along her inner thigh, deliberately avoiding where she will eventually crave it most. She writhes in the cuffs, the chain rattling softly over her stretched form.

"You're beautiful like this," I murmur, low and rough, as I trail the vibrator higher, brushing it just barely against her center. A moan escapes, hips arching toward me. I pull back, watching her squirm in the restraints, a faint sheen of sweat glistening on her skin.

With a flick of my thumb, the vibrator hums to life, its soft buzz filling the silence between her labored breaths. I press it lightly against the inside of her thigh, tracing slow patterns. Her head tips forward toward the bedpost, the gag stifling her sounds of frustration and need as I keep her teetering on the edge of pleasure.

"Keep your eyes on me."

I bring the vibrator closer, circling her entrance without settling there. "You want this, don't you?"

She lets out a whine, swaying forward in silent agreement.

Finally, I press the toy against her, letting the vibrations take over. Her body jolts at the contact, knees wobbling as she strains against the cuffs.

"Not yet," I whisper, pulling the toy away just as she begins to quake. The sound she makes is almost pitiful, a desperate, muffled cry that echoes through the room. I smirk, running a hand up her side, tracing the curve of her waist, bringing the vibrator back, slower this time, barely grazing her.

Her body is a symphony of reactions—shivers, gasps, the subtle arch of her back. I alternate between teasing and applying just enough pressure to push her to the edge before pulling her back again and again. Her skin glistens, thighs quivering as she fights against the cuffs, chasing the release I keep denying.

"You're mine," I murmur, setting the toy aside and replacing it with my hand. I trail through the slick evidence of her arousal, leaning in as my lips brush her ear while my fingers explore. "And I'll give you what you want," I whisper, "when I'm ready."

Chapter

FORTY-FOUR

Rainey

I'm in my room getting ready, trying to cover the marks Damiano left on my throat and wrists when Anya walks straight into my bathroom. She stops when she sees me, watching in silence. I lift a brow, meeting her gaze through the mirror.

"Yes?" I drawl.

"We need to get you out of here," she says finally.

I huff a laugh.

"I'm serious, Rainey. I don't think anyone realizes how bad Damiano is treating you."

I keep dabbing cover-up on my neck but turn slightly to glance at her over my shoulder. "He treats me fine," I say, shifting my focus back to the mirror.

"I followed you. Last night when Damiano took you. Boris slipped into one of the girls' rooms, and I trailed you back to his house. I saw what he did to you."

I shut my compact loudly, set it on the counter, and turn toward her. "I told you when you first got here to mind your own business, and I'm telling you again now. Mind your own business, Anya." I stride past her.

"He was torturing you!"

I spin on my heel to face her.

"I wanted it."

"You were crying."

"You know what? You're right. He's awful. I think I'd rather have… I don't know, Silvano would work." I say, knowing it will bother her.

Her eyes widen, mouth falling open before snapping shut. "I want to help you. But you're being a bitch, so I guess that's that."

"Then why are you still in my room?" I hold her stare.

She scoffs. "Whatever." Then she turns and leaves.

Damiano better figure this out fast. I never wanted to pretend to be her friend, and I definitely didn't want to actually start liking her friendship. Now I'm left without her.

As I make my way downstairs, murmurs spread about a lesbian arriving. They talk about making sure the men know, convinced she will end up earning triple what everyone else does. These men have a sick perversion, wanting to have sex with a lesbian just to assert dominance, believing their dick is so glorious it could magically convert her.

I pass the living room we were first brought into as Valentina strides toward me.

"Hi, sweetheart," she greets, pressing a kiss to my cheek. "Are you feeling okay?"

Her tone is soft, almost sympathetic.

"I feel fine."

I know she's referring to me watching Damiano kill Trixie, but I don't care. She was as evil as they get.

"We're meeting. Come." She turns and walks back toward the living room I was trying to avoid.

I don't bother sitting. Instead, I lean against the doorway.

Three new girls sit on the couch, nervous and uncertain. I remember being in their position. When Valentina starts giving the same speech she gave us, I tune her out. I hate this. I hate that she is fine with it.

Lorenzo is coming home today, and we have to have dinner with the entire family. It's times like this when I don't even want to be in the same room as any of them. Even Damiano.

Don't go pulling a gun on them again.

As soon as Valentina finishes, she rubs my shoulder in passing and walks away.

The new girls stay seated while most of the others disperse. Seven girls have disappeared in the last week. I don't know where they went, only that their rooms were cleaned out, and I overheard others saying they were "done." Damiano hasn't mentioned *taking care of them*, and nobody else has said anything. One of them had a developing thing with a man who plays poker in the casino. Maybe he bought her or something?

Tess glances at me, then steps toward the girls.

"The first day is always the hardest because you're getting used to everything. I know it's probably overwhelming, but we've all been through this, and we adjusted just fine."

They exchange looks before nodding at her.

"Which one of you is a lesbian?" I ask from the doorway.

A gorgeous redhead hesitates, glancing at the others, then slowly raises her hand.

"Have you ever had sex with a man?"

She shakes her head. "No."

Letting out a sigh, I push off the wall and stride out of the room. As far as I know, there was a meeting with the Volkovs. When I reach the large meeting room, it's empty. I continue searching the restricted part of the house, the area where they work from. We aren't allowed here unless called for, but I don't really care.

I keep searching until I reach Dante's office and hear voices inside. I listen until I recognize Damiano, then push open the door.

Dante sits behind his desk while Nikolai and Damiano occupy the chairs across from him.

Perfect. All the brothers I've been sexual with in some way or another.

"Babe…" Damiano says, looking confused by my presence.

I step inside and shut the door behind me.

"One of the new girls is a lesbian," I say, standing at the side of the desk, waiting for him to respond.

He keeps his focus on Dante, then shifts to Nikolai before straightening in his seat. "Okay." He rubs his hands down his pants, then back up.

"You need to take her back to wherever you stole her from. She's never even been with a man. You can't go through with this."

He raises a brow. "Go through with what?"

"The auction," I snap. "She's a lesbian. You can't expect her to—"

"We aren't attending the auction," he interrupts, his tone calm but detached.

"So, there won't be an auction?"

"I didn't say that. I said *we* won't be attending," he counters.

"*Us* not being there does nothing for the lesbian who doesn't want dick."

He sighs. "Baby, worry about your own pussy. You're not here to be a savior."

My mouth falls open. He wants to be a douche? Fine. So will I.

"Put me in her place."

He stares at me for a moment, then smiles, but there's nothing humorous about it.

"Fine. I'll take you again and make sure there are ten times as many people watching. When I get tired, I'll let these two have a turn until they wear out. Then I'll keep going until you learn to mind your own business."

My nostrils flare, and I clench my jaw. "She can't work here, babe. She doesn't belong here."

He leans back in his chair. "We don't get involved in those decisions. That's not our role."

My anger flares. I turn to Dante, narrowing my gaze. "Do something."

"Rainey, you don't know what you're talking about," he says.

My mouth falls open. "*I* don't know what I'm talking about?! You watched your brother fuck me on that shitty mattress in front of a room full of people. You saw the blood, sweat, and semen left behind. She doesn't like disgusting cocks." I snarl.

He sighs. "We *know* what she does and doesn't like."

My stomach churns. "You fucking pig."

Ever so calmly, he turns to Damiano. "Get her out of my office before *I* punish her."

"You're a fucking loser, Dante. All of you are."

Damiano stands and grabs my arm, but I jerk free. "Don't fucking touch me." Then I stride to the door, ripping it open and slamming it shut behind me.

As I stomp through the house, Em catches sight of me. She's doing the same thing she did on our first day, showing the new girls around, but when she notices where I just came from, she gives me a questioning look. I'm so angry I want to tell her not to put Dante on such a high pedestal because while he keeps her to himself, he's also fucking me. But Em hasn't done anything to me. She's actually only ever been good to me.

I lock myself in my room, too pissed off to see or talk to any-one. We aren't given any electronics to keep us busy, but Nikolai let me take a book from the library. I've attempted to read it multiple times, but I can't concentrate.

How can they expect a lesbian to be here? Disgusting men pay more for lesbians? That seems cruel. All of this is cruel.

I end up falling asleep while overthinking, only to be jolted awake by pounding on my door.

"Open the goddamn door!" Damiano roars from the other side.

I sit up, my heart pounding at his fury.

"Someone unlock this door now!" he yells, the words echoing down the hall.

A moment later, the door flies open, and he storms in, dark eyes blazing with anger.

"Get up," he snaps.

The murmurs outside confirm he has caught the attention of everyone on this floor.

"Get out of my room."

He strides to the bed, rips the blankets off, and yanks me up by my arm.

"Ow, you fucking prick," I say, trying to wrench free.

He's furious. I don't even know what set him off—was it me barging into his meeting with his brothers, or the fact that I locked the door?

"I can walk by myself," I say, annoyed, still trying to break free.

His hold stays firm as he drags me from my room. The hall-way is packed with girls, some peeking from their doors, others standing in the open to watch.

Anya stands frozen in her doorway, wide-eyed, as I try to keep up so he doesn't yank my arm out of its socket.

"This is no longer her room," he bellows. "Get her stuff out immediately."

Footsteps scramble to obey as he hauls me down the stairs and through the house. We pass his family seated at dinner, everyone watching as he drags me out the back door and slams it shut behind us, the force rattling the frame.

Chapter

FORTY-FIVE

Rainey

Tess and I sit in a quiet corner of one of the many sitting rooms, away from the central area of the house where everyone is gathered. Damiano is meeting with his brothers and dad, a requirement he wasn't thrilled about since he hates anything involving meetings. He told me each of them plays a key role in this operation, and his is beneath the house… extracting information by any means necessary and then… finishing them off, making his attendance in this meeting feel pointless. I told him to suck it up and get juicy gossip he can share with me later. Not even my silly half-joke helped his mood. Even the blow job I gave him before we came inside didn't fix it.

He and I have spent the last week healing. He wasn't pleased with me barging into Dante's office and disrespecting his brothers. I was punished for it, spanked so many times he actually bruised my butt. He tied me to the same spot at the end of the bed as last time, then called Dante and Nikolai, telling them he was going to teach me a lesson and that they were invited to watch. I was so mad I screamed that I would never forgive him if he let anyone come. They both declined. And after he was done and I couldn't even move, had he let his brothers see, I would have tried to beat the shit out of all of them.

The following night, guilt weighed on him. He never said it outright, but he handed me the same paddle and told me I could strike him as many times as I needed to make things right. So I did. I let my pain take control, swinging until my arm gave out. And he never protested. Not about the pain, the number of hits, or how hard I swung. He didn't make a sound.

Every time I caught sight of the bruises, I knew he understood exactly what I felt when I tried to sit. He had meals brought to us and made sure there were plenty of ice packs. There was no need for him to tell me not to do it again—it was implied in the way I was punished.

Tess takes a sip of her tea, her feet curled beneath her as I stare out the window.

"Em says you got in trouble." Her voice pulls me from my thoughts.

I turn to her, not registering what she means at first. Then I remember Em saw me storming down the hall, and I assume Dante told her what happened. *So that's cool.*

"It's disgusting that they have a lesbian here. It's disgusting that any of us are here," I reply, not even trying to hide the venom in my tone.

She shrugs. "Lesbian or not, she'll make more money than any of us because of that."

I scoff, shake my head, and turn back to the window.

"Enough about you and who likes pussy, cock, or all of the above. It's my turn. I feel like I can finally breathe again. Do you think I'd be foolish to sign another year-long contract?" she asks, as if renewing a gym membership.

"Contract for what?"

She lets out a soft laugh. "Well, I worked off all the debts the Volkovs covered. Another year would be enough to put me through college or buy a house, maybe even both. I could do anything I want for a couple of years, really—take my time figuring things out. I could probably check more boxes on the contract this time too, since I've experimented with a lot of new things since I signed the last one."

I blink, lost. "What debts are you talking about?"

Her brows knit together as if struggling to understand my confusion. "My gambling debts. The ones that got me into this mess. The ones I worked off by signing the contract. You know…" She waves vaguely, as if it's common knowledge. "To be a sex worker under Volkov protection."

The air is sucked out of the room, and my stomach twists. "What are you talking about?" My voice comes out sharper than I intended.

She tilts her head, now genuinely puzzled. "Did you not sign a contract?"

"No. Contract for what? What debts?"

Her face pales. "How are you here without signing one?"

"What is it for?"

"It outlines our hard limits—or, you know, how many men we'll take in a day."

"What?" I stammer, completely blindsided.

She fidgets with her glass. "It's not a big deal." She downplays the gigantic bomb she just dropped. "We're all here because of massive debts, and most of us were either already sex workers, strippers, or wanting to get in the business. It's just safest under Volkov protection, with their resources and clients. Once your debt to them is cleared, you keep everything else you earn. Since mine are paid off, I'd only sign for another year. Aside from their cut, all the money would be mine."

I shake my head, the room spinning. "You haven't even been here a year."

She studies me curiously. "Oh, are you talking about the auction?" she asks casually. "If you look young enough, a couple of stitches and you can be auctioned as a virgin a few times. That was my fourth. I hate that they go through the whole "kidnapping" routine every time they bring in a new girl, but it's part of the contract."

I can't even keep up with what's happening. "But I saw you guys. You were all terrified. And Boris hurt Lina in the van. She was bleeding."

"Boris is literally Lina's boyfriend, and that was an accident. They were having sex, and we went around a corner too fast—she fell and got hurt. And those rich fucks get off on fear. The more scared and timid you seem, the more they fight over you and drive up the price just to fuck you."

"But some of them had multiple men taking them…and their nipples were bleeding…"

She appears to not understand, then realization dawns. "Oh! Hannah? She loves that BDSM shit. Getting her nipples pinched gets her off. And her profile for those men said she'd take however many signed up. The total the buyer paid for her was multiplied by each additional participant. She made bank that night. But she can't go again because they can't sell her as a virgin anymore. Still, she's one of the highest-paid because of the kinky shit she allows."

My stomach turns. "Tess. *I* was a virgin."

Her eyes widen. "Like… truly?" she asks, voice hushed with disbelief.

"Yes!"

Her mouth falls open slightly, and she hesitates. "Well, that kind of makes sense. Maybe you didn't have to sign one because

Damiano wants you for himself? Have you guys ever discussed what you will and won't do?"

"No, not really." I pause, considering. Have we ever discussed it? Not exactly. It's always just been in the moment, and I mention what I like or don't like. "What did the contract say?"

She shifts, then starts ticking off on her fingers. "It asked for our preferences—how many men we're willing to sleep with in a day, our kinks, that we agree to get tested regularly. For each auction we participate in, we get 60% of the earnings, other games we get 50%. It also has a list of all the games in the *Fun House* with descriptions, and we check off the ones we want to participate in."

The room feels suffocating, and all I can do is blink as everything she's said replays in my head, but none of it makes sense. "You mean… all of this? Everything we've done? It's because of a contract? I've spent four months believing everyone here was being held against their will."

I scoff.

Tess chews the inside of her cheek. "I honestly thought everyone signed their own contract. I just assumed we were all on the same page. Part of it says we can't discuss the contract with anybody else."

"I don't have any debts."

Then I realize mom said she traded me for *her* debts. I was sent to work off what she owed with my body. Everyone else is repaying something and is here by their own free will. It's all bullshit. All the horrible situations we've been put in, my bones practically rattled the entire time we were brought to the *Fun House*. And these girls do this by choice?

"You purposely put yourself in the *Round Room*, knowing men could touch you right there in front of everyone?" I don't want to sound judgmental, but I'm judging… hard.

"Just for going down there, even if nobody touched us, we were paid five figures. That night, I made over six. Do you know how long it would take me to earn that kind of money on the street? I was a drug addict. I was brought here, cleaned up, and offered the contract. Now, I'm sober. And I don't have men promising to pay me, then fucking me, beating me to the edge of death, and leaving me with nothing. I like being here. I've never lived this well and I likely never will once I leave."

"You enjoy pretending to be raped?" My mouth hangs open.

"What happened to us should have never happened. But that's not the first time in my life. At least here, it's less likely. When girls resist and fight back, the men enjoy the thrill of it. I didn't fight. Only one touched me."

"This is all fucked up. You know that, right?"

She shrugs. "Who cares? Sex feels good, and the men coming in here are rich. The women who leave after their contract—or in the middle of one—go to be with a client."

"But every single client doesn't realize it's all a front? That the girls aren't actually trafficked?"

"It's part of our contract that we don't tell anyone the truth."

This is insane. My brain literally feels like it's overloading with information. "How do the girls willingly leave with men who sleep with them believing they are assaulting them? Or are they purchased?"

"They fall in love—whether with the money, the opportunity to leave, or something else entirely, who knows. The Volkovs take on our debts once we sign, ensuring no one comes after us while we're here. We can check at any time how much we owe and what we've earned after each party. If a man wants to take a girl out of here, he clears the remaining debt with the Volkovs, and then they ride off into the sunset. Sometimes, former girls return with their now-husbands for the parties."

"How do you check what you earn?"

"We can use the computers in the lab."

Now I'm really confused. I don't know anything about a computer lab. She must notice because she studies me, then leans back.

"They're obviously monitored. If we did anything suspicious, we'd get in trouble. But why would we? I've had my sights set on Marko Belkin. Once I leave, I want to leave with him."

"Why would you settle for a hitman?" I ask, surprised.

"I don't see him as a hitman. I see him as the love of my life."

"Does he know?"

"That I'm interested? I think I make it pretty clear."

"His job is literally to kill people. Every day, you'd have to worry he might not come home."

"Does that sway how you feel about Damiano?"

I sit here, thinking about her question. I've been so focused on passing judgment that I hadn't even considered the man I want to wait for every night is Damiano. But I was never given a choice. He chose himself for me. So whether I wanted it or not, I didn't have a say.

I don't answer. I just move on. "And he doesn't care that you sleep with other men?"

"He's never said one way or another. He's offered to pay off my debt, but now that I'm debt free, it's different. But I don't think he'll complain. Money is money."

"Does he sleep with other women?"

"Sure. If I'm busy and he has a break, he's free to."

I shake my head, unable to grasp how she's so nonchalant. I would lose my mind if that were Damiano. I nearly did when I thought he had sex with Trixie.

"Why don't the Volkovs care that they're viewed as sex traffickers?" I whisper, more to myself than to her.

Tess shrugs lightly. "They know they're not. If someone told you they hated the color of your blue nail polish, would it bother you?"

I wiggle my very sparkly, very red nails, then hold them up. "My nails are red."

She grins like I just proved her point. "And would it upset you?"

"No. Because they aren't blue."

"Exactly." She winks. "The contracts are signed voluntarily. We choose this. They provide rich clientele, and we still get to do the work we enjoy." She pauses, studying me. "As for you, I don't know why they didn't have you sign a contract. Everyone does. Maybe someone signed one for you?"

I sit there, trying to think who could have signed for me—then freeze. *She wouldn't.* My own mother would never sign a contract like this. But she had to have. She traded *me* for *her* debt.

I'm out of my chair in an instant, repeating the same reckless action I was just punished for.

I barge into the office where the Volkov men are in the middle of a meeting. My gaze locks on Damiano, and I stride straight to him.

"Where's my contract?" I demand, planting a fist on my hip as I glare at him.

He lifts his head from the papers spread across the table, glancing at Dante, who sits across from him.

"Don't look at him. I asked you a question," I snap.

His focus returns to me, then he gives Dante a single nod.

Dante exhales heavily, pushing back his chair as he stands.

Damiano rises as well, gesturing toward the door. "Come."

I trail behind Dante, my heart pounding. He walks to his office, straight to a towering filing cabinet against the wall. The drawer slides open, and he flips through the folders, pausing when he finds one with my name scrawled on the tab. He pulls it out, drops it onto the desk, and spreads it open, revealing a thick stack of neatly typed pages.

I step forward, hands trembling as I reach for it. "This can't be real," I whisper, barely audible as I skim the first page.

My vision tunnels when I flip to the last page. There, in bold print, is the debt amount: $1.9 million. My stomach drops as I read the bottom.

Two signatures glare back at me—my mother's and Ricardo's.

"No," I whisper, shaking my head as if that will make it disappear. My focus lands on the line above the signatures:

In exchange for the debt owed, Rainey Lane will work off the amount specified.

Tears blur my vision as I flip frantically through the pages, desperate to make sense of it. Each one is worse than the last.

Boxes are checked, detailing what I'm expected to do. Every vile, disgusting act spelled out in clinical terms, reduced to transactions. The more *'flexible'* you are, the more you earn, and the faster you pay off your debt.

And then I see it—the box that makes my knees buckle and my hands go numb.

Gangbangs (up to): My mother's handwriting ticks the highest option. 10+.

"She—" I gasp, my voice cracking as I skim the page. "She signed this. She checked these boxes. She gave permission for men to mutilate me!"

Dante says nothing as he takes a seat at the desk.

I flip through the pages again, searching for a way out, but the more I read, the worse it gets. My hands shake so violently I can barely hold the papers.

"She sold me," I choke out, tears streaming down my face. "She sold me to pay off her debt. How is that even fair?"

Dante leans back in his chair. "The thing with gambling debts is that most people don't know when to quit. They've been running up their debts again."

I blink rapidly, disbelief coursing through me. "And I'm just supposed to keep working like their own human credit card while they rack up more?"

"No," Damiano interjects, gesturing to the contract spread out on the desk. "It's stated here—if more than half the current debt is accrued during the agreed period, the contract becomes null and void."

I blink, processing his words. "How much have they racked up?"

Damiano's jaw flexes. "One-point-one million."

My breath hitches. "So… am I free to go?"

Silence fills the room. Damiano glances at Dante, who remains stoic, his gaze fixed on me. Then, he interlaces his fingers in his lap and finally meets my eyes.

"Yes." He almost sounds reluctant. "If that's what you wish."

Before I can respond, he stands, mutters something about needing to get back to work, and strides out of the room.

"Why did he take off like that?" I turn to Dante.

"Because he doesn't want you to leave." He rises from his desk. "If you're going, don't say goodbye. He'll take it harder."

He will take it harder?

He.

As in, all anyone cares about is how *he* is feeling.

I was lied to. I watched a van pull up in front of my house, two giant-ass men dragging me to it while I kicked and screamed, then throwing me in the back with other terrified girls. I was threatened—told that if I didn't shut up, I would be silenced the same way the girl bleeding in the corner had been.

Then, once we arrived at the Volkov Estate, I tried helping her, and I thought I got her raped before we even stepped foot inside. Meanwhile, Boris was just bending his girlfriend over the seat for a quickie.

The hair on my body was painfully ripped away, and then I was told I was being put up for auction. My virginity was taken in front of a room full of people. I was forced into humiliating outfits and chained up like an animal.

I was raped. I've seen men and Trixie killed. I've been threatened and feared that someone would sneak into my room to assault me.

All while it was fake.

And I was the only one in the house who didn't know.

The only one.

I sit in Dante's office for hours, reading the contract over and over, the words blurring together the longer I stare at them. How could my own mother do this to me? If Damiano hadn't wanted me, I would have been gang raped, and everyone would have believed I agreed to it.

I want my mother and Ricardo to pay for what they've done. None of this is fair.

And for the Volkovs to accept these terms, allowing someone else to decide another person's fate, wouldn't that mean I could just as easily decide Valentina should serve the rest of my sentence? That I could sign a contract, and she'd be forced to take my place?

At some point, exhaustion weighs me down. The fight drains from my body, and I sink deeper into the couch, the contract still clutched in my hands, allowing sleep to quickly pull me under.

A LIGHT TOUCH GLIDES DOWN MY CHEEK, STIRRING ME AWAKE. My eyes snap open to find Dante sitting on the coffee table in front of me, watching in silence.

"How are you holding up?" His tone is quiet, like he doesn't want to startle my senses any more than they already have been.

"Confused. Sad. Mad."

He nods, resting his forearms on his thighs and clasping his hands together.

"Rainey, do you remember five years ago on *Reach Me*, talking to someone with the username **DV_Ardent**?"

My heart hammers at the name. I signed up for *Reach Me* hoping to meet someone—even just a friend. You couldn't send pictures on the app, so every conversation was just words. I messaged with **DV_Ardent** for six months, all day, every day. We dreamed about running away together, living happily ever after. And then he vanished.

We had insane chemistry, and I had no idea what I did to make him disappear. A month later, I went to a New Year's Eve rave, and my *Reach Me* app dinged, notifying me that I was within ten feet of **DV_Ardent**. I thought I was going to faint.

At midnight, my phone buzzed and flashed red, signaling that I was a foot away from him. Then someone spun me around, and lips were on mine. I couldn't explain why, but I kissed him with everything I had. I knew it was him. I thought he had changed his mind.

In seconds, I convinced myself I was going to run away with him that night. When he pulled away, I barely got to see him before he strode through the crowd and disappeared. The app showed our markers overlapping—then the distance between us growing as he walked away.

I never heard from him again. His profile was deactivated, and I kept mine active for years, hoping he might come back. He never did.

I clear my throat. "No, I don't know who that is." I feign ignorance.

"Right," he says. "So then you also don't remember having sex with him at the rave on New Year's?"

My brows knit together, and my chin jerks back. "I didn't have sex with him." And just like that, I give myself away.

He holds his phone, staring down at it. "My phone." As if I don't already know what a phone is—or that I snooped through it. Then he pulls up the *Reach Me* app and turns the screen toward me. It's on a deactivated profile. *His* deactivated profile. **DV_Ardent's** deactivated profile.

I sit up, snatch the phone from his hand, and stare at the screen trying to process. Clicking on the messages, I see our conversation—the only one there. It's saved. "DV… Dante Volkov?"

"Yes."

"But why? Why did you ghost me? Why did you kiss me and then ghost me again?"

"Everything I said was the truth. Every conversation, every word—it was all real. Then my grandfather passed away, and Pa started needing more from me. When I told him I was going to marry you, it didn't go over well. They did a background check, thinking it would change my mind. It didn't. But I was forbidden from talking to you and forced to start preparing to take over the business.

"I lasted a month. One month before I had to see you in person. To get you out of my system. So I went to the New Year's rave. I watched you all night, dancing. Soaking you in, trying to make it enough to survive a life without you. And at midnight, I kissed you. Then I walked away.

"I tried not to think about you—never wanting to cause myself pain on purpose. But then Damiano stormed into our meeting one day, threw down a contract, and said he was going to marry you. When I saw your name and picture, it took everything in me not to puke all over the table.

"Pa agreed. He ended us and agreed to my brother marrying you. He knew who you were. He knew you were supposed to be mine.

"When Damiano left, I tried to talk Pa out of it. He said, 'This girl must have a golden fucking pussy to have all my boys on their goddamn knees,' then proceeded to tell me to let it go. Dom had been following you for a year, and they'd already asked Dr. Winn what she thought.

"She said there was no stopping him now—anyone who interfered would be killed. So we let it happen."

A tear slips down my cheek. I wipe it away, hoping he didn't see. "Is that what you meant in the *Round Room* when you said you should have never let me go?"

He stares down at his hands and inhales deeply. "Yes."

"Dom will kill us if he finds out what we've done."

He shakes his head. "He will kill *me*. And if I could go back to that day, the only thing I'd change is unchaining you from the wall so I could have stared into your eyes as I made love to you for the first time."

"Do you regret it? Letting me go."

He looks directly at me. "No. Because Damiano was dead inside. He has been for a long time. But you bring him back to life. And I love my family and my brother. Seeing him happy is what I want. And you're happy with him. You might feel trapped here, but you're not, Rainey. Once we get some things sorted out, you and Dom can take a nice vacation, relax, and laugh about this one day. Maybe we'll tell these stories to, I don't know, Andrei's future girlfriend or something."

He smiles, but it seems pained. "I've never wanted anything in my life the way I wanted you. Giving you up will probably be the hardest thing I'll ever endure. But I survived. Damiano won't. If you leave, it will likely kill him."

I reach out, lacing my fingers with his. Another tear escapes as I lean forward, pressing a kiss to his knuckles, then resting my forehead against them.

After the auction, I wondered why he kept staring at me. He was always staring at me. I thought maybe he was planning my demise or something. I never knew he was the man I once believed would sweep me off my feet and take me away from the hell I was living.

When I sit back up, tears glide down his face too. I reach out, wiping them away with my thumb.

"Can you help me with something?" I ask.

Chapter

FORTY-SIX

Rainey

Part of moving on from something that hurt you so deeply, something you never thought you'd heal from, is getting closure. Dante gave me that last night. I stayed in his room, and we talked until morning. **DV_Ardent** and **JaneDoe_Vixen**. We laughed, we cried, and then we just lay there, staring at each other.

I got the closure I didn't realize I so desperately needed. And what I've come to understand is that I'm madly in love with Damiano. Dante's role in this business is something I could never handle. It would drive me insane.

Tonight is another casino night, but multiple rooms are open this time. An auction is being held, and now that I know every girl in that room chose to be there, it only pisses me off more. My fear that night was real—I was *really* scared. And in the *Round Room*, I

was the only one who got fucked without fully choosing to. Grant-
ed, it was Dante, and I enjoyed it.

When he brought me here this morning, it was for one reason:
to work with one of the dancers in the strip club portion of the
Fun House.

He introduces me to Sparkle, their most requested dancer, and
I beg him to stay for a little while. He agrees, and she proceeds to
teach me how to use the pole and move seductively. Dante comments on the ones he likes, and Sparkle makes me feel confident
by telling me I'm a natural. Then she offers me a spot on the stage
anytime. He immediately shuts her down.

As night falls, my nerves get the best of me, and I debate
chickening out. This is my bold way of letting Damiano know I
choose him, and I will stay for him of my own free will. But now,
with the thought of smashing my nose on the stage or my heel
snapping and breaking my ankle, I really feel like I may have been
a little too ambitious.

There are more men here than usual. Way more. Tonight
is meant to bring in more money than ever. Security has been
ramped up, and there are more girls working that I've never seen
before. As I'm realizing now, any that seem scared are just putting
on an act.

Dante told me that Damiano thinks I left since I didn't go
home. He went there and found that I had never gone back. Nikolai, Giovanni, and Silvano had to drag him here, and they said he
had already been drinking.

I wait in the large, dimly lit room, the soft glow of the overhead lights casting shadows across the polished floor. A single stage
dominates the space, with a shiny stripper pole standing at its center. I know dancers will be working it tonight, but Dante said I can
have the room for as long as I need.

I'm wearing a black, skin-tight dress with a red lace thong tied
at the side underneath. Leaning against the pole, I reach behind

me and grip it. The DJ sits in the booth above, waiting for my signal to start the music I requested. For now, only quiet instrumentals play.

Damiano is practically dragged into the room and shoved forward. He looks like he's about to turn and fight his brothers, but as he catches his footing and straightens, his eyes land on me, and his mouth falls open.

I curl my finger, beckoning him. He strides toward the stage, weaving through the tables, and I point to the single chair I positioned in front of it.

"Sit," I command, allowing only the hint of a smile to show.

He arches a brow, intrigued, but complies. His tall, broad frame settles into the chair, leaning back as he adjusts the front of his pants.

Looks like we're off to a good start.

I glance up at the DJ, and the music instantly switches. A slow, sensual beat fills the room, the bass vibrating through the air.

Standing upright, I turn toward the pole, my fingertips grazing it lightly as I sway to the rhythm. The music takes over, guiding the roll of my hips. His lips part slightly, sheer arousal taking over his features.

I spin around the pole, hooking my leg around it and lowering myself in a controlled descent before rising again. Tilting my head back, I expose the curve of my neck, then ease one strap of my dress off my shoulder, followed by the other. The fabric glides down my body as I bare myself to him.

My hips sway in time with the music, lightly skimming down my sides as I move. Out of the corner of my eye, the door creaks open. A few men peek past the curtain, curiosity pulling them in. More follow, slipping into seats around the scattered tables. Their murmured conversations fade, attention locking onto me.

But Damiano doesn't look their way, not once. His focus stays fixed on the stage.

The men in the room emanate a mix of fascination and hunger. Some of the girls have joined, perched on men's laps, their bodies undulating to the music. Hands drift over arms and chests, their movements sensual and hypnotic.

Damiano stays still, but the way his jaw tightens and his fingers flex against his thighs tells me he likes what he sees.

More people enter, quietly taking seats at the tables. But none of them matter. All I care about is Damiano, the way his dark gaze consumes me, as if he is already imagining everything he's about to do to me.

My eyes drift over him, drawn to how he leans forward slightly, elbows resting on his knees, completely transfixed.

I spin around the pole, dipping lower until my knees touch the stage. Then, I crawl across it with feline grace. My stare never wavers, locked onto his as I move across the cool surface, inching closer. His chest rises and falls in sync with mine.

When I reach the edge, he leans in, and I grab his collar, pulling him toward me until our lips are just a breath apart. Our tongues meet briefly as I push him back with a single finger.

Turning on my knees, I face away from him. Leaning forward, I arch my back and press my cheek and shoulder to the floor, lifting my ass to direct his gaze exactly where I want it.

I find the delicate ties of my bottoms, tugging at them slowly. The fabric slips away, leaving me bare. I peer over my shoulder as his hands travel down his thighs, squeezing.

Behind him, the room shifts. The girls perched on men's laps grind provocatively, hips rolling in time with the music. The men hold them closer, their eyes flickering between the women in their arms and me.

I trail my fingers between my thighs, teasing myself. My moans start soft, then grow louder, more unabashed, as I press in deep.

I let the sensation take over, then add a second one in, my back arching as a soft, pleasured whimper escapes. He presses against the front of his pants, his erection straining against the fabric.

Easing out, I let the tension stretch, then roll smoothly onto my butt. My legs spread wide, bold and inviting, as I bring my fingers to my lips. My tongue teases the tip of one, then dips into my mouth, sucking gently, tasting myself with a slow, sultry moan.

I look up at Damiano, silently urging him forward.

His eyes blaze with raw intensity as he rises, his movements predatory. Tugging his shirt over his head, he reveals the hard planes of his chest, muscles rippling beneath his skin. The shirt is tossed carelessly onto the chair, forgotten.

His hands slide to his belt, unfastening it. The zipper glides down, and his pants drop, revealing his thick, straining length. He strokes himself once, gaze locked onto mine, the air between us electric.

"I can smell the liquor on you. Think you'll be able to perform?" I smirk.

Stepping toward me, he pulls me to the edge of the stage. "We're about to find out." His arms wrap around me, lifting me slightly as his lips claim mine in a heated, demanding kiss.

He tilts my hips, aligning us perfectly. The head of his cock presses against my entrance, and I gasp as he begins to push inside.

The stretch is exquisite, his thickness filling me. I cling to his shoulders, nails digging into his skin as a moan slips free, swallowed by his kiss. He trails down my neck, teeth grazing my skin as his hips rock into mine.

"Dom," I whisper, my voice trembling with need as he pulls back slightly, only to thrust deeper.

He grips me, holding me steady as he sets a pace that is both demanding and intoxicating.

I arch into him, my head falling back as he finds the sensitive spot at the base of my throat. His name escapes me again, louder this time.

Wrapping my legs around his waist, I pull him closer, urging him deeper. Heat builds between us, consuming everything in its path.

"Look at me," he growls.

I obey, shattering around him as my release crashes through me.

My cries fill the room, echoing in the charged air, but he doesn't stop. His movements grow erratic as he chases his own climax.

When he lets go, his groan is low and guttural, his body pressing into mine, holding me close.

He brushes a soft kiss against my lips as he withdraws, and I rise slowly, my legs trembling. Leaning over the stage, I glance back at him. "Scoot your chair closer."

He grins as he pulls it forward until it's just behind me.

I step back, straddling his legs, my hands braced on the stage for balance. Reaching down, I grasp him firmly, guiding him into position, then lowering myself onto him.

I start slow, dragging out each roll of my hips. His hands tighten around my waist as I set a rhythm.

As I take him fully, his breathing turns ragged as he struggles to maintain control.

Lifting myself slightly, I begin to ride him harder, the pace quickening.

"Don't stop," he groans, gliding his hands up my back.

Without warning, he lifts me, bending me over the edge of the stage. I brace myself for the shift in position.

He pumps in and out, each stroke deeper than the last, the sound of skin meeting skin filling the room.

The intensity mounts, pleasure consuming me until I can no longer hold back. My release crashes over me, and moments later, he finds his own, driving in one final time before pulling away.

I straighten with a satisfied smile. When I turn to face him, I find him sagging into the chair, dragging his forearm across his forehead.

"That was hot." He exhales.

I peer down at my legs, then back at him. "I need to clean myself up." I gesture vaguely toward the mess we've made.

He jerks his chin toward the corner of the room. "There's a bathroom over there."

I nod, watching as he stands and takes my hand.

I scan the room, surprised when I realize how many people are here. At least thirty pairs of eyes are on us, some seated at tables, others lingering near the back.

My gaze lands on Dante, Nikolai, Giovanni, and Silvano, all near the exit. Heat rises to my cheeks, and I quickly follow Damiano to the bathroom.

Chapter
FORTY-SEVEN

Damiano

She didn't leave me.
Even after she found out what I had done.
She didn't leave.

I went to the basement after she confronted me about the contract. I couldn't bare the thought of watching her go. I needed to release pent-up tension. I didn't bother wrapping my hands—quite frankly, I didn't care. I just drove my fists into the heavy bag, the impact rattling the chains suspending it from the ceiling.

Each punch sent a dull shock through my knuckles, but I welcomed the pain, let it fuel me. The bag swung wildly, jerking with every hit. Sweat dripped down my back, my breath turning ragged as I kept going, throwing every ounce of frustration into every strike.

My shoulders burned, my arms ached, but I didn't stop. Couldn't. I was the reason she was here. I caused her pain. I hit harder. Faster. Until my muscles burned, my hands were raw, my vision narrowing to nothing but the bag in front of me.

An hour later, my fists were throbbing, my body spent, but the rage hadn't gone anywhere. Because no matter how hard I hit that damn bag, nothing could erase it.

I know she needed to know. Dante has told me every day since she got here that I should tell her. But I didn't see the point. It was done.

I understand why she's upset about what her mom marked, but none of it mattered beyond ensuring I got to keep her. She wouldn't be with ten men. She would be with *me*.

Maybe she struggles to comprehend that the contract was just a façade to bring her here. Either way, I went to her room upstairs, and she wasn't there. I checked our house. Nothing. I waited all night. She never came home.

I was deep in a drunken stupor, pissed off, when my brothers barged in and dragged me out, telling me I was needed at the casino. The last place I wanted to be, especially in the mood I was in. I didn't bother changing, still wearing my sweaty clothes from yesterday.

I had never felt the muscle in my chest do anything but beat, maybe skip once when I saw Rainey. But the realization that she left… that muscle, it *physically* hurt.

I stood at a crossroads: drink myself to death or drag her back here, whether she wanted to come or not. The option I settled on, for the time being, was drinking myself to death. I didn't get far before my brothers stormed in and hauled me out.

When I was shoved through the doors of the dancer area, I figured they were trying to push me into finding someone else to take home. But Rainey was there, waiting. I had never felt such relief.

She chose to stay.

She chose me.

She chose *us*.

I watch her sleep, so peaceful, yet I know she's upset over what her mom did. I don't blame her. I can't fix it. But what I *can* do is let her confront her mom and Ricardo.

WE SIT IN THE BACK SEAT OF THE SUV WHILE SILVANO DRIVES AND Nikolai takes the passenger seat.

She stiffens as soon as we turn down the dirt road leading to the trailer park where she grew up. "What are we doing?" Her shock is evident.

We pull up and sit in silence. She stares at the trailer, either lost in a memory or gathering her thoughts, but says nothing.

"With the contract situation still haunting you, would you like to go say hi?"

"Fuck yeah." There is no hesitation as she swings the door open.

Passing Nikolai's door, she taps on the glass and motions for him to follow. Both he and Silvano step out, and we trail behind her up the stairs.

The front door has a giant hole in it, like someone put a foot through the thin material. She looks at it and lets out a humorless laugh. Stepping in front of her, I shove it open, pushing it wide as I duck inside, Nikolai and Silvano following close behind.

"What the fuck!" Darla yells, startled.

She takes in the three of us, scrambling up from the couch, hands raised in a defensive gesture.

Ricardo emerges from the short hallway, zipping his pants. "What the hell are you yelling about?" He stops in his tracks when he sees us.

"If she was useless, that's not our fault," Darla says.

Nikolai steps to the side as Rainey walks between us, standing at the front. She and her mom stare at each other, neither speaking, until Darla suddenly appears happy.

"Oh, sweetie, I'm so glad you're here." She holds out her arms and starts to step forward.

"Come near me, and I'll break your fucking nose," Rainey warns.

Darla studies her daughter. "We knew you would be fine and look at you. You were." She gestures up and down as if her appearance somehow justifies what she did.

"I got a facial for the first time in my life on my second day. My hair and nails were done, all at the estate spa—"

Darla cuts her off before she can get to the part where she hated every second of it. "Don't come in my house trying to act like you're fuckin' royalty."

"Royalty? Do you want to know what I was pampered for? I was put up for auction." She steps closer. "A large cement room. A single mattress on the floor. Every torture device and sex toy you can imagine. You're so obsessed with being number one, I would have made you proud since I was first up that night."

Darla swallows hard. Then, as if flipping a switch, she plasters on a fake smile. "You're fed and earn your keep spreading your legs like you've always done. It worked out after all."

Silence hangs in the air.

Then Rainey reaches out, swiping everything off the counter, sending it crashing across the room.

"I WAS SOLD FOR YOUR FUCKING DEBT, AND MY VIRGINITY WAS PUT UP FOR AUCTION!" she screams.

"Like you were still a virgin. You've been whoring yourself around this trailer park since you were in fifth grade," Darla spits.

"Does that make you feel better about your actions? Convincing yourself that your daughter was a whore, so it's fine that you sent her to a whorehouse? Because an eleven-year-old begging for food around the trailer park is a far leap from whoring myself out."

"Well, you satisfied these men since they're here to do your bidding," Darla snarls.

Rainey nods nonchalantly, as if mulling over her mother's words. "My bidding? They are my *only* family."

"You probably fuck all three of them at the same time."

"You wanna watch? Is that it? You're so pathetic that you want to see these three men fuck your only daughter?" She takes another step closer. "Well, guess what, you piece of shit. Part of the contract you signed to give me up stated that if you ran up any more debt, the agreement would be null and void."

Darla fixes on Rainey, confusion flickering across her face until realization sets in. Terror takes over her expression as she turns to Ricardo, who mirrors her fear.

Rainey nods, letting them both know they're fucked. "I'm no longer bound by your debt. In fact, you owe all the money back."

"That's not possible. The contract didn't say that. You didn't work off any of the money?" Darla demands.

"Oh, my legs have been spread since I got there. But not a single penny—mine or theirs—will go toward your debt."

"We brought a copy of the contract and highlighted the terms right here." I hold it up for her.

She rips it from my hand and starts tearing it to pieces, frantic and wild.

Silvano pulls a second one from his coat pocket and hands it to me.

Darla lunges for it too, but Rainey slaps the back of her hand, hard. "You're fucking done," she sneers. "I'd suggest you come get yourself fucked and earn your own debt freedom, but there's a standard. You need at least five teeth, and you're about four short."

Nikolai bursts out laughing, excusing himself outside to regain his composure.

"I don't want her back. Give me a new contract to sign," Darla snarls, rummaging through the mess on the floor for something to write with.

"The next contract she signs is our marriage certificate," I say.

Darla looks up, then at Rainey's hand, then back at me. "Are you two, like, an item?"

"Yeah," Rainey bites out.

Darla pushes herself off the floor, standing with one hip popped out. "Then why the hell are you coming to me for money? You wouldn't have her to marry if it wasn't for me. Quit being ungrateful and get out of my house. We should be discussing how much you plan on paying me for allowing you to marry my daughter."

Rainey stares for so long that I almost ask if she's okay, but then she speaks. "Apologize to me," she says to her mom.

"Apologize? For what?" A delayed laugh slips free.

"I was raped. Five men held me down and brutalized me. They beat me and I was forced to walk back into the house, where a hundred people got to witness the most traumatizing experience of my life. You may have birthed me, but I will never claim you as family. You were dead to me the day you signed that contract."

Darla remains indifferent, as if Rainey's words mean nothing to her.

"Do you want to know what happened to the men who touched her?" I ask. "One by one, I let them watch as I tortured each of them to death. I cut off their dicks and made them eat them. I sliced off their nipples, their fingers, their tongues. They thought there wouldn't be consequences. But there were."

"Good for them," she sarcastically remarks.

"I don't think you're understanding the predicament you're in," Nikolai interjects.

Darla scoffs. "We didn't do anything to you."

"But you did something to *me*. And you both are going to die for it," Rainey says coldly.

Darla falls to her knees, begging her daughter for mercy.

"You're so pathetic. You have a month to pay back your debts, or we'll come back and bring you to play with Damiano."

Darla's tears stop instantly, and she climbs to her feet. "Get out of my house, skank." She points to the door.

Rainey scoffs. "Gladly. It smells like shit in here."

"Can we rough them up just a little?" Silvano asks.

"Come on, Silvano," Rainey calls over her shoulder.

He sighs and follows.

Chapter

FORTY-EIGHT

Rainey

Damiano is "working," and most of the girls are too, even though it's mid-afternoon.

I hear Valentina on the phone with someone. It sounds important. She mentions a dress she needs for an event and how it has to be picked up immediately, but she can't leave because she's getting her nails, hair, and makeup done.

She passes by, still on the phone, heading to the spa when she suddenly stops. It seems like she wants to ask something, but then she mumbles, "Forget it."

"Valentina, is everything okay?"

She lets out a long sigh and walks back. "Can you do me a tiny favor? You can't tell Damiano. It can be our little secret."

"Sure. What do you need?"

"My dress for tonight's event is finished. I need to make sure the alterations are correct, but I have to get to my pedicure. My driver will take you to the boutique to pick it up. Just check that it's ready to wear."

"I'd love to."

She strides over and wraps me in a hug. "Thank you, sweetheart. Remember, our little secret." She holds a finger to her mouth.

This will be the easiest secret to keep. I'm excited to leave again. It feels like, slowly… very slowly, I'm getting my freedom back.

As I head outside to meet the driver, another car pulls up just as I'm getting into the back seat.

Niki jumps out and races toward me, barreling into a hug.

"What!" I gasp, shocked. "You aren't supposed to be home for another week!" I squeeze her tighter.

"I came home early. I couldn't wait to see you or my brothers. Even my parents." She releases me and grins. "Are you sneaking out?"

"Kinda. Sneaking in the sense that your brother doesn't know. But your mom asked me to pick up her dress."

"Fun. I'll come with!"

By the time we pull off the property, I can hardly contain my excitement. The windows are rolled down, and we let our hair blow in the wind.

When we arrive at the boutique, I immediately realize the Volkovs don't mess around with chump change. This dress is going to be expensive. I almost feel like I'll insult everyone just by stepping inside.

We are greeted by an older woman in a navy blue dress suit. Niki tells her we're here to pick up a dress for Valentina Volkov.

She studies us for a moment before asking for our names. "Niki Volkov. I'm picking up my mom's dress."

The woman's eye twitches, a barely perceptible reaction, but one I catch.

Odd. Maybe she doesn't like Valentina.

Her lips press together briefly, and then she says, "I was told Rainey would be coming."

Niki smiles, unfazed. "We made an adventure out of it."

The woman waits a beat, then nods and turns, guiding us to the back. As we follow, she explains that we need to inspect the dress and approve the design.

The room is large, lined with sewing stations and alteration tables. As I turn to wait for the woman to take the lead, I see a man injecting something into Niki's neck. She's out quickly, and he lays her down.

Then a needle bites into my neck.

My hand flies to the spot as everything goes dark.

THE ROUGH FABRIC OF THE BAG OVER MY HEAD SCRATCHES AGAINST my skin as I shift in the chair. My wrists burn from the ropes biting into them, arms aching from the awkward angle they're tied behind my back. Through the thin, coarse material, I can barely make out dim light filtering in, shapes moving in the shadowed warehouse around us.

My ankles are bound to the chair legs, and something is wrapped around my mouth, muffling any sound I might try to make.

Niki stirs, struggling against her restraints as she wakes from the sedative. Her chair scrapes against the cement floor as she rocks back and forth, testing the bindings.

The echo of measured footsteps bounces off the high walls of what feels like an enormous, empty warehouse, sending an eerie chill through me.

I freeze, pulse pounding in my ears, as the footsteps stop directly in front of us.

A hand grabs the bag over my head and yanks it off. The light blinds me momentarily, and I blink rapidly to adjust. As my vision clears, I see Niki doing the same.

A figure steps forward, their silhouette menacing under the flickering warehouse light.

"Ladies," a voice drawls. "Welcome to the end of your rope."

His presence is as sharp and calculated as the suit he wears. His tailored three-piece ensemble hugs his lean frame, every detail immaculate—from the crisp white shirt beneath the dark waistcoat to the glint of the pocket watch chain hanging at his side.

His chiseled jawline and unblemished skin are smooth and clean-shaven, adding to his polished appearance. High cheekbones and a straight, aquiline nose give him an aristocratic air, his light blue eyes cold and assessing. Dark hair is cropped short on the sides, the top concealed beneath a flat cap that sits snugly on his head. Any hint of softness is hidden beneath its brim, his expression a careful mask of quiet menace.

Everything about him exudes control. He isn't loud or brash like some men in his position. No, his power is in his silence—the dangerous calm before a storm.

Niki's gag is pulled away, and she glares at him.

"Nikita. You're an unexpected surprise."

"Cristiano," she grits out. "I'm sure."

I stare at her, then back at him.

Fuck.

Cristiano Fierro.